CW01506826

Darkness in the Light:

short stories

By

Lora Kay

A Demon's Destiny

He was just finishing a glass of red wine, which he had ordered along with dinner. It was a fine restaurant, one of his favourites. The staff knew his name and that his order was always the same, despite the varied menu they were offering. Damon was a regular customer mainly because of his lifestyle and inability to cook for himself. He was young and rich – but most importantly he was a demon.

The synchronicity with his chosen name wasn't a coincidence; on the contrary, he thought of it as a funny game of words. What a world it is where demons walk among people disguised as humans, someone might think. Well, that's not as important as Damon's story, a story of one demon walking the earth for many years: a story of his destiny.

After Damon left the restaurant, he headed towards the spot where he had parked his car. It was five minutes away on foot, which he didn't mind because a bit of a stroll would help his thoughts, on a small, not very well-lit street. Anybody else might feel unsafe passing along it but not him; he didn't mind that, either.

About halfway, he realised he wasn't the only one walking in that direction. There were three people across the street, though they didn't seem to be together – or at least one of them wasn't. It was a woman judging by the sound of her high heels. She was ahead of the other two who were definitely men from the echo of their footsteps.

Damon figured all that out without even glancing towards them. His thoughts were chaotic and he couldn't really focus, mainly because of the annoying sound of that woman's heels. She was speeding up, walking faster and faster.

It was one of those moments when Damon could sense

something bad happening. That was good for him, of course; he was a demon after all, and his purpose was to ensure as many bad situations on earth as possible. Not that he took his job so seriously these days, though he had at the beginning when he was eager to prove himself worthy of the cause. With time, he had become somewhat ... lazy.

Right now, though, he could feel bad energy on that small street and it drew his attention. He turned to look across. The two men were following the woman, most likely intending to rob her.

It wasn't in Damon's nature to feel pity because the victim was a woman, so he didn't. He stayed perfectly calm, trying to enjoy the bad energy that was vibrating in the air, thinking that he hadn't even had to work for this one because it was all happening naturally. The fact was that humans were generally bad, took the initiative themselves and did much of the demons' job for them. Not all of humans, of course, and that was when his efforts were required.

What Damon didn't sense, however, was the unexpected turn of events. The two men eventually reached the woman and were only a step away from her, but the demon didn't see her next action coming. Not that she surprised them with some secret karate skills or anything of that sort, but she suddenly stopped, turned around and pointed a little spray at them.

'I will use it – and I swear I will empty it!' Her voice sounded firm though Damon could sense that, behind the tough façade, she was shaking.

She used the moment of surprise wisely; it only lasted second or so, but that was enough for her to take her phone out of the pocket with her free hand. 'I'm dialling the police,' she threatened. Actually, she wasn't bluffing and her fingers were already pressing the number nine button.

The two men must have been amateurs because they exchanged brief looks then turned around and ran. 'Such a shame,' Damon muttered. They had been so close to going through with it and yet they had failed. That could have been his opportunity to act, to give them a little push and instil some courage into them, but he had stood there watching as if he were at the cinema. What was wrong with him? He had missed a precious moment to encourage something bad to happen, which was his only job.

Disappointment, almost shame, crossed his face. He really needed to get back into the game so as not to draw suspicion from the really bad guys, the demons in charge. They didn't come to Earth to do the dirty jobs but they observed what was done and passed judgments and punishments.

Damon had stopped and turned fully towards the scene across the street. Now he stayed there without moving. He could hear the woman breathing heavily; panic was starting to overtake . She must also have been still in shock because, instead of rushing away, she was standing motionless.

Their eyes met suddenly and they looked at each other for a long moment. He followed the changing emotions on her face while she was glared at his impassive expression. 'Hey,' she shouted angrily. 'Have you been watching the whole time? Why didn't you do something?!'

That was something Damon didn't expect and it surprised him even more than her sudden act of bravery. He was torn between walking away silently and shamefully – though for different reasons than one might have expected – or trying to entertain himself with this furious woman. She had fire in her, so maybe he could use his bad influence on her. Maybe she would respond positively to it. Perhaps she was hiding more surprises.

But it was too late for him to make a decision because she was crossing the street towards him. 'The decent thing to do when seeing someone in trouble, sir, is to help!' She was standing so close that, despite the bad street light, he could see every detail of her face. She was beautiful.

Not that that changed anything. Damon had been among

humans long enough to have seen plenty of attractive women and they hardly affected him unless he was feeling bored and in need of entertainment. But that was all; even though he had a human body, his essence was different. He looked at things differently, he experienced things differently; his reactions were not like those of regular people. Obviously he ate and slept, but that was to maintain the body he inhabited. Everything else about him was different. His mind was an entire universe; His knowledge was so extensive that if a regular person had even half as much, their brain would explode. The human mind was not designed to contain as much; it was developed with certain limits and rarely used at full capacity.

'I didn't catch what was happening from the beginning, but I admit I should have got involved.' A tiny smile stretched almost invisibly across his lips. It was his personal joke: the woman should consider herself very lucky that he *hadn't* got involved. She certainly wouldn't have liked it if he'd interfered.

They stared at each other for another brief moment. She didn't seem to like his answer, or she didn't trust it.

For the second time, Daniel acknowledged how beautiful she was.

'Well, I must say, you're not the best person to be around if one needs help,' she said sharply. Obviously deciding to waste no more time with this stranger, she turned to walk away.

His voice stopped her. 'In fact, you didn't really look like you needed any help. What you did was quite brave.' His eyes had an odd spark and the woman raised her eyebrows in surprise. She couldn't tell for sure because she was struggling to focus her thoughts, but she was almost positive that there was a sarcastic edge to his comment.

'You're calling an act of self-defence by a woman against two attackers brave? I call it an instinct for survival! You've got twisted ideas,' she responded in the same sarcastic tone.

4

She gave him the sharpest look she could then turned and walked off ahead of him

Yes, he was right about her: she had fire. And interestingly, she was heading in the same direction as he was. He had to carry on until he reached his car so he had to follow her; he just hoped she wouldn't consider him a possible attacker too and spray him. That would be terribly irritating.

As Damon walked, he kept his gaze fixed on her. Even though she was moving with small, fast steps, he somehow remained only three steps behind her. He could have slowed down to avoid upsetting her even more, but his good mood was suddenly back and he was planning on keeping it.

The fun didn't last long, though, because within a minute he had reached his car. And so did she because her vehicle was parked in front of his.

'You've got to be kidding me,' she said quietly to herself as she unlocked the door.

'I think you deserve to be in a better mood tonight,' said Damon, looking at her and holding his keys but obviously not in a hurry to get into his car. He seemed rather intrigued by the coincidence of their cars being next to each other.

'Excuse me?' The woman didn't get into her car either; instead she held the door open but turned towards him.

'If you think about it you won, so there is more of a reason to be happy rather than unhappy. But that's only how I see it – me and my twisted point of view.' He approached her slowly with a friendly smile.

Now that they were both under the street light, she could see that he was an attractive man.

'Perhaps you're not so wrong.' She smiled too; the fact that he had quoted her impressed her a little. She had always enjoyed word games and people who seemed interesting rather than just ... regular. In addition, his handsome face helped to soothe her.

'I'm Damon, by the way.' He stretched out his hand.

5

It took a second, but she finally gripped it. 'I'm Lisa.'

Her skin felt soft, pleasant, and for a moment he considered asking if she had plans for the rest of the evening. Maybe they could have a drink. It was a very open move, but he wouldn't bother playing around; his charm always worked like a magnet in the rare cases he felt like using it.

But doubt crawled inside him. Though she had fire, he sensed her goodness and light. Trying to shake those could be a waste of his time. Even if he had plenty of time, he never liked wasting it. Maybe it would be for the best to let her go on her way.

Lisa's mind was running in weird directions, too. She almost got the feeling that he was going to suggest they did something together, and what was most weird was that she was inclined to answer yes.

'I don't want to keep you any longer, Lisa, but it was nice meeting you even under such circumstances,' Damon said suddenly. He had decided it was better that way.

'Take care, Damon.' Lisa felt the moment of doubts and decisions was over and it was probably for the best, but the stranger had brightened her mood. She wasn't actually sure how that had that happened because he'd irritated her at first. 'Be careful in dark streets. There not only dangerous for women. You may need to take action another time.' She winked at him.

He couldn't believe that someone was joking with him because almost no one had dared to do that before. He was always giving the creeps to people, which unfortunately made it hard to have fun. But a game was starting at a moment when he wasn't even looking to play and it felt nice.

'That should have been my advice to you. He was holding the door open and already had one foot inside his car.

'But you didn't.' Lisa laughed through the open window

of her car as she started the engine. 'You missed your chance again.'

'Only because you didn't need it. I trust you to be safe after what I saw.' That was the last thing Damon said. She gave him a final look in her side mirror and drove away.

Damon found himself sitting in his car with the engine still off, looking after Lisa's car which had almost disappeared from the street. 'Have I really missed...?' he mumbled but didn't continue the thought.

Not practising his duty enough had made him soft. What had happened that evening was the weirdest thing he had experienced in – well, a long time. Probably that was why she had impressed him. Nothing more. She was just a regular woman, a beautiful regular woman, whom he would never see again. He shook his head quickly as if to remove all the weird thoughts and started the engine.

*

Lisa was home, taking a hot shower to relax her tense muscles. Now that she was alone, the realisation of what had happened hit her again and her body stiffened. The hot water helped, though she was still shivering a little; that was fear, which wasn't so easy to get rid of.

She had never considered herself brave, but she was proud of how the events this evening had turned out. She did it; she saved herself. The stranger, that Damon guy, was probably right: she should give herself more credit and be happy instead of upset.

The thought of him helped. He slipped suddenly into her thoughts and distracted her from the events that had led to their meeting. He was handsome, probably a few years older than her, perhaps around thirty. He seemed ... she wanted to say 'sophisticated' based on the fact that he was well dressed, had a nice car and all that, but she couldn't forget that he hadn't tried to help her. Was it out of fear for his own life? Maybe. Everything was possible. She shouldn't judge him too harshly; after all, she didn't know him.

Lisa had a glass of red wine to relax her before she went to bed. Hopefully she would have sleep deeply without nightmares. She didn't have to worry; her dreams involved only the tall handsome man with sparkling dark eyes.

*

Damon had his passions, just like every human. He loved art and, as a rich man, could afford to collect it. Paintings were his particular weakness. His home was very spacious for one person and he never had any visitors, but he had filled the space with luxurious furniture.

To outsiders, he appeared to have a good life, but he found it rather boring. Time was measured very differently in the Dark Kingdom from where he had come, and he had spent a couple of hundred years on Earth getting bored with his duties. He wasn't entirely sure how he had earned the 'honour' of being sent to Earth, but there must have been some reason behind it. But time was going so slowly that sometimes he feared they had forgotten him.

Damon had once been human but he had no memory of that life. He remembered opening his eyes and realising he was in hell – and finding he didn't dislike the idea. He didn't know what he had done to deserve hell but it didn't matter; he felt perfectly fine there. He was in quite a good position, too; everyone favoured him and soon they sent him back to Earth. He was told that he was being given an important task that wasn't given to just anyone and he felt honoured. That was why, in the beginning, he gave everything to keep up with their expectations and did as much harm as possible. He was a demon, after all, and his human past life did not matter. Soon his curiosity about how he'd landed up in hell vanished. It did not matter.

Time passed, year after year, and the excitement he had experienced at first cooled. He became lazy and avoided getting involved; he discovered that he could cover himself because humans were evil enough without his help. That was lucky for him because otherwise he'd have had to spend all his time working. Now he was comfortable, if a little bored, and passed the time by focusing on his hobbies and passions.

Damon was going to a gallery where he had scheduled an appointment in order to buy a painting he'd been interested in for some time. He parked his car in restricted zone but he didn't care; he wasn't planning on spending much time in the gallery. He crossed the street and entered the building.

The salesman was waiting. He offered Damon a glass of champagne and started polite small talk. Damon was not in the best of moods, firstly because he hated pretending to have good manners, and secondly because he hadn't slept well last night, so he cut to the chase and asked to see the painting.

Not having a good sleep was rare for Damon and he blamed that damned woman Lisa from the previous evening. Though he had considered her forgotten at the moment she had driven away, the strange excitement she had left in him didn't give him any peace for the whole night. Now his mood was one which no human wanted to be around to see.

'And this is it, sir,' the salesman said when they stopped in front of a painting with beautiful colours softly merging into a landscape. Damon quite liked the peaceful sensation it gave him.

'I'll take it,' he said flatly. He made no other comment, which confused the salesman who was expecting at least to have a discussion about the painting. 'Wait ... what's that?' Damon's gaze had slid to another painting almost hidden from sight.

'Oh, that's just something we are trying with a new artist, ah, a very talented young lady. We have an arrangement for a short exhibition...' He kept talking but Damon had stopped listening. His eyes were fixed on the painting as if something were drawing him towards it. He stepped forward slowly and examined it with an interest he hadn't given to the first painting.

The salesman saw the possibility of selling that one too, so he carried on talking enthusiastically, even though the second painting was probably the cheapest one in the gallery.

Damon stood silently; the painting had all his attention and he seemed to have frozen in front of it while the minutes passed. The salesman felt uncomfortable, so he decided to give his customer some privacy; it was more than obvious Damon was 'having a moment'.

Indeed he was. Damon was stunned by this painting, not because of the technique but more because of what it expressed: Heaven and Hell, with an angel and a demon both possessing light and darkness. There was something a little bad in the angel and something a little good in the demon. He finally spoke. 'I'll take that one too.'

'Great choice, sir. Young artists need to be supported.' The salesman was trying to keep the conversation going but it was a real challenge.

Damon was preparing to leave when his eyes fell on a figure, a woman with blonde wavy hair, blue eyes and full lips. She was so familiar, so beautiful. It was Lisa.

'Oh, that is even better,' exclaimed the salesman who was about to escort his valuable customer to the door. 'Here is the artist whose painting you just bought. I'm sure she will greatly appreciate your feedback on her work. Miss Adkins,' he called.

Lisa was talking with the gallery owner. They had just finished a meeting and he was leading her to the front door. She looked up when heard her name and the smile on her face immediately changed to shock when her gaze met Damon's. The interesting thing was that her expression completely reflected his at that moment – and Damon was almost never surprised by anything.

'I would like you to meet an admirer of your art, Miss Adkins. This gentleman just bought your *Good in Evil, Evil in Good* painting.' The salesman was now standing between Lisa and Damon, trying to introduce them; little did he know that they had already met the night before.

In daylight, Lisa looked like ... like an angel, Damon thought, and that idea almost made him shiver. That was another thing he had hardly experienced until now on Earth as a demon.

'Would you like to have lunch?' Damon asked to the great surprise of the salesman and the gallery owner, who both had their mouths open at his bold move. The man didn't even know her and it was totally inappropriate; there again, he was the type of rich person who was arrogant and had attitude. Neither man wanted to get involved.

'Well, since you're a fan of my work I don't see why not.' She smiled, not taking her eyes off his as she spoke. Then, realising they still had audience, she added, 'It's all right, gentlemen. We know each other.'

Both men gave a relieved laugh and quickly decided to leave this awkward scene and get back to business.

Damon hadn't really thought before making the invitation because he knew what would happen if he *did* think before speaking: he would have ended up not inviting her, exactly like last night. But he wanted, really wanted...

He opened the door and let Lisa leave first. He could afford that many manners without compromising his nature. 'Did you agree just because I bought your painting?' he asked as they headed to the restaurant.

'Did you buy my painting out of guilt for not helping me yesterday?' she asked provocatively. He was smiling and so was she. This was shaping up to be interesting, Lisa thought, and yet there was something odd about the man that she couldn't quite figure out. Perhaps this lunch would

11

give her some answers; she hoped so because she was really intrigued.

As for Damon, he didn't like this mysteriousness in the air that was pushing them together. He would stop this crush so he could avoid complications. Lunch was going to be the extent of it.

*

Lisa's hair was untidy and paint covered her face and arms in random spots. She was wearing only her favourite loose shirt and holding a brush. She was painting, though not successfully because she couldn't focus. Her thoughts were as chaotic as her messy looks.

It was already dark outside. She had returned from the lunch an hour or so earlier. She'd had high hopes for that lunch; she hoped to find out who this guy really was, if his looks reflected an amazing personality. Perhaps something nice could emerge from them meeting again...

But those hopes had been dashed. He was arrogant, he was not polite, he was everything she would never look for in a man to date. For example, when she'd asked what he did, he'd answered that he was a demon. What was that? Some kind of a joke on his own name? Perhaps that was his move with the ladies, but it didn't impress her. If anything, it gave her a chill because it fit perfectly with what she sensed about him. He seemed dangerous. Lisa didn't need that in her life; falling for bad guys was never her style.

And so after the lunch she had already decided – and not in his favour. Lisa had a strong character and never looked back. The only problem was that, despite everything, she felt a weird attraction to him. It must have been simply lust, some sort of low passion – she was human, after all, and it happened. But Lisa had masterful self-control and she would never allow herself to slip.

The doorbell rang. She wasn't expecting anyone, so maybe it was just a late delivery of her online orders. She opened the door and, for a second time that day, her face froze in surprise.

Damon was leaning against the wall. He didn't say a word, didn't explain why he was there or how he knew her address. He didn't even make a joke to break the awkward moment. Nothing. She didn't either; they just looked at each other for a very long moment. Anyone else would have felt uncomfortable, but not them.

*

Damon had tried his best during lunch to push her away, to push himself away from what was drawing him towards Lisa, and it seemed to be working. She didn't like his attitude and wasn't afraid to show it, something other people would have thought twice about doing.

The only problem was that, after the lunch was over and they had both gone their separate ways, Damon realised his plan hadn't worked, at least not for him. He wanted to see her again. Probably it was only lust that he was feeling; every once in a while that happened. As a demon, he didn't have all the needs that humans had – and the desire for sex was the one they were most obsessed with. He often described them as animals. Not that sex didn't mean pleasure, but humans really abused it. It was good for him, of course, because all those cheaters, rapists and those who sold their bodies for money were the ones who went to the place that he was from – Hell. But deep down, he thought they were acting like animals.

Occasionally he had experienced this 'pleasure' for the body, but it was more out of boredom than anything else. Maybe boredom was the reason he was attracted to Lisa. He hoped so, because once he'd got it over and done with he could continue on his way and forget all about the woman who had the looks of an angel and enough beauty to intrigue him.

When she opened the door, he didn't say anything

13

because she had a choice like all humans did. It was up to her; he could give a nudge but not force her. She had to decide – and eventually, she did.

Lisa stepped aside and opened the door wide as an invitation for him to come in. Still neither of them spoke a word.

The door closed and the sound of the turning key meant they were now locked in her flat. Damon scanned the room; she definitely had good taste, but he was most impressed by the place where the action was happening: the painting.

'Don't you have a special room to work in, a studio or something?' he asked.

'I do, but I never really have any inspiration there. Oddly, I feel more comfortable here in the middle of my living room, which is definitely not the right place to keep such a mess.' She was rather embarrassed he had caught her this way, not only because of the untidy flat but because of her appearance. She was nothing like how she had looked a few hours ago and she was practically not dressed.

'Can I get you anything?' Lisa asked, heading to the kitchen.

'What inspired the painting I bought today?' Damon didn't want to play nice, to play someone who he wasn't, so he spoke directly.

Lisa was pouring red wine into two glasses and she didn't rush with her answer. First she handed him the glass, then took a sip of hers, left it on the small table in the living room and looked him straight in the eyes. 'There is no inspiration behind it. It's simply my belief,' she said.

'What exactly is your belief?' Damon put down his glass too. It was always amusing to listen to humans speaking about good and bad, beliefs and religion, because they always got it wrong. But he was interested to hear what Lisa had to say because that would take his mind away from the fact that she was standing before him wearing nothing but a shirt.

'In every good, there is a little evil and vice-versa. Good and bad, by their very existence, create a perfect balance. A little too much good, a little too much evil, and the balance would be broken and there wouldn't be life if that happened. Good and evil need each other in order to carry on. They support each other.' She shrugged as if her explanation were obvious and couldn't be wrong.

It was too much for Damon – he couldn't handle any more of this, Lisa was too perfect and the magnetic force radiating from her attracted him more and more, creating tension in the air. He would explode if not he didn't have her at that exact moment. But she had to wish it first.

'What do you want?' he asked. More words were not needed, and Lisa got his hidden meaning.

Again, she didn't rush with her answer. She was confused. There was desire now, but life was so much more than desire. One-night stands were not her thing and neither were risky games with strange men like Damon. Danger was written all over his face.

She stepped towards him so there was little distance between them. 'I want to...' She stared into his eyes. Her look went deep inside him but also expressed agony. 'I want to feel your hands wrapped around me, to feel your skin against mine and your lips on my lips.'

Damon was breathing heavily; that was all he wanted to hear. But he could read uncertainty in her eyes.

Lisa slowly reached for his hand and put it gently on her waist. She stood on tiptoe, put her hands around his neck and pressed her lips against his, then she quickly stepped back again. She always knew what was right, and she was going to do the right thing this time. 'But I can't! This is doomed from its very beginning. We are too different.'

Damon was petrified. Had she just seduced and rejected him? That was his job; the roles were never reversed. But that was not important right now; what was really significant was the feeling he'd had when kissing her. It was a feeling of being complete, of being whole. He had never noticed before that a part of him was missing, but at that very moment he realised the full meaning of being complete. His sensations ran on a different level because he wasn't a human, so he could appreciate this feeling deeply. It was as if he'd been transported somewhere in the vast universe where there was only peace and tranquillity. That was what he'd felt when his lips met Lisa's.

'Please leave,' she said.

Damon could tell from her eyes that she was torn, but that was all right; he would give her some time to miss him, to think it over. This was not the end; of that Damon was certain.

He nodded and left. It wasn't easy when he wanted so much more, and it would be even harder to seduce her. That thought calmed him a little. It was just the beginning, just the beginning!

*

It was three days after that evening and there had been no sign of Lisa. Damon was starting to feel a little impatient, so he decided to take the first step and reached for the phone. Surprisingly, at that exact same moment it rang. Coincidence had worked in their favour so far, so he wouldn't have been surprised if it washer.

He picked up and heard a man's voice; it was the salesman from the gallery. 'I am terribly sorry to bother you, sir, but we have to inform you that the prices of all Miss Adkin's work that you want to buy have changed.'

After the other night, Damon had decided to buy all Lisa's paintings; he was quite satisfied with that move, imagining that would make her call him. 'The price is not a problem – I'm still interested in buying them all. But can I ask what caused this change?' Was it possible that she was so stubborn that she didn't want him buying her work and was trying to scare him with some high price?

'Ah, sir...' The salesman sounded really uncomfortable and he was definitely struggling to find the right words. 'She... Miss Adkins, sir, she passed away the other day. Terrible loss ... so young and talented... Involved in a horrible accident. We are establishing a fund and will donate the money from her paintings to charity because she was all alone, bless her soul...'

The man spoke on and on but Damon wasn't listening; he had dropped the phone. He couldn't breathe, his eyes were unable to see and all he felt was a horrifying, unbearable pain – not a physical pain but an inner one. It was like the moment when a person is drowning, but it was extended, captured in a loop. There was no escape from it.

A voice rose in his head, a voice he knew well. It was not a human's voice, nor was it a memory. Hell itself was speaking to him at that moment:

'Did you really think, Damon, that being in Hell would be pleasant? No, my friend, you all come here because you did something bad. Punishment awaits you all and there is no escape from it. We took extra time to decide the worst possible fate for you, and now here it is. Lisa is in Heaven and you will never cross paths again. Enjoy your eternal misery!'

The Wedding Day

It was days since it had happened, but Teresa still couldn't sleep. How could she, after what she witnessed? The scene chased her whenever she closed her eyes. She had even woken up screaming in the middle of the night from a nightmare that had taken her back to that place, although she wasn't completely sure the scream was real because neither of her parents had come to check on her. Maybe it had been part of the dream then, but it was so real that she could almost feel pain in her throat.

As well as the nightmare, something else unusual was happening: Teresa didn't want to leave the house. The family doctor explained to her mother that Teresa was 'experiencing shock or something similar'. Teresa didn't really understand what that meant because, after all, she was only eight years old and complicated words were still a challenge. The doctor had given her a document that excused her from attending school for a week so she could recover properly, but she had discovered that distracting herself and simply forgetting about it wasn't easy. The memory had sunk too deeply into her consciousness.

Teresa was aware how much her condition worried her parents, especially her mother, who was the most loving and caring parent a child could wish for. Her mother didn't know what else to do for her little girl; Teresa knew that because she'd overheard her parents talking behind the closed door of her room yesterday.

If Teresa could only have shut it out, she would have gladly done so for herself, for her parents... But how?

*

Six days earlier
Teresa was really excited because today the teacher was

taking the class to visit a museum. Out-of-school activities were always fun and now she felt full of energy, as if she had eaten a whole chocolate. That was something her mother wouldn't allow her to do because of something to do with teeth or health – Teresa never paid much attention to these explanations.

Today her father was the one taking her to school because her mother needed to be at her office earlier than usual. He was preparing her lunch bag, packing a sandwich, apple and juice, while Teresa was laughing at him. 'Mom is much faster than you,' she said jokingly as she followed his confused movements.

'Are you timing me, you little monkey?' He looked over his shoulder.

'I'm a flying pony, not a monkey,' she corrected him as she kept on brushing the hair of her pony toy.

'My bad ... flying monkey.' Her father pretended to correct himself and they both burst into laughter.

Finally, he was ready. Teresa's backpack was on her shoulder, the lunch bag was packed, and there was just one thing left to do: take her to school. Unfortunately, her father was not used to doing that because usually it was done by her mother, but he didn't mind if he had the time.

After he had kissed her on the forehead and promised the teacher that her mother would pick her up later, Teresa was finally at school. All the other kids seemed impatient and excited like her; they couldn't wait for the trip to the museum to begin. Her best friend, Lesley, was standing next to her while the teacher got all the kids in line.

'My dad said we might even see a mummy,' Lesley said seriously.

'What's a mummy?' Teresa asked, confused, as they walked in a perfect line down the alley to the school bus that was waiting to drive them to the museum.

'I think it's something very scary, because Mom told Dad to stop scaring me.' Her friend shrugged uncertainly.

'Then I don't want to see any mummies,' Teresa stated, slightly chilled at the idea of something frightening.

'Don't worry, I'm sure it won't be that frightening...' Lesley tried to convince her friend but was interrupted by the teacher who had overheard their conversation.

'Of course there won't be anything frightening, girls. Please don't say things like that and scare the others. Now get in the bus and take your seats,' she instructed them.

Ms Nansy was a young lady who had become a teacher just a year ago, and everyone loved her for she was kind and sweet. But at that moment Teresa noticed Ms Nansy was a bit nervous, something that happened every time she was responsible for them outside the classroom.

The two girls sat together and played Rock, Paper, Scissors to decide which of them would be by the window. Teresa was the lucky one, but she didn't want her friend to be unhappy so she promised to switch seats on the way back.

Ms Nansy gave her last instructions to the children then took her seat at the front of the bus. They seemed to be going on a long trip, at least with the speed they were doing. Teresa overheard Robert, the boy sitting behind them, call it a turtle ride. He wasn't wrong; her father drove much faster – even her mother – than the school bus. However, Teresa didn't mind; it gave her and Lesley plenty of time to discuss their favourite Disney princesses.

Soon after the journey started, probably not even halfway to the museum, the bus stopped very suddenly. All the kids were silent as Ms Nansy stood up quickly and checked them to make sure everyone was fine. Then, visibly irritated, she went to the driver to demand an explanation. If he'd been a student like them, Teresa thought, Ms Nansy would have scolded him.

Confused, the two girls looked at each other, not knowing why the bus was still not moving from the middle of the street. They were not the only ones; all the kids were whispering and looking around trying to understand. The sound of horns from the cars behind made the situation even more intense. The traffic was blocked, nobody was moving, and that made the students more anxious.

Soon, they heard another sound. It was approaching fast: a siren – ambulance or police, Teresa still couldn't recognise the difference.

'Where is Ms Nansy?' she asked her friend. She was starting to worry about the chaos that was forming around her.

Lesley stretched her neck to check; it was easier for her to see because she was in the aisle seat. 'She is still with the driver, but ... that's odd,' she said.

'What? What is it?' Teresa was already way too anxious. Whenever she felt this way, all she wanted was her Mom and Dad next to her, holding her hand, caressing her softly on the head and assuring her that everything was alright. Since they were not there, Ms Nansy was the person Teresa expected to soothe her. She leaned over her friend so she could look ahead herself.

The teacher was now standing sideways with one hand covering her mouth and the other making a quick movement, a cross in front of her chest. She seemed extremely upset, and the driver was advising her to take a seat and a sip of water.

What could possibly upset their teacher that way? Robert from behind was the only one who dared to ask, 'Ms Nansy, is everything all right?'

As if his voice had woken her from a dream, the question reminded Ms Nansy that there was a bus full of children depending on her. 'Everybody in their seats, boys and girls. I don't want to see anyone standing and moving around.' Her voice was shaking even though she was trying her best to sound firm so the students could understand this was not a game. 'Take out your school books and check on yesterday's lesson,' she ordered. It was essential to keep their eyes focused on something so they were not tempted to look through the windows.

'Ms Nansy, I can't open my water bottle,' a girl sitting at the very back of the bus called.

The young teacher went to assist her. She checked on all the kids as she passed by to make sure they were following her instructions.

Teresa took her book out of her backpack but she was really confused. Until now, she had never studied in a bus; studying was meant to be done in the classroom.

'I think Ms Nansy is trying to distract us,' Lesley said in a low voice.

'What do you mean?'

'Well, it's very simple. When I'm at home and there is something scary on the TV, my mom makes me close my eyes or turn around until it's finished. What we are doing now feels the same.' She sounded pretty convinced by her own theory.

'What do you think the teacher saw and doesn't want us to see?' asked Teresa. Her friend had no answer to that, even though she had managed to come up with such an interesting explanation right before that.

Teresa was as curious as every child; even though she scared easily, most of the time her curiosity overtook her fear. Her worry now was replaced by the impulse to go to the front of the bus and see for herself what was happening. She waited for the teacher to pass by their row and then, without even sharing her intentions with Lesley, she jumped up and ran towards the driver. She knew she had to be fast otherwise Ms Nansy would catch her before she could succeed in her plan.

Teresa stopped just behind the seated driver and tried to focus on the view outside. The siren she had heard a minute ago was from an ambulance. It wasn't easy to see much as there were a lot of police and paramedics around. The traffic had stopped but the school bus was right in front, so had the best angle for a close look – and that was why she could see it. See what she wouldn't have seen if only she'd done as she was told and sat as the other kids were doing. See what she wouldn't have seen if there hadn't been a museum visit today.

But she saw it and it paralysed her completely, making her unable to look away. What she saw would chase her in nightmares for a long time.

There was a car crash but, in the next second, she saw the most horrifying, blood-freezing thing. The paramedics had moved the victims on a stretcher but instead of rushing to the ambulance, they switched on some life-saving systems like she'd seen in the movies. Finally they covered the bodies.

The victims were already dead: the woman in the snow-white wedding dress and the man in the black wedding suit.

The Best Friends

Stories. Is there a person who doesn't like them? Not everyone enjoys reading, of course, but everybody likes to listen to a story being told whether it is fictional or real, to dive with our imaginations into another world and escape reality for a moment.

We are all storytellers, whether we are professionals making up fiction or simply just telling the story of someone's life. Even those people who are not fond of books are storytellers.

I will add one more story to the great book of the universe that collects them all. You, dear reader, can decide for yourself whether it is real or fiction.

*

Two friends, X and Y. Were they very close? Indeed, they were inseparable. As they were growing up together, X would often say, 'Our friendship is forever,' and Y would reply, 'Forever and ever.'

They knew what they had was rare; maybe even you, dear reader, would agree with that. No matter in what times a person lives, a devoted friendship is hard to find and very fragile. It often starts as pure and honest but somehow cannot continue on that road for long. Instead, a friendship can slip into one of the side streets of deception, envy or betrayal. And yet, though not often, there can still be a strong connection like the one between X and Y.

Do you want to know who they are? Or are you more curious about the essence of their story? Alright: I will reveal their faces and names to make it easier for you.

X was a good-looking young woman named Alice by her loving parents. Her ginger hair had naturally curls that were more perfect than even a professional hair stylist could have made them. The freckles on her face were very visible when she was a child, but with the years they had faded away and were now completely unnoticeable if she was wearing makeup. Alice's eyes were green and they charmed everyone who looked at her. She won their trust as if by magic, making them her friends because of her good heart. Do you think that, knowing her power, she would take advantage of it? As I have already said, Alice was pure-hearted and good, and wickedness of any sort was unknown to her,

Are you wondering already about Y? I won't keep you in suspense.

Everybody said that Y was like Alice's sister, though not because she had the same ginger hair (that would have been too great a coincidence). In fact, Y had straight blonde hair like the sun's rays and blue eyes like the ocean. She looked so much like a doll that this could mislead people, but for those who knew her her good looks were just a nice addition to her great personality. Her name was Sienna. It's important to know that her heart was made of gold the same as Alice's, and that was the reason why people often said they were like sisters.

How often does it happen in the universe that two so identical things attract each other and stick together? Even in nature, it is rare. I don't know about you, dear reader, but countless times I've seen a beautiful flower standing alone amid old grass and weeds, or a single beautiful tree in a wild field, or a sweet bird standing by itself on a tree branch, singing its song – to nobody. But when two identical things are like one, they shine even more brightly. That was exactly the case with Alice and Sienna.

Their childhood flew by, with its scratched knees and colourful markers used on white paper filled with nice drawings, many of which they still kept in a drawer; from time to time they opened it to smile at the old memories. And the school years flew away at the same speed.

Classroom, lessons, dreams and goals and, of course, the flickers of first love. After that, again together, they jumped into the life of being grown up. Always hand by hand, shoulder to shoulder, they supported each other. You may ask, dear reader, 'Support? what for?' because it all sounds so perfect.

Of course, life wasn't always easy for them. Life's obstacles are part not only of stories based on reality but also of fiction, where imagination is the master rather than life. One thing only connects a fairy tale and a real-life story: the uneasy path. Because life is easy on no one; don't fool yourself, dear reader; it isn't easy for me or for you, not even for Snow White or Cinderella. Even though we all want our lives to be like a fairy tale, it still isn't easy all the time. A happy ending would be a nice consolation but it is human nature never to be completely satisfied. Even a happy ending would bore us after a while.

But let us go back to our main characters and their story. Real or fictional, they also had their difficulties but, thanks to the fact they were keeping each other's backs, they could get through anything.

What would you like to hear now? Maybe that they remained friends until they both had grey hair, meeting for afternoon tea and remembering funny stories of their youth? Or would you prefer to hear that even the most perfect friendship always comes to an end because perfection does not exist? That probably the day came when they had a great fight and after that nothing could be the same ever again? That when they grew old, each of them would be sitting on her armchair in her living room, drinking tea and not even remembering her false friend from her youth? Well, I will have to disappoint you because their story is none of those.

Alice was celebrating her twenty-fourth birthday. As she was blowing out the candles, she made a wish to reach the top of the mountain of dreams she had this year – or at least to achieve one or two of her goals. She had her whole life ahead for the rest of the list.

Alice had just graduated from university in archaeology and was proud of her degree. Her next ambition was to become an assistant to a professor. Sienna had graduated in the same speciality. Of course she had; since childhood, they'd had the same interests so that was just a natural continuation.

Alice's parents, together with Sienna, were clapping hands joyfully and passing plates and cutlery for the cake. It was a small family celebration; afterwards the two girls were going to party with friends in a club.

'Darling, we are so proud of you.' Alice's mother was weeping from happiness.

'My life wouldn't be the same without your support, Mom. Thank you!' Alice replied emotionally and embraced her mother.

'The longer you both hug each other, the more cake there'll be for Sienna,' Alice's father commented jokingly. 'I can already see her licking her lips.'

They all laughed, but for a brief moment Alice thought she saw something strange in her friend's eyes, as if she were very thoughtful. But that odd sensation only lasted a second because then Sienna burst out laughing with the others.

After the family had finished dessert, the two young women went to prepare for the party, which was starting in an hour. 'It's adorable the way your mother always reacts so emotionally to everything,' said Sienna with a soft smile when they entered Alice's room.

'Yours is exactly the same. Even your father is, while from mine I can only expect a joke because he is too uncomfortable to shed a tear,' replied Alice, who was taking out her outfit for the night from the wardrobe. 'You know, yesterday I was checking out rented flats and I saw this absolutely amazing place. I'm sure you will love it!' she added enthusiastically.

Since they both were single, it was part of their plan after graduation to live together. They were so looking forward to the idea; it could probably have happened much earlier when they had started university, but their families had insisted they focus on their education; living together could distract them too much. Now, however, it was time to take their lives in their own hands and they were very excited at the thought.

'Sure... I mean great! You can show me tomorrow.' Again it seemed that Sienna was not actually there. Even her movements lacked energy and the excitement she should have been feeling about the evening was missing. She slowly smoothed the dress she was going to wear, which was short with a very revealing front.

'Are you alright?' Alice couldn't help but ask. It might have been just an impression, but if it was not then that was really odd. She knew her friend as well as the fingers on her hand; something must be bothering her.

Sienna smiled and Alice's anxiety faded away. 'Of course I am. I just need a drink.' She laughed and started getting dressed.

Alice did not reply immediately, not because she had nothing to say but because what she wanted to say was not a conversation for this evening. They were supposed to be in a party mood and she didn't want to ruin it, but the truth was that Alice had noticed her best friend reaching for alcohol far more than usual during the last year. Having fun was one thing, but Alice thought that Sienna was crossing the line.

In fact, many things had changed during the past year and they had not always been pleasant. During their last year at university, Alice's boyfriend Riley had been in a car crash that had changed his life and those of everyone around him. He was now in a wheelchair and the doctors predicted he would stay there for the rest of his life.

Riley was devastated and shut himself away from the world. He pushed away all the people who cared about him except his family who took care of him, and that effectively ended his relationship with Alice. She was crushed but she was forced to respect his wish; there was nothing else to be done.

They had not been together for very long, just year and a half after the first time they had met in the university cafeteria. But Alice had felt this special connection between them and she'd thought that he might be the one. After the catastrophic event, she had not much choice but to focus on graduating in order to suppress her sorrow. Even though time had passed, Alice wasn't ready for new dates because pain was still pulsing along with her heartbeat. She was keeping her love life on pause.

'That colour really suits you, you know.' Alice decided to change the course of her thoughts and go for a safe topic as she glimpsed Sienna's dark-blue dress on its hanger. 'Same as that blue blouse I'm always complimenting you about, though I haven't seen you wear it for ages. What happened to it?'

Sienna was half-undressed. She suddenly she pulled down her blouse again and buttoned up her jeans. Her face had the same lost expression as before, like something was really bothering her.

'What's wrong?' Alice couldn't be deceived anymore; there must be something, as she'd thought all along, but why was her friend not admitting it? They shared everything.

'Nothing – really, it's nothing... I just...' Sienna looked nervously for her handbag '...changed my mind about the outfit. I'll go home and pick something else to wear, okay?' She was acting as if she were out of her mind and that was really worrying her friend.

'What? But why? I was just saying what a good choice this dress is.' Alice's eyes were wide with surprise; she couldn't believe her friend was actually leaving now. 'But if you want another dress, take one of mine – we're the same size.' Surely that would be the most logical thing to do?

'Don't worry. I'll be quick, I promise.' Sienna was already halfway out of the room, holding the door handle.

'Sienna, for God's sake! It will take you half an hour to get to your place and we need to be at the club in less than an hour!'

'I'll meet you there on time,' were Sienna's last words before she disappeared, leaving the door open. In the next second Alice heard the front door close loudly.

Her mother had come up to find out what was going on. 'Honey, is everything alright?'

Alice nodded and gave a pale smile, but the truth was that she had no idea what her friend was thinking. Sienna had never behaved in such a way before.

*

Sienna was driving slightly over the speed limit. Tears were falling down her face, but she didn't wipe them away because she was alone and there was nobody to hide them from. She passed the street leading to her home and continued straight ahead.

Actually, Sienna had no intention of going home – at least not now. There was something else that had to be done, something that weighed on her heart like a rock, a rock that was dragging her down to the bottom of the ocean of sorrow. Was there anything heavier than unshared pain? She couldn't share her agony with anyone, neither with her loving family nor her best friend Alice who was like a sister to her. They had never, ever kept secrets from each other, at least not until this moment.

Sienna knew she had to give an explanation about her crazy behaviour, but she'd kept it inside for so long – a whole year already – that what had happened this evening was not unexpected. She had no control over it; no matter how much she tried, it was always there and she ended up with a glass of wine, two, three, a bottle. She knew that alcohol couldn't solve a problem, she knew her problem had no solution, but she was looking for something to take away the pain of that terrible night for a while.

Unintentionally, Alice had just reminded Sienna of what she couldn't forget and so she'd had to make an excuse to escape. The blue blouse was the one she had been wearing that night a year ago and had never worn again since then. She had thrown it away.

She parked the car and got out. Now it was necessary to wipe away the tears and make herself look better. She was standing in front of a house with a big garden that used to be so pretty but now seemed uncared for.

Sienna quickly crossed the alley and pressed her finger on the doorbell. There was no response the first time so she rang again; she knew it wasn't possible that nobody was at home. The door finally opened and before her stood a woman of her mother's age with sad and tired eyes.

'Mrs Cooper, I know it's late and I didn't let you know I was coming, but is there a chance I can see him?' Sienna's beautiful blue eyes filled with tears again, looking like a sea with a massive wave about to flood everything around it.

The woman stepped forward and closed the door behind her so they were both standing in the porch. Her tired eyes were pitying; she could see Sienna's pain– she could feel it too – but there was nothing she could do to help her.

'Dear girl.' She paused for a moment to modify her voice because it sounded too emotional. 'I beg you not to suffer. He wouldn't want that. It's enough that *he* suffers.'

Hearing those words, Sienna started to sob inconsolably.

'Go and live your life the best way you can and forget about him. If he ever feels ready, he will search for you – for you and all other friends on whom he has turned his back. Leave the pain for him to deal with and smile at the life he had.' The woman patted Sienna on the shoulder.

Sienna couldn't do more than that, but there was one last thing. After that, she promised herself that she would try to move on.

When Mrs Cooper turned around to go back inside, Sienna stopped her. 'Please, one last favour.' She took a piece of paper from her jeans' pocket. Though she'd kept it there, it seemed to have been folded carefully and to be of some importance. 'Give him this from me.' She stretched her trembling hand towards the woman.

Mrs Cooper smiled as much as she was still capable of and took it. There was something in that girl's eyes that reminded her very much of another girl. 'Of course,' she said.

Sienna headed back to her car. After she started the engine, she realised she could hardly see for tears. She wiped them away but new ones kept falling; there seemed to be no end to them.

What was important now was to get home as quickly as possible to change so she could be on time at the club. She didn't notice that she was driving over the speed limit. Her thoughts were running much faster than the speed of the car, making her feel dizzy. The memory was so clear, popping up in her mind as if it were playing a joke on her, trying to upset her more and more...

That night of the accident, she had been in the car with Riley. It was the last place she was expected to be because he was Alice's boyfriend and they seemed happy together. But actually they were not.

On that terrible fatal day when Alice had first met Riley in the university's cafeteria, she didn't know that Sienna was the one he had gone to talk to just minutes earlier. Alice seemed so enchanted by him that Sienna didn't want to spoil her happiness, so she had sacrificed the little spark between her and Riley for her best friend. Someone might think she had been very noble, but the truth was that it led to something awful. The attraction between Sienna and Riley didn't fade away, though as God was their witness they had tried really hard to destroy it.

The night of the accident, Sienna was in Riley's car because they'd met secretly to talk. She'd told him this was the first and last time they would meet, and that was only to set the boundaries. He seemed to agree with everything she was saying, but then he said that if that if this was the only time they would be alone together he might as well remember it forever.

Before she could react, Riley had leaned over and softly touched her lips with his; lips that she had dreamed of but accepted that she would never feel. But at that moment they were on hers, and so she responded instead of pulling away. She eventually withdrew, but not before imprinting the precious moment on her memory. Sienna then told him very coldly never to do that again and asked him to take her home.

The silence in the car felt heavy; they were both suffering. And then it happened. She didn't even know where the car that crashed into theirs came from. The terrible noise and sudden fright confused her, and for a moment she didn't know what was happening.

Riley was injured yet conscious. 'Are you alright?' he asked and she nodded because she wasn't feeling pain, though her face revealed fear as she looked at him. 'Okay, I want you to call an ambulance and get away from here.' He was talking with difficulty; the hit had caught him badly.

There was still nobody getting out of the other car – the driver was probably injured, too. Sienna started crying with panic and shock. She refused to go along with Riley's idea, but he tried to convince her that it would be much harder to explain why were they both together in his car at that time of the night. Everything would be just fine for him, and he didn't want her to suffer if Alice found out. In the end, Sienna agreed.

Nobody ever learned that Riley was not alone in his car

when the accident happened. Sienna had a few scratches, nothing serious, but the damage to her heart couldn't be healed. She couldn't find peace for herself because of her mistakes. She had allowed her heart to beat for someone who could never be hers; she had betrayed her best friend, and the sweetest kiss in the world had contradicted her moral values. She was sinful. If anyone deserved to suffer it was her, not Riley...

*

Mrs Cooper went back into her house and headed to her son's room to give him the note from the girl who had just visited. Before she entered, however, her curiosity took over and she unfolded the paper. *It should never been you, but me. I love you!* was all that it said.

*

Alice looked around nervously. She'd been at the club for more than an hour with the rest of her friends but Sienna hadn't shown up. Being late wasn't typical of her; neither was behaving in the way she had earlier in Alice's room. Alice was getting more anxious while her friends were trying to convince her to have fun. She couldn't listen to their advice; there was something wrong and she could feel it. Could her heart handle something else bad happening after what she'd been through already in the past year?

She went out and tried to call Sienna a couple of times but there was no response, and her anxiety started to mix with anger. Was her best friend really going to miss her party and disappear? As she turned around to re-enter the bar, her phone finally rang.

'Can I know where are you and what is happening?' She took the call without even looking to see who was phoning her or leaving a chance for the other person to speak. Then her voice suddenly changed from angry to confused. 'Mom, is that you?'

'Darling.' Her mother was sobbing. 'I'm sorry but I have some bad news for you... They called to say that Sienna was in a car crash and ... she didn't make it...'

*

Well, dear reader, that is all from this story. I'm leaving you to decide whether it is fiction or something real, whether it teaches us that people are not trustworthy or teaches us about moral values and bad luck. Are there victims in this story, or people who have a fault? Did they make the right choices or the wrong ones?

The Test

Maggie was covered with sweat; drops were rolling down her face, neck, and chest as if she had taken a shower with her clothes on. Anyway, it was of no importance to her.

Kevin stretched out his hand towards her but she didn't take it. She had no intention of doing so, though she could have used some help at that moment. Her feet felt weak and she was kneeling down with no strength to stand up. Her rapid breathing wasn't helping her regain her balance either. Nevertheless, her pride would not allow her to accept help.

'Maggie, stop trying to be a hero and let me help you, for God's sake!' Kevin's voice sounded almost angry, but even if it had been sympathetic it wouldn't have made any difference. The only response he received was an angry look, which was a silent way to tell him to leave her alone.

Oliver, who was standing almost the same distance from her as Kevin, didn't bother asking or offering help; he just put his arm around her waist and tried to lift her up.

'Don't touch me!' Maggie hissed at him in a weak voice. She made an effort to get up by herself.

'Leave her to do it the way she wants,' said Simon, who was standing by the door. His face was worried but he didn't go anywhere near Maggie. 'Obviously she doesn't want help.'

'Yes, smart ass, we can see that,' Kevin said sarcastically. 'But the faster we get back, the sooner she will rest properly. Plus, I really hate this place.'

'Why don't you cut the crap and say that you don't care about her? You just want to get out of here,' Oliver commented sharply. Despite having his help rejected by Maggie, he didn't leave her side.

Kevin and Oliver were glowering at each other, ready for one of their usual fights, but before they could start it

Maggie was on her feet and walking slowly. That was enough for them to follow her silently.

Simon was leaning against the open door with his arms folded. When she passed by him he asked softly, 'Are you all right?'

Maggie nodded without looking at him and hurried forward because she didn't want anyone to see her tears.

Her nod did not go unnoticed. 'Sure, she's nice to you – idiot,' said Kevin irritably.

Simon did not respond, though it was a real challenge for him to simply ignore the most annoying person on earth.

Maggie was already in the shower and the hot water was relaxing her tense muscles. It was also washing away the mask she had put on to cover her real emotions. Now, when she was alone, she let the tears run freely and merge with the water drops. The only thing that gave away her crying was her face, which was twisted in agony.

Maggie didn't know why all this was happening to her, how much more emotional torture she could bear. Would there be an end to it – and when?

It had all started three weeks ago...

*

When she opened her eyes, Maggie knew one thing for sure: she had no idea where she was. Fear and panic started to rise in her chest. The place was spacious and well-lit. There was a well-equipped kitchen, a living room and a couple of doors that Maggie guessed led to bedrooms.

She looked around anxiously, trying to recall how she'd ended up there, but her memory was betraying her, leaving nothing but a blank spot exactly where she was searching for a clue.

She wrapped her arms around herself and took a few uncertain steps to make sure she was completely alone. Maybe it would be a good idea to open each of the doors and see what was behind them; perhaps one of them led out of this unknown place. But before she could put her plan into action, one of the doors opened and she froze completely. She held her breath and stared anxiously at the figure that emerged. It was a man, not particularly tall but well-built and muscular. His dark brown, almost black, eyes seemed familiar – and he was looking as confused as Maggie.

'Kevin?' she said.

'What is that place...? Who...? Maggie, is that you?' He stepped towards her, still looking extremely confused. She stared at him open mouthed then her surprise and confusion were slowly replaced by anger.

She put her hands on her hips and demanded, 'What is this sick game? Is this your idea?!'

Kevin didn't look as if he were having any fun at all. 'What are you talking about? *My* idea? I could ask you the same thing.'

Maggie wouldn't buy his lie, no matter how well-disguised it was. She knew him well and telling the truth was not part of his nature – she knew that from experience. Of course, that was long ago and time had passed since then, but that wasn't a criterion for her to forget or forgive.

They had shared two years together, in which she was the naïve, blind victim and he was the skilful player, until the day the blindfold fell down like a theatre curtain and Maggie saw that he was cheating on her. She couldn't decide if she hated him for what he'd done or hated herself for being so naive. Now it didn't matter any more; time had pushed the memories away, leaving space for new, better ones. The truth was, though, that Maggie still felt angry towards him, a faded anger that wouldn't go away. For her, he would remain a monster from her past.

'I don't believe you!' she said, piercing him with a cold look.

'I don't lie! For real, I have no clue where we are and why!'

If she hadn't know him, she would probably have believed him because he sounded really honest. 'Yeah, for sure you don't lie...' She rolled her eyes but couldn't finish her sarcastic comment because something happened at that moment that made them both turn towards the doors.

The door next to the one from which Kevin had emerged was now open and there was another man standing there. His physique wasn't as impressive as Kevin's but he had a really beautiful face.

'Who are you? Are you the reason for us being here?' Kevin shouted rudely at the man but kept a safe distance as if he were afraid, which was ironic considering how strong he was.

'I honestly have no idea...' The newcomer looked as confused as Maggie and Kevin had minutes ago, which suggested that he didn't have any answers.

Maggie, her arms still folded across her chest, took a few bold steps towards the man and stared at his face as if she were making sure of something.

'Maggie? What are you doing here? What is this place?' The man spoke more confidently now he'd seen a familiar face.

'Do you two know each other?' Kevin asked, surprised.

'Of course, we do,' the newcomer answered sharply in the same manner Kevin had spoken to him. 'We were dating for half a year.'

'I don't think it was for that long, Oliver. Otherwise I would have been completely broke, without even savings, because you couldn't stop stealing from me!' Now that she had recognised him, Maggie had no interest in being near either of them so she headed to a chair in the small kitchen area.

As she sat down, she started massaging her temples with circular movements. It wasn't just the shock of being in some unknown place with no memory of how she'd got there; these people were ones she'd hoped never to see again. People who had hurt her, who had mocked her goodness and were the source of anger and rage that she'd not been able to shake off.

'You stole from her?' Kevin looked like a bull ready to attack. His eyes were wide open and his nostrils flared with every breath he took.

'Who are you to judge me? This is between me and her!' Oliver tried to cover the information Maggie had revealed about him with arrogance.

Maggie tried to maintain her self-control while the two men attacked each other with ugly words, but a sudden silence made her look up to see what had stopped them talking.

Another man had joined them. Judging by the expressions on the faces of the three men, they did not know each other – but Maggie knew every single one of them. The newcomer was Simon. Her stomach flinched unpleasantly.

If she really hated the other two, that was not exactly what she felt towards the newcomer. It wasn't hate, but it wasn't a nice feeling either. Maggie had met Simon a few months ago. Something about him had impressed her, not so much his good looks as an unexplainable attraction, often shown in movies as 'love at first sight'. She'd never got the chance to find out if it was love because after a few dates they had ended up in her bed – and the next day Simon had disappeared. He never called her back.

She'd tried to contact him but the only response she got was a text message that it wasn't going to work out between them. Dumped by a text message; that had never happened to her before. Even though she had to continue with her life after being deeply hurt, the question 'why' wouldn't let her rest. Maggie had thought they had a special connection, so but what had happened so suddenly that he had pulled away? She never got an answer.

Now Maggie was locked in a spacious flat with three

people who had hurt her. She didn't know if that was a nightmare or a punishment.

*

There were no other newcomers; it was just Maggie and three of her ex-boyfriends. They received some answers about what was happening the first day, but not enough and they made no sense. With no way out they were like prisoners except they had all they needed – food, bedrooms, comfortable surroundings. The situation was not only scary as hell but also very awkward; there was history between them, after all.

On the day of their arrival, a note appeared mysteriously on the kitchen table. That didn't make the situation any less confusing or frightening.

The next day, Maggie and the guys were woken up by something like an alarm. They already knew what they had to do. They opened the only door that didn't lead to any of their rooms and in front of them was a small hallway ending with another door. The odd thing about it was that it was made of glass.

The three men, followed by Maggie, walked the short distance to it and examined what was behind it. The glass was so perfectly clear that the only thing that indicated it was actually a door was the handle. Behind it was a room, not very big and unfurnished except for a chair in the middle like one in a doctor's surgery.

'And now what? We just go in there, sit on the chair and let someone whom we haven't met experiment on us?' Oliver's voice was shaking, but not with anger. He was scared; they all were.

'The note was clear enough,' Simon reminded him. 'It's not about experimenting. There won't be anything physically dangerous. The idea is to overcome our biggest fears, one for each passing week. Only then will we be free of this place.'

'Yes, Mr Know-It-All, we read the note. Thanks for reminding us what we already know,' Kevin commented sarcastically. The tension that had developed between the three men from the very beginning didn't seem like it would go away any time soon. 'But how would you interpret being held against your will in an unknown place and forced to do something that you don't want to do? It might not be for experimental purposes, but it doesn't sound like a vacation.'

The glass door opened automatically. Maggie, who until now had been standing silently behind the guys, stepped forward. Kevin's hand caught hers before she entered. 'Maggie, maybe would be better if...' he began softly but she interrupted sharply.

'There are rules. The note states that we all have our turns and today is mine.' She pulled away from his grip. 'And don't you dare pretend that you care! Don't any of you dare to!' She turned around and walked into the room.

The door closed by itself and Maggie felt goosebumps rise all over her body. But she had too much pride to show weakness, or at least she couldn't afford to do so in front of the audience she had at that moment. Kevin, Oliver and Simon had already seen her when she was weak; to hurt her the way each of them had done, they must have thought she was a loser. That was why she wanted to prove to them, here and now, how strong she actually was. She was stronger than them, even stronger than the three of them together.

Maggie suppressed her fear and sat on the chair, avoiding looking at the glass door where three pairs of eyes were staring at her. 'Act as if they're not here,' she repeated to herself, the same as she'd been doing in the apartment they were sharing.

'I guess now at least we can find out what methods they'll be using on us,' Oliver said quietly as he looked at Maggie.

'She is not your lab rat.' Simon was annoyed by the selfish comment.

'Come on, dude. At least be honest now that she's not here.' Kevin rolled his eyes like he couldn't stand any more of Simon's dramatics. 'Admit that you're glad not to be the first one.'

Then the three men stayed quiet, figuring that the tension between them could wait. It was more important to observe what was happening to Maggie. But even though they were staring at her, trying even not to blink, there was nothing to see. She was completely still except for giving a little shiver once in a while; it was like she was sleeping.

The minutes passed slowly. When Maggie suddenly took a deep breath and opened her eyes as if waking from a nightmare, the three men got scared.

She jumped off the chair. Even though she felt quite weak, the fear of staying even a second longer and letting the nightmare continue made her use all her energy to push herself up. She heard the door open and she wasn't alone any more; Kevin, Oliver and Simon had entered the room and were asking questions that she was too confused to answer.

'She must be in shock. It'd better to take her straight to her room,' suggested Simon. It seemed like a good idea; in fact, it was the only thing they could do for her. Kevin helped him and, supporting her from both sides, they led her back to her bedroom.

Maggie curled into a ball on the bed like a child, but she couldn't close her eyes. There was an awkward silence. Kevin and Oliver were standing beside the bed, waiting to hear about her experience so they could prepare themselves for their turn, but she was just staring into nothing without saying a word.

'I'll leave this cup of tea here next to you. All right?' Simon had returned from the kitchen bringing hot tea to soothe her nerves. She gave no reaction and he exhaled heavily and exchanged a quick look with the other two guys. 'Maggie ... I know you're upset, but can you tell us what exactly happened back there?'

She knew it had to be done sooner or later, whether she wanted to talk to them or not, because she owed them this information simply as one human being to another. The guys needed to know what was expected of them.

'It was horrible... I felt as if I were falling asleep, but it wasn't a dream – it was so realistic... It was so terribly realistic!' She closed her eyes for a moment and when she opened them again she asked, 'How long did it last?'

The three men had fallen silent, trying to imagine what they would have to go through. Simon was the one to reply. 'Ten minutes. Why? Did it feel longer than that?'

Maggie nodded, and that brought a new wave of terror to the men. 'I want to be alone,' she said. She couldn't bear their presence any longer; she couldn't have an audience at such a moment of emotional agony.

Kevin and Oliver didn't wait to be asked to leave again; it was a private moment for them too because they needed to prepare themselves mentally. Simon stayed behind for a moment. 'If you need anything at all, please don't hesitate to ask.'

He wanted her to know that she was not alone and to assure her of his good intentions. 'What was your fear?' His curiosity prevailed but he received no answer, not even a look from her: Maggie wanted him to leave. He decided not to push her, but as he placed his hand on the door handle to leave the room he heard her weak voice behind him.

'I can't swim,' she said. More wasn't needed; he could figure out the rest.

*

Every week, on a different day for each of them, they experienced one of their personal fears in an attempt to overcome it. The experience never lasted more than minutes for those who were watching it but felt like hours to the one experiencing it. The general mood got darker and darker.

The three men had only one thing in common between them – Maggie – and it wasn't bringing them any closer.

Maggie kept her distance; it would have been unnatural to pretend to be good friends or care for one another since they had all proved their disloyalty to her. Seeing them every day was adding salt to her old wounds, which she had mistakenly thought were healed. The constant reminders were making her agony even more unbearable.

It didn't seem to be as hard for Kevin, Oliver and Simon – or at least it looked that way to her. They tried to talk to her, to make a connection, but that only made her more furious. They had no right to act sympathetically now, not after the way they'd treated her in the past. She couldn't understand how someone could show the worst he was capable of to the one he loved then show care. That made her blood boil!

One question really bothered her: why had Simon disappeared without having had the courage to tell her face to face. That mystery was piercing her heart. She was rude to Kevin and Oliver but she was just cold with Simon, which was her way of being a little nicer.

In the fourth week, the fear Maggie had to face and overcome seemed hardest to bear. Covered with sweat, her arms and legs weak, her breathing rapid, it took her a while to realise it was over and she was already awake. She gathered all the strength to return to the kitchen, sat on one of the chairs and put her face in her hands.

'Maggie?' It was Kevin.

Of course they wouldn't leave her in peace, not until after they'd tortured her with pointless talk. What was this place? She couldn't handle it any more; she felt naked. Her mind wasn't a secret to the one who was putting her through these tests, and when she was most vulnerable her audience was made up of the people she least wanted to see. She felt like a volcano getting ready to erupt; it would only require the last drop of her tolerance and patience to drain away and she would explode.

Kevin was leaning on the side of the table, obviously planning to talk to her. Oliver and Simon joined him. 'We are all going through this and we know how difficult it is. We also know that you don't have warm feelings towards us – you've definitely made your point about that. But this doesn't mean we can't help each other in difficult times. Although you don't believe it, we do care about you.'

He stopped for a minute to make sure his words were sinking in then continued. 'I've never known you like this before – so stubborn and with such strong willpower. There are so many things I didn't know and am now learning. You are...'

With one quick movement of her hand, Maggie swiped at a glass on the table; it fell on the floor and broke into pieces. She stood up, the adrenalin from her anger giving her strength. Her eyes were red from the tears but, probably for the first time in these past weeks, she actually looked directly into Kevin's eyes. That was it: the last drop of tolerance had been drained and Maggie released the pain, sadness and anger she'd been keeping inside for so long.

'I am much more than you knew, yes! Do you know why? Because you didn't bother to discover it all. None of you tried.' Tears were running down her face while the three men silently stared at her. She was speaking openly to them for the first time.

'For you, Kevin, I was a stupid woman, satisfying your wishes out of love, something unknown to you. That was why my bed wasn't enough for you. And for you, Oliver, I was even more stupid because you thought that stealing from me was what I deserved. Neither of you respected me as a woman. And you want to convince me that you respect me as a human being now that you've got to know me better?'

It was the moment of the truth; there wouldn't be a better time and they all knew it so the least they could do was to use it.

Oliver started first. 'I'm sorry...' was the only thing he said, but it sounded honest.

'Not every relationship is destined to work out, Maggie.' Kevin had more of an excuse. 'You are an incredible woman. I know it for sure now, and I regret not treating you with the respect you deserved. But even if you were the most amazing woman on earth, even if I realise my mistakes, that won't change the fact that some people are just not meant to be together.' He shrugged and gave her an apologetic look.

Actually, his words made perfect sense and maybe Maggie already knew it deep down. But the truth was that she needed to hear it from *him*, from *them*, so she could find the peace she needed to let the pain go and continue with her life.

'Are you really going to skip me?' Simon asked her, surprised.

Maggie blinked away the tears that were blurring her vision. How could she skip the biggest question mark from her past? 'Why?' she asked, and for him it was clear how much she was covering with that simple question.

'I started falling in love.' He smiled softly. 'You are intelligent and funny ... the chemistry between us was so strong. I got scared. I wasn't sure if I was ready for something so big. But I know I am now.' He found that being open and honest wasn't that difficult after all; it was actually a relief. He waited anxiously for Maggie's answer. Would it be positive, or not?

Maggie exhaled and a smile appeared on her face. For such a long time she hadn't felt the way she was feeling now – free, light and happy, without bad emotions to suppress her, to make her doubt herself, to make her fear...

'I felt it too – but I don't need a coward next to me. I'm sorry.' She was now completely ready to leave the ghosts of her ex-boyfriends in the past. The questions had been answered, the fire put out and there was a sweet feeling in her heart.

'Hey, what's that?' Oliver broke the silence and pointed at something on the table. Four pairs of eyes turned in that direction. Another note had appeared as mysteriously as the previous one.

Maggie and the guys leaned over it to read it. It said: *Your last test is over. You are free.*

The Flatmate

Agnes was sitting on the sofa, stroking her hair and staring at the TV screen. A movie was on but she had muted it. She couldn't even remember how she'd chosen it; it must have been an automatic play of the first movie on her Netflix list.

She had a strong feeling of déjà vu but she couldn't quite place it. She was alone though, and that was a fear of hers from before; she didn't have that fear any more. Something had cured her of it – but the process had been scarier than the fear she'd had in a first place. Facing fears eventually proves that, no matter how hard one tries avoiding what one fears, life will deliver the lesson whether it is wanted or unwanted. And she knew that she'd see it coming although she'd tried everything in her power to avoid it.

Clementine had handed Agnes the keys after giving her an awkward hug and then closed the door. Agnes had locked it and gone back to the living room, sat in front of the TV, muted it and told herself, 'I am so damn lucky!'

A lot had changed. She could never have expected, even in her wildest imagination, that she would one day go through what she had done for the past half year. It had been one of the scariest experiences of her life – and the worst part was that she blamed herself for it.

*

Agnes had reasons to hate being alone. Some people would find it peaceful but it made her feel abandoned. Despite everything she knew about herself, she had decided to hide once again rather than fix what needed fixing – and that had been her biggest mistake. That is how her personal hell had begun.

Agnes's good friend, Clementine, had recently gone through a tough time and was currently living in a place she hated, so Agnes decided to invite her to be her flatmate. It was a promising move, a perfect fit and, most of all, something Agnes had always wanted to do – live with a friend. That sounded like so much fun, or at least according to the cheesy Hollywood movies – and Agnes was a true *Friends* fan. Of course, when she suggested the idea to Clementine, the answer was yes. There were no obstacles, everything was going so smoothly it was as if it were meant to be. Little did she know…

*

Clementine, or Cleo as Agnes called her, was a sweet young girl who was both Agnes's colleague and friend, though it was not one of those friendships where two people had immediately started vibing with each other.

At first, when they had started talking every now and then, Cleo was gentle and polite. Agnes admired the fact that she was probably the only person in the company who never seemed frustrated, angry or even simply moody because she was having a bad day. Cleo was perfect, with a perfect appearance and perfect reactions to everything. Agnes was really impressed; in fact, Cleo was so perfect she scarcely seemed human. Agnes, on the other hand, was more direct in her way of expressing herself; it was just the way she was and she considered it to be part of her charm.

Eventually occasional chats here and there developed into hanging out together in their free time, sharing their thoughts more openly and becoming what could be described as friends.

*

Agnes was having coffee with Deborah, another friend and colleague. That was rare in most workplaces; people usually considered themselves lucky if they could make one of their colleagues into a good friend. She was really lucky to have two, and she knew it.

'I can't wait for Cleo to move in, Debby, I'm so excited!' Agnes's joy was visible on her face.

'Are you sure that it's the best thing to do?'

Debby's question so conflicted with what Agnes was feeling that it puzzled and shocked her. It was true that Debby had piercing insights that quite often appeared to be accurate, so it was never a bad idea to listen to what she had to say, but at that moment it was not what Agnes wanted to hear. She wanted support for her decision because deep down her gut was trying to tell her something and she had purposely muffled it – until now. Carrying on with Debby's question would mean unleashing the voice inside Agnes's head, and that was not what she wanted.

'Why not, Debby? What could possibly be wrong with this plan? As far as I'm aware, it's perfect!' Agnes accompanied the last part of her sentence with a smile, which was her way of enforcing her positive attitude toward the decision.

'All I'm saying is that if you are doing it for some other reasons… Well, you'd better reconsider it.' Debby's words pierced Agnes's deepest hidden thoughts once again; it was almost as if she were an open book to her friend. 'But if you've taken the decision already then I'm happy if you're happy. Just … be careful.'

'What do you mean?' Agnes's alarm shifted to curiosity. It was the weirdest thing for Debby to say; after all, she was friends with Cleo too, so what seemed to be a warning made no sense. 'Cleo is struggling with money and moving in with me would help her.'

'I don't mean anything specific, just that I've caught Cleo lying many times…' Debby shrugged as if it were normal to say such a thing about someone considered to be the sweetest person.

Agnes was speechless for a few seconds; she even thought her jaw had dropped. But all she felt in that moment was one thing – certainty. 'Impossible!' she said so firmly that the exclamation mark could be felt in the air.

Agnes often went back to that memory because she believed that was when everything had begun. She'd had her first and most important clue and failed miserably to acknowledge it. She hadn't trusted the word of a good friend and dismissed the information so easily that she hadn't even examined it. No: instead she simply denied it. 'Impossible,' was what she said.

Happy to be blind, she'd ignored all the signs and moved to the next step, which brought her down with such speed that now she was facing evidence of her mistake she couldn't understand how she'd got there.

*

'Cleo,' Agnes said as she entered the kitchen where her flatmate was preparing lunch for herself, 'I left a spare towel out for you.' Cleo thanked her in the sweetest possible voice. Agnes rushed out of the kitchen and tried to avoid looking her friend in the eyes.

As she went into the bathroom to put her towel in the laundry basket and replace it with a clean one, she accidentally caught her expression in the mirror. It reflected perfectly what she was feeling and she couldn't hide it, but she had to try or she would offend Cleo.

The thoughts were overwhelming her and not giving the peace she wanted; question after question was fighting to be answered first. Why would Cleo use something that was not hers? Why didn't she ask to borrow? But what prevailed at that moment for Agnes was the feeling of having her privacy, her personal space and belongings, invaded. Her permission was taken for granted, and she felt oddly ashamed and vulnerable.

What happened made no sense so it was difficult for Agnes to apply logic or understanding. If someone had said, 'But don't girls share?' that would be not the concept Agnes had.

Agnes recalled a detail she hadn't paid much attention to at first. Cleo did not have many belongings and that led to her borrowing and using a lot of Agnes's stuff. But Agnes could excuse that because she knew how her friend struggled with money, although they both worked at the same place and had the same salaries. Agnes was dealing with everything on her own, much like Cleo, so it appeared odd for a brief moment that her friend always said she didn't have much cash.

The problem Agnes was facing now was that she had to find a solution without offending her friend. She thought she had done a pretty good job by offering a spare towel – surely that was hint enough? Agnes had hoped Cleo would explain what had happened, or maybe she would apologise, but none of those scenarios had happened. Cleo simply said in a sweet voice, 'Oh, thank you.' Nobody could be angry with that voice, that sweet expression.

As she left the bathroom, Agnes bumped into Cleo who smiled somewhat weirdly, her eyes wide with excitement. Agnes did not understand and, to be honest, she was a little frightened. And then she noticed. 'Did you just change your top?' A few minutes ago Agnes had seen Cleo wearing a different top but now they were both wearing exactly the same colour.

'We look the same now, don't we?' Cleo giggled, then she rushed to the kitchen where the kettle was boiling.

That was not a coincidence, it was intentional. A very unpleasant feeling ran through Agnes's gut and made her shiver.

*

Agnes had just come home from grocery shopping and planned to spend the rest of the afternoon having some 'me' time. She noticed that Cleo had left a real mess in the kitchen again. It was no longer a surprise as Agnes started to see her friend from a different perspective, though initially she had been shocked. How could someone who seemed so intelligent, well-mannered, sweet and delicate be so messy and even dirty?

The funny thing was that even if Agnes had told someone, nobody would have believed her; she wouldn't have believed it herself if she'd been told just few months ago. She exhaled heavily and decided to deal with everything later; now it was time for a face mask, and nothing else mattered.

As she entered the bathroom and opened the drawer that held her beauty products, she experienced a brief moment of confusion. Nothing was where she usually kept it and everything had been moved and obviously used. There was even a missing product!

That crossed all boundaries. Furious, Agnes grabbed her phone and wrote a message to Cleo. Not even a minute after sending it she received a response but, for some reason, she had the chills before even she read it. All it said was how sorry Cleo was and how it would never happen again. The message was filled with dramatic regret, which would make anyone feel sorry for raising the matter and upsetting sweet Cleo.

As Agnes read it, she held her breath in unpleasant expectation. She knew this would not be the only thing her friend would do.

The following day, Agnes found that all her make-up products had been destroyed by having oil poured all over them. That was the day she realised that she was dealing not with a friend, not with a colleague, not with a random flatmate, but with a psychotic person. She had known Cleo for three years without really knowing her at all.

*

A month passed and Agnes's living situation got much worse than she could ever have imagined. She had already avoided having an important conversation with Cleo twice, but today was the day it would finally happen. If she was able to, though she wasn't sure how, she would ignore things such as the personal boundaries that her friend Cleo had crossed, but she couldn't ignore the topic she was about to discuss. It was a financial matter and she couldn't postpone it any longer. It seemed as if Cleo had forgotten that food costs money, house supplies cost money – as a matter of fact, everything costs money. Money that Cleo never took out of her pocket.

'Cleo.' Agnes was sitting nervously on the sofa pretending to watch the movie that was playing on the TV but actually trying to remember the speech she had carefully prepared.

Cleo's focus moved from the phone in her hands and she looked up. For a moment Agnes could have sworn she saw something different in her; in fact, her whole expression was different: empty, as if her eyes were expressing something soulless. But even though that gave her the chills, Agnes had to have this conversation,

'I want to talk about something,' Agnes said, and her words triggered the immediate appearance of the familiar sweet expression on Cleo's face.

'Sure, what is it?' Even Cleo's tone of her voice changed to sweeter when she spoke.

At that moment, the doorbell rang. Agnes rushed to open it because she had been expecting a delivery any day now. Her mind was still focused on the conversation she was about to have when she realised it was way too late for a delivery. That made her check through the peephole first. There was someone outside whom she could not see clearly because he or she was wearing a hoodie and keeping their head down.

Agnes's blood felt like it was draining down to her feet. Her heart started pounding and instinctively she turned back to warn Cleo. A little scream came to her lips, but she muffled it quickly with her hands. Her flatmate had moved to stand right behind her so quietly that Agnes hadn't even heard her approaching. There it was again, the same empty, soulless look in Cleo's eyes. Agnes didn't know who she was more afraid of: the stranger outside the door or the stranger behind her.

'Don't worry.' Cleo spoke lightly, obviously amused as she recognised her friend's fear. 'If he doesn't go away, I'll beat him up,' she added with a wicked smile.

The stranger had walked away and there was no more danger outside the flat's door, but Agnes sank into deep thoughts. That night she connected some more dots to reveal Cleo's true personality. She no longer considered her a friend; the only thing that Agnes knew for certain was that Clementine was addicted to adrenaline. Tonight's situation had proved that and given her an honest, true smile, a smile Agnes saw for first time on a face she seemed to be seeing for first time. Clementine was anything but the person she was presenting to the world. Perfection did not exist after all.

*

The money talk did take place eventually. As every other time when Agnes brought something to Cleo's attention, she was scared what her reaction would be. But suddenly, to Agnes's surprise, Cleo showed that she actually had some money – which was completely opposite to the impression she had been giving. Every day Cleo returned home with bags full of groceries, cosmetics and clothes. The fridge was overloaded to the point where there wasn't space for the food; it went bad and had to be thrown away, something that Agnes hated – and Cleo knew it. The shelves in the bathroom were full of Cleo's products, most of which she didn't use but she seemed to want to show them off.

This behaviour looked like another attempt at deception, as if Cleo wanted Agnes to feel as though she had lost her mind and to doubt all her conclusions. It seemed like a punishment, a punishment for the person who could not be deceived, punishment for the person who saw through her. There were not many of them because Cleo was skilled in the art of deception.

To Agnes, the situation started to look like a game, entertainment for Cleo who was bored and had to spice life up to feel alive. Cleo needed to live on the edge by being nasty to those who opened their hearts to her – and there were many. There was not a single person who didn't want to be Cleo's friend or who had a bad word to say about her. In every person she met, she triggered the feeling that they needed to protect and love her because of her innocence. She was like a poisonous snake awaiting its victim but not attacking even when the victim was close; no, she would wait even longer to extend her satisfaction.

It was crystal clear now to Agnes that Cleo had no identity; she was someone who would absorb what was acceptable through observation and then she would perform like an actress. Nothing about her manners or behaviour reflected her real self. Life had damaged Cleo, as it surely has everyone, but people fall into two groups: those who cope and strive for a normal life and those who never heal, whose pain turns them into monsters who crave an extraordinary life they believe they deserve, a life where everyone owes them. A life where they are masterminds who win every time. Cleo was an attention seeker, a manipulator, a cold-hearted, selfish psychotic … and Agnes was scared.

*

'I'm so sorry – I know you're at work, but I had to… I just don't know what to do any more.' Tears ran down Agnes's cheeks one after another, as if chasing each other. She gripped her phone and tried to muffle the sound of her crying because she was sitting in the stairway of the building. She couldn't have this conversation in the flat because Cleo was there.

'It's alright. You know I always have time for you,' Debby said. 'Tell me what's going on?'

It had been six months since Cleo and Agnes had become flatmates and there had been a lot of changes. Debby had a different job now, so she and Agnes didn't see each other as often.

'I feel like I'm in a movie, one of those scary ones where nobody believes the victim.' Agnes lowered her voice through the crying hiccups. 'Debby, she is insane! She destroyed some of my things! She left garbage behind the sofa, then under my bed... She ... she stared at me while I was having a nap on the sofa and literally jumped away as soon as I opened my eyes!'

Agnes broke into sobs again, unable to continue. On the other end of the phone, Debby held her breath anxiously and waited for the rest of the story.

'I swear I was so delusional that I tried to justify everything, but she seems to have become more careless when it comes to me. Or maybe she just wants to get caught so she can enjoy watching me torment myself because I don't know what to do. She is sick, Debby, sick! I'm so scared, I'm freaking out...'

'Breathe. Take a deep breath.' Debby tried to slow her friend down because Agnes was talking faster and faster. 'Have you tried confronting her?' she asked.

'Of course I have, but she claims she hasn't done anything – and then she does something even more nasty and evil as a lesson to stop me trying to fight back.' Agnes's voice broke again. 'Every word she says is a lie and every move she makes is calculated and considered, yet nobody can see the monster I see. Everyone adores her the way I did six months ago. I just can't see how to get myself out of this situation...'

It seemed like a dead end but the solution presented itself a month after their talk, just as Debby had promised. Agnes didn't ask for many details; she didn't care as long Clementine moved out of the flat.

Apparently some guy was involved in Clementine's decision to move so suddenly – a new victim. Cleo grabbed her chance and moved out quickly. It seemed like it had all worked out for Agnes. Setting herself free had been surprisingly easy – but would she forget the trauma of the experience so easily?

*

Agnes unlocked the door, entered the flat and dropped the heavy shopping bags on the floor. There was nobody else there; it was months since Cleo had moved out and Agnes was living on her own again.

She walked into the living room to turn on the TV so she could watch her favourite show while she put the groceries away. As she was reaching for the remote control, her eye caught the frame with the photo her and Cleo together. She had tossed it out of sight somewhere as soon as Cleo had left.

It was now sitting neatly in the centre of the dining table...

The Passengers

I was fixing the little scarf around my neck in front of a mirror in the lady's washroom. I really hated that scarf.

I remembered the moments when I was a passenger taking a flight and thought how exciting must it be to work as a cabin crew, or even just stand firmly on the ground at an airport check-in desk. The interesting thing was that somehow I ended up working at the airport after all. It wasn't on purpose; on the contrary, it happened by accident. And, as with every profession, once you get to work in it, it's almost like going behind the curtains in a theatre: you understand it is nothing like it looked, nothing that you expected. Or at least for me it appeared to be a disappointment.

Sometimes, when I happened to have no queue of waiting passengers, I would let my gaze float around with no purpose and observe the whole dynamic of the airport. My thoughts, however, would be focused on deep topics that I wouldn't expect to think about at work. I wondered about things such as whether the behaviour of the modern man is worthy enough to be called evolved. I often answered myself with a firm 'no' because of the rude, arrogant attitude I regularly experienced from passengers. But I could be surprised sometimes, as well.

*

It was a busy day at work. The bad weather had led to many delayed and cancelled flights over the past three days, but today the airlines were operating normally again. Although it was a relief for the passengers, the same couldn't be said for me and my colleagues.

The queues at check-in seemed endless, like a snake whose tail could not be seen. The front of the queue – the face of the snake – was scary. Passengers were frustrated because of the inconvenience and discomfort, and they were expressing that very openly. Every now and then I heard a colleague exhaling heavily and simply surrendering in front of a passenger who looked like they were at war rather than about to get a boarding pass. Then the supervisor would come over to take the passenger aside and talk to them so as not to cause a scene but it would already be too late. The other people in the queue had seen the ugly behaviour and, like children in a kindergarten, repeated it when their turn came.

'Next in line, please,' I called from my seat. A moment passed and still there was nobody standing in front of me. Surprised, I called again, 'Next passenger in line, please.' Again nothing.

I leaned over the desk to see what was causing this situation and then I saw them: a woman and her teenage son supporting an elderly woman, walking slowly to my desk. I wondered why they hadn't asked for special assistance when the woman in the middle clearly needed it.

As they finally reached my desk, I gave them a closer look. They were dressed very simply, but that was not what caught my eye: it was their faces, their eyes, their expression. These were not going to be arrogant passengers; they were different.

The young boy greeted me shyly but the two women stayed silent with soft smiles on their faces. When they handed me their passports I finally realised why: they didn't speak English. That wasn't a problem for me; at an international airport I had to communicate with people from all over the world.

The boy answered a few routine questions in bad English, but it was enough for me to understand that they were going home. After tagging each of their bags, which were within the baggage allowance, I noticed there was one more. This exceeded the limit of the allowance so they would have to pay for it. The prices were not low, and something told me that for this family it would not just be a high price but an impossible one.

The two women were standing silently together, the mother of the boy supporting what I guessed was her own mother. I read sadness in their eyes, not the sort that comes when something bad has just happened but that is there constantly. 'They sure have a difficult life,' I thought. True, the same could be said about many others, but something about this particular family was making me emotional.

There was a massive queue and the last thing I should have been doing was making small talk, but I couldn't help it. I wanted to know more about them so I asked the boy if they'd been on holiday and had they enjoyed it. He answered me with some difficulty; he said that it was his grandmother's dream, which they had granted as she was now very old and sick and might not be with them for much longer. I felt my eyes watering. It was more than clear that they must have spent all their limited savings on this trip.

For the first time I found it hard to tell a passenger that they had to pay for an extra bag but I had no choice. I didn't know if they could afford it and I had no way of helping them out. When the boy heard the amount to be paid, he didn't translate it straight away to his mother. His young face expressed clearly what he was thinking as he calculated and realised they couldn't pay.

His mother urged him to tell her what was going on. When she finally understood, I expected to see the reaction I usually got when passengers who had to pay extra – normally they got way too upset, almost angry. Some would beg for a discount, others would make a scene. But not this woman. She was poor but proud, and she wouldn't beg. That was what her silence told me. But I could see from the tears shining in her eyes that she was trying to hold back just how difficult it would be for her to pay with money that probably meant survival to her family.

At that moment I hated how powerless I felt, how I couldn't do anything for these poor people. The woman took out a small leather pouch – it wasn't even a wallet – and started counting money. She was short by a little, so her son took the coins from his pocket and together they managed to find the right amount. I felt like my heart was breaking into thousands of pieces.

The boy left the money on the desk for me to take but I didn't want to. To distract them from this uneasy moment, I decided to ask another question: had they an original flight that had been delayed or cancelled as most other passengers had?

The boy explained that they'd had to stay at the airport for three days and had received nothing but a food voucher from the airline. I realised that they couldn't afford a hotel and had slept here. I tried as hard as I could to restrain my emotions as I imagined what a horrible time they must have had. They'd been through so much but still did not complain. Life was unfair and the evidence of that was standing right in front of me.

I tagged the last bag and tried to explain where they had to drop it off because of its dimensions, but the boy struggled to understand me. The least I could do was help him, so I left my desk and asked them to follow me. They did so silently but I knew they were more than grateful.

In less than a minute, we were in front of the belt for oversized baggage. The assistant responsible for it was an elderly Asian man. 'These passengers have a bag to drop off,' I informed him.

He nodded, looking pretty bored; apparently he couldn't wait for the end of his shift. Just as I was about to say goodbye to the nice family, he said, 'This bag cannot be transported like this. They need to wrap it first for safety.' He shrugged; they were not his rules but he had to follow them.

My eyes widened; I couldn't believe this unexpected turn

of events. These poor people had absolutely nothing and they couldn't afford to pay for the service, but the assistant was firm: he wouldn't accept the bag if it wasn't wrapped. It was a dead-end street.

I glanced at the family; they seemed scared and didn't understand what was happening. The boy probably understood, but he didn't want to worry his mother so he was looking at me hopefully.

I sighed. The assistant was sitting down, and I guessed he could no longer manage to stand for a long time – he was nearly sixty years old. I felt sorry for him, too. I imagined myself at that age being at home, not still working. But life often proves unfair.

I moved closer to him and whispered, 'Please ... I'm begging you to allow this bag through.' My eyes were watering again. What I was doing wasn't right, it was against the rules and I knew it, but this family was in need and depending on me. I was only a human, and compassion is meant to be part of us even though not everyone feels it. 'These people have nothing. I don't want to get you into trouble but please find a way to help them.'

The man didn't need much convincing. He looked into my eyes, then looked briefly at the family and he understood; rules could be broken sometimes. He nodded quickly and I placed the bag on the belt.

'Thank you so much!' were my only words to him, though I wanted to say much more.

I said goodbye to the family. The two women waved at me and the boy thanked me for everything. I hadn't done much but I'd managed to convince the old man to help them and that felt like a small victory.

I went back to my desk and reached for my water bottle. I needed a sip; I was still feeling too emotional. But before I could take a drink, the sound of passports being thrown on the desk made me stop and look up. A man was standing in front of me dressed smartly in branded clothes and wearing an expensive watch and glasses. Next to him his daughter, who was no more than ten years old, looked as expensively dressed as her father. She was focused on a game on her iPhone.

'This desk is not open yet, sir. I will call you when I'm ready—' I started to explain but he cut me off.

'I'm travelling in business class and I can't wait! Can't you see the madness that is all around while you're just standing here doing nothing! I want to talk to your supervisor right now!'

I didn't even bother to listen to him but immediately called my supervisor, not because of the passenger's demands but to let my supervisor know that I needed a minute's break. While he was being shouted at by the aggressive business-class passenger, I hurried to the washroom.

There, in front of the mirror, I fixed the little scarf on my neck. I didn't need to, I was just giving my hands something to do as I tried to hold back my tears. I wanted to cry so badly but that would have ruined my make-up; I wanted to open the tap of my tears and just let them pour.

Why was everything so unfair? Why was everything so sad?

The Choices

'Excuse me! Where are you going?' Meredith sounded rather rude, but at that exact moment she wasn't really considering her manners. In fact, her face was red from her emotions – a mix of being a little scared and a desire to be brave. Even if it was not the kind of bravery to be given a medal, for her it was a sign of courage.

The guy pointed towards the toilet sign with no expression on his face, obviously not bothered by her question. He was a teenager, the type you could tell wouldn't mind getting into trouble. In fact, he might try to pursue the image of being a 'bad guy'. Or maybe he really *was* bad. Who could tell?

'Well, you can't use it. Customers only!' Meredith pointed at the little sign on the door. She thought that would be enough; she had made it more than clear, so the guy had no choice but to turn around and leave. But to her surprise he didn't. He had a slight smile on his face as he turned around, completely ignored her and headed to the toilet.

Meredith couldn't believe it and stared at him with her mouth open. Such arrogance! But something inside her wouldn't let her walk away from the situation. She raised her voice and repeated, 'I said, customers only! Excuse me...' but the guy acted as if he hadn't heard The good thing was that there was nobody else in the shop, just Meredith behind the cashier's desk and the guy who was grabbing the door handle of the toilet. 'I will call the police!' she yelled.

That made him stop. It was too early for Meredith to have a victorious smile but she felt she was halfway there. Actually, she wasn't sure it made much sense to call the police for such a little thing – it was more a bluff than anything – but the words slipped out and, luckily for her, had the desired effect.

'For what exactly?' the guy challenged her sensing she was only trying to scare him. She didn't seem like a girl who would do that.

'For the fact that you are not a customer. I have barely opened the store and you are disturbing me!' Meredith improvised, hoping not to lose her advantage, but her words sounded about right. Once again she caught his attention – and that was the moment of victory.

'Fine!' he said. Obviously pissed off, he turned around and went out.

Meredith worked in a small bakery shop with a few tables inside. Most people bought take-away food, but in bad weather they would sit and eat there. It was a nice place to work, quite busy for a few hours a day but the rest of the time quiet enough for them to prepare the pastries.

Meredith wasn't the only one working there; there were three of them rotating on shifts. She'd expected her colleague to be there ten minutes ago, butthat colleague was Liam and he was always late. He didn't really take his job seriously, not like Meredith. She was very responsible, not because it was the job of her dreams but because she had just moved in with her boyfriend and they needed the money. The bakery was meant to be a temporary job while she found something more stable with better pay, but luck hadn't been on her side and she'd found herself stuck there for the last six months.

That morning it had been her job to open the store and get everything ready for the first customers. Five minutes after she had opened, Meredith noticed a small gang of guys; they obviously had not sobered up from the previous evening or maybe they had been drinking until now as it was 6.00am on a Saturday and still quite dark. As soon as they stopped in front of the shop without coming in, she knew she could expect trouble from them. And she was right.

Generally, Meredith was a very shy twenty-year-old

woman and situations like this one were nightmare for her, but she hardly had to worry about such things because she was almost never alone at work.

The little gang outside the bakery had gone, probably not willing to get into trouble with the 'crazy sales girl'. She took her phone from her apron pocket and quickly texted Liam, asking where the hell he was. Her hands were shaking a bit; obviously adrenalin was playing its part.

The first customer of the day was a regular, so Meredith knew what he wanted before he even ordered it. It was the old man from the house at the end of the street; every morning he came for some fresh pastries and coffee for his wife and himself.

'Here you go, Mr Adams. Have a great day.' Meredith sent off the old man with a polite smile.

Liam appeared behind her as if from nowhere. 'How is it possible they never get tired of the same breakfast every morning?' he asked, as if the question were a real riddle for him.

He took Meredith by surprise with his sudden appearance but she quickly shook it off and turned to look angrily at him. 'How is it possible that, even though you know what time your shift starts, you are always late, I wonder?'

'Come on, you don't want your favourite customer to see you angry. That will totally destroy his idea of you always being smiley,' Liam teased her. Mr Adams was now waving goodbye for the second time through the glass door and they both waved back with pretend smiles.

After he had finally gone, Meredith turned back to her colleague. 'Listen, I'm not gonna cover for you much longer.' Apparently some of her courage had remained from earlier. She didn't usually speak so directly, but Liam? Oh boy, he was really going on her nerves. 'And if you'd been here on time, I would have avoided a horrible situation.'

'What happened?' he asked, more curious than worried.

She explained quickly but his only comment was, 'Cool.' He gave the sort of smile that suggested he'd actually enjoyed the story and hadn't found anything disturbing in it.

Meredith rolled her eyes and exhaled. She couldn't deal with him any more. Sometimes she imagined that if someone opened his head they'd find a monkey clapping hands instead of a brain.

The day passed as usual. When Meredith finally arrived home, she rushed to tell her boyfriend Russell about her morning experience before even taking her jacket off.

'That's a really dangerous thing that you did, Meredith. Why don't you think before you act irrationally?' was his comment. That was a surprise; she'd been expecting more of a 'well done'.

'Why...?' she started when Russell continued lecturing her.

'He could have been mental or had some sort of a weapon, or ... I don't know, but you are lucky he went away quietly otherwise I don't even want to imagine what could have happened. Really dangerous!' he repeated before turning his disapproving eyes back to the television.

As she got ready to shower, Meredith started think that what she'd done this morning, probably wasn't brave at all. She'd wanted to do the right thing, to not let the rules be broken and not give in to her fear. Was that really such a bad thing to do?

The following day she was meant to close the shop, which gave her a whole Sunday morning to enjoy at home with her boyfriend before she went to work. They didn't have much time to spend together because of their different working hours; her shifts were flexible but Russell had fixed hours during the week. Luckily for her, today she was working with her other colleague, John. It wasn't that she disliked Liam, but... She really did dislike him.

Meredith went to work with a smile and worked all day with a smile because Russell had promised her a special evening and a romantic dinner when she got back home. They were really in love and she couldn't have been happier, though she sensed he might be trying to apologise for his reaction the day before. He'd noticed she was feeling a bit down after telling him the story and he must have felt guilty. Nevertheless, she was looking forward to the evening and nothing could ruin her mood.

At one point during the afternoon the shop got really busy, which wasn't unusual at weekends. John and Meredith hardly had time to catch their breath. After the queue ended, they started clearing up. The door opened one more time with another customer.

'I've got this one. You go have your cigarette,' said Meredith to John, who was dying to have one.

'Thanks.' He looked at her gratefully and didn't wait for second invitation. He quickly disappeared through the door behind them.

At that exact moment, however, something else happened. All the customers in the bakery exclaimed and a terrible noise made Meredith's heart jump. A new customer, a middle-aged man, was lying on the bakery floor. It looked like he was having a seizure; white foam was bubbling out of his mouth and there was blood underneath his head, expanding quickly and making the floor look like a crime scene. He had hit his head when he fell.

There was chaos. Customers were terrified and their screams pierced her ears. The man on the floor – it was one of the most horrific things Meredith had ever witnessed.

And then it happened: she was petrified. Suddenly she couldn't move an inch; only the heavy breathing that sounded as if she were drowning revealed that she was still alive. She didn't even blink as big tears rolled down her cheeks; her eyes remained open as she stared at the man on the floor and gasped for air.

The door behind her slammed open. John had come back when he heard all the noise.

'Oh my God,' she heard him say as he passed went to assist the man on the floor.

It was all happening so fast, but even if Meredith had had time to process the situation, she wouldn't have reacted differently. She knew it, but John didn't.

'Meredith, call an ambulance!' he yelled. Only when he shouted a second time did she make the effort to take her phone out of her pocket. It was an effort. She was not herself at that moment and, unfortunately, that made her of no help. But she tried.

'Hello...' She couldn't find her voice when her call was answered.

'Ma'am, what's the emergency?' The woman on the line had to repeat the question and sounded slightly irritated.

'Yes, it's an emergency...' Meredith's tears were now running down her lips. Her mouth was open as she tried to breathe and she felt she was choking with her own tears. But she had to pull herself together. 'I'm sorry... there is a man in the bakery where I work and he collapsed on the floor and...' She couldn't hold it together any more. She started crying and that did not help with giving important life-saving information. '...And ... there is blood...'

'Ma'am, I don't understand you. Could you pass the phone to someone else, please?' said the woman over the phone.

Meredith gave commands to her feet to move as quickly as they could so that she could at least do that. John was too busy providing help, so Meredith handed the phone to the person she found herself next to in the little crowd that had formed.

'What's that?' asked the woman, looking shocked as Meredith forced the phone into her hands.

'Ambulance...' she managed to say and ran to the back room through the door with the sign 'Staff Only'.

Half an hour later, John found her still there, sitting on the floor with her hands wrapped around her knees and her red face exhausted with crying. She was shivering and didn't lift her head when he knelt next to her. He put his hand awkwardly on her shoulder, hoping that would be enough of a consolation because he really didn't know what to say. It was obvious that there was a much bigger problem behind this sudden shock she had experienced.

Meredith felt his hand but was too ashamed to look him in the eyes. He had done what everyone should do, and she ... she was neither brave, as she had thought herself yesterday, nor helpful. In fact, she could have killed that man with her stupid behaviour.

'Hey ... here is your phone. One of the customers said it belonged to someone from the staff so I'm guessing that's you.' John tried to joke to break the tension and it worked.

Meredith lifted her head and wiped her eyes. 'I am so sorry...' she said.

He could see how difficult it was for her, and also that he would never know the reason. 'Don't be. The ambulance came surprisingly quickly and they took over. Everything is alright now. You know what, just go home. I'll finish here,' he said with a friendly smile.

'No, no.' Meredith took her phone, stood up and straightened her apron. 'I'll help you clean up.' She owed him that; John had done so much and she couldn't leave him do the rest on his own as well.

John offered to walk her home; she lived nearby but he was still worried about her. She refused. She could feel him throwing worried glances over his shoulder as they cleaned up the store before closing. She just needed to be alone for a while and that meant the fifteen minutes' walk from the bakery to home.

Meredith put her hands in her jacket pockets as she slowly walked home. She needed to calm down; she didn't want to cry all evening because she wouldn't be crying for the man who'd collapsed on the floor at her workplace. No: that had only unleashed a memory she was trying to bury somewhere deep in her mind, the memory of her father's death. Life had been difficult ever since for her family and for herself. The emotion might fade away but it would never really go. The pain remained, appearing at unexpected times like today.

Meredith had believed that she would finally accept and live with her father's absence, but it wasn't true. She was terrified by the fact that he'd been taken away from her so early, she was terrified of death itself ... there was no coming back from its grip.

But it was time to learn how to live with her fear because her lack of action today had actually put someone at risk. Yesterday she'd felt brave; she had defied that scary teenager and she'd been proud of herself even though her boyfriend disapproved. A bitter smile appeared on her face. Today, she had proved herself otherwise.

She felt the urge to talk to her mother and dialled her number. 'Mom...' was all she said but it was enough for her mother to sense that something was going.

'Darling, are you alright?' she asked. After listening to her daughter's story her reaction was unexpected. 'Well, darling, I'm glad nothing bad happened to you and I'm sorry you are upset, but you have to admit that was a terrible way to react. What if you'd been alone with that man and his life had depended on you? What if it had been Russell? You can't let your emotions lead you because, in a case like this, life is at stake! You need to be sure you can provide first aid and...'

Her mother went on and on. She was right, of course, and Meredith knew it. But that was not what she needed right now. She was feeling really guilty, ashamed and ... sad.

*

A week after that, during her late shift with Liam, a customer walked in. Instead of ordering, he asked her an unexpected question. 'Excuse me, were you here last Sunday?' He was tall with a very short beard and blue eyes. He had a soft smile which gave Meredith good vibes.

'Yes, I was. Why?' She tried to place him among their usual customers but she didn't succeed.

'I just wanted to thank you for your help. I can imagine what a scare I must have caused,' he said apologetically. Meredith was looking at him like he was a ghost and he felt the need to say something more. 'I'm better now but I owe you my life. Thank you so much.'

'No, I... My colleague who isn't here today was the one who helped you, I... I … just called the ambulance.' Meredith couldn't form a decent sentence; she thought she must sound like a complete idiot. Her eyes started watering again.

'That was more than enough help.' The man saw how upset she was. 'You know, it's a funny thing, but if I'd been in your situation I'd have been out of my mind not knowing what to do. I'd probably have panicked.'

Meredith lifted her eyes to meet his She smiled; it was nice of him to say that.

'It only takes going through something once and then it gets easier.' He winked at her and went out.

He was right, Meredith thought. She felt stronger.

The Perfect Family

She was watching them.

Sitting on a metal chair without a cushion to soften it, she was watching. It didn't really matter how comfortable the seat was because she didn't plan to stay long. The chair was in a small cafe whose staff had taken all the furniture outside for the customers because of the good weather.

The temperature was higher than what could usually be expected from the English weather. The cafe wasn't the most luxurious but, because of its location right on the riverside, on hot days like this one it was a real attraction. Every single one of the tables was occupied, and cheerful laughter and talk were filling the air.

The alley dividing the river from the cafe was crowded with pedestrians: families on a walk, children running, couples holding hands, people taking their dogs our, others cycling. All this noise and movement somehow created a feeling of blissful peace. Kerry looked around and felt indescribably happy.

Her table had still not been cleaned up after the last customer – most probably a man, judging by the lack of lipstick traces on the coffee mug. The staff were so busy with new customers that every time one of them passed by they didn't even notice her, so the table remained dirty. Or maybe they though the crockery was from her own order. She wasn't bothered; she didn't really feel like ordering anything so she stuck with the used mug and pretended it was hers.

Above the cafe was a small bridge with beautiful carving on its sides. In front of the cafe in the crowded alley there was a sign for renting boats. The young assistant had strong arms, not muscular but hardened from his work. He pulled in the returning boats and pushed new hires onto the river.

In between, he polished the boats that weren't being used and the sun caressed his skin, leaving its mark on it. Even he seemed happy, despite having to work. There was something almost magical about this place.

Something caught Kerry's attention: a family, a husband and a wife and their little son who was no more than six years old. What made them stand out was their clothes and the way they behaved. It was obvious that they were wealthy. Their clothing had been chosen to match: the husband was wearing white-linen shorts and a blue shirt with white stripes; the wife's dress was white with blue stripes, and the child had a captain's hat on his little head. They seemed to be full of harmony, love and joy.

Kerry followed them with her gaze until she lost them in the distance, then her thoughts drifted from the 'perfect' family and floated freely as she admired the beauty of the place.

'Excuse me, are you expecting anyone?' A man was standing next to her table. He wasn't a member of staff because he had no uniform. He was in his thirties and wearing sports clothes; he seemed to be enjoying the good weather the same as everyone else.

'No,' responded Kerry.

'I don't want to bother you, but all the other tables are occupied.' He looked around as if to prove it to her. 'This is the only one that seems to have a spare seat. May I?' He pointed at the empty chair.

'Sure,' she agreed easily. The temperature was more than twenty degrees so it was understandable that all the outside seating was taken. Not a single person had stayed indoors.

The man sat facing the river and for a moment there was silence. 'It's so peaceful,' he exclaimed. The comment suggested he might like to chat but he didn't want to disturb her. Kerry felt it was a cry for company; he seemed somewhat lonely. She noticed that, like her, he had no drink; there was just the dirty coffee mug on the table.

'The beauty of this place is that tomorrow it will be peaceful, the same as today. And the day after will be as well, whether it is warm or not, crowded or not,' Kerry replied with a soft smile without looking at the stranger. She was completely engrossed in her surroundings, almost hypnotised by them.

The comfortable silence continued, both of them sunk into their thoughts. Kerry felt like she had lost track of time or, more correctly, had lost herself in time. For once that didn't bother her. It didn't matter. Her eyes were hungry for more to feed her happiness: birds flying; the sun's rays playing on the water; the sound of laughter; a child smiling with lips covered in ice cream; a squirrel eating nuts from the hand of a girl; more laughter...

Here there they were again, the perfect family back from their walk down the alley. They stopped in front of the boats when the child pointed at them. Kerry smiled – she couldn't help it.

A sigh made her turn her eyes to the man sitting opposite her. He was looking at the family too, but with a sad smile on his face. 'Everyone's dream, right?' she commented.

'Not always achievable,' he replied and this time looked into her eyes. She could see his sadness.

His soul was definitely weighed down, but Kerry wasn't sure how appropriate it would be to ask why considering they had just met. She went for an easier question. 'Not having anything to drink on this hot day?' Her question not only distracted him but amused him, which she thought was odd.

'In fact,' he began as if he were about to tell a funny story, 'I had a cup of coffee earlier at this very table. I wouldn't be surprised if this mug is the one I've used.'

'What made you come back?' she asked curiously.

'By the way, I'm James.' Realising they'd skipped that part of the conversation, he introduced himself

'I'm Kerry,' she smiled back.

'Well, Kerry...' James exhaled and focused again on the family which was now rowing in the middle of the river. 'I received a phone call from my wife while I was sitting here. She said she wants a divorce and that she would stay with her family for a while.'

Kerry didn't know what to say; there was so much bitterness and sadness in his words. She looked across to find her favourite sight, the perfect family. They were moving further away but she could still see them. The husband was rowing pretty skilfully, the wife had leaned back to enjoy the sun and their son was dipping his hand playfully in the water. They looked so happy that it was impossible not to feel positive – or even a little jealous. They could easily be in an advertisement for the perfect life.

Some people think perfection is impossible in real life, but not Kerry. She had experienced it and, having done so, she felt sympathy for this stranger she had just met. Everyone deserved to find happiness.

'I'm sorry about what your wife told you – it's not the nicest thing to hear over the phone,' she said after a short silence.

James felt better having shared his pain. True, Kerry was a stranger but his story would now be locked right here, in this place and in this moment, with this woman he would never see again. That made it easier. 'All I wanted was to be happy,' he said with desperation in his voice.

Kerry knew that if they could have still seen the boat with the perfect family, he would have added 'happy like them'.

'Why did you come back here?' she asked.

James frowned, searching for the answer. The question seemed to have confused him. 'I don't know,' he admitted. 'After that call, I couldn't stay here. I had to go ... my head was full of painful thoughts, confusion and sadness. I was heading home… To be honest, I have no idea how I ended up here again.' He shrugged.

Kerry wanted to comfort him, but all the words she thought of sounded like a cliche even to her. Anyway, she couldn't do much more for this stranger, even though she already felt involved. For a while they sat in silence, sunk into their own thoughts but secretly just waiting for the boat with the perfect family to return.

And here it was. The boat stopped next to the stone stairs dividing the river from the alley. The husband with the white linen shorts and blue shirt with white stripes got off the boat and wrapped his hands around his child to help him. After he was sure the little boy was firmly on the stone stairs, he stretched his hand towards his wife to assist her. The woman took it with a smile and with her other hand held the edge of her long summer dress.

'Do you have a family?' James broke the silence.

'Yes I do.' Kerry smiled because the thought of her family made her smile every time. 'The most amazing husband, and a son more or less same age as that little boy.' She pointed at the child who was now holding both his parents' hands. The perfect family was leaving; their trip was at its end.

'Lucky you,' James commented with admiration rather than envy.

'It's not late for you. It's never late for anybody!' Kerry was filled with hope and she wanted James to see through her eyes. 'You need to fight for your relationship, to try and fix what needs to be fixed. Go back and talk to your wife – don't give up! There is happiness for everyone in this world.'

Sometimes a person just needed a nudge, she told herself, and she was excited to help this man take the path to his future happiness. It wasn't fair that everyone didn't have what she had. And if everybody were happy, what would this world look like?

'You are right,' he said, suddenly enthusiastic. His anxious features smoothed and he smiled. 'I will go and talk to my wife right now.' He was looking gratefully at Kerry, this total stranger whom he had just met and who had helped him.

At the same moment, a terrible noise made everyone – customers at the cafe and pedestrians on the alley – turn and look towards the bridge. Something had happened. Worried and curious, people started chattering.

Kerry and James, without even looking at each other to coordinate their moves, jumped from their seats and headed to the stairs leading to the bridge. They didn't exchange a word but both were very disturbed.

On the bridge, they got closer to the little crowd that had formed. It became clear there had been a car crash. Kerry and James anxiously made their way through the gathered people and that was when they saw it: one of the cars, a classic style like in the old movies from the sixties, belonged to the perfect family. An ambulance had just arrived.

The man with white linen shorts and a blue shirt managed to get out of the car, trembling but not seriously injured. He reached for his son who was scared and confused, crying loudly. 'My wife... my wife...' he shouted to the paramedics who had opened the door on the woman's side. She was not moving. The husband's face was twisted in agony as he squeezed his child tightly.

It seemed like the wife and the driver of the other car were injured. When the paramedics managed to put them on the stretchers, Kerry and James got a close look at their faces. It wasn't the blood covering them that made them hold their breath but the fact that the woman's face was Kerry's and the driver's face was James'.

'I can't catch a pulse here,' reported the paramedic who was checking on James' body on the stretcher.

'I've got a very weak one here,' said his colleague, reporting on Kerry.

Watching themselves, Kerry and James exchanged

frightened looks. 'Are we ... dead?' he whispered.

Kerry watched her body being pushed on the stretcher to the ambulance and her husband and child crying. It was a heart-breaking moment, but that was not the only sad thing. Her eyes moved to the other stretcher. There was nobody crying for James, the stranger whom she had met in the afterlife. The stranger who was miserable, but who now had a glimmer of hope ... which would never be more than that.

'Not yet. We are dead, but one of us still has a chance.' She looked straight into his eyes, smiled softly, turned around and walked away. With each step, her shape faded more and more.

'No! Kerry, come back! I won't let you do this... Come back...' James tried to go after her, but he felt heavy, as if he were being pulled back by some force.

The paramedics had just loaded the stretchers into the ambulance. 'Something is happening! We are losing the woman,' one of them cried.

'I've got a pulse! We've got him back. Hurry, switch the man onto the systems,' the paramedic handling James ordered.

The Store

Chocolates, candies, biscuits, all kinds of sweets in colourful, tempting packages were displayed here. It was just a small local store but, because of its size, it seemed to be overflowing with groceries. One could find everything here, or so it seemed to Lily.

She was a child, tiny for her age, to whom this small store seemed like a huge castle full of treats. However, the castle had its master – the owner who was also the salesman. He was a very tall man with a frowning face. He always looked angry, almost as though he had never known what a smile was like. This was Mr Nelson and Lily was afraid of him.

And here it was, right in front of the girl, inviting her: a bowl full of chewing gum on the counter. It was waiting for Lily to stretch out her little hand and take one. Just one; it was not much to ask. Her mouth felt watery.

'Can you pay today?' A sharp voice took the child's mind away from the daydreams of what the taste of the gum would be like. The owner was tapping his fingers on the desk having fixed his angry gaze on Lily.

'My mother thanks you for letting us pay for the food later,' she said in a voice so quiet that it was hard to catch the words. Lily was ashamed, even though there was nobody else in the store but her.

'Fine. And will you pay now for the previous time?' he asked, still frowning. The child was from a poor family that was always begging to pay for the groceries later. True, they were getting only essentials, but business was business after all.

The child's clothes looked very old and worn, and so did her shoes. She always wore the same dress and jacket; clearly, she had only those but they were always clean and her hair was nicely braided. It was obvious that, even though poor, this family tried hard – but lack of money was crushing their simple existence.

'Yes, I have the money here.' Lily stretched out her clenched fist and when her little fingers opened, the crumpled notes fell on the desk. Her mother had told her how important it was not to lose the money, and so she had squeezed it tightly while running to the store. 'And also I have to take bread.' Lily looked away because she couldn't bear the strict stare of the frightening man.

'It's enough to cover the previous bill but not the bread too,' he said, while counting the money and checking in his little notebook where he recorded how much someone owed him.

Lily was staring at the bowl with chewing gum, imagining taking one, unfolding the paper with the colourful balloons on it. She craved its taste so badly.

'I guess I'll just add this to the next bill,' continued Mr Nelson after a short pause. He passed over the bread, which Lily held tightly, and followed her with his eyes until she walked out of the store to make sure she didn't slip anything into her pocket. Not that this had ever happened before, but one could not be sure what to expect in some situations. Desperation could lead to a mistake.

Just three days later, Lily went back to the store. She was holding a list given to her by her mother of the groceries they needed, but of course there was no money. Mr Nelson frowned again, but this time it was not a surprise for him that the child couldn't pay; neither was it a surprise for Lily that the scary man didn't smile.

While the owner was filling the bag with food, the child was hypnotised again by the bowl of chewing gum so close to her and yet so untouchable. She was almost licking her lips. Flavours of cherry, strawberry, raspberry ... she wanted to try them all one day.

The owner noticed where the little girl was looking. He

folded his arms to show he was expecting her to leave once she had what she'd come in for. He wasn't going to tolerate thieves, no matter how young they were, and if he caught her stealing he was going to teach her a lesson. He was doing quite enough for the family already by postponing payment of their bills.

Lily felt the man's eyes on her and she felt goosebumps all over her body. Every feature of his face frightened her; he was so big and she was so small. Tears filled her eyes. The owner must have thought that she must be a thief because she was poor. And she was not; she was just a child dreaming about being able to afford chewing gum.

As she left the shop, Lily felt Mr Nelson's intense gaze following her to make sure she didn't take anything and her sadness and embarrassment turned to anger. Mr Nelson wasn't just scary, he was bad. How was it possible for someone who had everything to be like him, she wondered. If she had a whole store full of food, she would always be happy and smiling.

Lily's next visit was pretty much like the others except that she had made a decision, namely to steal one piece of chewing gum from the bowl on the counter. Mr Nelson was clearly a bad person, and he wouldn't even notice it had gone because of the many full shelves in his store. What would one missing piece of chewing gum mean to him? To her, though, it would mean so much.

She waited until he was searching the shelves to collect all items from her list. When would be the most appropriate moment for her to grab a piece of gum and slide it into the pocket of her old jacket? Could it be now? Or maybe right now, while Mr Nelson was taking a packet of flour from the lower shelf and had his back towards her? Her hands were trembling because she had never done anything like this before.

At that moment, the door opened and someone walked into the store. Both Lily and Mr Nelson turned to see who it was. The man seemed very elegant; he was smartly dressed and he smiled at the owner.

It was clear that Lily had lost her opportunity to proceed with her plan because now there was a witness. Once again, she would not be able to enjoy the taste she had dreamt of for days. Sadly she turned back to check if the bag with her groceries was ready – but then something surprised her.

The owner had stopped what he was doing and gone very pale. He was looking at the approaching man, who was now standing very close to the counter. Lily had thought Mr Nelson was the scariest man she had ever seen, but now he looked as if he were going to cry.

'Always a pleasure to see you, Mr Nelson.' The stranger started talking but without leaving time for a response, just like rich people do to show how precious their time is. 'I hope this time to be delighted by finally collecting my rent.'

Mr Nelson stood in silence. Lily could see something shining in his eyes: were they tears? He looked completely different; he had a look on his face that Lily had never seen before, a look that made him much less frightening. His lower lip was trembling and his face was twisted with unease.

'Please give me some more time, I beg you. My wife has been sick for a long time. All the money is going on expensive medicine but, despite that, she is getting worse. Each day seems like her last...' His voice was quiet and desperate.

Lily couldn't help but feel sympathy for him. She had known nothing about his life and now she realised it wasn't much different to her own.

'More time? I would usually agree to that, but considering you already owe me three payments I really don't think another delay is possible.'

Poor Mr Nelson laid his hands on the desk to support his weight because his legs felt so weak. The other man, still with a slight smile on his face, stretched out a hand and took a piece of chewing gum. Lily followed the action with wide eyes, but Mr Nelson did not even notice. And even if he had done, it wouldn't have mattered because at that moment very few things really mattered to him.

Already chewing the gum, the stranger spoke again. 'I will return at the end of the week – that is all the time I can give you. Oh, that seems to be tomorrow.' He giggled but his quiet laughter sounded evil somehow. 'See you then.'

The elegant man walked out of the store with the same smile that he'd had when he walked in. Outside he stopped for a moment and then mumbled, 'Some people have so little luck...'

Then he threw the chewing gum in the bin next to the door.

The Father's Love

Giselle's eyes were wide open. She couldn't believe it: Narcisse had raised her hand ready to slap her across the face! She had no right to do that for a number of reasons. First of all, physical aggression should not be accepted as normal; secondly, Narcisse wasn't even her mother but her stepmother, and thirdly, Giselle was not a child – she was twenty-five-year old woman. But most important of all was the fact that two weeks earlier Giselle had fallen, broken her leg and now had a cast on it. That made the physical attack even less justifiable.

But who could stop Narcisse from what she was about to do? Giselle's father, maybe? Paul was sitting comfortably at the table, not bothered by the disturbing scene in front of him. Not that Giselle expected any reaction from him, but she had *hoped* for one and hope always dies last. Or in this case, it had died with the sound of a slap that had reddened her face and knocked her off balance and onto the floor.

The pain in her leg pierced her and she screamed in agony. However, in this home where she was just a guest, nobody would feel pity for her tears. She wasn't welcome and she shouldn't expect sympathy or compassion. The question was, why had she fooled herself for so long?

'Take your stuff and leave. I don't want to see you set foot in this home again!' Narcisse yelled mercilessly, as though she didn't realise that Giselle couldn't get up and walk away. Or maybe someone else's pain was giving Narcisse satisfaction. Yes, that type of people did exist.

Giselle couldn't decide what hurt most, the physical pain or the humiliation. She just knew that she was in agony, physically and emotionally. She was already over-sensitive because of her broken leg and the fact that she was totally dependent on help, something she had always hated. She considered that a weakness, and it was something she had struggled to overcome all her life. Because of that, Giselle couldn't accept the incident with her leg as someone else would; for her it was a tragedy!

'Aren't you going to say something?' she asked her father desperately, even though she realised it was a long shot. Actually it would be better if he didn't speak; it would avoid rubbing , salt into the wound. But she had provoked him and, as she expected, the situation got worse.

'Yes, I will tell you to leave,' he said. He stood up and went to the sofa where Giselle had dropped her backpack.

'Who do you think you are to behave in such a way in my home?' Narcisse yelled, though her words almost didn't reach Giselle as her attention was on her father. Only his reaction mattered to her now.

Giselle held onto the kitchen counter for support and slowly stood up. 'Would you tell your wife who I am?' she provoked Paul for last time, hoping he would show a little humanity, but he was already holding her backpack in one hand and heading to the front door.

'Nobody. That is who you are, you are nobody!' he said, then opened the door and threw her backpack outside.

Even in her worst nightmares Giselle hadn't imagined a situation like this. Holding her crutches, she limped to the open door. She was off-balance because she was so upset; her hands were trembling, her head was aching painfully, her eyes were swollen from crying and she almost couldn't keep them open.

This must be the end, she thought. After today, she would probably never see her father again, so she might as well tell him all she'd been holding in her heart through the years. But would her words reach *his* heart? Probably not; he did not have one, or at least had no room in it for her.

When she finally reached the door, Giselle looked into Paul's eyes, though he was trying to avoid her gaze. 'One day you will get old. Do you think your mean wife will take care of you? You will remember me then and you will seek my help, but it will be too late. Goodbye!' She crossed the threshold and slammed the door behind her.

This page of her life had just turned and there was no going back. With difficulty Giselle bent to pick up her backpack then headed to the main street to call a taxi. And, of course, it started raining. Actually, that didn't make her feel any worse because she had reached the peak of despair.

Nobody had ever treated her so disrespectfully before and, now that it had finally happened, it was not just anyone but her biological father. That was probably the only suitable description for him: 'biological'. He had failed to prove himself as anything else.

Giselle waited for the taxi without trying to hide from the rain. Once she got into the cab the driver made a comment about the bad weather, intending to chat, but quickly realised that his passenger's face was wet from tears. He left her in peace and she sank into deep, dark thoughts.

She had hoped never to get to this moment. When she had renewed contact with Paul, with whom she hadn't kept in touch for most of her life, she had known it wouldn't be easy. He had left her with her mother when Giselle was a child, and growing up with his absence had affected her deeply. It had left its mark on her, and she desperately needed a father's love – or at least a father's care. Unfortunately, it appeared all she got was a father's slap.

When they had met for a coffee three years ago for the first time after so many years, he seemed uncomfortable, willing the meeting to end quickly. Even then his second wife, Narcisse, had been with him. Sometime later, Paul had admitted to Giselle that Narcisse had forced him to see her.

For the past three years, Paul had always acted nervously around Giselle, almost as if her presence was unpleasant to him, though Narcisse had always been kindly and friendly, inviting her over for lunch or dinner. At first, Giselle thought it was very noble of her stepmother to try and help their reunion but, with time, Narcisse revealed her dark side . She was nowhere close to being a saint, so why was she helping a father and daughter to strengthen their relationship?

Giselle held back her tears during her ride home because she didn't want the driver to witness her drama; for the same reason, she didn't call her mother until she arrived back and was completely alone. None of this would have happened if she'd still been living with her mother, but long ago Giselle had decided to go and study in the big city. She didn't know anyone there; she was aware that her father lived there, but she didn't know him well. Despite her efforts, it was clear that he'd never loved her and could not be forced to love her.

Inside her small flat, she threw the backpack to one side and sat crying on the kitchen chair. She cried for a long time until it was almost dark outside; she felt as if she could cry for days because so many tears inside her had collected over the years.

Her cell phone rang; it was her mother. Giselle couldn't postpone speaking to her because her mother would worry and think the worst. She had to talk to her and tell her what had happened. 'Hey, Mom,' she said, trying to keep her voice even.

'What's wrong? Are you alright?' Her mother couldn't be deceived; she sensed the sadness in her daughter's voice right away.

Giselle exhaled, knowing she would have to relive the whole scene again as she related it to her mother. If she didn't, her mother wouldn't leave her in peace.

'Narcisse invited me for lunch today. I guess Paul approved, but you know how I can never tell if he really wants me in his home. Maybe his wife forced him into it. They didn't know I had broken my leg and were surprised to see me with the cast. I explained to them that I'd slipped and fallen and it was very challenging for me to deal even with the easiest thing alone at home.'

'Of course, of course,' her mother mumbled supportively.

'I asked if I could stay with them for a while because, much as I hate to admit it, I really need some help.' Giselle's eyes filled with tears again. 'They refused, said that they didn't have the time, and if I'd been stupid enough to break my leg I should deal with my own mess. I couldn't hold it in, Mom.'

Giselle's voice broke as her mother waited to hear the rest. 'I said I'd never been able to rely on his support throughout my life and ... they both flipped out.' She continued with the rest of her story then waited for her mother's reaction.

'It's your own fault! You have too big a mouth! You've provoked them with your silly words and you got what you deserve,' her mother said coldly.

That was Giselle's other problem: she'd never had a father's love and she'd never had her mother's support. Whatever she tried to do, her mother would be there to discourage her. Was this normal? Did every person have parents like hers?

Giselle pressed the red button to end the call. It wasn't the first time she'd had to end a call in the middle of the conversation – it was the only way to let her mother know that she had crossed the line. In a few days it would be forgotten and they would be talking again as if nothing had happened. But the problem remained: Giselle felt alone despite having two perfectly fit parents. What made her any different to an orphan?

Usually in situations like this, people are advised to look on the bright side. True, if Giselle dug a little she could find one: it was the fact that her parents' mistakes had taught her to be strong and independent, to never depend on anybody. Giselle hadn't asked for this life and she'd been forced to deal with it the best way she could.

There were times she looked in the mirror and asked what she could offer to the world. One time, she had overcome the bitterness when looking at her reflection and thought that life was more about giving your soul the opportunity to grow through experience, and having the upper hand in the deciding how that experience shaped you. But if she looked at her reflection now, she would see tears and sadness and loneliness hiding this strong woman looking back at her.

Sitting alone in her little kitchen with a cast on her leg and her face covered with tears, with a mother and father who not only lacked parental instincts but also human kindness, the only thought Giselle had was that not every person should be allowed to be a parent!

Sam

'Come on, Sam! How long are you going to take in there?'

Sam opened the toilet's door and tried to pass his father as quickly as he could without meeting his gaze. He kept his head down because he was ashamed, but unfortunately some things couldn't stay unnoticed by a parent.

'Hey, is everything alright?' asked his father. 'Why are your eyes red?'

'Of course! Everything is fine,' Sam replied, supporting his answer with a casual smile. 'I had something in my eye, that's all.'

'Fine. Well, get yourself ready, we're going out soon,' his father reminded him and went into the toilet.

Sam didn't need a reminder; that just made it worse. There was no chance for his mood to improve if even crying in the toilet couldn't release the pressure. In fact, as had become clear, the toilet could no longer be counted as his secret place.

Sam's thoughts were annoying as he tried to tie his shoelaces. Tears were about to break through the pretend enthusiastic mask on his face.

'Darling, let me help you.' His mother appeared from the kitchen and noticed his unsuccessful attempt to deal with his shoes. She was smiling softly as usual, her eyes full of love, her hand caressing his cheek. Sam loved his mother beyond anything; he loved his father, too, but not as much. It was odd because most boys were attached to the strong figure in the family who set them an example. It should have been the same for Sam, only he didn't want that.

'Don't spoil him, Clara,' his father muttered, standing by the door with the car keys in his hand. 'He is a man and, as such, he should be able to deal with everything by himself. Isn't that right, Sam?' he added more loudly, as it were an important statement to be remembered and he wanted to be reassured that his son shared the same point of view.

Sam smiled again, showing a line of white teeth – probably too many because the smile was forced. But he knew that his father wouldn't notice. 'Of course, Dad. I'm a man,' he said to satisfy his father.

His mother did not comment; 'Sometimes silence is the best move,' she often said. Sam wasn't sure he entirely agreed with that. He would hide when he desperately needed to let the pressure out, when he needed to cry. He hid because, if his father saw him, Sam wouldn't be able to avoid the slap.

'Men don't cry,' his father would say angrily, ashamed of his son. Sam could read the pride in his father's eyes when his only son behaved like a 'man', and the shame when Sam acted like a 'woman'. Sam didn't know how many things his father judged to be 'womanly', but he'd learned to recognise many of them and avoid doing them.

His father was a tough man, very strict, but not like other parents by forbidding stuff and giving orders. No, he was strict in what he expected from Sam. All these expectations were a heavy burden on the child's shoulders, but what choice did Sam have except to carry it?

And today Sam again had to pretend for his father. He had to go with him to a football match, support the team by shouting and afterwards comment on the players. Even though that would make Sam's father happy and proud, it was not what Sam wanted.

*

The outing went well, as did the next one and the one after that through season after season. Sam was growing up; he was not a little boy any more but a young man. A lot changed during that time. Much more was expected of him, not only at home but from society as well.

At school, the teachers expected him to run for miles. If

he struggled, the other guys laughed at him for being weak and the girls laughed at him for not being more manly. At home, his father would give him a slap for embarrassing him. Sam was a man; he had to be strong and cocky and cool, to like fights and aggressive games and beer. When he helped his father carry heavy stuff from the garage and the weight almost paralysed his muscles and the rough materials pierced his skin until it bled, he dared not complain or make a sound to suggest it was too much for him. He was a man, and weeping was for girls.

Did 'strength' mean everything to his father? Could only that make him proud of his son? Or was Sam being strong by trying, even though being strong did not come naturally to him? Was it shameful to show emotion during a movie, to refuse to go fishing, or not to like football? Were all types of art 'just for women', as his father said? Was there a real difference between what men and women should like and do?

So many questions filled Sam's head when he went to bed, yet answers and solutions seemed impossible to find.

*

Sam passed his driving test. Choosing his first car was an exciting moment for him, even though it was not his choice that mattered. Sam was well-aware that his father would not approve of whatever caught his eye. He had to have a car that would show in every possible way how manly he was.

His father made a whole speech about how grown up his boy was, how he was already a tough man. His mother, on the other hand, admired him silently with tears of pride – tears that she was allowed.

'How many stories will your car have to tell one day, son?' his father joked. 'You probably can't wait to drive the girls around.' He winked and laughed. His mother did not comment and Sam just smiled awkwardly. Why could some things never stay unnoticed by a parent?

'Come on, tell us about the girl you'd like to drive first in your new car?' His father didn't want to change the topic; he wanted to make sure his son was popular among the girls at his school.

But Sam could not satisfy his father's curiosity. 'I don't have a girlfriend, Dad,' he answered simply, hoping it would not affect his father's good mood.

His father frowned. He fixed his eyes on Sam's, looking disappointed, ashamed, disapproving, a look his son knew very well.

'How is that?' his father almost yelled, his face slowly turning red. Sam's mother exhaled and decided to start preparing lunch; she clearly didn't want to witness her husband's grumpy mood.

He continued, 'Explain to me how it is possible for a man, athletic and with a shiny car, not to have a girlfriend!' He stepped closer, his face only centimetres away from his son's, and yelled rudely, 'What's wrong with you?'

Sam did not flinch; he kept his eyes on his father's, but his silence made the situation even more tense. Clara was arranging the plates on the table but her movements were slow; she was wondering what her son would do.

'Are you gay?' his father shouted, his nostrils moving as he breathed heavily.

Sam remained silent. No, he wasn't gay; he liked girls, though not the popular ones at school who reminded him with their arrogant attitude that he would have to wear a mask for them, too. He didn't want to do that ever again; he wanted to be free to express himself, not follow a stereotype.

The girl who had his attention was not popular, but why would that matter to Sam? She was a talented painter and a love for art was what connected them. They had a date today, though he wouldn't take his car to impress her because neither of them cared about cars. Instead, they would walk around her favourite park where she loved to sit and draw. Who was to say that a man could not have a delicate soul?

Sam's father had reached the limit of his patience and he yelled once more, 'I asked you – are you gay?!' He raised his hand to grab his son by the collar of his shirt.

What happened next was completely unexpected. Sam caught his father's arm and pushed him back with such force that the man lost his balance. He didn't even try to stand up again, he just stared at his son with wide eyes, not knowing what to say.

'There is nothing wrong with me! Even if I were gay, there would still be nothing wrong with me.' It was the first time that Sam had felt strong in the true meaning of the word.

His father was amazed and speechless. His mother, who had now stopped what she was doing, had a little smile on her face. The look in her eyes expressed victory. She was proud of him, and Sam knew how much more important his mother's pride was than his father's feelings.

He grabbed his jacket and went out.

She and Them

Ruth couldn't wait to grow up. She saw the displays in the stores for St Valentine's Day, the attractive pink and red colours, the balloons, decorations, colourful lights, huge teddy bears holding hearts, the couples in love holding hands and exchanging kisses, the red roses and gifts wrapped in nice paper. She couldn't wait for this day to come for her, too. The women were like princesses and the men were princes. She wanted to be one of the girls with a smile on her face and a red rose in a hand given by a man who was in love to her. It all looked so perfect and magical.

And here she was, grown-up already, a young woman in her prime like a blooming flower. Only there was no flower in her hand; neither was there a teddy bear or a balloon. The prince had not arrived yet.

'It's alright,' she would say to herself. He would find her soon and they would hold hands and walk under the lights and exchange a kiss.

And then, there he was: the prince. Tom had stolen her heart as can happen only in a movie. He made her blush, touched her hand lovingly and said beautiful, sweet words. It seemed like Ruth was living in a pink bubble, even though it was not yet St Valentine's Day yet.

She allowed Tom to touch her passionately, allowed him even more than that. 'Why not?' she thought. 'One day we are going to marry and love each other forever.'

But Tom left. He walked away from her and he crushed her heart which he was holding in his hands, returning it in an unrecognisable state. He left without saying why, without caring for her tears, her pain, her sorrow.

Her friends gave her tissues, patted her back and said stuff like, 'Of course he left – he got what he wanted,' or 'You should have known better!' Those words, despite being said with love, were not soothing. They could not help Ruth to understand why, could not stop the fire burning in her heart.

But then Ruth was back on her feet, ready to try again. Her heart was back in its place; it had a few stitches but at least it was still beating. The smile was back on her face and the dreams were back in her head.

A new man crossed her path who smiled charmingly and spoke beautifully. She smiled, too. 'Why not?' she thought. 'Maybe he will be the prince.' And they held hands and walked around the streets feeling love and exchanging kisses, even though it was not St Valentine's Day yet. And Ruth allowed him more.

That man left, the same as Tom had done. Ruth's heart got a few more stitches. Her friends wiped away her tears saying, 'He was no different – only one thing he was looking for,' or 'You should have known better!'

And this too had passed. Ruth got up on her feet, smiled again and carried on her search for the one. St Valentine's Day was coming up; maybe this time she would celebrate it as she had always wished to since she was a little girl. Red roses, chocolate candies, fluffy teddy bears, a walk in the alley of the lovers decorated with beautiful lights, holding hands with her prince.

Another man crossed her path: new hope, a new open door suggesting happiness. And he spoke beautifully at the beginning, as every other man before him had done. She smiled and thought, 'This could be the one.' But then, instead of holding her hand, he started raising his. The words became ugly, the happiness vanished like smoke and the dreams broke into pieces like crystal. Which hurt more, the words or the red mark on the side of her face from his hand?

This time Ruth was the one to leave, but it did not make much difference; the feeling was the same, the pain familiar.

Her heart was like an old coat, all covered in patches. Her friends said, 'They are all the same,' or 'Don't give up... probably the next one.' But how many more would there be? How much longer could she search and fall and stand up again? After the last time, she needed invisible crutches to support her heart and the soul.

It was St Valentine's Day and Ruth was rushing down the street. She no longer enjoyed seeing the beautiful displays in the stores or on the streets. Those couples holding hands and staring into each other's eyes full of love no longer looked like princesses and princes, as she had once thought. The princes had turned into scary monsters with sharp teeth and nails like devils.

'Ruth!' Someone called her name from behind. She stopped and turned around. It was Tom, the same Tom she had once loved so purely and naively. The same Tom who spoke beautiful words, words that turned out to be lies. Tom, whom she'd trusted when she shouldn't have. Tom, for whom love was just a game. Tom, her worst teacher, who had showed her what would come next.

'Ruth,' he said her name again. 'I'm so glad to see you. In fact, I wanted to call you to tell you how sorry I am. I was a fool. If you can give me another chance, I promise to make you happy. Will you forgive me?' They looked into each other's eyes for a brief moment.

'I forgive you,' she answered, 'so I can finally let go of you, not to bring you back into my life.'

She turned back and carried on her way without saying anything else. The invisible crutches supporting her heart were no longer needed; they vanished and a smile appeared on her face. She felt as light as a feather, and the decorations looked beautiful again and the couples were princesses and princes again. But this time Ruth would buy her own sflowers to brighten her room, and she would buy herself some chocolates as a treat. And there was nothing wrong with that.

The Stranger

April. It was neither hot nor cold but cool enough for me to wrap my hands around myself even though I was wearing a jacket. I was just getting on the bus and I was not in a good mood, but that was hardly surprising considering where I was coming from – my boyfriend's home. Or more accurately a guy who I was trying to date. 'Trying' doesn't always mean success.

He had upset me again. Actually, it wasn't his fault, it was mine for being so stubborn and refusing to give up. People say the first step to overcoming a problem is to realise there is one, and then to fight it. But what happens if someone gets stuck on the first step?

That had happened in my case. I had realised my so-called relationship was already dead; in fact, it never should have started. But ... we all make mistakes, right? I never liked comparing myself to others and the fact that everyone makes wrong choices didn't make me feel any better.

The question was why I continued agonising instead of just putting an end to it. It was out of sentimentality, not love. He was the first man I'd ever been with, but soon after that we broke up because of our immeasurable differences.

A couple of years later our paths crossed and the old fire started burning again. It was easy to forget the reason for our separation in this sweet moment of temporary passion. I even convinced myself that we were both more mature now so it would work better than the previous time.

God, I wished I could give myself a slap for being so naive and having such poor judgment. I had more experience with life and I should have known better. Of course it was a mistake going back to him. I could see clearly that I must put an end to it again. I didn't want to be in one of those 'toxic' relationships. But sentimentality was pricking my heart like a needle. Not that my heart hurt – the guy didn't deserve that much – but it was still an unpleasant feeling.

It was 8pm and almost dark. There were not many people on the bus so I had a good choice of seats and took one next to the window. I always did that if I could, staring through the window was a great method for escaping my thoughts. Though to distract myself I had a plan for the evening to look forward to. Getting home and watching some favourite romantic movie so that I would convince myself love does exist, just I haven't found it yet. Weird thing to think about but at that moment I also felt glad for not having my own car, I was way too upset to stay focused on driving.

'Hi.' I turned from the window in the direction of the voice; not that I was considering talking to its owner but it was instinct to react . On the double seat in front of me was a guy, leaning against the window so that he was facing me – and yes, he was talking to me. He was smiling as though we were friends but it was the first time I'd seen him.

He was cute and probably younger than me by about two or three years. However, lessons one learns as a child don't go away, and that was the case for me. 'Stranger-danger' an alarm in my head was saying. I didn't respond to his greeting and turned my head back to the window. My technique for dealing with crazy people was to ignore them. Sooner or later he would leave me alone.

'I think you are very beautiful,' he said.

That was crossing the line; he was being arrogant allowing himself such freedom towards me. Wasn't he too young to behave that way? I turned back to him, this time with a piercing gaze. I planned to say something rude to him so he wouldn't mess with me, but before I could open my mouth he continued: 'Relax, I'm not some maniac.' He rolled his eyes. 'But I see nothing bad in saying what I think.' He shrugged innocently.

I had never experienced a situation like this before. What

was odd was that he seemed honest; if he'd really wanted to bother me inappropriately, he would have sat next to me but he kept his distance. Anyway, I wasn't a fan of 'talking to strangers', though a friend of mine was; this guy just proved she wasn't the only one, I guessed.

'Yeah, it's nice being open but that's usually with people you know.' I decided to reply after all, but sarcastically, so he wouldn't accept my answer as an invitation to start a conversation.

'I'm Mike, from Michael. So there, now you know me.' His smile wasn't going away. I wondered if he might be high.

'Well, I'm not telling you mine, so it doesn't count as a real introduction,' I said.

'I haven't asked your name. Considering your attitude, if I do ask you will give me a fake one, so there is no point.' Judging by his tone, he was pretty sure of getting a score on his side after my sarcasm.

Again I didn't know what to say. He was completely right: I was either going to tell him to leave me alone or, if I was in a good mood (which I wasn't) I would come up with some fake name. I was intrigued by the fact he'd guessed that, and also that he wasn't insisting. My mood was definitely brightening, and I started considering that maybe this guy wasn't crazy or a pervert after all, but just someone who enjoyed talking to people.

'You're right there,' was my only comment, along with an almost unnoticeable smile.

'No worries. My girlfriend does the same thing.'

'So you have a girlfriend?' I couldn't hide my surprise.

'Yes!' He sounded surprised by my surprise. 'I'm on the way to her place now, taking the food for her fish,'

'And what does she think of your "friendly" behaviour with random women?' I was sarcastic again. He should have seen that coming when he admitted being in a relationship. All men were jerks.

'And what if I'm talking to you? I'm not hitting on you. I'm just looking for someone to talk with until I have to get off the bus,'

It was impossible not to laugh. He was just so laid back, and oddly honest given the fact he was talking to a stranger, that I suddenly wished I had that skill every once in a while. Maybe then everything would look easier to me. Being stiff wasn't one of my best qualities and it could stand some improvement.

'And you are bringing your girlfriend food for her fish?' There was nothing for me to lose; I might as well just make the ride in the bus a bit more pleasant.

'She studies a lot and her exams are soon, so I decided to help her since she doesn't have much time to go out,'

'That's sweet...' I smiled. Indeed it was. In the last three minutes I'd changed my opinion about this stranger a couple of times but, if I had to be honest with myself, this unexpected situation was actually quite nice.

'My stop,' he informed me. 'It was nice talking to you ... beautiful girl with no name. He stood up. 'Just kidding! Cool off.' He winked at me and got off the bus.

I searched for him through the window – I don't even know why – but it was as if he had vanished. It didn't matter anyway; I wouldn't see him again, but I was grateful to him for bringing back the smile on my face when I thought the day had already ended badly.

*

September. It was raining. I was holding my umbrella, waiting for the green light so I could cross the street. The summer had passed and much had changed. I had ended the relationship that wasn't making me happy but, frankly, I wasn't any happier after that. I was in a loop: single, not satisfied with my job, slightly depressed. Not a good combination.

I was trying to keep my distance from the street so I didn't get splashed by a passing car, but it was pouring down and the light was about to turn green any moment now so I made a small step forward.

'Hey, you! Beautiful girl with no name.' The words struck me. I turned around but couldn't see anything from the umbrella but there was nobody next to me. I moved the umbrella away so I could see better view and saw someone walking away down the alley. Was it him...?

No, I doubted it could be Mike from the bus who had started a conversation with me so many months ago. I had almost forgotten about him. At that moment the figure going further and further away turned around and smiled at me and I recognised him. It was him, Mike. What was odder, it appeared he had recognised me as well, even remembered what he had called me back then. But he didn't stop. He just waved at me and carried on his way.

Really strange guy. Obviously my first assumptions about him being crazy or a pervert were wrong; instead, he had intrigued me with his behaviour. Free, careless and friendly; I could compare him to one of those little birds that get close to a person, making him smile just with its presence and then fly away leaving nothing behind but a smile.

I turned back towards the street to cross. I had a smile on my face. The light was red again; I had missed the moment to cross and I had to wait some more. Nevertheless, the smile was still there on my face.

*

December. The holidays were getting closer and it was definitely time for being in a good mood. Well, I still didn't have a boyfriend but that problem could wait until after Christmas. At least I had changed my job for a better one, so I'd crossed at least one thing off my complaints list.

Judging by the frosty pavement it would be no surprise

if we had snow at Christmas, right on time like a special delivery, and I would lose my bet against my father. I was stepping very carefully trying to avoid slipping, but even if I hadn't been watching out I couldn't have moved faster because I was wearing so many layers of clothing, including a huge winter jacket. I must look funny, I thought.

I looked up, as I did from time to time so I didn't bump into someone. It was one of those awkwardly funny moments when two people are in each other's way and as one steps left, the other steps right. I was about to apologise when I looked at the person's face. 'Mike?' I couldn't believe it.

'The beautiful girl with no name from the bus?' He laughed and so did I. It was unbelievable how we kept bumping into each other in this big city!

'How are your girlfriend's fish?' I asked jokingly. I had no problem having a conversation with him now, even being the one to start it.

'Actually, they died, and the girlfriend has changed, too. I have a new one now. She has a dog and the dog is doing well. Thanks for asking,' his smile was infectious and I liked his sense of humour. I was smiling as if I had met an old friend, not just a stranger.

'I'm sorry for the girlfriend ... and for the fish.' I tried to show some sympathy, not sure if it had been one of those dramatic break ups that often happen among young people.

'No worries, that's life. Actually, I'm in a hurry before all stores close. It's my only free time to shop for Christmas gifts. I'm guessing I'll see you around.' He smiled; it was already our private joke.

'Sure, see you soon somewhere around the big city,' I answered, also smiling.

He had just gone on his way when I heard him shout, 'Happy holidays, by the way!'

*

Actually, our paths never crossed again; I guess the city is that big after all. We had never exchanged any contact information to keep in touch, but I don't regret it. Those coincidental meetings with Mike were exactly what I needed.

The Riddle

Gerard exhaled heavily. Sometimes it was really difficult to practise this profession. He was a psychologist and he loved what he was doing; his passionate interest was, in fact, the reason for being where he was today – in his office. Years of constant studying and hard work had paid back with success; his name was well-respected in the field, and Gerard couldn't wish for a bigger reward. Sometimes, however, even all the knowledge he had did not appear to be enough. Some patients were just a big question mark, a puzzle where no standard pieces would fit. But after all, wasn't that exactly why he loved his profession?

The new patient was what had caused Gerard to exhale. Of course, he waited to be alone to do that, otherwise it would have been extremely unprofessional. But he was sunk in deep thoughts as he prepared to leave his office at 5pm, when he said goodbye to Hilma, his secretary, and also while walking home.

Gerard didn't like bringing his work home, not only because it deprived him of the sweetness of free time but also because Agnes, his wife, would ask questions. His profession didn't allow him to share information about what happened inside the four walls of his office, but he never felt that was a heavy burden because many other professions had the same regulations.

Gerard hoped his thoughts would be distracted, like a rainy cloud going away before the bright sun, left behind on the street as he crossed it. But as a professional, Gerard's inclination was to analyse, and since he was his very own first patient he knew himself to the core. His hope to leave the riddle at the threshold of his home was in vain.

Gerard and Agnes lived in a spacious house with a back garden. It wasn't very modern; they both preferred vintage style. Their living room contained a big library, a tall wooden clock and a gramophone next to a small side table with bottles of nice whisky. It was a cosy home, but since their daughter Elsa had left for college it seemed emptier, with a nostalgic feeling floating around like a ghost.

Agnes was a primary school teacher, and her affection for children was what made the hole in her heart even worse. Gerard, on the other hand, tried to explain the feelings overtaking them both by the fact that their little girl wasn't little any more. He used terms from his books to make it seem normal, but the truth was that he was hiding his own sadness.

When he opened the front door of his home he almost collided with his wife. 'I just spoke with Elsa.' Agnes's joy made her look like a balloon that was about to burst. She was waiting for him at the door so she could deliver the news right away. The few quick phone calls per week that their daughter could manage were a big event, or at least Agnes made it look that way.

'Great! Anything new?' Gerard was secretly thankful for having this call today as he desperately needed something to distract his thoughts.

'No,' she answered shortly, without realising how disappointing that was for her husband.

Nevertheless, while setting the table for dinner, Agnes didn't stop talking about their daughter. It was her favourite topic, but she was just repeating what they both already knew.

Gerard tried to follow his wife's words, to clutch desperately in their meaning, so that the riddle about his new patient wouldn't invade his mind again. But how could he focus on something he had already heard?

'Darling, are you listening to me?' Agnes had stopped eating and was looking at her husband curiously.

I didn't do a very good job at disguising, Gerard thought. 'Yes, of course, I am. I just got distracted for a moment.' He tried to reassure her with a smile.

'When will you finally understand that you have never learned how to lie?' Agnes gave him one of those looks as if he were an open book to her. 'A patient?' she asked, quite confident in her guess.

She was right; there was no point in going around the subject when it was perfectly clear what was troubling him, so he nodded. 'Don't worry darling, please. It's nothing that I can't deal with. I just need some more time to figure it out.'

Agnes did not respond to his soothing words, but Gerard knew what she was thinking. It was something that she had stopped herself saying out loud for years because they both knew it wouldn't make any difference. She hated the fact her husband couldn't share with her because she loved him, and naturally she was worried. Countless times she had told him that she didn't need to be a psychologist to know that, because he was a good person, Gerard took each case personally. But he was also human and needed to share the heavy weight on his shoulders.

The dinner continued in silence, as did the rest of the evening. Agnes was well aware that, even if her husband couldn't speak openly about his work, he needed peace to think and solve the riddle.

Gerard was sitting comfortably in the armchair by the window, looking out at the quiet night brightened up by the streetlights and holding an unopened book. Questions, questions, questions... Why did people act or think in a certain way? He couldn't remember at what age he had started thinking about that question, but certainly he was still a child. Once it was triggered, the curiosity did not leave him.

While he was growing up, his friends joked that the most suitable profession for him would be psychology, and they all counted on him for emotional support in moments of need. It was somehow easier back then; they were all close friends, he knew them, but even though he had gained knowledge and experience over the years, it had become harder. Each patient who came into his office was hiding a whole unknown universe within themselves and often wouldn't let him in, would not tell the whole truth, would skip important details or would even lie to him. That didn't make the process any easier; it was like stones on an even road.

Sometimes the patients would be completely open, would reveal each secret drawer in their soul and hand it to Gerard to analyse. But when he did his part, they seemed to lose the strength to follow his advice. When they left his office, there was nothing more he could do for them; it all depended on them. Actually, it had always depended on them, the patients. Gerard was there just to remind them of that.

Even after long years of practice, Gerard had been surprised by his new patient. People were strange creatures, full of dusty drawers filled with buried memories, some of which were destructive. But what system was the mind using to handle those memories? Some people could leave behind even the worst experiences and live happily, while for others their worst experiences became nightmares that haunted them.

Gerard didn't feel his wife's presence until she lightly put her arm on his shoulder and his mind came back from the deep ocean where it had been floating in search of answers.

'It's late, I'm going to bed,' she said softly.

Gerard kissed her hand on his shoulder. 'I will join you soon,' he said.

But Agnes did not leave right away; she remained beside him for a brief moment to show him that she had something to say. The silence felt tense; perhaps she was searching for the right words.

She finally spoke. 'Not everybody has the will to fight their demons and not everybody wants help. Some people choose the easy way and give up... You can't help everyone.'

Then she walked away, leaving him alone.

Her words did not help Gerard; on the contrary, they made him sink even deeper into his thoughts. Could it be possible for a person to sabotage themselves? It happened often; it was described in books. But Gerard was now questioning himself not as professional but simply as a human being. Why would a person not want to be happy?

Next morning, Gerard was at his office at the usual time. He hoped the new day would bring some answers, which his sleepless night had failed to do. Perhaps the session with the patient today would be more successful, he would break the invisible shell, discover where the problem originated and take a step forward.

Hilma, his secretary, greeted him with a smile. 'Ms Bakker called to cancel her appointment for 10am. The next patient is scheduled for 12pm.'

'Thank you, Hilma.' Gerard forced a polite smile, but he was unpleasantly surprised and slightly upset. It meant that he was doomed to spend another two hours in the same way he had spent his evening: thinking over the riddle.

Gerard sat on the sofa in his office that was meant for the patients, closed his eyes and tried once more to analyse his first and only meeting with Ms Bakker the day before...

*

Lea was sitting on the sofa opposite him and, contrary to most patients, she appeared to feel comfortable there. She had a fixed, polite smile on her face but her eyes, the window to her soul, revealed emptiness. Gerard had already discreetly scanned her and his professional eye had caught a few details. She was twenty-five, good-looking, and the way she was dressed showed she was neither rich nor poor. Her perfect manners did not reveal anything odd at first sight. What could be the problem be, then?

He started with a few standard questions, but soon after he was forced to get to the point because his patient was giving perfectly satisfactory answers. 'Are you feeling confident in sharing your reason for coming to see me?'

'Yes, of course.' Lea didn't hesitate with her quick response, which appeared as another question mark in Gerard's mind. 'Actually, I'm not even sure this is the right place for me to be, but I decided to give it a try.' She shrugged. 'I want to find answers about myself.'

'Very well.' Gerard nodded approvingly. 'And what exactly are the questions you are looking for answers to?'

'Well, the main one is why do I not have feelings.' She glanced at him, expecting amazement, but Gerard gave no reaction. He just carried on with another question.

'Could you be more specific. What sort of feelings do you think you are missing?'

There was a brief silence as Lea searched for the right words. 'All kinds of feelings... It's as if I am indifferent to everything. I know that's not normal though I feel fine with it.'

'What is your family status? Relatives, friends?' Gerard continued.

'Big family. I can't complain about lack of friends and I have a partner with whom I live.' She almost felt as if she were completing one of those forms that asked personal questions.

'And what are your relationships like?' Gerard was pleased his patient was so open with him, so he tried to get as much information as he could.

'My boyfriend, Simon, is loving and caring, and my family are too, but they all complain that I don't give them enough attention and I act as if I don't care about them and their feelings.' Lea sounded uneasy; her eyes were a little sad – and there was also something else.

'Is that true? Are they correct?'

'I love my family and Simon, but... I feel as if someone has surgically removed my emotions. How is that possible?' She gave Gerard a questioning look, but he encouraged her to carry on talking. 'I'm not excited about things like I should be. I don't get emotional when I see Simon upset. If it were up to me, I'd call my parents once a month but I know that would break their hearts.'

Sensing he was on the right track, Gerard knew exactly what to ask next. 'Have you been feeling depressed lately? Perhaps a bit more closed within yourself, irritated by everyone surrounding you?'

'No, nothing at all.'

Lea almost couldn't wait for the end of the question so she could give her honest answer. That puzzled Gerard, who was almost ready with his diagnosis. He had already spotted a few signs that suggested the young woman's problem.

She continued, 'I don't find anything different in my behaviour and neither do my family. But I know there must be something wrong with me. I sadden my loved ones with lack of emotion, I just don't know why...' She seemed completely calm and under control, this type of person that someone would rarely suspect had any emotional issues.

And yet here she was after all, a riddle for herself and for Gerard.

Milton Keynes UK
Ingram Content Group UK Ltd.
UKHW022122161023
430741UK00005B/65

@ReiraShiver

NATURE'S TRIBUTES

JADE FORD

CRANTHORPE
—MILLNER—
PUBLISHERS

First published by Cranthorpe Millner Publishers (2025)

ISBN 978-1-80378-259-1 (Paperback)

www.cranthorpemillner.com

Cranthorpe Millner Publishers

Printed and bound by CPI Group (UK) Ltd
Croydon, CR0 4YY

MIX
Paper | Supporting
responsible forestry
FSC
www.fsc.org   FSC® C013604

TRIGGER WARNINGS

Death

Violence

Torture

Death of a parent

Death of an animal

Mention of suicide

To all those needing to escape, I give you the keys to my world.

The door is always open; you are never alone.

And if my fae bite...
BITE BACK.

CHAPTER ONE

The sharp tang of ashy woodsmoke breaks me out of my slumber and I blink dizzily, unable to focus. Groaning, I try to peel myself off the hard, wooden floor, stretching out my aching muscles as I check for damage. Struggling into a sitting position, my hand encounters something soft and plush beneath my outstretched arm.

My eyes snap open, meeting two blue ovals.

A heartbeat later, they blink.

I realise they're attached to a man, lying on his stomach in front of me, and I lurch back in shock, clumsily scrambling upright.

Smirking, he folds himself into a crossed-legged position in front of me. "Finally awake, Sleeping Beauty." His smile doesn't match the piercing vibrancy of his gaze as he studies me curiously. "You're the last one."

He gestures around the room with a flamboyant sweep of his arm, and I realise there are other people here, wandering about or speaking in hushed voices.

He leans in closer, a frown of concern painted across his brow. "Perhaps they gave you too much sleeping draught. Is your voice not working?"

I instinctively pull away, watching him warily.

He leans back, giving me room to breathe, but his consideration is swiftly marred by his words. "With such a

1

pretty mouth, it would be devastating if it wasn't."

I shuffle away from him, reaching for the back of my head; it aches, but I can't feel any lumps or bumps. *Thank the Nature I'm not bleeding.* I can't remember drinking anything powerful enough to knock me out so soundly. Then again, I'm struggling to get my thoughts in any kind of order; it's like there's a box where the information is locked away, and I no longer have the key.

I let out a slow exhale, trying to focus my breathing and regulate my fluttering heart rate so I can think clearly. Anxiety is a familiar, unwelcome companion, and the gentle breathing exercises come to me instinctively, even in my confused state.

Five inhales later, and my heart rate is finally beginning to slow. Until a wave of realisation sweeps through my body, a sinking feeling travelling down my spine, dousing me in an icy-cold shudder of understanding.

The blue-eyed man gets to his feet in one swift, nimble movement, extending a hand to help pull me up.

A hand which I ignore as I stubbornly stand unaided, albeit with a slight wobble.

He retracts his offering, raising one neatly curved eyebrow in question, his annoying smirk still lingering.

I avoid his gaze. "Nature's Trials," I whisper, swearing softly as I gingerly pat down my body again, checking once more for any damage I may have missed.

At least I'm still wearing my own clothes. The thought comforts me as I trace the ivy design stitched into my simple woollen dress with a finger. My feet are bare, but my long red hair remains gathered in a messy bun atop my head. I pull a long strand of straw out of it and cast it onto the floor without a second thought, barely catching the brief frown that streaks

2

across the man's face before it erupts into a grin once more.

I decode his incessant smirking is reason enough not to trust him.

"Indeed. *The Sin Trials*. Did you only just realise?"

He grabs me by the hand, ignoring my sharp flinch at the unexpected contact as he leads me to a railing of clothes that stands in the corner of the room.

"I feared you might have lost your mind for a minute," he whispers into my ear, sending a shiver that isn't entirely unpleasant down my spine.

He studies my face briefly, as if searching for something, before sighing softly and stepping back. I don't understand why, or what his purpose is, but there's a lot I'm ignorant of right now. Currently, he's the least of my problems.

I take another deep breath, letting it out in a firm exhale as I try once again to calm the frantic pounding of my heart. *Why isn't anyone else panicking?* I wonder as I study the people around me, hoping for some kind of clue. Perhaps they are all here wilfully, since I'm the only one behaving as though I've been abducted. It certainly seems like I'm the only person here who isn't *happy*.

Idiots, I think to myself, before nearly jumping out of my skin as a pair of startling blue eyes suddenly re-enter my field of vision.

"What are you thinking?" the man asks, studying my face intently, looking genuinely interested in my response.

He waits for a moment to see if I'll answer, before turning to run a hand through the rows of luxurious outfits hanging on the silver railing in front of us. There are rich velvet and flowing silk dresses that drape to the floor in a riot of colours – greens, blues, purples – all elegantly gathered at the waist,

3

alongside an array of white shirts and expertly tailored trouser suits in dark damask purple and thunderstorm grey.

The man's hand rests on top of a shirt that looks like it's been sewn out of seafoam, the pearl-like fabric catching the light in a swirl of rainbows as he gently moves the garment back and forth.

"That they've picked the wrong person," I murmur, finally answering his question.

His gaze flickers to mine and I meet his intensity with my own, daring him to explain the situation I've fallen unwillingly into.

"What makes you think that?" he asks, letting go of the shirt and running a surprisingly cold finger down my cheek.

Annoyingly, I find myself flushing; it takes only the tiniest amount of embarrassment for a blush to form on my pale cheeks. I can't help raising a hand to my face, frowning at the telltale warmth, frustrated that my body has betrayed me in its immediate reaction to a single touch.

I flick his hand away, instantly irritated. In his defence, he looks chagrined, almost as if he regrets infringing on my personal space.

"I never wanted to be chosen for the Trials," I explain, struggling once more to control my breathing as the enormity of the situation threatens to overwhelm me again.

My new companion gives me a sympathetic look, placing his strong hands on my shoulders, and for a second, I allow myself to be comforted, wanting desperately for the fear, shock, and confusion to be displaced onto someone else.

I don't let it last long, though, shrugging his hands off me moments later.

"What about the prize if you win?" he asks. "What about

4

the fame? What about..."

I'm examining the room as he speaks, but his pause brings my attention back to him instantly.

His expression is eager as he continues. "What about... you know... *them*?"

I roll my eyes, understanding what he's really asking. "The *fae*?" I reply tartly. "What about them?"

The man leans back on his feet and claps his hands together gleefully. "Yes, the fae!" He laughs, seeming both surprised and delighted by my response. "Do they not excite you?"

He swirls me around in a dizzying half circle so that my back is pressed against his chest. He has one arm looped casually around my waist, his earlier chagrin apparently forgotten. It's as if he can't resist being close to me.

"Are you not seduced by their beauty? Their magic?"

He spins me around faster and faster, before stopping abruptly, making me sway clumsily on my feet. I hold my stomach, feeling decidedly sick.

"Look," he whispers in my ear, his breath tickling against my neck, prompting me to shiver again. "Look at how the other contenders polish and preen in anticipation and hope. Hear how they chatter excitedly among themselves like a flock of shrieking birds. Look, Rosalind!"

His voice is suddenly deep and full of a power that I am unable to resist, my eyes widening against my will.

My heart, however, remains heavy; my mind full of questions that I imagine are not going to be answered any time soon.

CHAPTER TWO

The room is light and airy, despite the lack of any obvious windows, and circular in design; large enough to comfortably fit the other people present: two men and five women.

What I'd originally assumed were simple wooden floorboards are richly polished slabs of mahogany, decorated with opulent rugs, and I quickly realise that the room is split into six separate sections, each with their own theme.

One section features an array of plants in an assault of green hues: vibrant emeralds, jades, and viridians, alongside softer tones of fern, pistachio, and pine. It almost looks as if light is shining behind the foliage, with sharp, sunny yellows and golds breaking up the picture. Wrapped around the clothing rail is a long, trailing vine, erupting sporadically with bright orange flowers.

In the corner sits a young man, upon what appears to be a giant pink orchid's head, its petals open and curled around him. He sits with his eyes closed, his hands placed neatly in his lap. He reminds me of May, my cat back at home, who has an almost supernatural ability to blend into the furniture by simply remaining still.

From his attire, I'm guessing he's already raided the clothing provided. No human would choose to dress so outlandishly themselves, surely? His moss green trousers have been paired with a black shirt, topped with a shockingly vibrant peacock green waistcoat and decorated with an orange flowerhead in one of the buttonholes. His black boots have been neatly laced all the way to his calves, the laces as bright orange as the flower's petals.

Like a cat's flickering tail, the only sign of him being awake is the impatient tap of his boot against his leg. That, and his occasional shivers, during which his eyes flicker open and look over to the area next to him, where round, plump clouds are floating. Gusts of wind keep erupting seemingly out of nowhere, wafting cold blasts of air into the space's immediate vicinity, his zone included, ruffling his clothes and no doubt prompting his shivers.

A couple stand bickering in that adjacent zone, though they don't appear fazed by the breeze tugging on their clothes and hair. Every now and then, a cloud floats in front of their clothes rack, and one of them impatiently nudges it aside as they continue to peruse the garments and argue between themselves.

My eyes follow a drifting cloud that joins a clump of others, adding to the cluster that makes up a peculiarly lumpy but soft-looking chair.

A chair made of clouds.

Realising my mouth is hanging open, I close it resolutely, trying to hide the incredulity I feel as I take in my surroundings. I've heard about the magic of the fae from stories, but knowing is entirely different to seeing such unnatural sights in person. I suddenly feel *very* far from home... and painfully alone.

My mind flickers to Nature – the reason our interactions with the fae began in the first place. Despite being a magical being herself, Nature favours living in Sora, the human lands, so she can keep a direct eye on her work. I suppose it is easier

7

to ensure that the plants continue to flourish and the weather remains stable if she is closer to the action.

Fae are creatures born of her magic, so have access to some of her power, though as I understand it, they are restricted to a particular element – water, air, earth, fire, light or dark. Their magic also starts to wane with prolonged separation from Nature, so I'm told, forcing them to visit Sora to replenish and regain their strength. I'm not sure exactly how it's done; whether they have to visit Nature in person, or simply visit an area that Nature has had a hand in restoring. Perhaps water fae can simply bathe in our seas and allow the tides to soothe their weary magic-depleted bodies?

Of course, the Trials allow the winning fae court unrestricted access to the human world for an entire decade, until the next set of Trials commence. I would feel sorry for those fae not permitted to visit but there must be a reason that Nature chose to punish them by asserting control over their access to magic?

I should have paid more attention to the travellers passing through the village, I think to myself. *My lack of wanderlust is really coming back to bite me.*

By staying in Samania my whole life, I've prevented myself from meeting any fae before today. At least, as far as I'm aware. No contestant from my tiny southern village has ever won the Trials, and it's been five centuries since a contestant was even *selected* from Samania. I highly doubt I'm going be the first one to rectify our losing streak.

Why was *I chosen?*

My knowledge of the fae is limited to what my mother taught me before she passed and idle village gossip, which can't be trusted at the best of times, particularly when delivered via my best friend, Jack. I don't even know what happens to the victor of the trials; can't even recall whether a man or woman won last time. *Figures.* The first human from Samania they've selected in years, and it's one who doesn't worship at the altar of the fae.

So many others *dream* of being whisked away by a fae consort, making their homes close to the fae portals in the hope of increasing their odds of selection. The wealthy even send their offspring to private classes, designed to teach humans how to make themselves more appealing to the fae, spending disgusting quantities of gold and silver on ensuring their children know how to dress for each fae court; how to speak eloquently; how to understand the riddles in which fae converse; how to dance elegantly and seductively; how to recite poetry, both prewritten and self-created, and how to sing and play various musical instruments. For those interested in more than a marriage arrangement – namely winning the Trials – pains are taken to improve logic-based knowledge and physical strength as well.

Idiots, the lot of them. If I had that kind of money, I certainly wouldn't be wasting it on making myself appealing to the fae. They're fickle creatures, fae; just as likely to curse you as bless you. Far better to buy more hardy seed varieties and prepare for the harsh weather changes that happen in the years leading up to the Trials, when Nature restricts her magic in the human world, culminating in one disaster after another.

Glacial, bitter frosts sweep across the land; crops refuse to grow; the youngest and oldest of the villagers fall asleep at night, never to wake in the morning. Droughts come next, with crops bleached to nothing but husks in the harsh sun. Then the sudden blackouts begin, contrasted with days where the sun doesn't set at all, and the confusion sets in, villagers fighting against one another because of arguments that they cannot even remember starting. I suppose it's no wonder that so many humans are desperate for the trials to start and end, so magical balance and peace can resume.

I can understand the appeal of an easy life amongst the fae; a long life, too. Fae magic is said to work wonders, after all. But personally? I'd rather spend all day standing in the rain selling our vegetables than be married to a fae.

Hells, my stubbornness is going to be the death of me.

I close my eyes, both hating myself for not being the same as everyone else and commending myself for at least knowing I won't die as a fae-obsessed clone. I don't have a hope in all the hells of getting through this and going back home. I can't sing, dance, perform, or write more than the simple shopping lists I fill out when my father sends me to the market to buy the produce we can't grow on our small farm. I've no interest in – nor am I stupid enough to entertain the idea of – a love match, but neither do I have the capabilities to survive a physical challenge. There'll be no white knight in shining fae armour for me, despite the fact I'm little more than a damsel in distress.

I take a breath, letting it out slowly. I have never yearned for anything more than the life my parents have given me, and I refuse to die regretting that.

"Let's work this out," I mutter, unable to break my habit of talking out loud when I'm thinking through a problem. "What of *me* has appealed to one of *them* enough for me to be considered their champion for these trials? Which fae court's interest have I captured? If I can work out which court I'll be championing, maybe I can think up some kind of survival plan..."

A sudden movement in my peripheral vision prompts me to shift my gaze to another corner of the room. A girl is pacing alongside one of the clothing rails, the colours of the outfits all rather muted compared to the other sections, though equally beautiful in design. Every now and then she stops to pick up a random piece and holds it against her body, before rejecting it, adding the garment to an ever-growing pile on the chair next to her.

I watch as she repeatedly flicks her long blonde hair away from her face, indecisively twisting one of the dresses back and forth in front of her as she considers it. It's a long, trailing chestnut brown gown, with a bodice that appears to be formed of sharp twigs. She disappears behind the chair in her section – a vertical tree trunk half hollowed out to form a tall, throne-like seat – presumedly to try on the dress, if the layers of clothing flying over the back of the chair are anything to go by.

In the adjacent section, a young woman is looking disdainfully at the girl behind the throne, not bothering to hide the contempt in her eyes. There is a sharp, fierce beauty to her – a cliche I assumed was exclusive to novels – and her figure is sensual in its voluptuousness. She seems to have curves everywhere it is possible to have curves, and wears them proudly, showing off her figure in a skin-tight black jumpsuit. Stunned by her beauty and confidence, I can't stop myself from staring at her, taking in the long, luxurious coal black hair that cascades down her back in numerous plaited braids, her dark skin glowing despite the dim lighting.

Beside her, a clothing rail in the form of a sharp iron trellis protrudes from the floor, upon which hang a host of trailing black gowns, their skirts adorned with feathers; precise pinstriped black trousers with strange metal loops protruding

11

from their seams, and unapologetically short dresses studded with metal buttons. There is no chair, and the whole area seems to be sucking the very light out of the rest of the room, though I can't decide if that's to do with the space itself or the woman occupying it.

It's a sharp contrast to the section immediately to the right, where the air is erupting with blooms of light and heat. A fiery red rug embroidered with images of the sun in swirls of orange, gold and ruby sits in the centre, beside a curious chair, formed from what appears to be a large, copper dragon, its curled tail acting as the chair's feet. Two red garnets the size of my fist are nestled in the gaps where the eyes should be.

A woman rests regally upon it, trying on the shoes scattered haphazardly around her. She ties a long red ribbon around her leg and up her thigh, trailing from a glittering gold heel that is staggeringly high. I know that if I even attempted to walk in such shoes I would instantly faceplant the floor.

I wriggle my bare toes self-consciously, realising that I'm currently standing on my own warm, thick rug. Looking down, I am met with a cacophony of blues, like an ocean beneath my feet. Little white fish dot the rug, peeking their heads out between the crests of the waves.

I guess that answers the court question.

I sigh, nudging one of the fish with my bare toe. Water magic is favoured by the Winter Court... pity I've never really liked the cold.

Another chair sits to the left of me in the form of an open shell, with a pearlescent interior that shines in a swirl of rainbow hues as it catches the light. A plum purple blanket is invitingly placed in its concave interior, offering a hint of warmth in contrast to the harsh, curving angles of the shell.

My eyes widen as I remember the man standing behind me... and that he knows who I am.

I step forwards, turning to look up at him. "How do you know my name?"

He holds up his hands, palms open, shrugging in innocent surrender, a slight smirk tugging at his lips. "Should I not, Rosalind? Or perhaps you are simply distraught that you do not remember mine?"

With a sudden nimbleness he clasps my arms and turns me around, swinging me onto the shell chair before nonchalantly strolling away. When he reaches the centre of the room, he turns back, giving me a reckless grin and raising his hand in farewell. I flush again, embarrassed to be caught watching him walk away.

No one else seems to give him a second glance. Or even a first.

I suddenly wonder if I'm the only one who can see him.

"I'll be seeing you again soon, Rosalind. Take care now," he says, and I'm surprised that I can hear him just as clearly as when he was standing next to me.

In less than a blink, he's gone, and I flinch at the suddenness of it, the image of his piercing blue eyes and wide, perfect grin seemingly burned onto my retinas.

"Fae," I hiss, disgusted with myself for not realising sooner. *How am I going to survive if I can't even recognise one when they're standing right in front of me?* "Idiot," I mutter under my breath. "What did he mean 'you don't remember mine'. How am I supposed to remember his name when we've never met before?"

A soft, breathy laugh echoes in my ear and I swiftly spin around in the shell, struggling to gain purchase on the slippery sides as I check to see if he's somehow returned.

There's no one there.

I gulp miserably.

I hate fae.

CHAPTER THREE

"You better hurry and get dressed, unless you want to go as you are."

The girl from the fire section locks eyes with me, snapping me out of my inner turmoil. When I don't move straight away, she sighs and strolls across, heading straight for my rack of clothing.

"Look, we're competitors, so this is the only time I'm going to help you, understand? Here – try this one." She thrusts one of the outfits into my hands, before walking back to her own seat without a second word or backwards glance.

Struggling to get into a sitting position due to the curving sides of the chair, it takes me a moment to settle enough to look at the item of clothing she's selected.

I'm pleasantly surprised by her choice, given her own clothing selection. It's a simple garment, meaning I'll stand out less than the other contenders. Of course, that might be her intention, but it suits me fine. After all, I don't want to draw attention for the wrong reasons. Too much fae scrutiny could be dangerous, even deadly. I only need to do enough to get through the trials and return home.

I don't need to win, just survive.

Is that too much to ask for? To hope for? Is it even possible? I'm still not sure what happens post-trial to the challengers. Only the sole winner, or 'survivor', is celebrated, and their home 'blessed' by the fae. I haven't really thought about the losers before; I'd just presumed that no one likes to talk about losing. *Where do the losers go?* I wonder. Do they reside in the fae world? Do they die? Or do they return with their memories wiped so they don't give future contenders an unfair advantage? Are the family members and friends who are left behind conveniently memory-wiped too?

I can't imagine the fae wiping a human's memory just to spare them the pain of losing someone close to them. But surely people can't be so stupid as to want to compete in these challenges if failing means death? I shake my head firmly. I refuse to entertain the idea that losing means I'll never see my family or friends again, especially when I didn't get to say goodbye.

I massage my scalp, wondering just how much draught I was drugged with – my head is throbbing. I can't even remember what I was doing beforehand.

I sigh as I stand and pull my dress up and over my head. Wallowing will get me nowhere. All I can do now is hope for the best, and try to prepare for the worst. If I keep my wits about me and my heart guarded, I'll be fine, right?

Unfortunately, there is no one I trust enough to ask.

Slowly, with trembling fingers, I begin to dress, pulling on trousers before carefully fastening a blue waistcoat over a pearl white shirt. The buttons are in the shape of tiny seahorses, fashioned from a type of stone in the same pearlescent shade as the shirt. It takes several attempts of nervously placing the buttons out of sync before I manage to do it up properly.

Stretching to check the give of the fabric, I am pleasantly surprised that the soft velvet of my indigo trousers allows full movement. I look down at myself bemusedly. I look ridiculous,

16

but I suppose this is the type of fashion the fae like. Better to try and fit in, given the circumstances.

I pull some silly poses, checking the give of the fabric some more, before pulling on some simple boots. They are white, and highly impractical; they wouldn't last a day on our farm. I grin to myself, imagining my father gifting them to me, and me returning home after a day with the cows.

My head starts pounding again, my heart suddenly heavy as I try to shove thoughts of my family out of my head and focus. At least the boots fit well, and have a reassuringly tight grip on the soles. I tap one heel on the floor, begrudgingly accepting them.

Around me, my fellow humans are moving to stand in the circles at the edges of their sections. I suppose I ought to start thinking of them as contestants, if only to remind myself not to get too attached. No point befriending someone who might die the next day, or worse, betray me and bring about my own downfall.

As I ponder this rather depressing thought, the dainty pink and white spotted mushrooms around the edges of the circles begin to glow.

Summoning circles.

I roll my eyes. Would it kill the fae to lose the theatrics and use doors like everyone else, instead of showing off with magic at every turn? Perhaps I would become lazy too, if I had access to magic all the time?

Stepping over the mushrooms surrounding my own circle, I feel, rather than hear, the low hum that starts from my feet and travels up my body. Icy hands seem to trek across my body, but strangely, I don't feel cold.

Before I have time to consider this peculiar contradiction,

my spine jerks sharply, as though I am being yanked by an invisible string. Immediately, my vision turns black, and the humming vibrates across my body. It's like being stuck in a swarm of giant moths.

Somehow, I resist the urge to slump to my knees as a wave of nausea threatens to lurch up from my stomach and into my throat. I blink against the sharp, bright light, a second wave of noise overwhelming me. I can hear groans from the other circles nearby, but when I try to take a step over the glowing pink mushrooms, they immediately shrivel into black spines, lashing out with long, green tendrils that shoot up into the air at an alarming rate.

"What in the Nature?" I hold my arms close to my body, protectively shielding my face as the vines launch themselves into the air, crisscrossing over one another before arching over the top of me and back down.

I'm in a rudimentary cage. *Great*.

The pink mushrooms pop up again around the base of the summoning circle and the vines begin to shimmer, what was once dense foliage becoming a faint haze of green light. It's like looking through a coloured glass window – I know I can't step through, but I can see everything around me, albeit with a green tinge.

Several contestants have gone through a similar experience, while others seem to have known what to expect, or perhaps had simply been cautious enough to stay firmly within their circle's boundary. For them, the circle hasn't bothered to make a cage, leaving them free to survey their surroundings unhindered.

In front of us is a large open room, with multiple platforms jutting out from the sides of the walls, somehow held up by numerous narrow, twisted pillars. The room has three floors, giving the space an almost theatre-like appearance. Maybe that's what it usually is, if the crowds of people standing in every available space are anything to go by.

Hells.

My sharp inhale stabs at my lungs.

I'm in a room full of fae.

The ones closest to me look almost normal; like stunningly beautiful humans in elaborate outfits that either cling to every gorgeous curve or swoop around them in dramatic swathes of fabric. Large, colourful gems dot all available skin space: fingers, necklines, ankles, wrists, ears... I gasp again as I realise some of the fae have even adorned their tails and horns.

All their faces are striking, with sharp high cheekbones, expressive hypnotic eyes, and full plump lips painted in rich golds, reds, and purples, often pulled up into teasing, arrogant smirks.

I'm struggling to take it all in; as soon as my eyes focus on one thing, something glitters elsewhere and my brain struggles to catch up with what my eyes are showing me.

A wave of dizziness washes over me, and I close my eyes, trying to breathe deeply, though I'm not sure even my trusty breathing exercises are enough to help me now.

CHAPTER FOUR

I open my eyes to find a tall, honey-skinned woman grinning viciously at us as she strolls up and down the platform we're caged on, her long plum hair swinging in cadence with her movements.

Realising we're on stage, I snap to attention as the woman begins to talk.

"Before us are this year's brave contenders." Her musical voice twinkles like raindrops on a windowpane, whilst somehow reverberating loudly around the room. "Let's give them a big round of applause!"

The fae most closely resembling humans merely raise their glasses, their drinks producing an array of colourful bubbles that float into the air and dissipate in a musical arrangement of pops.

Behind them is where the bulk of the noise erupts from.

The further from the stage they are, the more shocking and less human the fae appear. Some have flowers blooming from their skin, others long, twisting horns and short stubby spikes that curl from their heads and arms. Emerald green and cobalt blue seem to be the most common skin tones, but I notice a few fae with ethereal dusky rose-pink skin, little pink snub noses, and full red lips. It's these fae that erupt in screams, woops and cheers, leaving me feeling completely overwhelmed, the myriad of colours assaulting my eyes inconsequential compared to the ringing in my ears.

The woman twirling around the stage appears unfazed by the noise. If anything, her boundless energetic spinning is fuelled by the chaos.

"As Nature demands, these six contestants—" She pauses, realising one of the cages holds two humans. "Seven contestants! Someone's been naughty!" She giggles conspiratorially. "But don't worry." She lowers her voice to a breathy whisper and the crowd leans in as a collective, spellbound by her every word. "We'll get rid of the extra one soon enough!"

I try to keep my expression blank as the crowd cheers again, the woman clapping her manicured hands together joyfully. Inside, I'm screaming.

"Perhaps this one!" She points to the girl adjacent to me, wearing the impossibly-high-laced gold sandals.

The girl gasps, shaking her head frantically.

"Just look at those obnoxious shoes she's chosen," the woman mocks, giggling manically as she pirouettes easily on one pointed toe. "Or what about two for one!" The laughing fae spins again and leaps elegantly across to the human couple, their former argument seemingly forgotten as they cling to one another tightly.

I don't hear the rest of the fae's taunting comments, the thumping of my heart in my ears drowning out any sound. For the first time, I wish I'd paid more attention to what I chose from the clothing rail, instead of going with the other contestant's advice.

I should have taken this more seriously, I think desperately as I try to belatedly straighten up my outfit and stand a little straighter. *Surely the fae won't hurt us just because we didn't dress correctly?*

Panicking, I try to covertly look at the other contestant's clothing while simultaneously focusing on what the fae host is saying as she introduces the other human contestants. I've already missed the details of the first three, other than what court they've been designated to. The boy with the orange flower in his buttonhole is introduced as a Champion of the Light, the girl draped in brown as an Earth Warrior, and the couple as Swords of Air.

I struggle to recall the lore I learnt growing up, cursing myself for not paying attention. *Too late now*. I shake my head. Perhaps the draught hasn't worn off yet – my memory still feels strangely hazy, and I'm left wondering, yet again, why I was chosen. Someone somewhere is clearly enjoying a laugh at my expense. I just hope I'm not eliminated before I have a chance to prove myself.

My thoughts are interrupted by a loud snap and a scream that is brutally cut off before it's even fully started.

I watch in horror as the girl from the air couple, still desperately clinging to the boy next to her, is dragged from their cage.

"Makani, save me!" the girl screams as she is flung over the shoulder of a grinning rose-skinned fae, who is evidently stronger than they look.

I turn my head away, unable to watch, but it's not long before more human cries force my eyes back. The boy left in the cage is desperately trying to reach his beloved, tearing his way through lashing vines that are slicing chunks out of his skin. Tears pour from his eyes as blood erupts from the welts in his skin, splattering the floor of his cage with red as he tries again and again to tear through the tendrils that reknit themselves back together as quickly as he tears them apart.

The vines seem to pause then, the glimmer of hope on his face wrenching at my heart, before one lashes out in a sharp crack and strikes him straight across the face. He yelps, holding his now blood-misted eye as he staggers back to the floor of his cage, watching helplessly as the fae carries his lover away.

Seeing his resolved defeat, the girl screams all the louder, her eyes widening in shock and pain as the rose-skinned fae suddenly puts her down and slaps her, leaving her with a mark across her face.

"I like my prey silent," the fae woman says in a strangely deep, gravelly voice, shocking the girl into gulping sobs as she looks desperately around for any kind of help.

Met with nothing but smirks and grinning looks from the surrounding fae, the girl seems to finally realise the hopelessness of her situation. With silent tears trickling down her face, she takes one last look back at her beloved, mouthing 'I love you', before the fae swipes one long nail across her throat in a neat sharp cut.

When she slumps to the floor, the screams truly start.

She must be alive. She can't scream if she's dead, I think desperately, before realising with a sickening lurch that I'm the one producing the ear-splitting sound.

Panicking, I gulp in air as I struggle to regain composure. I know I can't risk drawing attention to myself, yet I can't contain the torrent of emotions that are cascading through my already weary body.

"Only one contestant per court, please! Let's not be greedy."

The melodical tinkling of the fae host's voice makes my breath catch, and I hold it, hoping I can assert enough control to make the screaming stop.

The fae woman waggles a finger tauntingly, smiling at the

23

crowd and gesturing for the rose-skinned fae to carry the girl's blood-spattered body off the stage. She doesn't seem bothered by the streaks of red now painting the shiny white marble stage, instead turning ominously to the boy, who breathes heavily through his nose, one hand held to his eye as he cowers at the back of his cage, clearly terrified.

Slowly, she bends down until she is eye level with him. "See? We told you that *only you* were selected. That only *your* heart was needed." She punctuates her remark with a stab of her finger towards the boy – it is nowhere near him, but he violently flinches, nevertheless. "But you didn't heed the warning, did you? What did you say? That *your* heart and *hers* beat the same?" Her head tilts to one side, as if she actually wants an response.

"Don't answer, don't answer," I chant softly under my breath, praying that the boy knows enough about the fae to remain silent when faced with an indirect question.

Unfortunately, the boy appears to be too weary, too frightened, too heartbroken, or a horrible combination of all three, to care about that age-old adage.

"She is my *everything*," he replies, gasping as the fae reaches forward, the vines parting so that she can grasp his face between her hands.

It clearly hurts, for the boy's eyes roll back in pain, one leaking droplets of blood down his pale cheek.

"I think you mean *was* your everything," the host trills, grinning manically again. "Perhaps it's your time too? The Roses will be more than happy to receive more fresh blood to blossom their cheeks with."

A cheer erupts from what I assume is the Roses' corner of the crowd as I close my eyes, unable to hold back my dry heave at the realisation that the rose-skinned fae gain their beautiful complexion from *blood*.

"Now, now."

His voice snaps my eyes back open.

It's him.

The blue-eyed fae man from earlier saunters past my cage, giving me a jaunty wink as he goes, and places a hand on the host's shoulder, gentle but firm. "Air deserves their chance at victory too, Remora. Leave this one be, for now."

The host, Remora, turns back to look at him, her hands not leaving the boy's bleeding face.

"Aalto." Remora raises one perfectly poised plum eyebrow, her eyes glinting, daring him to come closer. "Do you have to be such a bore? It's such a *human* trait."

I didn't think I had the capacity to feel relief anymore, but when the woman finally drops the boy's face, my tense muscles relax a fraction. The poor boy is shivering in shock and barely moving, watching the two fae like a mouse studying a cat and an owl – not sure which predator is going to pounce first.

Aalto gasps dramatically, bringing his palm to his chest as though her words wound him, his piercing blue eyes glittering with mirth as I try to subtly take in of the rest of him.

Like most of the fae seem to be, he is taller than an average human, his broad shoulders framing what his expertly-tailored clothes suggest is a slim, muscular abdomen. His periwinkle blue shirt almost looks dull when compared to his eyes, though the silk material screams luxury, and despite having clearly been neatly pressed, the slight wrinkles at the hems suggest the shirt was haphazardly thrown over his head without a second thought. The top four buttons are undone, revealing the top of his chest and a simple woven cord around his neck, that seems to be missing its charm.

As I study him, he tugs on the rope, like it's an unconscious habit he can't quite kick. The gesture feels strangely familiar, though I can't understand why.

I shift my eyes to his hair, struggling to name the colour. The strands look like shafts of spring morning sunlight, some almost white, others a soft, buttery yellow. They fall in a tousled mess of waves down to the nape of his neck, curving around his slightly pointed ears.

If not for the ears, and the faint shimmer to his skin, he would pass as a very handsome human. Though if the arrogant smirk that lingers around his mouth is anything to go by, he's clearly aware of his beauty.

"On the contrary, dear Remora, one more human, especially one so deliciously emotional, will makes things all the more interesting." He holds out a beautifully manicured hand to Remora, who begrudgingly takes it to pull herself to her feet.

With her elegance, she doesn't need the extra help, but I get the impression that very few fae say no to Aalto, although there is clearly no love lost between these two.

Back on her feet, Remora smiles and brushes past him, ignoring the human boy that had moments before captured her interest, ready to face the crowd once more. I'm reminded of how short fae attention spans really are. One of the worst offences you can commit is to bore a fae.

"I suppose we'd best get the introductions out of the way, hm?" Remora waves her hands, shushing the crowd when they playfully start booing her.

I tear my eyes away from the sobbing, shaking boy and reluctantly return my attention to our fae host.

"Settle down, settle down. Now..." Remora turns to face us for a moment. "... brave contenders, may I present my beloved home court, and our reigning champions – Summer!" She bows her head humbly as the fae of the Summer Court cheer and whistle raucously. "Our icy neighbours – Winter!" An equally hearty cheer erupts from the excited crowd. "Our colourful friends – Autumn! And our energetic brethren – Spring!"

Less is heard for the smaller courts, but there is still enough of a cheer to make me cower at the noise.

"Of course, irrespective of our home court, we all favour our own magical disciplines."

At this, Remora flutters her fingertips and whisps of orange-red flame flicker between them. She raises her hands and aims her power towards the crowd, and with a sharp crack a giant whip of fire flicks out, the smell of smoke filling the room as sparks dart across the gathered fae. Several of the fae closest to the stage move their own hands in a soft wave and a cloud of salty ocean spray counters the flames, resulting in a soft hiss as the airborne water droplets sizzle against the specks of fire.

"Fire being my own speciality." Remora winks. "But what beautiful, hot-blooded female would choose otherwise?"

The crowd respond with cheers and wolf whistles.

"Of course, we also have the other disciplines: Water; Air; Earth; Light; and Dark." Remora pauses between each discipline, watching as the corresponding fae show off their talents.

As each magical discipline competes to make the biggest spectacle, the riot of sounds, colours and lights crescendos to a point that I can barely see beyond the front of the stage.

Above my head, dragons made of water tousle in the air playfully with dragons made of white light, creating a rainbow of colours as they twirl and twine their bodies in and out of one another. Parts of the room disappear completely into pure black nothingness, before miniature tornadoes blow apart the curtains of darkness. The ground rumbles beneath our feet as Earth wielders shake the very foundations of the room.

I shiver; so much power in one space. How could they commend this magic to 'Nature' when it all feels so unnatural?

The crowd calms as Remora gestures to us. "Each of these humans have been selected by Nature to prove, on behalf of their race, that they are worthy of keeping her magic in their land. But they cannot compete alone." She sighs, throwing a look of exaggerated sympathy our way. "They are only human, after all, so they will each require a guide. A fae who will help them navigate the trials."

Remora beckons onto the stage a group of fae that I realise have been standing off to the side, slightly hidden from the crowd.

"Each court has selected their own champion, as have our blessed Light and Dark wielding brethren, who choose to wander freely and not align with any court. As the host of this decade's Sin Trials, it gives me the greatest pleasure to present: Idalia, the Summer champion!" A woman from the hidden group walks onto the stage to join Remora. "Corentin, the Autumn champion! Dhara, the Spring champion!"

After a man and another woman have joined her on stage, she gestures to Aalto. For the briefest of seconds, I think he looks in my direction, but he's facing the crowd again before I can blink.

"Aalto, the Winter champion!"

I have to hold back my gasp as she introduces two other women, Nora and Amaya, the Light and Dark wielder champions. Aalto isn't just any fae. He's the Winter Court's champion. *What in all the Hells was he doing talking to* me?

A hush smothers the crowd, and I swallow nervously. I feel like something serious is about to happen. Anxiety swirls like a nest of snakes in my stomach. I'm still in shock from the death of the girl mere moments ago. I start to feel dizzy, my vision blurring at the edges as a strange heat spreads through my body.

No. Not here. Not now. My nails dig into my palms as I recognise the familiar sensations. I try to focus on my breathing again – in through my nose, out through my mouth – but a roar from the crowd startles me and I instantly revert to hyperventilating.

At the rate my heart is thumping in my chest, I'm surprised I'm able to hear anything over its frantic beat, but as I struggle to assert control on my panicking body, I'm semi-aware that the fae champions are being matched with their human counterparts.

A pair of startling blue eyes suddenly appear in front of me, and as Aalto places his hand against my cage, I instinctively cower backwards, remembering only too well what happened to the girl. But before I can move any further, I feel a sharp stab in my stomach. Doubling over, I look up at Aalto, crying out as my stomach lurches, like I'm being yanked viciously forward through my navel.

All I can see is his eyes, before everything turns black.

CHAPTER FIVE

I wake feeling strangely at peace.

I'm lying in a plush bed with several velvety blue blankets layered around me, and as I look to my right, the source of the hazy purple glow that lights up the room becomes apparent. A rounded, pebble-shaped lamp sits neatly on a white wooden table, beside a vase full of wildflowers in vibrant blues, soothing pinks, and sunny yellows. I guess by how hard the light has to work to chase away the shadows in the corners of the room that it's late in the day, though not yet night.

Propping myself up in bed, I shift the pillows around for back support. The room is simple but elegantly furnished, the pearlescent walls curiously rounded, as though the room has been scooped out of the side of a mountain.

I swallow, conscious of how dry my mouth is, and wonder briefly if this is how it is going to be for the foreseeable future? I'd rather not be knocked out without warning, forced to wake up in a strange environment every day. How is my body so relaxed when the situation is so threatening? Did they drug me again?

The air feels warm and heavy, with a heady, lingering smell of honeysuckle. I take a deep breath in, and immediately feel the tense muscles in my shoulders and neck ease up.

I realise as I take a second breath that the scent is the reason behind my false sense of security and I immediately want to hold my breath. But this just makes me take a deeper one when I eventually run out of air and I sigh, losing the will to fight against it.

It's a relief to feel calm, even if I can still feel the lingering fingers of nausea in the pit of my stomach as my body tries desperately to wage war against the soothing scent; to tell me that no, everything is not all right.

A flickering in the corner of my vision snaps my attention to a slim piece of paper, wedged under the pebble lamp next to me. Hesitantly, I give the room another quick scan, finding nothing more than the bed, table, and wardrobe. Before anyone can tell me otherwise, I pull the note out from under the lamp. It is folded neatly in two, with my name written simply in cursive script across the top, the paper so thin I'm surprised that the note isn't transparent. Cautiously, before I can think of a reason not to, I open it, relieved that it doesn't tear in the process.

A sudden, booming voice echoes joyfully around the room, shocking me into dropping the note. Now closed back up, the noise is immediately silenced.

"Fae magic," I breathe, wondering how many more shocks it'll take before I get used to it and stop expecting normality. "Just fae magic. There's no one here," I reassure myself as I ease my body off the pillows and twist my torso, leaning over the side of the bed so I can peek underneath.

As I suspected, there is no one hiding.

Shifting myself off the bed entirely, a cursory look in the wardrobe reveals the same, so I cautiously return to my mountain of pillows and wrap the blankets around me before I return to the note.

Don't jump this time, I coach myself, before opening it.

Once more, a booming voice permeates the room, filling all corners of the once tranquil space. I'm prepared this time, so don't drop it, and the message continues.

"You have been cordially invited to a *feast*!" it exclaims excitedly.

With a sinking feeling, I recognise the voice of the blue-eyed fae man.

Aalto.

I all but growl upon hearing his voice and force myself to take in a deep breath of the honeysuckle scent, using the calming sensation to unclench my fingers that have tightened around the paper.

"A feast of great proportions, such that you have never seen in your human realm! Tonight, you shall join us in celebrating all the fae have to offer! There will be food, dancing, music..."

I can almost see Aalto dancing around in jubilant circles as he penned, or perhaps recited, the message.

"The trials begin, and they begin in *style*!"

A loud round of applause has me dropping the paper in fright again, and Aalto stops talking as it flutters to a close. Breathing deeply as I wait for the honeysuckle scent to resettle my heartbeat, I open it for the third time.

"You have been cordially invited—" It promptly goes back to the beginning, and I sigh, frustrated, my temper building in a strange war against the calming honeysuckle smell.

I focus on taking deep calming breaths as I listen to the message back, to the point where it previously stopped. Steeling myself – I don't want to drop it and relisten all over again, particularly as Aalto's voice is grating on my nerves as it is – I try to pay attention to the instructions.

"Your fae partner will shortly provide you with a selection

of opulent outfits and finery to choose from for this evening's festivities. Will you select lace or silk? Gems or pearls? The choice is yours! Just remember – every decision matters in this competition, so make sure to decide with more than just your eyes! After all, Nature demands that you prove yourselves to be stronger, smarter and more daring than your human traits suggest; to prove that you are deserving of her grace and magic!"

The note disappears in a puff of smoke and I flinch instinctively, relieved to note that it hasn't immediately set fire to the bedspreads I'm currently cocooned in.

"How patronising," I grumble, wondering where my 'fae partner' is and what monstrosity I'll have to get dressed up in. Though perhaps I should be sensible this time, and actually don the outlandish clothes they prefer. I hate their fashion, but dressing up isn't exactly an arduous task, for which I can only be grateful.

Suddenly, Remora's teasing of the girl who donned the high-heeled golden sandals flashes through my mind, and I wonder if I even *know* what constitutes as fashion to the fae. Maybe I *should* seek advice from Aalto?

"What did he mean by 'human traits'?" I ponder.

Was he referring to the traits that make fae and humans different? Kindness, compassion, empathy? I highly doubt it. The fae seem to be out for blood and would quickly grow bored if made to watch a series of challenges based on those characteristics.

"Gold for your thoughts?" A soft breath tickles the tip of my left ear.

"Argh!" I startle, scurrying backwards until my back hits the headboard of the bed with a solid thump. I rub my spine and groan miserably.

Perched in front of me, legs crossed neatly in front of him and flicking a golden coin up and down, sits Aalto. Grinning manically, as per usual.

"How do you do that?" I cry out, flustered that once again he has caught me unaware. I'd literally been staring at the very spot he was now sat in and hadn't noticed him until he had spoken.

"Well, it's quite simple really – it's all about balance. You flip it up" – he flicks the coin into the air, and I watch as it spins a glorious five times before he catches it again in the palm of his hand – "and then catch it in the other hand." He raises an eyebrow. "I thought even a human was capable of that, but..." He sighs dramatically. "I suppose I shouldn't overestimate you." He grins, as if sharing a personal joke that he expects me to get.

"You know I didn't mean the coin!" I'm getting more and more tangled in the bedcovers as I try to extricate myself and climb out of the bed.

Aalto's grin widens. "How is one to presume what anyone means? Maybe you should be more direct in your questions if you seek more direct answers."

He gets up off the bed in a sophisticated, sweeping movement that further aggravates me as I promptly tumble onto the hard floor, my legs still entangled in the covers.

He bites his lip flirtatiously as he smiles down at me. "Normally women wish to *stay* in bed when I'm around."

I choose to ignore him, deciding that he looks more ridiculous than seductive, though annoyingly, I can't ignore the warmth that spreads through my veins as his eyes sweep up and down my body.

"Stupid honeysuckle," I mutter, wanting something else to blame for the lustful thoughts that briefly dance across my mind.

Why is my body attracted to him when he's so absurdly irritating? It's infuriating! I try to ignore the embarrassed flush warming my cheeks as Aalto bemusedly watches me dust myself off and straighten my tangled dress.

"As much as it pleases me to see you care about your appearance and demeanour, little human, you won't be wearing those rags for much longer." Aalto smirks. "A sight I, for one, can't wait to see."

He winks, but before I have a chance to admonish him, ask any more questions or even agree to anything, he raises two fingers and pokes me square in the forehead. My eyes cross as I try to look at his fingertips, but my stomach merely lurches in that annoying way I'm almost beginning to get used to, and my vision promptly goes black.

This time, to my relief, I come to within seconds. It takes me a moment to realise that Aalto's strong arms are holding me firmly before I push him away and try to take in where he's transported us to.

"Welcome, little human, to your dressing room." He gestures to the room with his arms, unbothered by my earlier rejection of his proffered help.

"Not 'little human'. Rosalind," I insist, disliking the patronising nickname he's chosen for me enough to risk it, though I'm worried I'll hate seeing his lips form my real name even more. Still, Rosalind is better than my preferred 'Ros'. I don't think I could stand for him to be *that* familiar with me.

Aalto turns to me, smiling wolfishly. "Ah, she's braver than she looks. Not concerned that I'll be able to control you, now

I have your name, hmm?"

I don't know how he cleared the distance between us so quickly, but I roughly stumble back, disgusted when he goes to run a finger through my knotted hair.

"Myth," I mutter, ignoring Aalto's gleeful celebration in response. I may not know everything about the fae and their customs, but I'm at least sure of this. Only given names have power, and as a human, I don't have one. At least, not one I'm aware of.

Turning away from my patronising host, my attention swiftly shifts to the other side of the room, where a long, white marble table is pushed against the far wall. The shimmering surface of the marble makes the rest of the furniture look dull by comparison, but when combined with the vast array of sparkling pendants, bracelets and brooches spread across the table top, the sight takes my breath away. I walk over, mesmerised, hesitantly holding out a hand over one of the necklaces, briefly looking at Aalto to judge his reaction.

I'm wary of touching anything fae-made, particularly as it's calling out to me in this way, yet I just can't stop myself. I've never seen jewellery such as this before. After all, such excesses are not necessary for survival. Delicate silver chains won't feed a hungry mouth. Elegant pearls won't clothe a cold back. Glittering gemstones won't heal a deathly disease.

Not unless you're selling them, that is.

I gulp. *How much money would I make, selling these back home?* I return my outstretched hand to my side, clenching my fist tightly. Fate is cruel – always too little, too late. If only I had access to this kind of wealth last winter season.

Perhaps then my mother would still be alive.

The winter right before the trials, when the magic in our

world is at its thinnest, is always brutal, and last winter was no exception. There was barely enough food to feed myself and my sister, let alone our parents, and my mother had always been frail. Helpless to do anything but starve ourselves in her place, we pressed our meagre scraps into her hands, hoping it would be enough; that our hunger would be worth it. But as the harsh winter progressed, I watched her continue to deteriorate, every inhale painting a thick line of pain across her forehead as her lungs crackled and struggled to keep her heart going. I could do nothing but wait, powerless to help her as she gradually lost her battle with life.

Money would have easily paid for the medicine we needed to make her better. Hells, money would have kept her from harm in the first place.

My thoughts turn bitter as I look down on the finery in front of me. Surely with all this access to wealth and magic, the fae could do something to help us? Or intervene with Nature and stop her from withdrawing her power from the human lands at the end of each decade? Stop us from having to enter these trials? Yes, humanity abused our power before, but surely we have more than paid for it now? Haven't enough of our ancestors died for Nature to forgive us? For her to allow us to live in harmony alongside her magic?

I reach a hand back towards the table. It may be too late for my mother, but I can still do good for my father and Tasmin. I can still protect *them*.

I glance up at Aalto – I'd almost forgotten he was here, he's been so uncharacteristically silent – before reaching to pick up a long, heavy gold chain with a thick golden cage on the end, enclosing a red ruby the size of a hen's egg.

Out of the corner of my eye, I see frown lines appear on his forehead. I hesitate, but he waves an impatient hand forward, encouraging me to continue, even as his eyes narrow in silent warning.

"What is it?" I ask, then quickly reform my question before he can tell me 'it's a necklace'. "Should I not touch the jewellery?"

The yearning to scrape all this wealth into a big bag and hoard it away until I can get back to my family is undeniably strong, but I wait for him to respond.

"You can take what you wish, Rosalind," he says simply. "It is not for me to say what you can or cannot wear. Rather, it is interesting to me to see what your *human nature* leads you to."

Infuriating fae, I think bitterly. Life would be so much easier if they just said what they meant. I look back at the garishly large ruby, suddenly wary again. *Do I really want this?* I doubt I'll be able to keep it safe throughout the trials... taking it home with me once I'm done likely isn't realistic.

If I even make it home.

Perhaps it *would* be safer to pick something smaller? Even a tiny jewel would be enough to feed my family for months, and would be easier to keep safe. A large, conspicuously visible gem might put a target on my back.

My hands linger over a set of gold bracelets with garnets inlaid in their bands, and before I can second guess myself, I clasp one onto my wrist.

I hesitate for a second, waiting to see if any magic takes hold, letting out a shaky breath that I hadn't realised I was holding when nothing happens. I wonder if the first trial is to assess whose fashion choices are most in line with the fae? Or perhaps they want to see if we can match our partnered fae? If we belong by their side?

I steal a sneaky side glance at Aalto, studying his clothing.

He has changed out of his previous outfit and is now dressed in a simple white shirt, with ruffles along the hem like the crest of a wave. His trousers are neatly pressed, as before, but are made of a simple, dark material. Before, he had adorned his body in multiple gems, but now all I can see is a blue circlet, nestled amongst his curls, and that same strand of rope around his neck that he seems to favour. The crown is simple enough – a golden band twirled around three blue sapphires. Well, simple enough for a fae, anyway.

I sigh. I suppose I best match him, seeing as he *is* my partner, however much I hate reminding myself of that.

"Can't you tell me *anything* about this trial? Would it not be easier for us to win if I knew what to expect?" I demand. "Aren't you meant to guide me through this?"

"The rules dictate that I *take no active participation in elaborating on the trial instructions*," he recites, as if reading from a manual.

I startle, having not expected him to respond, though the frown on his formerly cheerful face and the sweat beading on his otherwise pristine brow reveals that he isn't any more pleased about the situation than I am.

"If I release information that will even inadvertently help you win, it will result in my removal from the competition." He breathes heavily, as if pushing the words from his mouth is causing actual physical pain.

"Removal? You mean I can go home if you leave the competition?" A seed of hope blossoms within my chest. "Without a fae partner, I can't compete, surely?"

"No." He snuffs out my hope with one word. "By removal, I mean death. And if I die, then you also die." He looks down at me as if I'm stupid. "Please tell me you at least remember how this competition works, little human? Your memory can't be *that* damaged, Rosalind."

Aalto briefly looks concerned, before his usual arrogant smirk returns. I assume the brief glimpse of sympathy that fluttered across his face must have been concern for his own wellbeing, rather than mine. After all, if our fates are intricately tied together, my understanding *is* critical.

Does he truly expect me to remember everything that was said during the fiasco last night? When that girl was killed right in front of me? I'd barely been able to keep my sanity together, let alone retain information. Perhaps he assumes I was told before I came here? But he was there when I woke up the first time. He must know I'm from Samania; that no champion has been selected from my village in five centuries? I'd never knowingly met a fae in my life until yesterday. He can't expect me to know anything.

Aalto sighs at my thoughtful silence, running a hand through his hair; tousling it further as he waits patiently. When I don't say anything more, he continues speaking.

"It is what it is. Sadly, I cannot enlighten you any further. It's presumed that all human tributes know at least the basics of our relationship with one another, but it appears not, in your case. I forgot how shallow humans can be."

I scoff in anger, about to tell him exactly how I feel about his insult, before he holds up a hand, interrupting my angry outburst.

"Let me put it like this." A strange expression contorts Aalto's face, as if he's trying to speak but someone has placed their fingers over his lips. He swallows, running a hand across his eyes, clearly frustrated, before shaking his head, as though trying to physically expel his thoughts. "At least I know we get some kind of warning before sharing something we shouldn't." He sighs. "Just know that these trials will be tough. They may not be what they seem." He pauses between each sentence as he tests what he is and isn't allowed to say. "There are seven in total, the same as the number of basal human urges. You must overcome each trial, to prove that you are worthy of becoming fae." He breathes deeply through his nose, sweat beading his forehead.

Clearly that simple explanation took more than it should have. Did he push the boundaries just to help me? I ponder over his words. At least I know for sure that there are only seven challenges – even I can survive that, I hope. Especially if they are all to be as simple as attending a party.

"What do you mean 'basal human urges'?" I eventually ask, frowning.

Aalto all but groans as he tries to push the words from his lips. "Gluttony. Greed. Wrath. Sloth. Pride. Envy. Lust," he spits out, panting slightly once he's done.

I save my thoughts on that revelation for later. "And 'becoming fae'? What if I don't want to be fae?"

Aalto winces, before sighing again. *He seems to do that a lot.* I hope desperately that he'll answer; that I misunderstood his explanation. Unable to keep my hands still, I run my fingers over a tiara on the table. It's similar to the one Aalto wears – a simple copper band, twisted as if to resemble a tree branch, with the tiniest sapphires twinkling in-between the whorls like little flower buds.

This one will do, I decide, as I resolutely place it on top of my messy curls.

Before I can blink, Aalto removes my tiara, smoothing

down my curls before placing it neatly back on top of my head. My skin tingles at his touch, and I struggle to suppress a shiver. *He must just have cold hands... he is a Winter fae, after all.*

"You must only prove that you are *worthy*. It is not a literal 'becoming'. You cannot become fae unless another fae wills it, and even then, such transformations come at great detriment to the fae themselves. Hardly any humans are turned fae nowadays." His expression turns introspective, almost melancholic, though I can't understand why.

Before I can probe further, he turns his back to me, striding across the room. Giving a frustrated sigh of my own, I swallow back a retort and follow him, casting one last lingering look back at the table of jewellery.

He stops in front of a giant square screen that cuts the corner of the room off neatly, shielding whatever is behind it. It's an elegant blue colour, with silver swirls etched along the bottom. Small silver fish are hand painted onto the screen, darting in and out of the waves, their fins inlaid with shards of pearls; their eyes formed from specks of gold. Aalto taps the screen, clearly impatient for us to continue. There is only so much talking he seems to be willing to put up with.

"You'll find everything you need behind this screen," he informs me, resuming his role as patronising fae prick. "Do hurry, though. I can only give you so much time, so choose quickly and choose wisely. We have dallied long enough."

He taps my copper tiara and nods, locking eyes with me intently, as if to relay some information that he cannot speak of.

"I'll return shortly," he adds, before vanishing into thin air.

I stare after him in confusion and frustration. I appreciate him trying, but his words mean absolutely nothing to me. I take a breath, shaking myself down to try and release the tension in my limbs. *Focus*. I need to focus.

Noticing a slit in the centre of the screen, I pull the edges apart, quickly discovering that there are two screens linked together. Gently, I push them to the side and enter the adjacent room.

I can't hold back the tiny gasp that escapes my lips. The room is far larger than I imagined, and houses more clothes than I've ever seen in one space. Unlike the racks that held the garments yesterday, strange, twisting, emerald-green seaweed grows out of the floor, intricately interlinked and plaited together to form railings. All the outfits are of the same colour scheme, grouped so that the colours blend beautifully into one another. Soft whites fade into delicate greys, shifting to pale turquoises before brightening to vibrant electric blues, then darkening to indigos so saturated they are almost black. I start to walk, my eyes wide, wanting to take it all in, before Aalto's warning echoes in my mind. I don't have much time.

I stop before the closest rail and, grounding myself with a few bounces on the balls of my feet, I begin hurriedly flicking through the garments. I'm pleased to find that there are trouser suits as well as dresses, and I linger over them briefly. I'm much more comfortable in trousers, and for all I know, this trial might require freedom of movement. Then again... the invitation did say there would be dancing. A dress would almost certainly be deemed more suitable.

I wonder whether we'll be expected to dance with our fae partners? I somehow doubt the annual Harvest Festival barn dances back in Samania are even comparable to a fae ball... I likely won't even know the right steps, not to mention that I have no experience following a partner; I've always taken the lead. Still, I imagine that Aalto is much the same way inclined.

Thinking of Harvest Festival reminds me of Isabel, and I feel a familiar icy stab in my chest. It's been months since we last spoke, after yet another messy breakup, to the point that I don't think our relationship is worth saving this time. But my lingering feelings clearly haven't got the message yet.

One of the dresses catches my eye, pulling me out of my melancholy. It's a floor-length, silver-white gown, the bodice made up of hundreds of tiny sequined opals in the shape of miniature snowflakes. Several layers of tulle cascade down, with pristine white feathers sewn into the seams like layers of freshly fallen snow. I sway the skirt softly from side to side, mesmerised as it catches the light, the feathers emitting a shimmery sheen. It's quite simply exquisite.

I try to lift the dress from the railing, unsurprised to find that, with all the elaborate finery, it's insanely heavy. I chuckle to myself. As much as the idea of shocking Aalto by becoming some kind of winter queen appeals to me, I would prefer to be able to actually move whilst I dance. I'm far from trusting any fae, so being able to move quickly is an essential, non-negotiable requirement for any outfit.

Fearing that Aalto will reappear any second and sling me over his shoulder, I begin to hurriedly shrug off my clothes, grabbing the next dress along on the seaweed rail. Cold air is starting to permeate the room; icy fingers gripping at my hair, urging me to move faster. Shimmying the fabric up my legs and over my body, I look down at the outfit I have randomly selected. The bodice fits snugly to my frame; the small pearls sewn along the hem of the sweetheart neckline glinting softly in the light. The skirt flows down from my hips to my knees, affording me easy movement whilst still retaining my modesty, and the long sleeves make me feel less vulnerable.

I was right to hurry along, for no sooner have I done up the last button, neatly hidden in a fold along the side of the dress, than Aalto returns. His eyes sweep over me hungrily, lingering on the bracelet around my wrist that I'm still fiddling with. I fidget under his scrutiny, unsure whether or not he is pleased with my choice, for his facial expression doesn't change. Before I can open my mouth to ask, he places a hand on either side of my shoulders, and I feel that same tugging sensation as we are both plunged into darkness.

CHAPTER SIX

Sounds reach my ears before my sight returns, and I stumble slightly, this time grateful for Aalto's firm grip on my shoulder as I readjust my balance. We're stood at the top of a sweeping staircase that curves down like a steep tidal wave into what can only be a ballroom. The noises overwhelming my senses are coming from the centre of the dance floor, where a collection of fae sit, playing an assortment of harps, cellos, violins, and other stringed instruments that I do not have a name for.

The music is haunting but beautiful; sweeping and darting like the dancers who are swirling around the orchestra in a strange, alternating slow-then-fast tempo as they keep up with the song's dips and dives. I can barely contain my gasp as I gaze upon the seemingly countless varieties of fae, fabrics and outfit styles. And the jewellery! I've never seen so much wealth in one space. Rubies the size of my fist; sapphires twisted together into thick, sparkling necklaces; brooches constructed of solid gold with glinting obsidian décor. I fiddle with the simple bracelet on my wrist, wondering if perhaps the choice I made earlier was wrong.

A warm breath in my ear makes me jump, snapping me out of my musing.

"Are you ready to make your entrance, little human?" He seems to hesitate, before stroking a long finger down my cheek, lifting my chin so our gazes meet. "You look truly beautiful," he murmurs, looking at me intensely, before backing away swiftly, his smirk returning; his hands drifting back to his sides.

I fail to hide my shiver at his touch, and only just manage to bite back a scathing comment, instead contorting my face into a rictus smile. I have to remember where I am; who my companion is. I can't trust that Aalto is genuinely complimenting me, but it wouldn't do to push him too far either, despite my desire to argue with him. After all, one of my fellow contenders was ripped apart and by another fae last night. I shiver again, this time in horror, and struggle to regain my focus.

I can't afford to get distracted by maudlin thoughts. I'll need all my wits and more to get through this soirée.

Aalto holds his arm out to me, his eyes flashing with mischief, and I resist the urge to arch a mocking eyebrow at him, looping my arm through his as I've seen the other attendees do. As soon as we make to step forward, a bearded fae dressed simply in a short bronze dress bows and extends a tray filled with multiple crystal glasses, each containing a twinkling, hazy blue liquid.

"Dragonfly Dew?" the waiter offers, handing us each a glass without waiting for an answer, before turning and disappearing back into the crowd.

Aalto raises his glass to mine, chinking them together before I take a tentative sip. My tongue is immediately flooded with warmth, but rather than being hit with a taste, I'm hit with sensations. The feeling of lying in a warm field, as the sun slowly caresses my cold body, easing out all the aches and pains as—

The feeling suddenly stops when I swallow the liquid. I look curiously at my glass and instantly raise it to my lips again hungrily.

"Be wary, little human," Aalto admonishes, grinning. "Forbidden tastes always lead to more."

I flinch as I feel his arm tighten around my own, looking up at him in surprise, but his gaze remains fixed firmly ahead as he leads us down the stairs, bowing his head to the fae he recognises as we pass.

I go to take another sip of the delicious blue concoction but manage to stop myself as I study Aalto curiously. He hasn't taken much more than a sip himself and I'm suddenly afraid of the way the drink has made me instantly want to seek out more and more. I decide to follow his lead, and avoid sipping further, despite the temptation.

It seems that perhaps there are games already in play, although what exactly this one entails, I still haven't the slightest idea.

"Care for a dance?" Aalto asks politely with a slight bow.

I glance reluctantly towards the dance floor, where couples slowly swirl around in graceful circles, pulling away from each other before returning and clasping hands. It reminds me of the peaceful motions of the tide lapping against the shore. I'm definitely not that elegant.

"I'm not sure I'm one for dancing. Perhaps we could sit and enjoy the music?" I offer, not wanting to make a fool of myself in front of everyone.

Aalto leans down, whispering in my ear, "Come now, Rosalind. I know for certain that isn't true. Dance with me; I promise I won't let you fall."

He looks at me with such intensity that I can't help but avert my eyes, and before I can protest again, he's swept me onto the dancefloor.

"Aalto!" I hiss, chastising him as he smoothly spins me around, catching my stumbling body as if he's done it countless times before. "I didn't say yes!"

"Yet you didn't say no, either." He laughs, clearly enjoying himself.

I supress a groan. He's entirely right: I didn't say no directly. Why do fae choose to take things so literally only when it pleases them?

For a while, we dance in silence, as I attempt to follow his lead around the dance floor, dipping in between the other couples that swirl around us. Despite being unfamiliar with following a partner, I'm finding it a pleasant change of pace, as I have a chance to listen to the music rather than having to intently focus on the dance steps.

"Enjoying yourself?" Aalto asks, taking the opportunity to whisper into my ear as he dips my body towards the floor.

"The music is magical," I respond honestly, surprising myself when I manage to match his sudden increase in tempo as the song quickens before slowing down again. "And easier to follow than I was expecting." I smile genuinely for the first time since I arrived in the fae realm, and for a moment I think Aalto looks pleased, though a quick twirl has me wondering if I imagined it.

All too soon, the music comes to a stop, and before we are swept up in the next number, Aalto deftly removes us from the dancefloor.

I follow him quietly, my eyes eagerly seeking out the other human contenders. I find the girl who helped me get dressed before our first introductions standing on the stage, this time dressed in a vibrant purple pantsuit, with two simple purple gems decorating her ear lobes. She stands close to her fae partner, who is elegantly clothed in a long purple gown. I blink when I see it move, and realise it's made from hundreds of live butterflies, woven together.

I feel bile rising in my throat and quickly swallow it down, turning back to look at Aalto. He's stopped in front of another fae, a beautiful woman with icy white hair, who is accompanied by a young man. Another tribute. The two fae begin chattering excitedly, leaving me to introduce myself to my fellow contestant. He raises an eyebrow and shrugs, as if to say 'how rude', and I can't help but smile back, silently agreeing.

"I'm Kieran," he says, holding out a hand, which I take. He grasps it between both of his and places a chaste kiss on our enclosed palms, which would have seemed odd if I didn't recognise it as a Duli custom. Seems I *have* learnt something from my history lessons, after all.

"Rosalind," I reply, touching my forehead to our enclosed palms before stepping back.

His warm smile reassures me that I completed the custom correctly.

"You've been to Duli?" he asks curiously. "No offense, but you don't look like someone who would fare well in the sun." He grins, his bright, sky-blue eyes twinkling mischievously.

"Why's that?" I ask, crossing my arms, pretending to be annoyed despite his words being true.

He tugs one of his blond curls, then indicates to my hair. "We don't see many redheads. They find the Duli sun too strong for their delicate skin." He steps forward, after giving his fae a quick sideways look. "I miss it already," he whispers conspiratorially, and I find myself nodding, unwilling to mention my homesickness out loud, not wanting to give the fae any ammunition that they could use to make my time here more miserable.

A brief flicker of what looks like disappointment drifts across his face, but his expression is quickly wiped blank when his fae companion looks down at him. Grabbing him roughly by the scruff of his collar, she leads him away without a goodbye or even a glance at me.

I force myself not to roll my eyes, though the fae's lack of manners doesn't come as a surprise to me.

"Let's join Nora and the others at the banquet table," Aalto suggests, nodding after Kieran and the fae I assume is Nora. "Though I imagine you're not all that hungry," he adds, giving my shoulder a firm squeeze as he directs me to a long table and pushes me down into a seat.

I grimace, resisting the urge to shrug off his grip as I sit down, annoyed at his presumption, though he isn't wrong. My nerves have left me feeling too sick to have much of an appetite. How he could possibly know that though, is beyond me.

In front of me is a long wooden table, unadorned aside from the food, which is extravagant and bountiful enough to more than make up for the simple decor. Despite my nausea, I can't help my stomach from releasing a quiet grumble, which prompts Aalto to raise his eyebrows and smirk again.

"Stupid fae hearing," I mutter under my breath, knowing full well that he'll hear that too.

Still, there's more food here than my family has seen in a month... yet another reason for me to be disgusted by the fae. So much of my life has been spent with hunger gnawing at my insides; watching my father give up his food just so me and Taz could eat. It's these thoughts alone that stop me hungrily reaching for the food and shovelling it in, like I can see some of the other contenders doing.

Interestingly, the fae themselves are more reserved, but I suppose this kind of feast is something they are used to indulging in. Seeing as it is for our benefit, it might even be less than their normal fare. I can't imagine they'd go to any additional effort for a group of humans.

I pick up one of the simplest looking bread rolls, almost moaning when I bite into it, the sweet honey and tangy spiced raisins in its centre oozing out into my mouth, contrasting deliciously with the warm, soft texture of the bread that almost melts as I tear into it. I manage to stop myself from reaching for another, taking a chunk of white, crumbly cheese instead to contrast against the sweet taste.

I look around curiously, watching the others and studying the rest of the food on offer. The table must be six feet in length at least, and every inch is crammed with a different delicacy. Some food I don't even recognise, which I imagine must mean it is either native to the fae lands or from a far distant region of Sora.

There are a selection of roasted meats, dripping with golden crispy fat; whole partridges dressed with tiny red berries; some kind of fish, speckled with a green herb I don't recognise, and a massive spit-roasted boar in the centre of the spread. Giant bowls are filled to the brim with crispy potatoes, rounded red grapes that look like they'll burst the second you bite into them, and mounds of leafy greens with various dressings. And the cakes... My stomach grumbles again as I turn my eyes away from the dainty little animal-shaped delicacies: swans with little currants for eyes, hedgehogs decorated with sharp quills of chocolate, and owls with tufted buttercream for feathers.

I look to Aalto, who has barely touched anything. He's placed some potatoes and a slice of meat on his plate, but is twirling his wine glass as he watches the rest of us. I take another slow bite of the bread roll, once again resisting the urge to grab another one... hells, another three. Perhaps I'll regret my hesitation later, but I can't push down the deep-seated distrust I feel at the fae's supposed kindness.

I watch in silence for a while, lost in my thoughts, amazed by the speed with which some of the other tributes are devouring the food in front of them. One girl –I hear her fae partner call her Seraphina – can't seem to get enough of the cakes, nibbling into each one before discarding them, seemingly desperate in her urge to try everything before it's taken away. I wonder if, like me, she is used to the pangs of starvation.

I turn to say something to Aalto, but he shakes his head, suddenly looking serious as he stares off into the distance, as if he is listening to a voice I cannot hear. He stands abruptly and places a firm hand on my back, helping me up and leading me forward. Looking around, I notice the other fae and their tributes are also standing up and are being herded in the same direction.

It seems our feasting is already over.

CHAPTER SEVEN

Aalto swiftly deposits me with the other tributes, and I wait silently as we're gathered, then led to the stage in the centre of the room, now clear of musicians. My stomach somersaults in trepidation for what's to come, and I'm grateful that I decided not to eat much in the little time we had.

A tall, silver-haired fae with sharp features and piercing green eyes steps into the middle of the stage and crouches down. I feel a rumble beneath my feet and watch, fascinated, as green, inky tendrils swarm up his bare arms, twisting vines swirling beneath his skin. He places his hands on the floor, and the rumbling intensifies as the ground in front of him begins to crack open.

A round, green door slides out of the floor, rising above him, devoid of adornment except for a hollow circle in the centre, surrounding by a glowing blue ring which sparks as he brushes his hands briefly across it. He reaches out a hand as if to grab a doorknob and one magically appears underneath his palm. With a sharp, twisting motion, he opens the door, leaving it ajar just a crack, before stepping back, bowing to Remora before leaving the stage.

I notice curiously that the once green etchings under his skin have muted, now pale mint in places, completely gone in others.

No wonder they're so desperate to replenish their magic if that's how fast it depletes.

I turn once more to face the door, wondering what the sparking blue circle is for, if anything at all. No doubt behind the door is our next location, and I'm praying that it's going to be some kind of lodging, where we can all rest after the party. Though hoping for the best when the fae are involved is always foolish.

"Place your hand within the circle, then take a step back," Remora, instructs, gesturing towards us. She sighs theatrically when none of us step forward. "Come along, humans. Don't be shy! It's simply going to assess how gluttonous you've been before we move on to the next task." A wide smile stretches her lips, but doesn't quite reach her eyes.

When still no one steps forward, she reaches towards the closest human – Makani, the boy whose partner was killed before – and drags him towards the door, forcing his reluctant hand into the glowing circle. She steps away as tendrils of blue light spark out from it and wrap around the boy's hand. He lets out a gasp as the tendrils sprout into the air and then suddenly lunge back down, bypassing his skin and going straight into his hand.

"What's happening? What is that?" he exclaims, fighting to remove his hand by pulling his whole bodyweight back and digging his heels in. But whatever magic is at work, it's keeping him firmly in place.

It ends just as suddenly as it started, and Makani is taken by surprise, falling to the floor with a groan.

His eyes flicker to Remora. "Well... did I pass?" he asks, hesitantly.

Remora quirks an eyebrow and gestures back to the circle. The blue ring around the edge is filling up with a more vibrant

55

blue light; it stops when it reaches about halfway, flashes once, and then returns to its original colour.

"Next!" Remora demands, as Makani steps back in line with the rest of us, looking confused.

"I'll go," I find myself saying before I can think it through, and I step forward towards the circle. I'd rather get this over with, whatever *this* is. I hate the anxiety of waiting.

The circle feels surprisingly cool as I place my hand within it, and I experience the strange sensation of having put my hand straight into cold, wet mud. The blue tendrils start curling around my hand, touching my skin almost thoughtfully. I was expecting to feel electricity, but I feel little more than if I was being stroked by a feather.

Still, it's rather disconcerting when I see the tendrils disappear into my hand; even more so when they almost immediately re-emerge and release me.

"They're done already?" I ask in a whisper.

The ring barely fills up with any blue light, before returning to its starting colour. I step back and look to Remora, who rolls her eyes and gestures back to the group.

"Well, that wasn't so bad," I mutter, wondering why on earth this supposed task was even classified as a trial.

I watch as the others step up, one after another. Some fill up the circle more than others; Delaney doesn't generate any blue light at all.

It's not until it's Seraphina's turn that anything of note happens.

Confidently, she walks over un-encouraged and slams a hand onto the circle, where the tendrils immediately get to work, tasting her skin. They drift in and out, hungrily swirling.

"Is it just me, or is this taking longer than usual?" Kieran whispers.

I agree with him, but dare not answer, too nervous that we'll get told off for conspiring.

"Hey, why isn't it letting me remove my hand?" Seraphina demands as the circle begins to fill up with blue light.

Remora claps her hands with delight. "It looks like we have ourselves a winner!" she trills, bouncing on the spot gleefully.

"A winner?" Seraphina turns to Remora, her hand still trapped inside the circle. A beatific grin lights up her face. "What have I won?"

Remora smirks, shrugging. "Why, your removal from this competition, of course."

I turn away at the last second, realising a heartbeat too late what the fae means, but I can't hide from Seraphina's piercing screams as the blue light erupts from the circle and engulfs her in a hazy fire.

When I eventually look back, there is nothing left.

"What a fitting end for a tribute of the Summer Court," Remora trills.

I feel a rush of hatred flood through my body, making me tremble, and I almost lunge out before Kieran grabs my arm to steady me, shaking his head before he drops my arm back to my side. Idalia, Seraphina's fae partner, is led away, a grim but resolute expression on her face. I care little for her fate. At least she's alive, unlike Seraphina.

"Now that's out of the way, please step through the door. You next trial awaits!" Remora proclaims jubilantly, making me jump, shocking me out of my thoughts.

"Already?" I exclaim. "Do we not deserve a break after that? After what you did to her?" I can't stop my outburst, and my heart all but stops as Remora cocks her head and steps towards me.

I wince as she pinches my face between her two fingers, looking at me with her piercing, vibrant eyes. It takes all I have not to look away or spit in her face.

"The blue drink and the feast, my dear human," she says, stroking my hair tenderly. I cannot help the flinch, which makes her laugh as she lets me go. "She drank the most, and then ate the most, so she must go. Gluttonous, disgusting human," she playfully sings, before turning back to the door.

I watch her go, unable to mask the hatred in my eyes, biting my tongue till it bleeds to avoid saying something I'll regret.

"Well... come on! I'm bored, don't make me ask again," Remora chides, nudging the door open with the pointed toe of her foot and turning back to look at us.

I hesitate, reluctant to go ahead after what just happened. I glance around for Aalto, surprised to find myself seeking comfort in his presence. Perhaps it's simply because he's the most familiar face in this unknown world? My eyes eventually find him in the crowd of other fae partners. He must read something in them, for he begins pushing past the other fae, ignoring their irritated looks as he makes his way to my side.

I look up at him in dismay, wanting him to answer all my questions but not knowing where to start. Perhaps he senses this, but before I can talk, he shakes his head, and places a firm hand on my shoulder, squeezing it gently. I gulp, taking strange comfort in his contact; I can feel his magic transversing through his hand into me, sending a powerful feeling of warmth through my body. However indirectly, it was thanks to him that I stopped myself from drinking too much of the blue elixir, and I can't help the unwelcome spark of gratitude I feel towards him after witnessing Seraphina's fate.

He gently pushes me forward, urging me to follow the others, and our contact is broken. The last thing I see is his eyes, fixated on me the whole time as we step through the door and into a large empty room. The round curved door shuts with a solid finality, breaking our eye contact and leaving me feeling entirely alone.

CHAPTER EIGHT

I look around the room we've entered, immediately claustrophobic. I know there is no point in trying to open the door we came through, but I'm half-hopeful as Makani gives it a firm tug.

"Locked," he groans, turning back round to face us.

"Guess we've been left on our own," I mutter, wondering what this next challenge will involve.

I stubbornly plant my feet, suppressing the urge to walk around the room, tired already of the many tricks the fae have played on us and unconvinced that this is not another trap. Several of the other contenders are evidently more trusting, or perhaps just not as tentative, for they begin to actively explore the room.

Idiots, I think to myself, as I watch Makani pace around in ever increasing circles.

"What do you think the challenge is?" he says, having seemingly come to no obvious conclusion.

I look around hesitantly. To the right is yet another large table, positioned directly underneath two tunnels that are carved into the wall. From my position, I can't see how deep they are or how far they run, but I'm not keen on how narrow they appear to be. With my simple dress I should be able to crawl through if needed, but some of the others might face more of a struggle.

Makani points at the tunnels, noticing my line of sight. "They're too high to have any purpose relating to us. Even the tallest of us couldn't reach them."

"I guess," I say, rather unhelpfully.

I find his disruption of my train of thought rather irritating. Perhaps he realises this, as he doesn't try to initiate any further conversation and instead goes back to pacing around the room. I return to contemplating the tunnels, proud of myself for staying calm despite our current situation, until a sudden shout snaps my attention back to the centre of the room.

Two of the girls are exclaiming and pointing up at the ceiling. It's beginning to crack as it slides open at the sides to reveal another long pipe. I shiver, and like many of the other contestants, sensibly back away from the centre of the room to stand with my back against the wall.

Mere moments later, a loud whooshing sound, like that of a waterfall tumbling over the side of a cliff, precludes a sudden torrent of water that sprays out of the ceiling tunnel and onto the floor.

Luckily, my dress is knee-length, and I go to pull my shoes off as the water begins to pool around my feet. Others are not dressed quite as practically, if their squeals are anything to go by. I wriggle my now bare toes in the water, flinching at the sharp, ice-cold bite as I wonder how wise my decision was. Still, I would prefer to stand barefoot in cold water than wade through it in waterlogged shoes.

I study the room again, my eyes drawn back to the table; the only thing other than us in the room. Previously bare, the wooden surface now holds a single piece of white parchment. I set out towards it, pushing past one of my squealing comrades who is foolishly complaining about her hair getting wet, but

I'm beaten to table by Kieran.

"What does it say, Kieran?"

He simply holds it open, and a voice, one that unfortunately I recognise as being Remora's, fills the room.

"Welcome, contestants, to your second challenge! Are you ready to discover the consequences of your greed? Better hope you didn't succumb to the temptation *too* much, for it is your will to overcome your basal desires that will determine whether you survive in the challenges to come!" A little tinkling laugh concludes this ominous statement. "Do our fae gems weigh upon you, pathetic humans?" Her voice suddenly changes, sneering with malice as she continues, "Is your life worth your weight in gold?" A giggle echoes around the room, marking the end of her eerie message.

The parchment incinerates in a flicker of flame, and with a shocked yelp Kieran drops it into the water, where it immediately extinguishes and dissolves into a little floating island of ash.

"Well, that was helpful," Kieran mutters, putting his hands into the pockets of his golden waistcoat as he stares at the point where the note has disintegrated.

I cry out, distracted by sudden sharp pinch on my wrist. I look down in horror at my bracelet, where a thin trickle of blood has appeared on my skin from where it's fastened. I try to pull it off but find that it's firmly clasped around my wrist. Another sharp, stabbing pain brings my hands frantically up to my head, where my diadem is perched. I go to pull it off, starting to panic, but find my hands suddenly firmly enclosed in Kieran's.

"I wouldn't if I were you." He holds my wrists steadily, nodding towards another girl, Dionne, who is hysterically trying to yank off a much larger crown from her head. Tears are streaming down her cheeks as little rivulets of blood trickle down to intermingle in messy puddles across her face.

I nod numbly in horror, showing I understand, as Kieran cautiously removes his protective grip around my hands, seemingly reluctant to let me go.

I lift my fingers up to feel my diadem gingerly, noting that it's done the same to me as Dionne's crown has to her. Where the clasps sit against my hairline, sharp thorns of gold have grown, pushing into my skin and effectively pinning the diadem to my skull.

Strangely, it doesn't hurt; it's more uncomfortably heavy than anything, and I'm suddenly very conscious of the extra weight pressing down against my head. Noting Dionne's reaction, I realise how painful it would be if I tried to rip it off.

"Quick!" Kieran pulls me towards him, pressing me back up against the side of the wall, shielding me with his body.

My immediate reaction is to push him away, but then I hear a whooshing sound and recognise it for the warning it is.

"Move! Now!" I scream at Dionne, who is still far too close to the centre of the room.

I watch in horror as another burst of water floods out of the pipe and sweeps Dionne off her feet in one vicious wave. I'd been so fixated on the magic placed on our jewellery that I hadn't registered that the water has kept up to our calves already.

At this rate, I realise with a gulp, *we are all going to drown*.

I begin to frantically scan the room, looking for an exit, but the door we came through has sealed itself back into the wall, with only a faint line indicating that it was ever there.

A voice pierces my panicked thoughts. "This way!" Kieran

yells, pointing to the table, but I'm already striding across the drenched floor to get to Dionne, who is floundering in her dress and struggling to get to her feet.

I reach down and pull the girl up, helping her untangle herself from the mass of fabric that is now damply clinging to her.

"Thanks," Dionne begrudgingly mutters as she puffs out her wet dress, her eyes wide and frantic.

I'm amazed that she's still attempting to make herself look presentable. Does she not see the danger we're all in? I guess we all panic in different ways.

Remora's voice suddenly refills the echoing cavern of the room and collectively, our eyes flicker back to the table, where Kieran is holding open yet another piece of parchment.

"Feeling like the weight of the world is upon you, vile humans? Hope you weren't taken in by the finery of the clothes on offer. Garments only mask the wearer, and it is oh so heavy to wear such an elaborate costume. Will you sink, or swim?"

Once again the parchment disappears in a cloud of fire and smoke.

Kieran is quicker this time to throw it away from him, and the ash flutters on the air before settling on the quickly rising water.

Dionne huffs in frustration, slumping to the floor. I look at her in surprise, before feeling a dragging sensation of my own. For a moment I hope it's transportation magic, ready to zip me out of the room, but with a sickening feeling I realise it is another magic entirely.

My clothes have tightened around my body, and the buttons that were etched along the side have disappeared. I'm well and truly trapped in my outfit, and my dress suddenly feels unusually heavy. I look over at Dionne with increasing dread pooling sickeningly in my stomach. *If this is how weighed down I feel...*

"Help! I can't get out of it! I can't stand! It's too heavy!" Dionne frantically claws at her dress, then when she realises it's getting her nowhere, she grasps onto the next closest thing, which unfortunately happens to be me.

I stumble against her as she tries to use me to pull herself up off the floor. Gritting my teeth, I grimly pull back, trying to help her to her feet, but it's no use. It's as if she suddenly weighs several tonnes.

"Let me go!" I scream in terror as another whooshing sound echoes from the pipe above our heads.

It's no use. The terrified woman has a frantic hold on me, and when another wave crashes down upon us, we are both slung against the side of the wall.

I groan as I slump against the side, quickly stumbling to my feet as I realise the water has helped release me from Dionne's desperate grasp. I can now feel the waves tugging at the edges of my dress, almost reaching my knees. *Once my clothes become waterlogged, I'll barely be able to move.*

Placing one foot in front of another is a struggle as I try to shift my weighed-down body, and I lean against the wall for support as I follow a pathway around the outside of the room back to the table. The other contestants appear to have had the same idea.

Kieran has beaten us all to it and is already standing on the top of the table, trying desperately to reach the empty tunnels above.

"It's no good, they're too high!" he shouts, clearly frustrated as he pulls at the tight collar of his waistcoat.

Finally reaching the table myself, I grit my teeth as I attempt to pull myself up onto the surface. I have little upper body strength and I can feel my muscles protesting as I try to lift myself up. I'm grateful when, with a grunt, Kieran leans down and helps me up onto the tabletop.

Sweat is beginning to dot his forehead, and I imagine I don't look much better. I can feel my hair beginning to plaster against the back of my neck. I daren't turn around as the whooshing wave of water begins to sound again.

"Conserve your energy," Kieran murmurs, slumping down onto the tabletop.

"We can't just give up!" I exclaim as I study the smooth wall beside us for rough patches; anything to help us climb up into the tunnels.

"It's no use – I've already checked," Kieran explains, surprisingly calm considering that the water is already beginning to tease the underside of the table. "I presume they want us to swim with the water as it rises and then slide down out of the tunnels. There is no other way of reaching them that I can think of or see." Kieran lets out a resigned sigh, scooting to the side as Delaney, the girl representing the dark fae, nods to us, joining us on the table.

"Can't we stand on one another's shoulders?" I don't like the idea of waiting until the water fills up the room enough for us to reach the tunnels. I feel claustrophobic enough as it is, and the idea of waiting until the last moment fills me with dread.

What if it isn't the correct solution? We'll be out of time to come up with anything else. And what about the contestants like Dionne who are too heavy now to swim?

"Wouldn't work," Delaney mutters, lifting a corner of her dress and dropping it with a loud sodden thump against the tabletop. "Our clothing is too heavy. We'd run the risk of squishing the person at the bottom and not being able to lift everyone up once we're inside the tunnel. We've just got to hope we'll have the strength to swim. If I were you, I'd sit and conserve my strength for what's to come." Delaney brushes a stray black braid out of her eyes, surprisingly calm despite the situation.

She turns to study me, sharp appraisal in her eyes. I gaze firmly back, determined not to waver under her scrutiny.

"You were right for taking your shoes off earlier," she comments, stretching out her legs and clicking her thick heeled platform shoes together. "Mine are welded on now." She pulls at one, but immediately stops with a grimace, before turning to give me a suspicious glance. "You didn't know about the challenge in advance, did you?" She glares at me, seemingly prepared to start an interrogation despite our predicament.

A loud scream interrupts us, and we both turn at the sound.

Dionne.

CHAPTER NINE

I struggle to my feet once more, moving to the side as other contestants jostle to get onto the tabletop. The water now reaches most contestant's shoulders, and I can see Dionne's panicked eyes as she struggles to keep vertical in the water.

"We have to do something," I exclaim, repeating myself a little louder when the others on the table look away, refusing to meet my eyes. "She's going to drown if we just stand here and watch! You can't tell me you'll all be able to live with yourselves if she doesn't make it out?"

I try to roll up my sleeves in preparation for re-entering the water, grimacing in frustration when I realise that I can't even do that.

"You won't live if you try to help her. It's as simple as that," Kieran says seriously, directing my face with his hands so that I'm looking at his. "The fae want to lose a contestant in each challenge. Better her than you."

I can see the brutal horror of his words reflected in his eyes, but his gaze remains unwavering with cold hard truth. I shake off the calming hand that he moves to my shoulder, not appreciating his touching me despite the comfort he is trying to offer.

"It doesn't matter. I won't be able to live with myself if I don't try," I reply as I push him aside, bracing myself on the edge of the table.

"Stupid girl," Makani mutters somewhere behind me.

I close my eyes, ignoring him as I try to acclimatise myself to the cold water tugging at my ankles. Out of everyone here, Makani should understand the need to help others. Though I guess maybe losing his partner in such a violent, shocking manner has left him too traumatised to spare any emotions for anyone else.

"You won't live if you *do* try!" Kieran insists, exasperated with the situation.

I take a deep breath, choosing to ignore him as well, and keep my eyes firmly closed. Dionne's screams are getting increasingly desperate, stiffening my resolve to give her whatever aid I can. I lean forward to push myself into the water, steeling myself for the drop, when a loud splash and a spray of water erupts across my face, shocking my eyes back open.

"Come on then!" Kieran has jumped into the water and is holding an arm out ready to help me in. "Perhaps we'll live if we work together."

He helps to steady me as I slide into the water next to him, gritting my teeth firmly. Despite bracing myself, the icy coldness of the water still takes my breath away.

"If we can't save her, I'm still getting out of this – with or without you. Understand?" Kieran's grip on my arm is firm and I blink away the tears that have sprung to my eyes from the cold shock of the water.

I nod, accepting Kieran's words, grateful for any help he is willing to give me.

Satisfied that I've accepted his limits, Kieran uses the momentum of his arms to swing himself through the water towards where Dionne is flailing. She isn't far away, but it feels like for every step we take forward, the push of the water's currents and the heaviness of our bodies forces us to take a step further back. With every flounder of my arms, I'm pushing the waves more frantically around myself, effectively propelling myself further back as I struggle to get close.

I'm conscious of the silence in the room, listening out for the whooshing warning with bated breath. If another wave comes and sweeps us all from our feet, it wouldn't just be Dionne in danger, but all three of us. I couldn't bear it if Kieran got into trouble because of my newfound hero complex and apparent lack of self-preservation.

Eventually, I get within an arm's length of Dionne. I gulp as she panics and slings her arm around my neck, effectively closing off my airway and plunging me underwater. It takes Kieran yelling at Dionne and then unapologetically slapping her around the face for her to let go of me and cooperate with us in starting the long, hard slog back to the table.

I can see the rest of the contestants beckoning to us frantically, pointing to the tunnel in the ceiling, but I can barely hear anything. The blind panic that has overtaken me as I desperately try to help Dionne wade through the water seems to have blocked out any sound but the ringing in my ears.

With barely moments to spare, we reach the table, and the others quickly lean down, helping to pull Dionne up onto what has become our life raft. I hold my arms up so that hands can reach down and drag me up too.

Panting heavily, I lie motionless on the table for a few brief moments, trying to regain my breath and control the shaking that has overcome my body. The fear and adrenaline intermingling with the damp icy press of my heavy clothes against my body is starting to make me go into shock.

I focus on Kieran, who I suddenly realise has my hands

held in between his own, rubbing them together vigorously. On seeing that I'm back to my senses, he drops my hands and begins rubbing his own together instead. I quickly follow his lead, rubbing my legs and arms, trying to regain sensation in the areas where pins and needles are starting to take over.

Dionne is rocking, her head resting on her knees, thick, ugly sobs shaking her body. I desperately scan the room again but for what I don't know. It's no different than before; we're in the exact same situation as five minutes ago.

At least we don't have to listen to Dionne's screaming anymore.

I watch the water whooshing again through the tunnel, noticing that it is starting to pool over onto the tabletop's surface. It's coming a lot faster now and it won't be long before we'll be forced to swim. At least the water is clear, so we can see the floor beneath. Looking down, I note that the four table legs are anchored to the floor with metal plates, eliminating the one and only idea I have: to use it as a kind of boat.

Kieran is right; the only way out of here is to swim as the water rises and hope that we don't tire before we reach the tunnels above us. Then we'll have to pray that they actually lead to safety.

I gulp, a horrifying realisation hitting me now that I've calmed down and am thinking more rationally. I look up, meeting Kieran's resolute stare. Clearly, he's reached the same conclusion – perhaps that's why he was so against trying to rescue Dionne in the first place.

I look across at the sobbing young woman. She has no chance of swimming up and out; her clothing and jewellery are simply too heavy. I watch as the other contestants edge away from her; she hasn't moved from her scrunched up position on the tabletop, despite the water pooling around her. No doubt they don't want to risk Dionne pulling them back down when they attempt to swim to the top.

I stand up, as do the other contestants, as the water begins to flood over the tabletop and around our ankles. The water is flowing from the ceiling tunnel at a terrifyingly rate now, rather than the intermittent whooshing of water from earlier.

Surely there has to be something *we can do?*

I look over at Kieran, who slowly shakes his head. We struggled enough dragging her through the water in the first place. There's no way, even with our combined strength, that we'd be able to swim upwards with her in tow.

I want to scream.

How can the fae be so cruel? We weren't even warned that this was to be a test of greed, how were we to know that the simple act of donning clothes and jewels would be the death of us? Surely for a party it's natural to expect everyone to dress up? There must be *some* way out of this predicament where everyone survives?

I feel the water tugging at the hem of my dress and I prepare to start treading water. Loud splashes imply that other contestants have already jumped from the table into the water to begin the swim. I stay where I am, not wanting to tire myself out, waiting until the very last possible second.

I glance over at Dionne, whose eyes are closed, tears streaming down her face, as she blindly scrapes at the walls with nails that are beginning to tear. She no longer looks to the other contestants, seemingly aware of her own fate.

I feel sick. We saved her, only for her torment to be prolonged. There aren't even any weapons here that she can use to make her end swift.

"Help!"

A loud repetitive banging noise catches my attention, and I turn to look at Kieran. In his hand is one of my shoes; he is repeatedly raising the sharp, pointed heel above his head and smashing it down onto the table.

Dionne understands his idea quicker than me, for she immediately begins trying to pull the wood apart with her bare hands, ignoring her bleeding fingertips that stain the surface.

I finally catch on. It's grim, but I can see what they're attempting to do, and it's certainly better than doing nothing. I glance around, searching for the other heel, dragging myself over to it and reaching down into the water to drag it upwards. Tensing my muscles, I bring it over my head, aiming the sharp heel at the wood next to where Kieran has already started smashing. I'm grateful that the table is flimsier than the pointed heel, despite it being well known that fae wood is stronger than what we have in Sora.

"Try and break a piece off, Dionne!" Kieran shouts between grunts as he frantically smashes away. The shoes are heavy because of the magic upon them, and its strenuous work lifting them over and over again. "If you hold onto a piece, you might be able to use it to float!"

Dionne resolutely nods, not saying anything as she concentrates on hacking away at a slowly loosening piece of wood with grim determination.

Oh. Relief floods through me. The wood is to be used as a floatation device. I flush, uncomfortable. I had thought Kieran was creating some kind of weapon that she could mercifully end herself with.

The motion of the water helps loosen the wood further, and with a gasp, Dionne finally grabs firm hold of a long, slender fragment that is starting to break off. Leaning back, she puts all her weight into tearing it completely from the table.

I go to help, but find myself being dragged to the edge of the table by Kieran.

"We need to go now," he mutters under his breath. "We've done all we can for her. If we help too much, the fae may penalise her, perhaps us too. We can't risk her pulling us down too if it doesn't work. We can't all drown trying to save her."

I shake my head. I understand the logic behind Kieran's words, but I can't be so cold hearted. If I leave her, I'll be just as bad as the fae I despise.

I'm about to say so when he tugs on me harder, and we fall into the water together.

The cold steals my breath, all altruistic ideas of saving Dionne leaving my mind as the icy cold tendrils sweep over my head. The urge to take a deep breath is overwhelming, and I struggle to resist opening my mouth and taking in a great gulp of the swirling water. Instinctively, I begin kicking my legs back and forth, panic choking me as much as the lack of air. My dress feels heavy and tight around my legs, constricting my movement and further fuelling my terror.

Suddenly, my head breaks clear of the water's surface, and I take in a deep, gasping breath of air. Frantically, I look around, noting various other contestants equally floundering. But I don't have long before another tidal wave of water pulls me back under like a massive, heavy hand pushing me down, and I'm once more fighting for the surface. I focus on moving my legs back and forth but can already feel that I'm starting to tire.

This time, when I reach the surface, I hurriedly look around for the tunnels in the wall, and am surprised to see that their entrances are now almost level with the water. Indeed, some of the others have already reached them, clinging to the edges with their fingertips, their teeth gritted as the current threatens to pull them back off course.

I take a deep breath and focus on swimming in the direction of the wall, rather than merely trying to break the water's surface. It's easier said than done; I've never been good at opening my eyes underwater, so am effectively blinded every time I go under. It's disorientating to say the least.

Every now and then, I feel something brush up against me – a sharp heel to my side, or a hand grazing my leg – and I flinch, my energy renewed for a second as adrenaline flares and I envision cold hands dragging me down into the cold depths below.

A solid thump echoes in my head as my body connects with the wall and I grimace at the sharp pain down my side. I've gone slightly off course and haven't hit the wall head on as I was aiming for, though I suppose I should be thankful. Giving myself concussion would not end well.

Breaking the surface once more, I see a foot kick out in front of me and disappear.

The tunnels! I've finally reached one of the tunnels!

Without a second thought, I grasp the edge, grateful that it's smooth, and slide on in.

A brief wave of claustrophobia overwhelms me as I squeeze my body inside, but I'm grateful for the air, welcoming it with big, heaving gasps. The water has only just begun to trickle down the tunnel that, thankfully, as we suspected, slopes slightly downwards. It's dark, and I have no idea how long it stretches for, but I'll take anything in this moment rather than drowning in a locked room.

I scramble down the tube like a frightened crab that has

been unearthed from under its rock, realising too late that I'm going headfirst and have no way of controlling my speed. The water propels me forward and I close my eyes, shielding my face with my arms, as the current and gravity takes me faster down the slope. I feel a faint stinging sensation on my bare legs – no doubt I'm grazing them against the tunnel walls – but admittedly that's the least of my worries.

Sensing a soft glow on my face, I open my eyes, struggling to see against the water's misty spray.

A light.

I realise I'm nearing the end of the tunnel.

Gritting my teeth, I remember that I have nothing to slow down my propulsion and I'm likely going to fly out of the other end. My last thoughts are to shield my head with my arms, before I feel my body leave the tunnel at speed.

A sharp snap sounds, like a branch snapped in two, then a punch slams into my whole body, making me see bright white.

Bile rises in my mouth, before all fades to black.

CHAPTER TEN

I wake with a frown, my face contorted into an expression that is becoming all too familiar. The last thing I remember is whizzing down the water tunnel, then overwhelming pain that swallowed me up at the end.

I stretch out my arms in front of me and point my toes. Why don't I feel any pain? I run my hands up and down my body, checking for lumps, bumps, grazes – anything that would indicate the trauma I went through.

There's nothing.

Was it just a bad dream, concocted by the fae? What about Kieran? Dionne?

Looking down at myself, I notice a hazy, throbbing blue glow, travelling up and down my body, like little snakes slithering on an invisible breeze. My stomach lurches as one of them dips beneath my skin, disappearing momentarily before returning to the surface and continuing its explorative journey.

I stroke a tentative finger over one of them and feel something akin to warmth exuding from it. Strangely, almost as if its alive, it shivers, seemingly repulsed by my touch, before darting down my body away from my hand.

"Get off!" I hiss, flapping my arms at the mist snakes and lurching to my feet.

I'm lying on a bed of thick cotton blankets, and I stumble as I clamber roughly out of them. The bed is raised high off the ground, and it takes me a second to orientate myself.

My sudden movement must have scared or irritated them, for the air snakes hover above me in their original position for a moment, before shifting into a writhing mass of sharp bristles, like the fur of an angry cat.

It takes a few moments for my body to catch up, but a short while after losing contact with the air snakes, I suddenly feel as if I've run headfirst into a wall. My muscles ache so much I can barely lift my arms, and red patches of damaged skin appear all over my legs.

"Ugh," I moan, slumping off the bed and onto the floor in a heap.

I watch in horror as my arm starts contorting in an unnatural way, accompanied by horrifying cracking, snapping sounds. My stomach heaves, my mouth filling with bile and my vision blackening as my arm breaks all over again. Sweat dots on my forehead as I desperately struggle to hold out my broken arm towards the air snakes.

"Please," I manage to gasp out between waves of crippling pain. "I'm sorry."

The air snakes ignore me, fluttering further out of my reach; still collectively bristling. I try to crawl towards them.

"Didn't... realise," I murmur, gasping as one slightly smaller than the rest tentatively leaves the group to poke at my arm curiously.

I feel a gentle numbing where it touches, but it isn't enough to take away the pain; just a teasing hint of the magic that these creatures possess.

"Oh? So *now* you want their help? Yet before you knew of their power, you judged them blindly and sent them away? Tsk, I expected better from you, little human – and you wonder why the fae don't want to help your kind?"

My stomach lurches again as a strong pair of arms lift me into the air and pull me to settle against a warm, solid chest. I can just make out Aalto's gentle smile through the haze of the pain. His words may have been harsh, but I can see true concern in his eyes, though he is trying to mask it with mockery.

"Help," I manage to gasp as he places me back onto the bed. I'm barely able to take in his admonishments through the cloud of my pain.

Aalto cocks an eyebrow at me, seeming amused by my predicament, before waving one of his manicured hands towards the air snakes. "Humans are foolish. Please do continue, Vielheim."

The air snakes – Vielheim – bristle again, before whizzing around his hands, emitting a soft humming sound. Seemingly satisfied, they reluctantly resettle above me, resuming their healing journey up and down my battered body.

Immediately, I feel the pain leave, and my bones begin to knit back together. It's not unpleasant exactly, but the cracking sounds make me flinch.

"Thank you. I'm sorry." I try to gently stroke one of the snakes travelling across my arm, but it squeezes its body almost completely flat to avoid my touch. "They hate me now, don't they?" I sigh, saddened by their reaction, but understanding it. "I am truly grateful, though." I look across at Aalto, humming in contentment as I bask in the healing light of their quivering bodies. "I'm surprised something so good is friends with a fae such as yourself."

I smile at the snake on my shoulder as it quivers in a rhythm akin to laughter.

"Ah, only a human would imply that something is

inherently good or bad. Life isn't as black and white as all that." He perches on the edge of the bed, causing the covers to slump slightly under his weight.

I shift my body, carefully realigning myself. If Aalto notices my attempts to move away from him, he politely doesn't say anything.

"Although it is funny you say that. Vielheim and I are one in the same, after all."

He begins playing with one of the air snakes, watching as it slithers in-between his fingers. Bringing his hands up to his lips, he blows on the air snake softly, and to my surprise, it glows a soft periwinkle blue before it doubles in size. He places it gently onto my broken arm and I can't withhold a sigh of pleasure as a warm, tingling sensation permeates my skin.

"What do you mean?" I breathe, eager to finally learn more about the fae. Better to know your enemies then go into a fight blind, after all.

Aalto lifts another air snake from my leg; this one is starting to fade, and it waggles the end of its body sadly as it tries to attract his attention. He repeats the same gentle blowing motion, causing it to swell and regain its vibrant, electric blue hue. Aalto grins as it mimics a quick kiss to his cheek before joining the others.

"They are the essence of my magic. Vielheim just means essence. Water fae are generally good at healing, but not as good as the Light fae. So, I must keep regenerating them with my own breath," he tries to explain.

A brief frown skitters across his face, and I have a sudden strange urge to run a finger over his forehead and brush it away.

It's just so at odds with his usual mischievous grin.

I suppress the thought firmly; what am I even thinking? It's probably a side effect of being overwhelmed with his healing magic. With his essence. *Gross.* I try not to think about it too much as I sink into the soft bedcovers and allow the creatures to heal my weary body.

I only wish they could heal my tired heart, too.

CHAPTER ELEVEN

We sit in silence for a while, me watching the Vielheim and Aalto occasionally scooping one up to regenerate it with his breath, his brow furrowed. If the action is draining him, he shows no signs of tiring.

"Why are you frowning?" I can't resist asking, finally breaking the silence.

I say it so quietly, and he pauses so long before answering, that I assume he hasn't heard me, until he takes a deep shuddering breath and begins speaking once more.

"I didn't realise how little you knew of our magic," he says, fiddling with the bedcovers in a manner at odds to his usual confidence.

I hold my breath, not wanting to interrupt him if he is about to share important information.

"The Vielheim, for instance. Did you know Nature has control over all of them?" At the shake of my head, he continues. "She chooses which fae court is blessed with which form of magic. Many centuries ago, we had boundless power; could use whatever type of magic we pleased. Until Nature barred our access to the human world, restricting the use of the portals. It's rare to find fae who have natural ability with more than one Vielheim. They have to be truly old to have been born before the time of Nature's wrath." He refuses to meet my eyes, focusing intently on the Vielheim in his hand.

"Why did Nature take away your full power?" I ask curiously, surprised to discover that the fae have suffered their own rough dealings with Nature.

Aalto rubs a tired hand down his face, as if made weary by our conversation. "There was a great battle, a fae rebellion that destroyed our relationship with Nature. Though not all of us fought against her, she continues to punish us for the rebels' choices."

That's what Kieran was afraid would happen, when we helped Dionne. I sit quietly for a while, wondering what happened to the other contestants; trying to process everything he's just shared. When I look up at him, I find him watching me, a frustrated expression on his face.

"That doesn't explain why you're frowning at me," I say tartly. He can't blame *me* for Nature punishing the fae, surely? I've suffered just as much, if not more.

"You honestly don't remember anything?" His gaze is so piercing that I can't help but look away, unsure what he is hoping to hear.

"What is there to remember?" I ask. "I barely know anything about the fae."

"Never mind..." he sighs, leaving me feeling even more confused. "I just thought... maybe..."

As his stutters dwindle into silence, I almost prompt him to continue, but before I can do so, he swiftly relapses into recounting fae history, like he's trying to deflect.

"You ought to know that each court has their own pool of secular magic, but now, only the court whose human tribute wins the Sin Trials gets to replenish it fully. They also have access to *all* the magical elements, during the decade between the trials." He fiddles with one of the Vielheim between his fingers, gently stroking it, increasing the intensity of its blue colouring.

"So only one court can replenish their magic? Is that why fae take part in the trials too? Because winning is the only way you can open the portals from the fae lands to Sora and access your missing powers?"

"Eleria," Aalto replies, rolling his eyes when I look up at him perplexed. "The land of the fae is called Eleria."

His vibrant blue eyes are studying mine intently as he waits for me to say something, and I find myself, without thinking, lifting a hand to his face and brushing away the strand of hair that has flopped into his eyes.

"You still haven't told me why you're frowning," I say, refusing to let it go, my hand lingering on his face. I feel like I'm on the verge of understanding something important, but I can't work out what.

He grasps my hand tightly in his own, stopping my gentle exploration of his face but not breaking our contact. Rather, he almost leans into my hand so that I'm cupping his cheek; I can feel the sigh of his warm breath on my skin, causing goosebumps to travel deliciously across my arm.

"You really don't remember, do you?" he says once again.

My breath hitches in my throat; I hadn't realised how close we'd become. I can feel his soft breath caress my lips and the perfumed honey of his skin is warm against my own, reminding me of languorous summer days spent traipsing along the beach, hunting for shells.

I shake my head softly. I don't know what he means; I don't know what he wants me to remember.

My eyes are wide, fixated on his lips as he speaks, and I only vaguely register the flicker of pain that sweeps across his eyes before he pulls away, standing abruptly.

He silently surveys me some distance away, his hands placed in his trouser pockets, effectively cutting me off with his body language. I blink, confused by the sudden shift in his demeanour. It's almost like a curtain has swept down, cutting off our brief emotional connection, and I come abruptly back to my senses.

I shiver, repulsed that I allowed myself to get so close to him. *What's happening to me?* For a second there, it seemed almost like we were about to— *no*. I shake the thoughts from my head, causing some of the Vielheim to flutter around my neck in a panic before resettling. I won't let anything happen between me and a fae. They are tricksy, immoral, and if the challenges so far are anything to judge them by, downright evil.

The challenge.

I feel like I've been zapped with a cattle prod, and I sit bolt upright in bed. Why didn't I react like this earlier? What fae spell has the man put me under? Images of Dionne; of Kieran; of struggling to swim against the current flash across my mind in terrifying snapshots.

"The trial— what happened? Where are the others?"

"What of it?" Aalto asks, shrugging nonchalantly. He walks over to the other side of the room and rather sullenly leans his back against the wall, his legs braced apart and his arms folded defensively against his chest.

"What do you mean 'what of it'?" I shout. "I almost died! We all almost did! And for what?" I stab a finger in his direction. "Because the fae are desperate to have more power and refuse to be content with just one form of magic."

I fist my hair in my hands, my body shaking from the array of emotions coursing through my body. Anger at having been forced to do this, fear for what is to come, disgust at myself for getting close to a fae and failing to recall why I'm even here in the first place. I just want to sleep and forget it all.

"Did Dionne make it?" I ask weakly, my body exhausted from the whirlwind I'm putting it through.

Upon hearing no answer, I look up at Aalto, who merely lifts an eyebrow in question and shrugs again.

"Did. Dionne. Make. It?" I enunciate harshly, feeling tears prickle behind my eyes. I grit my teeth; I will not cry in front of a fae – I will not give him the satisfaction of seeing me break down. "Don't you dare tell me you don't know who I'm talking about! I bet the fae were all sat somewhere safe watching everything that went on. You disgust me." I angrily wipe at my eyes with my sleeves, trying to stem the flow.

Soft silk fabric brushes away my tears, and I feel disorientated all over again. Looking down, I realise I'm dressed in a simple nightgown. No adornments; just azure silk and comfort. I wriggle my toes and am relieved to discover that it reaches all the way to my ankles, before realising that it doesn't matter how modest it is... someone must have stripped me of my clothes to put me in it in the first place.

I break.

"You care nothing for us," I sob messily, great wracking heaves that tear from my chest. "You have no respect for us; give us no dignity. You treat us as playthings and expect us to just go along with it. I can't do this!" I breathe heavily, scrunching the bedclothes in my hands, staring blankly at the pattern across the fabric. "I can't do this anymore."

"Are you quite done?" Aalto's firm voice snaps me out of my wallowing.

"Done?" I can barely breathe through the choking sobs. I

look up at him, shocked. *How dare he!*

He holds up a hand before I can continue berating him. "You say we fae 'care nothing' for you; treat you like 'playthings', but what have humans ever done to deserve our care and attention? You destroy all that is put before you – why do you think Nature is in the state she is, if not for you?" His eyes glint angrily. "Why do you think we keep links with the human world when we'd rather just cut off all ties completely? Because. We. Care. To. Tidy. Up. *Your*. Mess." His voice is calm, but his clenched hands and piercing eyes betray the simmering anger barely restrained beneath the surface.

I suddenly remember who he is; *what* he is. The screams of the Makani's partner echo in my mind.

"We have magic because we can be entrusted to maintain the balance Nature requires. You ask why the fae are involved in the trials? Because we must prove to Nature that there is still *some* good in you; that you are *worth* saving. She may have a soft spot for your species, but that doesn't mean she wouldn't give you up in an instant, like you have given up on *her*." He pushes away from the wall and begins pacing around the room, enraged. "She demands human tributes because it is you *humans* who have caused her harm."

He gestures wildly as he walks, spitting out his words passionately. I can only watch, wide-eyed; terrified of what he will do to me once he has finished his tirade.

"Can you not see what you have done? You pollute her waters, suffocate her earth, and you expect her to keep giving? Humans always expect something from nothing, and when they are asked to atone for their sins, they act wounded. Like it's someone else's fault. No, Rosalind, it is you humans who disgust *me*!" A vein throbs against Aalto's neck as he paces over to me, reaching me in two long, furious strides.

I flinch and press myself up against the headboard, gulping. Has he been supressing his rage all this time, or have I just hit a nerve?

"Nature blesses us with magic because we take care of her, and now, it is *our* benevolence that keeps her tied to your world, that stops her from raging war against humanity. Without the trials; without our dedication to proving that humans are worthy of her continued blessing, your world would descend into chaos. You are *nothing* if not for us." Aalto ignores my cowered state and brushes a cold finger down my cheek.

I shiver, terrified of the man bristling with power before me.

"Yes. Dionne *died*. Greed overcame her and Nature deemed her unworthy of survival. Her fae partner died with her. The moment Dionne lost, she ceased to be also." He cups my cheek gently and runs a rough finger across my lips.

I find them parting, mesmerised by his passionate words, my body acting on instinct rather than conscious thought.

"Do you really think we don't care? Death is the ultimate price we pay for helping you humans keep your world. Sometimes, I wonder if you even deserve it." He halts, his final words coming out almost as a whisper, the fight seeming to finally drain from his body.

I back away from his touch. "If fae are so blameless in all this, why did Nature take away your magic?" I whisper, afraid but determined to at least try and understand. "You just admitted that Nature is punishing you too, for rebelling against her. You say humans are the reason for Nature's wrath, but we are not to blame for your magic being taken from you."

He tuts and looks away, his eyes clouding as some memory

or other drifts through his mind. "That rebellion was started over *your* species," he growls, trying to rein in his anger. "There are some fae who feel humans aren't worth saving."

I can tell from the disgust in his eyes that he is not one of those fae. At least I know he doesn't want *all* humans dead.

"When humans began to destroy Sora, some fae decided that they should take your land, claiming it as their own. Why look after you when you were so intent on destroying your world?" He hesitates, closing his eyes as he remembers. "Those fae harmed many humans: those who revolted against the idea of being ruled and those unfortunate enough to be caught in the crossfire. It almost descended into war between us before Nature stepped in." He shakes his head. "We aren't all like that, but we all suffered the same punishment. Now we must prove that we can work alongside you, if we want to keep our magic. Some fae resent this; they think humans should suffer. Rest assured, they aren't the ones who volunteer as partners in these trials."

"Not all humans are like that either. Not all of us destroy. My family are farmers," I whisper, hugging my body to myself, feeling suddenly incredibly homesick. I choke back a sob and look up at him. "Why did you volunteer?"

He either doesn't hear me or chooses not to answer. I try to speak again; ask a different question, but when I open my mouth, a squeak is all that comes out.

I clear my throat and try again. "What was her name?" I whisper.

"Who?" Aalto queries, confused.

"Dionne's fae partner. What... what was her name?" I stutter, fixing my gaze firmly on Aalto, daring him to belittle me for asking.

Aalto blinks in surprise. "Her name was Dhara, from the Spring Court. She was kind; gentle; helped seedlings to grow with just the tiniest hint of encouragement. She volunteered as a representative of Earth magic." He shudders. "Now she's gone." His eyes are sad as he looks away.

"I'm sorry," I say, knowing those two words will never be enough, but not knowing what else I can offer. I take a deep breath. *I have to try.* "I'm sorry the world has lost Dhara. I'm sorry the world is in such a state. Sora *and* Eleria. But we aren't all like that. *I'm* not like that. We don't get to volunteer for this, and yet..." I look at him, fire in my eyes. "If this is what it takes to stop even more people from dying, to stop all-out war, then it's a sacrifice I'm willing to make." I pause, taking a shuddering breath at the realisation that I've just accepted by own fate. I meet Aalto's gaze again. "I respect that you chose to fight alongside us. You and the other fae volunteers. And I'm sorry, that you have to."

Aalto sighs softly, a gentle, almost awed expression on his face. "When you speak like that... you remind me of someone," he murmurs, so quietly that I wonder if I've imagined it.

Without warning, Aalto blows a breath of air towards me, and I feel the Vielheim collectively shudder before sinking into my body. Tentatively, I move my limbs, testing to see what still hurts.

"I'm afraid you've been recovering for quite a while. It's day three already; you've only just recuperated enough for me to risk bringing you back round," Aalto informs me grimly, abruptly changing the conversation yet again. "The next challenge will start soon. I advise you to stay here and rest until then."

I simply nod. I imagine he feels just as drained as I do, and I can't blame him for wanting to stop talking.

"Would it be okay if... are you allowed to leave me alone for a while?" I ask quietly. "I'd... like some time to mourn Dionne." I close my eyes, completely exhausted. "And Dhara," I add in a whisper.

When I reopen my eyes a mere moment later, surprised at his silence, I find the room empty and cold.

He has already gone.

CHAPTER TWELVE

It's not long before I've learnt every inch of the room.

There's no door that I can see, meaning I'm trapped, *again*, but this time I feel strangely comforted by the lack of entrance or exit. It's like Aalto has given me my own space to heal and recuperate, though the thoughts that swirl around my mind in a continual dizzying storm make it hard to relax.

Whilst I'm pleased, and surprised, that he's heeded my wishes in leaving me alone, another part of me yearns for his company. At least he was another voice to talk to, and as much as I don't want to admit it, I'm starting to warm up to him. Not all fae can be judged the same, that's for sure.

Occasionally, Vielheim of different colours zap into the room. I look forward to the green ones, bearing bowls of succulent round oranges, chunks of sweet pineapple on little skewers, and thick doorstop chunks of bread slathered in thick, rich honey. The red-coloured whisps bear gifts of hard-boiled eggs and slabs of ham, but they often appear after the green Vielheim, by which time I'm often full already. They gently tap me until I take some of their offerings and I smile, thanking them as I try and eat their offerings too. I can feel my strength slowly begin to return; Aalto's healing magic has done its job. I can walk around the room now unaided, free of pain.

Which is all I've been doing.

I've been pacing for at least the last hour or so. There are no human measures of time – no clocks on the bare walls – but I notice that, despite being windowless, the light levels in the room change throughout the day, gradually darkening as time goes by, until the walls are pulsing a deep, sea blue. At first, this terrifies me, giving me flashbacks to drowning, but over time I relax and eventually learn to drift into a deep sleep whenever the light starts to dim.

It isn't long until I get bored and begin to crave company again; I'd even welcome another difficult conversation with Aalto at this point. My body now fully healed, I'm tired of looking at the same unadorned walls constantly.

I try asking one of the Vielheim for an update, but it quickly gets flustered, bristling angrily when I try and contain it in my hands. I watch frustrated as it sinks into the walls of the room, wishing I had the power to walk through them too.

I can feel my anger beginning to build at being contained; even another trial would be a welcome reprieve at this point. I'm quick to chastise myself at this thought, even if it is somewhat true. I'm at the point where I'm considering smashing some of the furniture just for a change of scenery, when a silver line begins to sketch the shape of a door on the wall. I run over to it eagerly, barely waiting for it to finish its construction before I grab hold of the doorknob and turn it, my urge to be free overriding any caution.

I startle when I notice Aalto leaning expectantly against the opposite wall, his arms crossed and an expectant grin on his face. I try to backtrack into the room, but my back is met with the once-more solid wall.

"Oof." It knocks the breath out of me, which only causes Aalto's grin to widen.

"Is a locked room really preferable to spending time with me?"

Aalto holds out a hand, his smile faltering slightly when I don't immediately reach out to grab it. It seems that, despite our heart-to-heart talk, I can't shake my wariness of him.

He hesitates, before retracting his hand, and gesturing down the hallway. "I know you may not be ready yet, and I'm sorry to rush you, but I've stalled the next challenge as long as I was able to."

He stares off into the distance, ruffling his hand through his hair as he thinks, an action I realise I've seen him do several times now. I shudder. *Hells, I'm even starting to recognise his mannerisms.*

I take a moment to study him; he looks the most dishevelled I've seen him so far. His blue shirt's vibrancy almost hides the fact that it's completely creased, but his trousers are what gives away his distress: simple and black, they are marred with smears of dirt and torn thread, making me wonder what he has been up to in my absence. He turns to look at me expectantly, and I realise I've been silent for too long.

"I guess I don't have a choice," I say bitterly, slightly regretting my tone when his eyes reflect my pain. "But I appreciate you giving me the time to rest."

I need to remember that I'm not the only one affected by these trials.

He nods, looking down as if he's about to grab my hand again, before changing his mind and setting off on a brisk walk down the corridor. I hurry to follow, his long strides a challenge to keep up with, even for me.

As we walk, we pass various closed doors, the corridor eerily silent. The pulsating blue light I found comforting in my room seems almost threatening as it lights up the walls with its throbbing glow.

Aalto eventually stops in front of one of the doors. It looks the same as all the others we passed. "Your fellow humans are in here."

I go to open it, but he holds out an arm to stop me, and I look up at him curiously. He seems to be struggling to speak. I'm reminded of when he tried to share some insight into the trials, but the magic restrained him.

"Your heart hasn't always been angry," he says eventually, with a frustrated grimace. "If you remember anything, remember that."

Before I can reply, he opens the door and pushes me gently into the room. I turn to look at him, to ask him to explain, but I'm met with a blank wall again. I trace a finger across the smooth surface contemplatively.

"Good to see you're still alive."

The feminine voice snaps me to attention, making me jump as I realise that Aalto was right; I'm not alone in this room.

I turn to meet the remaining tributes: Delaney, Kieran, and Makani, pleasantly surprised to find that their familiar faces make me smile instinctively.

It had been Delaney who spoke, and she offers a little wave of her fingers. Kieran grins at me and raises a glass he is holding in my direction. Makani is the only one who doesn't react to my entrance; he remains still, his head held in his arms, elbows against the table they are sitting around.

"Oh, don't mind him." Delaney lowers her voice, though Makani doesn't move when she gestures towards him.

She pats the seat next to her and whispers the name *Celestia* to me as I sit down. My hands clench involuntarily as my memory is jolted violently back to our first day on that stage, when Makani brutally lost his partner to the rose-skinned fae.

"Is he okay?" I whisper, before realising what a stupid question that is. Of course he isn't okay.

Delaney doesn't answer, perhaps understanding that there isn't an appropriate response. She hands me a drink instead, which I would have assumed was water if not for the pink bubbles that occasionally appear on the surface.

"Oh, don't worry, it's perfectly safe," Delaney says, taking a sip of her own as if in demonstration. "I always see Amaya drinking this, and she's as fussy as they come."

I take a small sip of my own, hiccupping in surprise when I feel a pink bubble pop on my tongue, releasing a sweet nectar.

Kieran laughs at me, leaning across the table opposite. "I did the same thing the first time I tried it," he says, reaching forward to clink his glass against my own.

I can't help but frown at his celebratory action.

"I know it's not easy to relax," he adds, noticing, "but my mother always told me to face fear with a smile. Perhaps then it might not bite back."

He let out a self-deprecating laugh, and I find myself reaching forward to give his hand a comforting squeeze.

"You think we're here for the next trial then?" I ask hesitantly, trying not to sneeze as I take another sip of the drink.

Delaney nods, twirling her own glass between her hands. She taps her coal-black nails against it as she talks. "We're only ever gathered together when there is a challenge looming." She grimaces. "Like sheep being herded to slaughter." Standing abruptly, she begins to pace the room. "I'm sick of it!"

Her sudden movement and bitter words snap Makani out

of his trance.

"If I could kill every last one of them, I would," he snaps, his voice full of pain and anger.

Glaring at the blank wall where the door had been, he hurls his empty untouched glass against it, watching silently as it shatters into brittle shards. I flinch, swallowing back my retort that not all fae are bad; that Aalto said some of them had even taken the humans' side during their wars. My stomach churns: have I really been taken in by the fae so easily, after one conversation? I don't even know if Aalto was telling the truth, and if he was, that still doesn't change anything. He may think he has good intentions, but after what happened to Dionne... to Celestia...

I glance at Kieran and Delaney; although they're not saying anything, they seem to be silently agreeing with Makani.

Letting my eyes drift around the room, I try and find the words to break the silence, until I notice coloured lines appearing across the walls. I watch, fascinated, as doors begin to appear and solidify: one blue, one yellow, one white, and one black.

"Look." I gesture towards them, approaching the closest one: the yellow.

"Wait!"

Kieran's strong voice snaps me out of my dream-like state, and I turn to see him unfurl a piece of parchment.

"Where did that come from?" I ask, stepping away from the door and back towards the group.

Kieran merely shrugs as Remora's voice echoes around the room.

"No one but you can control your actions, but are you ruled by your mind or your heart? Beyond these doors, we shall find out."

We all look to the doors, with more trepidation than before.

An engraving appears on each door as she speaks: a bowl that slowly begins to fill with liquid, moving somehow despite being seemingly carved into the wood.

"As you face your inner demons alone, so must you face this challenge alone. Enter the doorway that matches your fae partner's essence and begin your trial."

The parchment disappears, without the usual puff of smoke or spark of flame, and Kieran clenches his fists, staring at the doors resolutely.

"I want to see all of your faces when I come back out that door," he says firmly, meeting each of our gazes, before squaring his shoulders and choosing the yellow door.

The water in the bowl upon his door is still, with strands of green light swirling throughout. We all try and lean around to see past him as he opens the door, to get a glimpse of what's to come, but we are temporarily blinded by a piercing light.

I startle when I feel two arms wrap around me, turning and pulling me into a deep hug. I'm even more surprised when it causes a sob to escape my lips.

"Enough of that." Delaney raises my face to look at hers, offering me a soft smile that does nothing to hide the fear in her eyes. "He's right, we *will* see each other soon. I want to get to know you better." She winks, offering a moment of joviality, before taking a deep breath and opening her door: the black one.

Shadows twist out of the opening pulling her inside in a strange, twisted embrace. I watch the bowl on her closed door fill with water that slowly freezes, before cracking straight down the middle. I shiver, and look across at Makani, who is staring angrily at his door. He offers me no words, picking up one of the shards of glass from the floor as he passes and slamming open his white door, before disappearing without a backwards glance.

His bowl bubbles with an angry, swirling substance.

I look back at the other shards of glass, considering whether I should take one, but I'm too worried about breaking a rule that might have me instantly disqualified.

A wintery chill sweeps through the room, forming ice on the surface of our drinks left on the table, and my mind flickers back to Aalto's last words.

"My heart hasn't always been angry," I muse, wondering what he meant, as I watch my bowl fill with a murky blue liquid.

Realising I can't afford to hesitate any longer, I reluctantly open the blue door, stepping through into the unknown.

CHAPTER THIRTEEN

I'm no longer surprised to end up somewhere that defies all rational possibilities.

Taking in the gently rolling hills, the scattering of trees and the luscious green fields bare of livestock, I find myself drawn to a narrow trickling river. I was always taught to follow the current, so I begin to walk alongside the path of the water, trying to take a moment to enjoy the peaceful tranquillity; the rhythmic bubbling of the river as it brushes the pebbles; the melodic tune of the birds flitting between the trees and shrubs that line the shore.

I decide to take my shoes off, having always enjoyed the squelch of wet mud underfoot; hoping the familiar sensation will help to ground me when the trial begins. My eyes scan the shoreline as I walk, looking for any indication of what I need to do. I find myself humming the same song my father does when he works; it has no words, but it brings a homely comfort to me as I try to avoid the dark thoughts that flicker in my head.

As my eyes focus on the horizon, I make out a figure wading in the shallows at the bend of the river. The possibility that it might be another contestant, despite having been told we were to complete this challenge alone, brings energy to my feet that I didn't realise I still had.

"Hey! Wait!" I yell as they make to move further into the depths.

I feel my bare feet slip and slide on the pebbles; a sharp scratch on the soft point of my sole as I scrape it against a rock in my hurry to catch up to the figure.

Eventually, I stumble to the bend, panting, my hands resting on my knees as I catch my breath. The figure straightens up in the water and turns to look at me, her dark brown eyes, almost dark enough to appear black, meeting mine with an eerily blank stare.

I blush and look away.

The figure is not a contestant, but a tall slender woman with long green tendrils of hair that fall about her skin in waves. She's completely naked, standing in the waist-deep water, and her nails are stubbed and caked with dirt, It is these that she's scrubbing in the river.

"I-I'm sorry I interrupted your bathing," I stutter, continuing to avert my eyes, feeling intimated by the woman's cold expression.

She doesn't say anything in response, and eventually I hazard a look back up. The woman has gone back to scrubbing at her nails, ignoring me completely.

The water is faster here, and I'm surprised that she isn't struggling more to stay upright; I can see it pulling at her hair as it swirls past her.

"Are... are you alright?" I eventually ask, attempting to instigate a conversation, still wondering what I'm meant to be doing here.

The woman tips her head forward and dunks her hair into the water, smoothing it out with her fingers, now clean from the grime.

"Why don't you join me, child? The water is pleasant enough."

The woman's voice surprises me, and I shiver, though I can't explain the sudden feeling of dread that travels down my spine like a droplet of icy water. It's a throaty, low voice that rises and falls much like the movements of the water around her.

"Um." I hesitate, taking a step back when the woman's eyes lock onto mine. "I think I'll stay here. I've already been in the water, and my shoes are still drying off." I hold them up, wriggling a bare foot in explanation.

The woman wrinkles her nose, whether in disgust or some other feeling, I'm not sure. For a few seconds the only sound is the gentle trickling of the water, and it takes a moment for me to realise that all the birds and wildlife that had been happily chirping, whistling, and rustling in the background have grown silent.

The woman smiles, but it doesn't quite reach her eyes. "My queen requests your presence."

I find myself taking another cautious step back. "Thank you, but I'm afraid I can't stay. I have to head this way... I'm meant to be completing a trial." I turn to gesture towards the pathway I've just come down.

In the seconds that my back is turned, several things all happen at once.

The woman, who is not a woman at all, lunges out of the water, rearing back onto her hindquarters, which had been previously covered by the water. I realise her abdomen tapers down into a set of four hooved legs, which canter towards me at spine-chilling speed, leaving me little time to prepare as her preternaturally long arms reach for me, her nails having elongated into sharp claws. I scarcely have a moment to breathe before she is pulling me towards her body in a sickening, crushing embrace.

Her once beautiful face is contorted into a menacing imitation of a grin, her teeth now sharp, needle-like points in her mouth, cutting into the corners of her lips and causing a strange black substance to leak down her face.

"It wasn't a request," the monster hisses into my hair as she tightens her grip on me and begins dragging me back to the water's edge.

I try to dig my heels into the ground, but the mud is wet and slippery and I'm barefoot. Even if I had my shoes on, I don't think I would have stood a chance against a creature that has the lower body strength of a horse.

"Let me go!" I scream, pushing desperately against the arms that shackle me, but she only cackles, her breath rolling over me in waves of salty seaweed tang and rotten fish, making me retch.

My eyes begin to tear up from the acidity, and I choke on a panicked sob as I feel the soft loamy mud give way to the gentle lap of waves around my feet.

I'm running out of time; once we reach the middle of the river, I'll have little hope of ever escaping.

"Don't fear, child, it will all be over soon," the monster's hot breath heaves into my ear.

I feel myself lose grip on the ground as I'm pulled backwards into the depths of the river. The waves lap at my waist, whipping my clothes tight around my body, further escalating the suffocating feelings of entrapment and confinement that overwhelm my senses.

"Please let me go!" I whimper, straining to take in a deep breath before the water finally reaches my neck. It takes just one wave for it to sweep completely over the both of us.

At first, I strain to keep my eyes open, but the water is gritty and the need to blink soon becomes overwhelming. I try to kick, but my clothes have wrapped so tightly around me that I can't properly gain momentum. I feel my chest burning as my body desperately tries to persuade me to open my mouth and breathe. The monster places a hand over my lips, sending me into a further wave of panic.

I can't believe I escaped drowning in the test of greed, only to drown in a different challenge.

"Relax, stupid human," the monster hisses, trying to simultaneously hold her clammy hand over my mouth and propel us further down into the dark depths of the water.

No! I think frantically. *I'm not going to die without a fight!*

I rekindle my efforts to try and release myself from the monster's grasp, pulling at her arms that hold me in a lock. I close my eyes, not wanting my last memories to be dark swirling water and the manic grin on the creatures' face.

I feel the current swirl forcefully around us, and I briefly flicker open my eyes.

Instantly I regret doing so.

In front of me are several of the river creatures. Two appear male, their pearlescent skin glimmering: one rich ruby red, the other cerulean blue. Their shoulder length hair wafts around their faces in the current, a shade lighter than their skin, and both have piercing green eyes that betray their bemusement at my predicament.

Darting in and out of the males, swimming in rapid circles, is a smaller, female monster. She looks younger than the other three, if her cherub-like cheeks and smaller proportions are anything to go by. Like the creature holding me, she has green skin, though in a softer tone, but her teal hair has been shorn short, leaving only a few tendrils wafting in the water.

I flinch as she suddenly darts up close, flashing a grin mere inches from my face. The two sharp fangs jutting down from the centre of her mouth have my heart rate accelerating, yet it's clear that her smile is one of joy, not menace.

Perhaps these creatures find amusement in playing with their food before killing it.

I panic.

I can't die. Not here.

Then I realise something.

The atmosphere feels... strangely lighter.

As I focus on the creatures swimming around me, I stop fighting enough for my body to take in what's happening. I realise the pressure in my chest has eased, and I blink rapidly. *How am I breathing?* Confused, but no longer in a state of fight or flight, I reach for my mouth, realising it remains covered by the creature's hand.

The monster grins.

"Finally, she gets it!" a voice exclaims. "I can't remove my hand; it's the only thing trapping air around your mouth. So stop trying to fight me, unless you actually *do* want to die."

The monster tuts, and although I'm still terrified, I'm able to focus enough to realise that the monster is the one talking to me. Not out loud, but in my mind. Which makes sense, considering that we are still underwater.

"I'm Esmeralda. Although I'd prefer it if you just called me Esme. We're almost there, so you can go back to doing your normal human breathing again soon. Just hold on a little longer," Esme instructs as we swim in and out of some tall, jutting rocks that protrude from the riverbed.

I'm slowly getting used to the sensation of water streaming

past my face and I try to keep my eyes somewhat open so I can take in my surroundings as I'm pulled along, if only to take my mind off what the creatures plan on doing to me once we arrive at wherever we're heading.

They may be trying to keep me alive, but I haven't forgotten that they dragged me down here without my consent in the first place.

Besides... what can a monster queen possibly want with me?

CHAPTER FOURTEEN

As we journey along the riverbed, the natural rock formations are replaced by giant, jagged structures covered in strange carvings. It's difficult to pick out the details at the speed we're travelling, but I'm convinced I see shapes that look like the monsters escorting me, alongside human-like figures. The carvings glow a soft, golden hue, almost as if they've been painted over with sunlight.

As we near the end of a tunnel of rock, lit by engravings of tiny starfish that glow a soft, soothing green, we are met with curtains of seaweed, draping down and hiding whatever lies beyond.

"We're here, little human!" Esme trills as we push past the last curtain of seaweed and swim upwards.

Esme breaks the water's surface with a shake of her long green hair, and as she pulls me with her, she finally releases her hand's grasp around my mouth.

Despite realising that I've been safely breathing underwater for the last however long, I can't hold back the instinctual gasp as I gulp in lungfuls of air. Dragging myself onto dry land and slumping to the floor, I refocus my breathing, my palms flat on the ground. The sensation of the cold damp stone through my skin gives me something to focus on.

Once my breaths are coming out in steady exhales, I go to wring out my sodden clothes, only to find they are completely dry. I reach for my hair, finding my curls not only dry but undamaged by their stint in the grit-filled river. I fling a confused glance over my shoulder, looking back at the water.

Esme laughs, a deep throaty chuckle that sounds less ominous now that I'm not being dragged against my will, but it still makes me jump all the same.

"You humans are all the same." She stretches out her two back legs before beginning to braid her green hair into one long plait over her shoulder. "You never trust what is right in front of your eyes. Haven't you seen enough magic by now to feel that it's real? Why is everything always such a surprise to you?"

Esme kneels on her front two hooves, bringing her eye level with me. She looks like she's settling in for an amicable conversation between two friends, but I feel far from friendly towards her.

"You almost drowned me! What in the hells were you thinking?" I know I'm at her mercy, but I'm still pissed off. She could have explained what she was about to do rather than just lunging at me! I don't understand why the fae seem to expect us to go along with everything in their crazy world.

Esme raises a thin green eyebrow and goes back to plaiting her hair, a faint smirk teasing at the corners of her lips. "You would be wise to be more careful with your tone of voice, considering our current company." She gestures with a twitch of her shoulder and my eyes swiftly follow her movement.

I gulp, my mouth suddenly dry, as I finally take in my surroundings.

We are in a large, cavernous room; the walls shine with a pearlescent sheen, and inlaid into the stone are little green gemstones, arranged in the shape of seaweed fronds. Dipping in and out of the fronds peek miniature topaz fish, with singular ruby gems as eyes. White marble statues stand at each corner, shaped in elegant forms – a dolphin suspended in a graceful dive, accompanied by some of the river-creatures; a towering, craggy rock formation studded with golden starfish; a giant bronze octopus with cascades of tentacles. The final statue is simple by comparison: a pedestal holding a giant spherical orb that appears to change colour when looked at from different angles. I squint when I notice my own eyes looking back at me through its milky white surface, flinching in surprise when my reflection gives me a jaunty wink.

Looking away, I ease myself upright, walking tentatively forwards and curling my bare toes in the seaweed mats that decorate the cold marble floor. Before me sits a throne of tarnished copper – surprising considering that the rest of the décor favours gold or silver – the umber metal emphasising the importance of the occupant currently sat upon it.

Her lips curl up in a slight smirk as our eyes finally meet, her chin resting nonchalantly against one delicately bejewelled hand; legs thrown over the other arm of her throne. The deep emerald skirt of her dress clings tightly to her toned body, ending rather abruptly at the top of her thighs.

I blink, begrudgingly respecting her for being comfortable enough to sit in a dress that way, when one thoughtless movement might reveal more than intended.

The bodice of her dress is the complete opposite, layers upon layers of blue and white tulle making for a startling contrast to the tight fitting green of her skirt. The sleeves float around her arms in voluptuous swathes of fabric, trailing far beyond her fingers on the arm not currently holding up her chin. It looks like she's been swallowed by a crescendo of foamy white waves.

On the top of her head, nestled within her mess of thick green hair, rests a simple copper circlet, featuring a singular emerald gem that is almost entirely lost amongst her curls.

The strange realisation that Aalto would probably approve of her choice of jewellery flickers through my mind, reminding me that I'm currently in the midst of a trial, and should really be focusing on working out what it is that I have to do.

Movement brings my attention back to the woman I assume is the queen, and I blink in surprise when I notice her feet. She's tapping one bare, dark brown foot against the side of the throne. Not a hoof – a foot.

Clearly, she isn't the same as the creatures who have brought me here. Although I'm starting to wonder if I'll ever be able to confidently identify anything 'clearly' again.

"You seem confused, my dear."

Though her words are kind, her tone hints at her power, and I have to swallow a few times before I can get my vocal chords to work.

"This whole situation is a bit confusing," I offer, somewhat croakily.

I'm not sure what's intimidating me so much about this woman; she looks far more approachable than the horrifying river-creatures that brought me here, yet something about her has me tongue tied. Then again, I've always struggled to speak when faced with women I find attractive. She's undeniably gorgeous, and the aura of power that surrounds her isn't helping. *No.* I can't keep being led astray like this. She's probably fae; I can't let her looks sway my reasoning.

That thought spurs a spark of fire back into my voice. "I don't know why I've been dragged here. Who are you? Where am I? Is this part of the trial?" I question, holding up my arms, which I realise have nail marks gauged into the skin from where Esme held me tightly.

The woman on the throne swings her legs around in front of her, clapping her hands together in delight. "Now there's the passionate human I've heard so much about!" Her smile is sincere, as if she is genuinely pleased that I'm beginning to become frustrated. "Your trial will begin soon, have patience."

I raise my eyebrows. "Aren't you human then?" I ask, my eyes travelling down the woman's legs and back up to her eyes again. I feel my face flush warm, most likely a hearty pink, when her eyes meet mine and she gives me a wink, seemingly enjoying my once over of her body.

"You mean these?" She swings her legs to-and-fro in the air playfully before suddenly leaping off the throne and into the air at a height that should be far from possible from a sitting position.

There are no sparks of light or loud bangs, but something must have happened when the woman jumped, for I've barely blinked before she lands, and what were legs have transformed into neatly cloven pink hooves. She clops them up and down on the spot, gleefully giggling at my obvious confusion.

"Oh, you poor dear!" She trots over to me and cups my cheek in her hand, before dipping forward and planting a sweet, chaste kiss on my lips.

I stare at her, stunned, as I watch the reverse happen. No sparks. No noise. A mere blink and the woman is back on her throne, lounging with two human legs intact.

"We're Lonakh. We can transform at will, though only in our horse shape can we breathe underwater. It's all rather boring really." She pretends to stifle a yawn, rolling her eyes.

"Somewhere along the line, one of our fae ancestors fell in love with one of our kelpie ancestors, and thus we are allowed to walk the line between fae and kelpie." She waves her hand at her legs. "I'm indifferent to which form I take, but from what I know of humans, I presumed you would feel more comfortable talking to me in this form. Humans are so judgmental of anything different." She smiles encouragingly, her round brown eyes twinkling despite the insult she's just nonchalantly chucked my way.

I shiver; I'm not sure whether from exhaustion, fear of what is to come, or simply lack of substance, but I suddenly feel bone-achingly drained.

"Oh, you must be worn out from your swim!" the woman exclaims, once again leaping from the throne with a speed that is dizzying to me. She wraps a companiable arm around me. "Come along now."

I allow myself to be led across the room, towards a series of thin green fronds that look like they've simply been painted on the wall. As the woman runs a gentle finger across them, the plants give an almost human shiver, before parting like a pair of curtains and allowing us to pass through.

The woman pauses briefly to nod at Esme and the other Lonakhs, their eyes narrowing as they replicate the gesture before diving back into the water and swimming away. I wonder at their reaction, but I'm too tired to give it further thought as the woman leads me through the archway.

"And there I was whittering on about my tribe's history! Dear dear. You see, it's been so very long since I last met a human." The woman runs a dainty pink tongue across her lower lip in thought. "Such beautiful creatures, but I forget how delicate you are."

112

She pinches my arm, not altogether unkindly, but I pull away, the pain shocking me out of my fugue state. I need to wake up; stay vigilant.

"We haven't even been introduced! Queen Toriana the Third, Ruler of the Dark Lonakhs and Lord to the Kelpies of the South. You must forgive me, dear, my manners have rather left me."

She grips me in a tighter embrace when I try to step away, restricting my movement, and I struggle to contain my spike of panic. I can barely keep up, stumbling over my own feet as we hurriedly stroll down the corridors, passing multiple locked doors that I barely afford a second glance.

"How can you be both queen and lord?" I manage to ask, as another stone protruding from the ground threatens to have me falling head over heels. If it wasn't for Toriana's sharp grasp of my upper arm, I would have done just that.

"Whatever do you mean?" Toriana looks perplexed for a moment, looking down at me, reminding me of the vast difference in our height.

"Well, aren't queens women and lords men?" I ask, glancing frantically back down the corridor.

I wish I'd had the foresight to count the doors as we passed; if push comes to shove and I need an escape route, I've no idea how to find my way back. Though even if I do make it back to the throne room, I'll never be able to hold my breath long enough to swim back out to the surface without the Lonakhs help.

Hells, I'm trapped here.

"Oh, how very deliciously silly you humans are! I can be anything I want to be. I may very well decide to be King tomorrow! As long as I rule my people with a just and fair hand, am the first to ride into battle, and the one to carry them safely home again, who cares if I do so as queen or king, or lord or lady?" Toriana shakes her head in bemusement, the rounded gems around her neck tinkling against one another at her movement.

She stops abruptly in front of a door that looks no different to the rest, but clearly has some significance. It's made of the same solid pearl sheen, with a simple circular knob for a handle, a vine motif etched in a spiral pattern around it.

A faint light glows under the lip of the door, but I hear no sounds other than our soft breathing. Still, I find myself holding my breath in anticipation as, with a gentle smile on her lips, Toriana opens the door and pushes me inside, her palm flat on the small of my back.

"Here's your room, I hope you find it to your liking. This is where it starts. Good luck."

"Wait— what?" I spin on the balls of my feet. "What do you mean my room?"

But Toriana has already left.

I hurriedly pace to the now-closed door, thinking I must be missing something, when I hear a sound that causes my stomach to roll in revolt. With a desperate couple of twists to the knob, my fears are confirmed.

I'm locked in.

"Hells," I breathe, leaning my head against the door and taking a few deep breaths in to try and smother the panic that is threatening to erupt. "What do they want with me?"

I turn to face the room, hoping that an answer will present itself to me.

It's only then that I realise I'm not alone.

114

Chapter Fifteen

The room is narrow, bare aside from a bed, desk, and chair, and there are no windows. Though my logical mind tells me this is because we're probably underwater, I can't shake the feeling of terror that grips me. More softly glowing starfish are inlaid into the walls, their haphazard scattering across the room managing to light it well enough for me to see where I'm walking, but not enough, it appears, to wake the occupant of the bed.

They are lying on their side, turned away from me, the white sheet covering the bed pulled all the way up to their chin. All that remains visible is their long purple hair, matted at the top, as though they haven't had the energy to brush it in a long time. Perhaps they're one of the Lonakh people, in human form? I wonder what's wrong with them. They're breathing rather heavily, with ragged inhales, and faint perspiration dots what skin is visible.

I hate myself for it, but immediately start looking around the room for some kind of weapon with which to defend myself. I'm aware that I seemingly misjudged the Lonakh initially, yet kidnapping and then locking someone in a room isn't exactly a friendly thing to do. Not to mention I still don't know what this trial entails.

As there's only the chair and desk to explore, I decide to start with the latter, creeping towards it with bated breath and quiet steps. It's equally simple; made from thick white stone with no drawers and four solid, trunk-like legs. But there are several items sitting neatly on top, almost as if placed there ready for me to study.

I don't need any further encouragement.

I pick up the first item, twirling it around delicately in my hand. It's a glass flask with a tapered end, making the contents easily pourable. There is a tiny amount of clear liquid pooling in the bottom that looks suspiciously like water, but I don't risk sniffing or tasting it to find out. I place it down carefully, not wanting to break it. Beside it is another flask, with some kind of green, mossy vegetation residing at the bottom; I shake the flask curiously, but the contents are too dense and it makes no sound.

Next, I pick up a long, thin object. If I look closely enough, I can make out engravings on the marble handle: images of tiny humans holding swords that they are using to draw green swirling circles on their arms. The end of the object tapers into a sharp point. My eyes flicker over to the figure in the bed. Perhaps this tool would be a good defence if they wake up and attack me.

I place it back down on the table, within easy reach, before I lean over to grasp the largest and final object: a wooden chest. It's about the size of a hardback book and has a curved top, with a silver clasp keeping it closed.

I give it a curious tap on the top; the thud is solid, indicating that the trunk isn't empty, but thankfully nothing judders in response to my tapping, so I presume that there isn't anything alive inside.

The fae have made me suspicious of everything.

I flick the silver clasp and the lid back, before quickly retreating my hand and peering inside at a safe distance.

It contains one of the curled up scrolls I'm beginning to recognise, although made of purple paper this time, and tied up neatly with a lime green ribbon that curls up at the edges.

Hesitatingly, I pull the scroll out of its container. Should I listen to it and risk waking up the occupant of the bed? Feeling some trepidation, but not knowing what else to do, I quickly untie the ribbon before I can talk myself out of it. I chuck it back onto the table, expecting it to deliver its traditional verbal message, but instead there is an empty, anticlimactic silence.

I guess this isn't fae magic, then.

I lift the scroll from the table and unroll it, so I can read it normally.

'How far will you go to help someone in need?
Will you risk yourself?
Can you ignore the pain in your heart?
To ease the pain of another?'

The scroll shoots out some angry sparks once I've finished reading it, zapping my finger.

"Ow!" I exclaim, shooting a hurried glance across to the figure in the bed, to see if my shriek has woken them up.

I've no idea how the paper recognised that I'd finished reading. *Maybe there was some magic involved, after all.*

A flicker on the scroll catches my attention; new words are beginning to form where the previous ones had been.

'All you need to save the woman in this room is on the table.

Rinsgh moss can cure blood poisoning, but will cause tremendous pain when taken.

Pour the liquid onto the moss when you are ready.

Addition of human blood to the concoction will act as a sedative and counteract the pain.'

Once again, the words disappear with a sharp snap of

sparks, though this time I grit my teeth when I get to the end of the paragraph, so I don't cry out.

Yet more words appear, and I hurriedly read them.

'This woman is a prisoner of our people – she has killed several humans, harvesting them for their blood.

Will you choose to save her, despite this?

Will you offer your own blood to ease her pain?

Or will you simply wait out her death?

The choice remains with you.'

The parchment disappears in a cloud of lime green smoke, leaving me waving my hand in front of my face to dissipate the gas. It smells of nothing, but I don't like the idea of breathing in a noxious-looking cloud all the same.

I close my eyes, trying to process the barrage of information I've just been presented with as a tirade of thoughts wash over me like a tidal wave. Wrapping my arms around my chest, I hug myself tightly, trying to ground myself in the present, though all I really want to do is curl up and cry.

What is this trial attempting to test? Do fae see having empathy a weakness? Do they want me to leave without helping the woman? Compassion and kindness are human traits, after all, but I know they are testing our sins rather than our virtues, so it can't be that. A wave of acid swirls in my stomach. Does this woman even deserve my help when she's hurt so many humans? I close my eyes, trying to swallow back the resentment, an angry bubble forming in my chest, the pressure making it hard to breathe. What have the fae ever done to deserve our compassion?

My eyes snap open as I remember my conversation with Aalto. He might have been lying, of course, but what if he wasn't? His behaviour towards me certainly suggests he cares

118

about my wellbeing, at least to a certain extent. I can't judge this woman based on my feelings about the fae as a collective. I don't know her. She isn't to blame for Dionne's death, or Celestia's, or my mother's. I grit my teeth in frustration. But the note said she had killed humans. Does she really deserve to survive without experiencing some kind of retribution for her crimes?

I could just add the liquid to the moss and give it to the woman – that way she will survive, but she'll still suffer.

I shake my head, horrified by my own thoughts. How am I even contemplating this? What the note said might not even be true! I can't let someone suffer needlessly when I have the tools to help them, regardless of whether they are human or fae or something in between.

No longer worried about waking up the sleeping figure, I pick up the curious marble object, finally understanding the pictures on the side of it.

I cast one last thoughtful glance over to the bed's occupant, and without another second's hesitation, I pour the liquid from the first flask into the one containing the moss. Clenching my hand around the instrument lying on the table, I swipe firmly down along the blade, whimpering as it slices into my delicate skin. Shaking, I hover my hand over the flask containing the mixture and let my blood drip down the funnel's opening.

It takes a while for the blood to trickle down the sides and reach the moss, and I hold onto the side of the table with my other hand, the marble instrument lying forgotten on the side. I feel dizzy and slightly sick, although I'm not losing blood quickly. It's just not a particularly enjoyable process.

As one drop after another splashes onto the moss, it sizzles softly before flashing a vibrant purple colour and releasing a pungent cloud that smells vaguely of sage. The purple light splashes against the side of the flask, lighting the interior with a soft pulsating glow that I find mesmerising.

I almost knock the whole thing over when a voice suddenly breaks the silence.

"That's more than enough blood, please don't waste anymore."

I hurriedly grab the trembling flask between both hands, wincing slightly at the soreness in my left palm where it rubs against the cut.

I turn slowly to look at the woman on the bed, who has now turned towards me. She's leaning on one elbow, tilting to one side as she struggles to watch my activity. Her lips are pale, and she pants softly; every now and then pain streaks across her face, her forehead puckered with a frown.

"Please?" She reaches out a shaking hand towards me and the flask, causing me to take an instinctive step backwards, cradling the flask against my chest.

She coughs into her hand, purple flecks of blood splattering onto her skin and the sheets.

The sight of her blood spurs me out of my frozen state and across to the bed. No longer concerned with any danger I might be putting myself in, I support her head with one hand as I lead the flask's funnel up to her mouth.

At first, the woman struggles to swallow, but after a few ragged gulps her frown smooths out, and she pulls herself a bit more upright. Her eyes open to look at me – eyes that shine warmly with gratitude. She gently places a hand on my arm, her eyes begging me not to take the flask away from her mouth, as she swallows down every drop of it.

I watch in abject fascination. Part of me is repulsed by the

120

idea that someone is drinking down my blood, but the fact that it no longer resembles the thick red substance that flows through my veins certainly helps.

Once finished, the woman pulls herself fully upright into a sitting position, the bedsheets pulled neatly around herself. We stare at each other, studying one another thoughtfully for what is only the barest of moments but feels like much longer.

Finally, the woman breaks the silence.

"Thank you," she whispers. "I truly didn't think I would make it. I cannot begin to tell you how grateful I am." She brushes her sweat-damp hair out of her face, rubbing her eyes tiredly.

I merely nod, unable to resist looking towards the wall to see if the door has reappeared. I made my decision; I saved her life. Does that mean I passed this trial? Or failed? What was the right decision to make?

The woman notices my gaze and is suddenly full of a fervour. "Please! You must listen before you go!"

I make to back away, but with a speed that shocks me, she grabs my hands within her own.

"Please, let me explain! It's not what you think. I didn't kill anyone, not intentionally. I was trying to save their babes."

Her hands tightly grasp mine, but I wouldn't have moved even if she'd let go. I can't look away from the pain in the woman's eyes.

"It's difficult for my tribe to reproduce successfully... we often shift forms unintentionally when in severe pain – we are stronger in Lonakh form, after all; it's our natural defence mechanism – but to do so during childbirth can rip the mother apart." She shakes her head miserably. "The greatest sacrifice a mother can give is her life."

"But... but the note said that you harvested human blood, not that you killed Lonakhs," I whisper, distressed by the trail of tears that are travelling down the woman's face.

The woman nods, wiping at her cheeks as she recalls what must be painful memories. "We return to our human forms when we die, so the blood I took was human blood, in essence. When the mother dies so swiftly, the only way to keep her babe from joining her is to collect the mother's blood; to use the nutrients it provides to keep the babe alive. I was unable to rescue the mothers, but that was not an intention on my part, just the cruelty of life's cycle."

"Why wouldn't your tribe heal you? Why go through this elaborate charade when I could've just as easily let you die?" I wave my hand angrily around the room, furious on this woman's behalf.

"Because the mothers I left to die were royalty, and you don't let royalty die, irrelevant of the impossibilities." There isn't a trace of resentment in her voice; she clearly accepts this as a just and fair fact. "So, I was used as an example, with which to test your human heart and the wrath that resides inside it. They poisoned me deliberately."

I let out a sharp, bitter laugh. "I suppose royalty can be just as obnoxious in the human world," I concede begrudgingly, despite my disgust and not wanting to excuse the Lonakhs for their horrifying behaviour. "But to use you as a pawn for these trials... it's inexcusable."

The woman sighs and pulls away from me when she hears the anger in my voice. "Your mind doesn't think as clearly, when your heart is clouded with anger," she responds cryptically. "And yet, you still did the just thing...why?"

I shuffle awkwardly, feeling uncomfortable under her direct

scrutiny. "Just because one person does a bad thing, doesn't mean everyone else in that group is bad. And even if someone *is* a bad person, it doesn't mean that you should lower yourself to their standards. It just didn't feel right to knowingly cause you pain when I had the ability to stop it." I struggle to explain my reasoning. Putting complex emotions into words has never been my strong suit.

When I meet her gaze, though, the woman's eyes are warm. "You are a kind-hearted person. I'm glad to have met a human such as yourself." She bows her head slightly.

I blink, taken aback by her formality. "My name is Rosalind," I offer. "I know some magical creatures don't like sharing their names, but I would appreciate knowing yours? I think it's important to remember those whose paths we cross." I meet the eyes of the woman, who looks apprehensive at my question.

I sigh. *What is it with magical creatures and names?* It's not like I was asking for her given name.

"Forget I asked." I wave a hand in the air, as if to brush away my question. "I'm not asking for anything in return for curing you. I'm not asking for your name as a way of gaining power over you. It just means something to me, to remember those I meet." I turn away from her, pulling my hand gently out of her grasp as I realise the blue door from the beginning of the task has appeared. "I must go. I don't regret saving you, but I need to know if I passed this trial. And if my friends survived."

Filled with a sudden desperation, I walk briskly towards the doorway.

"It's Cerise."

The woman's whisper startles me, and I spin around to face her.

"Cerise Flist of the Highwater Clan. My given name is Mires."

I double over, feeling a wave of power stun me as Cerise shares her given name. It feels like invisible tendrils are wrapping themselves around my chest and restricting my breathing, before soaking into and under my skin, settling as a warm glow. I take in a large gulp of air when the sensation finishes washing over me, leaving me with a strange tugging sensation – almost as if someone has put a leash around me that connects to Cerise.

"I didn't mean for that," I whisper in shock, meeting the resolved gaze in Cerise's rich brown eyes.

"I know you didn't. That is why I gave it to you." She offers a small smile, its warmth lighting up her skin, and for the first time I notice how pretty she is. "If you ever have need of me, you can call on me, and I will aid you if I can." She shrugs. "Of course, my skills are primarily in midwifery, but you never know." She winks, and I smile weakly back, struggling not to grimace.

Of all things, *that* is definitely *not* going to happen any time soon.

Reluctant to just walk out on Cerise after she has performed a very personal, sentimental ritual, I fidget on the spot, unable to stop my gaze from flicking to the door. My anxiety for my fellow tributes, and myself, is steadily increasing, becoming a loud buzzing in my head.

"Go." Cerise smiles warmly, noticing my anxiety. "But know that me sharing my name was something I did on my own terms. Not on instruction."

Spontaneously, I reach for Cerise and envelop her a warm hug.

The woman stiffens beneath me, and I briefly regret my impulsiveness. "Thank you, Cerise," I say awkwardly, feeling a slight nudge in my mind, reminding me that I know this woman's given name.

Cerise nods, her eyes sparkling as she realises that I will not use her given name rashly, and finally returns the hug.

I nod my farewell and finally step back through the door, curious as to why the engraving of the bowl on the front is now filled with clear liquid.

Chapter Sixteen

I re-enter the room from before and immediately find myself enveloped in a fierce hug from Kieran, before I even have time to register his presence.

"You made it," he exclaims, relief evident in his voice. "I've been waiting so long; I was started to worry that I was the only one who would."

He clings to me tightly as I awkwardly pat him on the back.

"Delaney and Makani haven't come back through?" I turn to look at the remaining two doors, ours having disappeared completely. Worryingly, ice is beginning to form around the edges of Delaney's door, and Makani's is emitting a sulphurous smell.

"I guess their wrath is stronger than ours?" Kieran mutters, wrinkling his nose as a puff of noxious gas starts curling under the white door.

We both take a step away.

"What did you have to do?" I ask curiously, as I consider that everyone might have had personalised trials.

But Kieran's reply is interrupted as Delaney's door slams open and she storms through. Her ordinarily composed face is streaked with tears, her clothes dripping with water. She holds out shaking hands, and I step forward, catching her as she falls into my arms with noisy sobs.

"I w-wanted to k-kill her, but I-I c-couldn't." She trembles in my arms, making little sense.

I silently stroke her hair, allowing her to compose herself.

"Makani's door is gone," Kieran interrupts, and I look over Delaney's shoulder, noting the blank wall. "I guess he didn't make the right choice." Kieran sighs. "He was full of hatred before we even started. It wasn't a fair challenge for him." He swallows. "At least his soul is with Celestia now."

Kieran rests his hand on my shoulder and I turn to meet his gaze.

"You asked me what happened. I had to oversee a trial; decide whether to commend a fae man to death. I don't believe in the death penalty, regardless of the circumstances, so it was an easy decision to make." He shrugs. "Don't get me wrong, I hate what they're putting us through, but it's not the fae's fault that Nature is punishing us."

"Doesn't mean that they're blameless either," I can't help adding, as I help Delaney to a chair and take off her wet outer clothing.

She's left in just a slip of a black dress, and I'm pleased when, without prompt, Kieran takes off his jacket to wrap it around her shoulders. In similar attire myself, I have nothing to offer her.

"I also had to decide whether to let someone live or die, but it was more complicated than that. I was kidnapped; imprisoned by half-human water creatures. Whoever planned the task tried to convince me that the woman I had to save was cruel; had harmed humans. I had options too: whether to heal her painlessly or not. And she wasn't fae, she was Lonakh – the same as the creatures who kidnapped me."

Kieran tilts his head as he thinks this through. "Maybe your heart and mind are too conflicted and it wasn't easy for the magic to devise a clear-cut test, so there were extra variables?"

"I... I saw my former lover," Delaney whispers, interrupting our conversation, tears filling her eyes again. "I fell in love with her when she passed through Ramk, my home." She stares off into the distance, as if travelling through her memories. "We were inseparable. She promised me she'd love me forever; that me being human didn't matter; that she could always turn me fae. But it was all a lie." She angrily brushes away her tears. "I was just a challenge, to see if a *pathetic little human* could be convinced that a *beautiful* fae loved her." Delaney chokes on her words. "I thought I was over it; that I'd regained my confidence in myself. But seeing her just brought it all back."

Kieran steps forward, placing an arm around her shoulders. "Do you want to tell us what happened?" he asks softly.

Delaney shudders. "I was at her court, watching her dance with some other fae. I... I felt angry, all over again. It was like I didn't even exist; she didn't recognise me when I tried to approach her. I was offered the chance to give her a drink and given the option of adding berries to it."

"Berries?" I interrupt, but Kieran shushes me.

Delaney looks up at me, moving to rest her head against my shoulder. "Min berries. They're native to Ramk and cause a deep sleep when mixed with drink... one that you won't wake from. It's fairly peaceful, as death goes. Our elders use them to help ease cattle that are at their end." She sighs. "I hate her, but not that much. I couldn't do it, but I couldn't bring myself to walk back through the door either. Instead, I tortured myself, watching her be happy with others." She clenches her fists. "I guess I haven't moved on as well as I thought." She offers me a weary smile, pulling away slightly from Kieran's hold.

"It's never easy, moving on from love," I reassure her,

thinking of Isabel. "But it does get easier."

We all startle when our fae partners suddenly appear in the centre of the room.

"Did Makani make it?" I ask instantly, taking a step towards Aalto.

He shakes his head solemnly.

I look away, unsurprised but disheartened all the same.

Nora steps toward Kieran, reaching for his shoulder. "Well done for battling mind over heart," she says simply, without a trace of a smile upon her face.

They disappear in a flurry of sparks.

Amaya merely nods silently at Delaney, who wearily gets to her feet and holds out a hand. They too disappear, wrapped in a blanket of shadowy tendrils.

Aalto steps towards me. "I was worried," he says simply. "I underestimated you, again. I'm sorry."

His unexpected apology halts the retort I might otherwise have thrown his way.

"I know you're confused." He brushes a stray tendril of hair away from my face with the base of his thumb. "But it seems that your heart remembers what your mind cannot."

I frown, not understanding a word; frustrated by his tendency to hide behind convoluted riddles.

He takes advantage of my confusion, grabbing hold of my shoulder and whisking us away from the room, leaving just the lingering smell of a salty sea breeze.

It surprises me to find us back in what I'm starting to think of as *my* room, even though I had been so desperate to leave it earlier. There are so many questions tumbling through my mind, but when Aalto leads me to a table, set with a simple fare of warm bread, juicy looking red apples, and crumbly cheese, it's all I can do but sit upright and eat. I'm just so tired.

He sits opposite me in companionable silence, seemingly not expecting anything from me, for which I am glad.

Eventually, however, I can eat no more, and I finally take note of him. He hasn't changed from earlier; if anything, he looks more dishevelled than before.

"You were worried about me?"

He blinks in surprise at my question. "Yes," he responds, as if no other answer makes sense.

I suppose he had a right to be. If I had failed, he would have died with me, if his words from earlier are to be believed. His grief over Dhara seemed too genuine to have been faked, but he is fae... I'm not sure I can truly trust anyone in this strange reality.

"You didn't think I would pass the test?" I ask, running the tablecloth between my hands, worrying the lace.

"No, that I wasn't worried about. I know you have a good heart, Rosalind. I knew you would never cause anyone pain, no matter how angry you were."

What? Then why was he worried? "You only met me a few days ago, how can you know that?" I drop the tablecloth to fiddle with an apple segment instead.

Aalto looks away, frowning deeply. "Magic, I guess."

I feel like it's a copout answer, but I'm not sure why he's giving one to me.

"There's confusion inside you, yes, but not true hatred. Unlike Makani's bubbling volcano of emotions..." He places a hand over mine, stopping my hand as it reaches for the white lace again. "Can you please not take your frustration out on the tablecloth?"

I sigh. "Fine."

130

His answer still doesn't explain why he was worried about me, if he knew I would pass the trial, but given his evasiveness, I doubt he'll explain anyway.

"Can I sleep now?" I look longingly at the bed, wishing to escape into its warm embrace.

Aalto strokes his thumb across the back of my hand briefly, before pulling away, perhaps finally accepting that I don't fully welcome his touch, no matter how much I crave comfort.

"It's probably advisable. I'm afraid delaying this trial so you could rest means the next one is imminent." He looks down at a circle indented into the ground. "When this begins to glow, you must step inside, and it'll transport you to the next trial. I won't see you before then. They— I am needed elsewhere."

He looks me over, as if trying to remember everything about me and I find myself flushing under his attentive gaze.

"Fare well, Rosalind."

He smiles, and before I can respond, I am left with the tang of salty sea-breeze and an empty room.

I feel almost disappointed that he ended our conversation so abruptly, but my exhaustion soon wins out, and it doesn't take me long to strip off my clothing and collapse into the bed, falling into a fretful, agitated slumber.

CHAPTER SEVENTEEN

I continue to pace back and forth in front of the round circle in my room, watching as the smooth stones set within it take turns to flash a comforting blue. A note that arrived earlier, nestled beside a plate of oranges, commanded me to sit inside the circle when all the stones turn golden, to be transported to the next trial.

I also received a leather backpack, the meagre contents of which I've curiously securitised several times over, delivered by a group of excitable blue Vielheim, making me wonder if Aalto sent it. It is empty save for a single piece of blank parchment, which I presume will utter instructions once I arrive at whatever destination the fae have planned for me.

The wait is making my anxiety flare; I feel nauseous, and the urge to curl back up in bed is almost overwhelming. Hence the pacing. After each length of the room, I stop to rock on the balls of my feet, trying to nullify my pent-up energy.

I do this with my backpack firmly on. The instructions do not say how long the stones will stay golden for, or how much warning I'll get when they finally change colour, so I don't want to risk accidently missing the sign.

When I get bored of resting and pacing, I try to make words appear on the parchment, with little success. I've tried drizzling water on it and even using a finger dipped in orange juice, but nothing has worked.

During my isolation, I've explored every corner of the room. The wardrobe is filled with nightgowns, and when a group of red Vielheim deliver a deep, round tub of steaming warm water for me to bathe in, I hurriedly swap my old one out for one of the soft, clean ones after a luxurious soak.

It's as I'm pacing again that I hear a loud bang sound from inside the wardrobe, which has me diving for the comfort of my bed. After eyeing it suspiciously from the safety of my nest of blankets, I gingerly walk over to it, leaping back after I whip open one of the doors.

Rather anticlimactically, the nightgowns have simply been replaced with more practical clothing. I can only presume that the next challenge is imminent, and I need to get dressed.

I select a pair of lightweight trousers with several pockets along the legs. They are tight fitting, but whatever fabric they are made from allows me to move easily in them. An equally tight-fitting top accompanies them; black with long-sleeves and no embellishments, which seems unusual for fae clothing.

Some yellow Vielheim tied my hair neatly back into an intricate plait after my morning soak in the bath; I had attempted to brush them away and do it myself, but they gave my fingers a surprisingly sharp static shock, stunning me so much that I'd sat compliantly for the ten minutes it took for them to tie up my tresses and pin them neatly back.

I must admit, it's much neater than what I could have done myself; not a single strand is out of place. They even coated it in a luminous golden substance that has so far miraculously kept every strand flat, rather than it fraying in little curls like it normally does.

I touch my hair dubiously; it doesn't even feel greasy despite whatever they smoothed through it; if I hadn't been watching them, I wouldn't have even realised there was any product in it at all.

The stones begin to glow a soft gold and I swallow hard.

"Here we go," I mutter, as I grab the lightweight jacket I had placed on the bed whilst I'd been pacing.

With my nerves frayed, I've already worked up a sweat, and hadn't wanted to put it on earlier. But there's no way I'm not taking it with me if it's something explicitly provided.

As I step over the stones and into the circle, I feel the magic begin to take hold, fluttering my clothes in an invisible wind. I close my eyes; the tugging in my stomach is disgustingly familiar already, but it doesn't make it any easier, and I'd rather not throw up when reaching my destination.

It wouldn't be the best first impression.

"What the—" A warm breeze has me snapping my eyes open, and for the first time since entering the fae world, I feel pleasantly surprised.

I'm in a massive meadow, filled with gently bobbing poppies, though they are a sunny yellow colour rather than the traditional vibrant red I'm used to. The sky is a comforting aqua blue, caressed with several plump, fluffy white clouds that are drifting merrily along. To the edges of the meadow is a set of towering pine trees that get denser the further away from me they are, but rather than feel threatening, I feel that warm sensation of coming home after being away for far too long.

I sigh, feeling my muscles relax as I breathe in the rich floral aroma, watching lazy fat bumblebees bob from one flower head to the other, their pollen sacs heavy as they buzz drunkenly.

A tittering sound has me spinning around, but I can see no one nearby. I'm definitely alone.

"Am I finally losing it?" I ask the air, wondering where the other contestants are.

A vibration along my back has me hurriedly slinging my backpack onto the grassy floor.

Watching it shake, I kneel to look closer, noticing that the tittering is getting louder. Realisation finally dawning, I grab the bag and fling open the top. Still with a tiny bit of trepidation, I peer slowly inside, but immediately, my theories are confirmed.

At the bottom of the bag, the rolled-up piece of parchment is fluttering angrily, trying to break free of the tie that is wrapped around it. Struggling to hold it firm as it bucks against my grip, whilst simultaneously pulling off the ribbon tie, I end up clenching it between my legs and finally manage to wrench the tie off.

It immediately flips itself open and takes what can only be described as a deep breath, before it leaps into reciting the message it had been trying to shout at me before. Finally, I understand why it had been blank, with no message written upon it.

"You have been dropped within a fae passage. Bound at the end of the road lies your partner, who is in great danger. Covered in chains, locked by key, they await the fate that is travelling towards them. Their outcome is in your hands; *you* are their key. Be quick, but don't take shortcuts."

I yelp as, with another gasp, the parchment message shudders and bursts into a shower of sparks. I wish that fae messages gave some kind of warning before reaching the end, so I could throw them away before they explode.

I stop to survey my surroundings once more, perplexed that none of the other contenders are around. Perhaps they've been dropped off in a different passage?

What will happen if I'm the last to reach Aalto? Or worse, if I don't reach him in time at all? How much time do I even have? The note wasn't clear. Was that why he was unable to visit me before the trial? Was he taken in preparation?

Aalto might be infuriating, but he's also been far kinder to me than he needed to be. If everything he's told me is true, he's opened up to me more than he probably should have, and after hearing him speak so passionately, I can no longer say that I hate him. I wouldn't go so far as to say that I like him, but I certainly don't want to see him hurt. Besides, I'm painfully aware that my fate is intertwined with his during these trials.

These sobering thoughts finally inspire me to get a move on and I begin walking forwards in the direction I've been placed, not knowing where else to go.

"At least the weather is reasonable," I murmur, noting that the sun is high up in the sky. I can only presume that this place mimics Sora, and that the position of the sun means its roughly midmorning.

The grass is soft and springy beneath my feet, making for easy walking terrain, and the flowers exude a subtle relaxing scent. But I've grown used to things not appearing as they seem, and my muscles remain tense with trepidation, my heart beating as fast as a marching drum.

I feel the ground begin to slope slightly upwards and am reminded that I have no water on me. I've no idea how far away Aalto is, so water is going to quickly become an essential factor in my survival if this journey is prolonged.

As I continue to walk, I spot a solid wooden panel inserted into the ground ahead of me, with two arrows pointing in different directions. It's the first thing I've come across that gives any clue as to where I am, and I pick up my pace, almost breaking into a jog in my eagerness to reach it.

I swiftly realise it's a lot taller than I initially thought, and as I come to a halt, I strain my neck back to try and read what is engraved into the two wooden pointers. Ivy-like leaves trail around the post, but luckily they have yet to reach the top. That, or someone regularly attends to it, keeping it clear.

One arrow points towards a path that slants slightly upwards, formed of pretty, clear blue pebbles that create a rather precarious route up a hillside. It looks like it gets steeper the further you go, but I can't see past the bend to confirm. It is simply named 'Sight'.

The other pathway, labelled 'No Sight', is formed of the same stones, but weaves through a glade of flowers. Like the hillside path, it curves around a bend and out of my line of vision.

Helpful.

I tap a finger against my lips in quiet contemplation. The added ticking of a clock in my head, counting down to Aalto's demise, and therefore mine, isn't helping me to think logically.

Not that I have much to go on anyway.

Typical fae.

I sigh, feeling that anything I come up with would be mere guesswork. All I can hope for is that both paths lead forward.

"The 'No Sight' one is an easier path," I murmur to myself, rationalising my thoughts aloud, "but I might be able to see more of the landscape if I take the hillside one. Maybe that's what the 'Sight' sign is hinting at. But if I get to the top of the hill and it's a dead end, I'll have to scramble back down again. But then the note did say to be quick, but not to take shortcuts; does taking the lower path count as a shortcut?" I shake my head, frustrated.

I can't let my second guessing distract me. If Aalto is in danger, I must focus on getting to him as quickly as possible. My decision firm in my mind, I take off down the straight-lined pathway entitled 'No Sight'. I swear I hear a sigh in the wind, but I shake my head and continue, not wanting to risk self-doubt.

As I'm walking, small shrub like trees pop up along the pathway, gradually giving way to larger bushes and towering, leafy trees that shelter me from the sun's rays. At the start of the journey, I'd enjoyed the warmth of the mid-morning sun, but after a good hour or two of walking, I've naturally warmed up and am starting to resent its persistent glare overhead. Still, I'm reluctant to take my jacket off, deciding it will be more tiring to carry than to wear.

Little pink butterflies are drifting in and out of the bushes, landing on succulent, round, juicy blue berries. They aren't like anything I've seen before, so I initially ignore them, though my mouth is starting to feel dry and they look so succulent they would simply burst in my mouth.

I tear my eyes away and focus on the path, ignoring the nagging voice in my head that warns me that I might not find another opportunity for nourishment further on. I've learnt the hard way that the fae like a show, so I doubt they'll let me simply die of thirst or hunger in the wilderness, though this isn't as comforting a thought as it should be. Dying by more extravagant means doesn't make it any more appealing. Death is death, after all.

It isn't long before I reach the bend in the path and turn the corner. I stop, startled, the sight in front of me completely at odds with the lush meadow and shrubbery behind me.

For as far as my eyes can see stretches a vast, sandy expanse.

A soft wind is blowing across the ground, sweeping little flurries of sand along in gentle whirls. The only vegetation is an occasional spiky plant, reaching no higher than my ankles. They have little red flowers embedded in their thorny stems that shine enticingly against the endless gold.

The sun beats down like a drum on my head. Why does it feel so much harsher here, when a minute ago it was so pleasant? I can immediately feel that my ears are beginning to burn, and I hurriedly pull off my coat, deciding finally that it is time to shove it into my backpack.

I sling my bag to the floor, unzip it, and am just squeezing my jacket into it when I notice a small fabric hat, folded up neatly at the bottom. *That definitely wasn't there before.* Shrugging, I pull and shake it out, gratefully putting it over my head. Simple and beige, it has a wide brim that shadows my eyes, protecting them from the intense sun's glare.

Feeling a sudden strange sensation of someone closing a door behind me, I turn around, only to be met with a sheer cliff face. The meadow is no longer there, nor are the shrubs, trees, hills, or pathway.

I fiddle with the brim of my hat nervously. I really wish they would give us some warning before doing things like this.

I hesitate, running a finger against the rock. It's completely solid, not a vision like I'd assumed. My hat's brim flutters slightly in the wind, tugging away from my eyes and allowing the sun to temporarily blind me.

Removing the hat, I repeatedly look away from the cliff and back, but it's still there. Clearly whatever magic has transported me is not going to revert itself.

"I guess the only way is forward," I announce quietly to myself, trying not to think about what I've potentially missed by not going up that hill.

Maybe it would have given me an eagle's eye view of this desert terrain, and I could have planned a way forward? Or maybe there had been food or water at the top, which I could have replenished myself with before continuing.

I hope I don't regret not tasting those berries. The thought of food finally gets me moving again. Maybe the red flowers are edible? At some point I'll have to risk poisoning myself if I don't find anything to drink soon. A low grumble in my belly further emphasises the point. If I'm going to keep on trekking, I'll have to address my mortal requirements.

I pause, an idea taking root. "Drink? Food?" I say out loud, feeling silly as I shake my bag hopefully.

As I open it, I'm not surprised to find that my pleas have gone ignored. It's empty. I put a hand inside the bag, feeling around, perplexed that I haven't even noticed the weight change of my jacket disappearing. Still, at least I won't be carrying the dead weight of something I don't need. I can only hope that if the weather changes – or Nature forbid, I'm still searching for Aalto come nightfall – that my jacket reappears as suddenly as it disappeared.

"Best make a start," I sigh, tugging my backpack back onto my shoulders and tightening the straps.

Squinting at the sun, I try to judge where it is in the sky so I can keep track of the direction I'm walking in. The last thing I need is to end up walking a full circle and finishing right back where I started.

Chapter Eighteen

The repetitiveness of the never-ending golden sand, hazy dust clouds and little spiny plants is making me dizzy. I want to groan with frustration, but my mouth is too dry, and the sun's rays are unforgiving.

My hat is beginning to feel unpleasantly warm where it sticks to my head, and I can feel a thin band of sweat beginning to build up between my hair and the rim. My shirt is sticking to my back, and my shoes are starting to pinch at the toes and rub against the balls of my feet. I no longer look ahead to the horizon, sick of feeling disappointed when nothing new appears, and instead concentrate on putting one foot in front of the other.

"Am I even going in the right direction?" I mumble to myself, my tongue sticky against the roof of my mouth. "Or is this just another challenge? A test of endurance designed to never end?"

My thoughts tumble one after another through my aching head, like pebbles splashing into a murky pond, the water's surface too dark for me to make any sense of them or come up with any answers. Yet I cannot stop them circulating, round and round.

My eyes are beginning to feel sore and gritty, and I stop for a second, rubbing them vigorously as I try to focus.

"Ow!"

Blinded by my own palms, I've managed to step forward straight onto one of the spiky plants. One sharp thorn wedges itself into the skin around my ankle, visible above the flap of my shoe. I kneel and, gritting my teeth, pull it out, flinching as a small dewdrop of blood wells against my skin.

My patience finally wrung out, I fling the thorn away from myself, anger and frustration tightening their firm grasp as the thorn merely flutters to the ground in front of me instead of travelling the distance I'd anticipated.

I glare at the opposing plant that is silently staring back at me. The little red petals flutter in the gentle breeze, and I blink hazily, irritated by the sand swirling around me, threatening to blind me again.

My lips are sore, and I lick them to salvage some moisture, but my tongue is so dry that I've only added to the problem. I want to cry, but I'm too dehydrated to be able to produce any tears. Frustrated, I reach out and pluck one of the red flowers, carefully avoiding the thorns. It feels silky, and for a moment, I contemplate eating it, just to see if the glossy petals make my mouth feel any less scratchy.

I scrunch it in my hand and reach out to pluck another one, but as I do, something tickles against my palm. I drop the scrunched-up petal in surprise and bend down to look at it more closely. It just lies there, moving very slightly in the gentle breeze, but otherwise not showing any sign of being more than a simple red flower petal.

Am I delirious? I worry that the lack of water is beginning to get to me, but I don't feel faint yet, which is a positive sign at least. I study the rest of the flowers still attached to the plant, before selecting the largest one, perched at the very top.

I hold it in my hands and grin. *There: it isn't moving! I'm not going mad!*

"Argh!"

The tickling sensation is back, and my eyes widen in disbelief as one long, black, spindly tendril uncurls from underneath the giant petal, followed swiftly by another and then another. My hands shake as I force myself not to throw the thing as far away from me as possible.

What in all the Hells? I watch, unmoving, until six long and wiry tendrils have fanned themselves out and around the petal. The petal shakes, fluttering, as what can only be described as its *legs* straighten around it, pushing the petal up.

"Argh!"

This time I do throw it away from me as, from the dead centre of the petal, with a disgusting sucking sound, a bristly round black head pops out, blinking at me with three glaring red eyes.

Unfortunately, the petal acts as a windcatcher, and as it puffs outwards it catches the wind like an umbrella, leaving the creature hovering eye level with me. Its three red eyes blink slowly as it bobs in the wind, using the petal like bellows to puff itself up and down.

I realise I'm holding my breath when a flicker out of the corner of my eye causes me to gasp. The rest of the flowers on the plant – twelve in total – are unfurling to reveal more of the little creatures, all taking to the air and surveying me ominously.

Slowly, so as not to trigger any sudden movement, I inch backwards, struggling to get up from my kneeling position. With a sinking feeling, I watch as the creatures rise in the air with me, not letting me out of their sight for a second.

I'm so focused on their movement that only as I'm

stumbling to my feet do I realise they're softly humming, all at slightly different pitches, weaving an altogether sinister melody. The largest one, that I'd disturbed first, seems to be the leader; all the others hover, grouped around it.

Abruptly, the song becomes louder and faster; the large one angrily buzzes and flutters more vigorously in front of me. Its red round eyes have stopped blinking, almost hypnotising me with their staring glare. I go to take a step around the creatures, hands held up placatingly in front of my face, when without warning they collectively lunge, diving for me.

I've just seconds to take in the little black hole under the creatures' eyes that opens to reveal hundreds of thin, needle-sharp teeth before I feel a burn across my arm.

Whipping my arm away, shocked, I swipe blindly at the air in front of me with my other arm, pushing the cloud of creatures away as I examine the damage done. For something so small, it's pierced a substantial amount of flesh. A circle of holes decorates my lower arm, little droplets of blood welling up at each point of incision. I hurriedly press my other hand to the wound, trying to stem the flow, but each mark stings like a tiny papercut, spurting a shocking amount of blood.

I dive out of the way as another of the creatures lunges for my arm. The sight of blood has spurred them all into a fury, and they all begin taking turns to buzz in close and take neat, vicious slices out of my skin.

"Please stop!" I cry as the ringleader delivers a sharp ripping puncture to my neck.

No longer caring about my arm dripping blood, I concentrate on batting the creatures out of the way as I try to press forward and past them. Despite my earlier conviction that I was unable to cry, my eyes well with tears as I register the pain from the bites and the danger I'm in.

It seems that the ringleader's change in attack is enough to encourage a free-for-all, and they attack any available bare skin they can land on. I immediately regret taking my jacket off, grateful for the hat protecting the soft skin around the top of my head.

I feel their spindly legs tickling me seconds before their sharp piercing stabs and it spurs me into a frightened frenzy as I desperately try to escape. One particularly nasty petal creature lands on my eyebrow, tearing at the sensitive skin before I have a chance to whack it away. Blood instantly begins pouring into my left eye, partially obscuring my vision.

I start to run – it's all I can do – feeling a spurt of satisfaction when I feel one of the creatures squish under my foot.

But it doesn't take long before it's replaced by another.

As I pass more of the spiny plants, more of the 'flowers' wake up and accompany their brethren. Lured by my blood, they quickly snap out of their sluggish, peaceful state and join the chase.

I panic as I run blindly forward, hoping that I'm going in the right direction but caring little; just hoping I can get away.

Wiping away the blood from my left eye, I try to focus on the landscape, but there is nothing, just clumps of those blasted plants and miles upon miles of sand.

I choke out a sob, feeling despair start to leach in, threatening to slow my pace as I come to terms with my reality.

I have to keep running.

Ahead of me, the endless flat desert seems to change, a darkness rising from the sand, though I'm unsure if I'm actually seeing something or if it's just the blood and sandy grit obscuring my vision.

Maybe the creatures can't go beyond it? Change surely means something *in this place?*

Spurred on by this tiny flame of hope, I press forward, aiming for the cloud of sand that is hovering above the dark blot on the landscape.

CHAPTER NINETEEN

As I get closer, the shape begins to take form, and with my heart in my throat, I realise it's a crouched figure and a horse, kneeling on the ground. The horse is weary; panting heavily with flecks of spittle foaming at its mouth, dripping to the ground where it lies. The figure appears to be a man, with a slight curve to his back. Too old to be any of the other contenders, but at this point, I don't care if I'm running into the hands of even more danger.

As the buzzing creatures nip at my skin and blood runs stickily down my body, I'm intent on just getting away from my current problem.

Namely: crazy, rabid petal creatures.

I'm finally close enough to make out the man's face, surprised to discover that he looks neither shocked nor concerned to find a blood-soaked girl running towards him, followed by a hoard of angry, red, buzzing monstrosities.

"Help!" I scream, retching as one particularly vicious creature tries to enter my mouth and ends up tearing the side of my lip wide open.

I taste the iron rich tang as blood pools in my mouth.

The man gestures for me to stop, but there is no way I'm going to turn around now. Surely, he won't refuse to help me?

"Halt, child!"

The man's voice is deep and gravelly and sends pinpricks of

unease trailing down my spine. Despite being smaller than me, when he grabs my shoulders, I feel the power of his muscles. His hands are big and firm in their grip, covering my shoulder blades and firmly pinning me in place. He is wearing a ragged travelling cloak, and it is into one of its many pockets that he reaches, pulling out a small vial containing a swirling clear liquid.

He flicks the stopper out with one hand, the other still holding me tightly, and without preamble he pours the contents over my head. A cold mist settles over me, and my senses are stormed with the strong aroma of peppermint. I shiver, my eyes clenched firmly shut and my muscles tense as I wait for more bites to shock my delicate skin.

Nothing comes.

I open my eyes in shock. The creatures are no longer buzzing around me, and the sudden silence is disorientating to say the least. I meet the deep brown eyes of the man in front of me; he simply raises an eyebrow and points to my feet.

"Urgh!"

I swiftly take a step backwards, stumbling over my feet, my hands anxiously clasped to my chest as my heart pounds. The petal creatures with their red eyes and spindly legs are no more. Instead, scattered around my legs are twelve red flowers, with vibrant green stems protruding from their centres, all rooted back into the sand. I stare at them, too apprehensive to move in case their legs suddenly reappear and the little demons swarm once more.

"W-why?" I finally breathe, ignoring the trickles of blood dripping from the bite marks across my body as I focus on steadying my heart rate.

The man pats the horse's flank gently, stroking its back in

comforting rhythmic circles. "Why does anything do what it does?" he responds, paying more attention to the horse than to me.

I only just restrain myself from rolling my eyes in exasperation.

He must be fae, I realise. *He sounds just like Aalto.*

Despite my apprehension at being around a fae stranger, my heart sings with gratitude that he managed to stop the creatures, and that I'm no longer alone. I study him whilst he is distracted by the horse, waiting for him to notice me again and say something else.

Now I have time to look at him closely, I can see clearly that he is not human. His skin is mottled purple and raised in unusual bumps and dips. Where the lumps protrude, a gentle lavender glow is pulsing, yet rather than be repulsed, I find the soft glow almost hypnotic. His ears are finely pointed at the ends, much more so than Aalto's, which means he must be one of the older generations of fae, if I'm remembering my very limited understanding of fae lore correctly.

The lavender glow of his skin helps to calm me, and my heart rate slowly starts to return to normal. Despite my pain, I find myself pleasantly relaxed.

"Here," the fae says simply, handing me a small round jar that he procures from his cloak. "It soothes wounds."

I open it and watch as he gets out another, similar shaped jar and begins rubbing the colourless ointment onto the horse's flanks. Without thinking, I move to the horse's other side and begin gently smoothing the ointment in my jar onto the animal's skin. Perhaps I should be continuing my journey, rushing to save Aalto, but I can't force myself to leave when my help is so clearly needed here.

The fae raises an eyebrow in surprise, but doesn't say anything, and for some moments we tend to the horse in companiable silence. Every now and then, the horse lets out a whoosh of heavy breath, and the fae wipes away the spittle at the corners of its mouth before continuing. The horse closes its large, rounded brown eyes, relaxing under our administrations, flicking its tail occasionally.

"I thought you would have applied the ointment to your own wounds before tending to my horse," the fae eventually comments, shaking me out of the peaceful reverie.

"Oh." I look at the ointment in surprise. I hadn't even considered that it was for my use. "Your horse seems a lot worse off than me," I explain, before returning to my task. The animal has a particularly nasty red welt on its foreleg that I'm trying to be extra careful around. "Did he get attacked by those creatures too?" I ask, breathing in the sweet, fruity scent that doesn't quite match the colourless form of the ointment.

"Something like that," the fae replies, choosing neither to confirm nor deny my theory.

I don't know if it is the fae's company, not being chased by rabid creatures, or something about the repetitiveness of tending to the horse whilst breathing in the rich aroma of the cream, but rather than become annoyed at his lack of response, I just mentally brush it away and continue rubbing the ointment in.

The fae eventually proffers some information without being prompted. "His name is Jumpfer, and mine is Zaidan. I care not much for names, but I know humans find it hard to interact without them." His eyes meet mine. "It's been a long time since I have conversed with one; you must forgive me if I forget the relevant customs." He places a hand over mine, stopping me from reaching back into the jar. "I can only harvest so much of that cream. Jumpfer will be as well as can be now, please attend to your own wounds."

I find myself obediently following his suggestion, unable to hold back the slight moan of relief as I rub the first dollop of cream gently onto one of my injuries. I'd been afraid it would sting, but it feels like putting a cool compress onto a burn. I can feel it enter my skin and sink deep into my muscles, pulling out the pain within them and un-tensing the tightened ligaments.

I hurriedly sit down, rolling up my trouser legs and shirtsleeves to ensure that I reach all the bite wounds. I especially pay attention to my neck, which the creatures had a particularly sadistic affinity for.

"Thank you," I finally say when I've finished coating my wounds with the cream.

I screw the cap firmly back on and go to hand it back to him.

Zaidan shakes his head, curling my fingers up and around the jar so that I'm tightly grasping it. "Please, keep it. Jumpfer would have wanted you to have it." He smiles. "You made his last moments pleasant."

There is something so welcoming and unthreatening about Zaidan, that I can't help myself from smiling back, mirroring him unconsciously.

Until my brain catches up with his words.

CHAPTER TWENTY

I hurry to Jumpfer and reach out a hesitant hand, placing it softly on his flank. My eyes dart back and forth from my hand to his body, my brain not willing to rationalise what my eyes are seeing.

Jumpfer's tawny chest has stopped moving up and down, and his once heavy snorts are no longer puffing from his mouth.

He is no longer moving at all.

I jump when I feel a heavy, warm hand on my shoulder as Zaidan guides me gently away. I stumble to my feet clumsily, turning to look at him.

"He is gone, but we took away his pain at the end. We did the best we could for him," Zaidan explains kindly.

I don't understand why I'm more distraught than him; I've been with the horse for no more than an hour, and Jumpfer must have been a long-term companion to the fae if the relaxed way he had around him is anything to go by.

Perhaps the fae knew all along that the horse was due his time?

"Does... does that mean?" I stutter, a terrifying thought blossoming in my mind like an ink stain spreading across thin paper.

"No. He died of other causes. The creatures that attacked you, whilst dangerous, have not poisoned you. Of course, you may feel weakened from blood loss, but that is all," he reassures me, looking up at the sky with a contemplative expression. "Although, this does leave me in rather a predicament."

I watch quietly, confused, as Zaidan presses a finger to one of the lumps on his forehead, waiting for it to pulsate before pulling his finger away. A fine lavender mist forms, which he trails through the air with a gentle flick, directing it down the horse's body.

Jumpfer begins to glow the same soft lavender colour, the light gradually brightening in intensity until I have to look away, holding my hands in front of my eyes to protect myself from the glare. When it eventually dies down, I'm shocked to find that the horse has completely disappeared.

"He is resting now." Zaidan pre-empts my question.

Though his answer is lacking, I can see from the stern glint that has entered his eyes that it would be too much for me to expect any more than what he has already given.

I swallow, remembering that despite all his help so far, he *is* fae, and if appearances are anything to go by, he's a particularly old one. *Not someone I should anger or mess with.*

"W-wait!" I stutter, as Zaidan begins walking off without a word of goodbye.

Not knowing what else to do – I'm still just as lost as before, and the desert still appears just as endless – I break into a steady jog to keep pace with him.

Despite his hunched appearance and small stature, Zaidan moves fast. I fear if I take my eyes off him for even a second, he'll disappear, and its only now that I'm no longer alone that I realise how badly I don't want to be.

"What should I do next? Where do I go? Do you know where I can find water?" I pepper him with questions, scared of missing anything before he leaves whilst remaining hopeful that he'll stay.

"I cannot answer your questions," Zaidan says simply, not turning around, seeming to pick up even more speed.

"Please, don't leave me." I stop jogging, my throat tight as I choke back the tears leaking from my eyes, like clouds dripping before the onslaught of a sudden downpour.

Zaidan stops too.

For what feels like a long time, but is probably no more than a minute, we simply stand there, Zaidan staring straight ahead, not moving; me standing behind him, staring at his back, silently, desperately willing him to stay.

Eventually, he turns back and looks me up and down.

"Will you help me?" he asks.

"What?"

"Will you help me?" he asks again.

I start to utter a desperate yes, but he holds up a hand, stopping me before I've even begun.

"I don't want a human 'yes'," he warns. "I want to know that you will help me."

He punctuates each word firmly and I gulp, horrified that, once again, I've allowed my emotions to override my cautiousness. I'm surprised he stopped me and didn't just let me agree to something without thinking it through.

"I want to know that you will continue to help me, even when it gets hard," he continues, pointing to a pile of wood on the sand next to him, which I should have noticed straight away, but I swear only appeared the instance he pointed to it.

Almost as if its very existence was dependent on the fae recognising it into being.

I close my eyes: my go-to for grounding myself. Yes, I'm

154

nervous that Zaidan will disappear when I reopen them, but I need to focus my thoughts before I answer him. The swirling repetitiveness of the sand is distracting me, sending my heart into a fluttery panic, leaving me feeling inexplicably claustrophobic despite the open space.

I think of Aalto, wondering if I even have time to help Zaidan. But I've never been one to shy away from hard work, and seeing as the trial's instructions didn't give me a set deadline to rescue to him, I can only hope that I'm making the right decision. Zaidan might be my best chance at finding a way across the desert, and if I have to help him in the meantime, so be it.

"Yes," I state upon opening my eyes, pleased that he hasn't disappeared whilst waiting for my response.

Zaidan merely studies me for a brief heartbeat more, then nods. He touches one of his lumps, this time on his chest, and points towards me.

"So be it," he says, flicking the lavender mist at me.

It snakes towards me at a speed that is too fast for my eyes to follow and latches itself around my wrist, tying itself into a bracelet before seemingly sinking into my skin. It isn't unpleasant, just a shock; I can still feel it, despite it no longer being visible, though I can see no obvious mark.

"How can I help?" I choose to ask, instead of the numerous questions that are threatening to overwhelm me.

Perhaps I should have asked this before agreeing to help him, but I was reluctant to say anything that might risk angering him and sending him away.

"We need to carry these across the desert." Zaidan bends down to the eight planks of wood beside him. He slings two under each of his arms, and I kneel to do the same.

With the planks under my arms and my backpack firmly on, I feel my back complain as I straighten back up again, but I say nothing as I focus on putting one foot in front of the other and following Zaidan onwards.

I desperately want to ask how far we need to carry them, but I'm getting the sense that fae don't do well with conversation, and I'm keen to keep him happy. He might be my only chance at survival and not getting hopelessly lost.

As we are walking, I try to keep myself motivated by ticking off in my mind all that I've achieved so far. My father always told me that if the road ahead looks difficult, then look behind you to see what you've already accomplished and that will make the journey ahead seem easier. I don't know if this is true, but it at least helps distract my mind from worrying about the challenges ahead.

Perhaps the petal creatures were the challenge? But in that case... surely I'd have reached the end by now? I've seen no sight of Aalto yet.

There is a part of me that worries he is in serious danger; if I think too much about the fact he volunteered as my fae partner, I start to feel strangely guilty, knowing that if I don't do well, he'll suffer too.

This isn't just about my life anymore.

Still, guilt won't help me now, so I begin listing achievements in my mind again. *I was chosen as a contender, so they must see something special in me. I survived the trial of gluttony; I escaped that hellish water room and I didn't let anger overwhelm me in the test of wrath. My family are safe at home.*

I stop. I've been so focused on being trapped in this fae world that I haven't even considered how my family are coping without me. Ashamed, I swallow my guilt. *It's not my fault I was taken. I just have to hope the neighbours are helping them out.* I'm sure my father is perfectly capable of managing without me and prioritising the less hardy crops. It's not like we have a massive farm, we just grow a few different vegetables and fruits that we can sell on at market or eat ourselves. If they are sensible and ration, their food supplies shouldn't take too big a hit, and if worst comes to worse and I'm stuck here for a while, my father can always send out Taz to work on non-market days.

Taz may only be fourteen, but she has a sharp mind and could easily be trusted to go foraging for wild berries and mushrooms to help keep their bellies full. She wouldn't be happy skipping school though, not like me; I always took every teacher's turned back as an excuse to sneak out the door.

Maybe this whole façade is an elaborate punishment by fate for not paying attention in class?

"Ow!"

I drop all the wooden planks as I bump into Zaidan, one falling onto my foot and stubbing my toe. Lost in my thoughts, I hadn't noticed he'd stopped.

"This is where our time together ends." Zaidan turns to me, placing his planks of wood on the floor.

He brushes me down and gives me a smile that lights up his face. I realise he hasn't properly smiled at me until now.

"No! You can't go!" I exclaim, suddenly overwhelmed with panic.

"But we are here," he replies, gesturing directly ahead.

Looking beyond his still form, I realise we've reached the edge of the desert, the land sloping down gently before me. I can even see a thick blue ribbon of water and I squeal in delight, clapping my hands together.

Spontaneously, I grab the fae before me, pulling Zaidan into a tight hug.

I feel his muscles tense up under my hands, and for a brief second, I panic that I've perhaps made the biggest mistake of my life so far, before I feel him relax and reluctantly hug me back.

Well, if tapping me on the back awkwardly counts as a hug, that is.

I pull away from him, giving him an equally radiant grin of my own.

"You don't know how much I've been yearning for water," I say breathlessly. "Is it safe to drink?"

Zaidan nods. "I presume you collected the water bottles at the top of the hill before you entered the desert? You can top those back up if you have finished them already. Though I'd recommend some restraint and pacing going forward."

I shake my head and take a deep breath, frustrated. *Of course there were full water bottles at the top of that stupid hill.*

"I... I didn't climb that hill," I reluctantly admit, ashamed. "I was in too much of a hurry."

Zaidan blinks, surprised. "It is not good to neglect opportunities for the sake of rushing," he admonishes me. "Surely that is every traveller's first lesson?" He wags a finger sternly, like a concerned and protective father.

"Why was the signpost marked 'Sight' if the hill wasn't simply a vantage point?" I mutter, ignoring his question.

I can't take my eyes off the strip of water, suddenly reminded of how dry my mouth is. My very pores feel tight, my skin pulled taut across my face.

"Because if your eyes dry out too much, you can't see. You need water for sight," Zaidan explains, in such a way that I can tell he isn't making fun of me, though I can't help feeling frustrated by the sheer ridiculousness of it all.

I bite my tongue, trying not to issue a sharp retort. *It's not his fault I chose to take the other path*. I return my gaze to the water. The desire to run straight down the small slope to the river is difficult to resist. I can even hear the slosh of the spray tumbling over the rocks at the bottom.

"Do you have to leave? Can't you travel along with me? Are you not thirsty too?" I stumble for reasons to persuade him to stay.

Zaidan merely shakes his head. "My path with you ends here. Look for the door that will take you where you need to go. I thank you for your time and companionship, human." He bows his head at me solemnly. "And for not taking the easy option," he adds with a smile, a slight twinkle in his eyes as he looks from me to the planks and back again, seeming to hint at something which, in my dehydrated state, I can make neither head nor tail of.

"Thank you for your company, and for rescuing me," I say respectfully, without a hint of the sarcasm I usually reserve for conversations with the fae. I nudge one of the planks that is resting on the ground with my toe. "What should I do with these?" I ask, realising I never thought to question why Zaidan needed to carry them across the desert.

When he doesn't respond, I repeat my question, but the silence reigns.

I look up, curious as to why he's ignoring me, only to find that he's gone. All that remains is a fine, hazy lavender mist. I cautiously reach out, and it shifts around my hand briefly. I feel a snap, the bond around my wrist flickering into being once more, before re-joining the rest of the mist in front of me.

No sooner has it parted from me than the mist evaporates. It's as if Zaidan was never here at all.

CHAPTER TWENTY-ONE

Blinking back to reality, I consider what to do next. It seems strange for Zaidan to have asked me to drag these planks all the way here for no reason, and I wonder whether I should take one with me. Then again, it could just have been part of some ambiguous fae task. What had Zaidan said? 'Thank you for not taking the easy option'. Maybe I'm supposed to take the planks with me, to help rescue Aalto? Or to prove that I'm willing to do this task the hard way?

Resigned to my fate, I turn to pick them up, when I notice the fine lavender mist has returned, drifting around the planks. I carefully reach out a hand through the fine haze to touch one, associating the magic with Zaidan, but still reluctant to trust anything magical. But as soon as I make contact, the plank disappears, and I stumble clumsily to my knees.

Confused, I barely have time to think before a greater worry takes over, the lavender mist hovering around me in a glistening cloud. I can't help but feel apprehensive, especially when some of it concentrates into a point and dips beneath my skin. I lift my arms, intently studying myself, but feeling and seeing no difference.

Weird.

Hoping that the mist is just Zaidan trying to look out for me in his own strange, fae way, I decide to head down to the river and search for the door he mentioned.

As soon as I reach the water I immediately stumble to the ground, taking deep gulps of clear, cool liquid. The sensation is heavenly, deliciously easing my parched throat.

Unable to hold myself back, I walk into the lazy current, washing off the sand and grime of the last however many hours. It feels so good to be clean again.

With nothing to collect the water in, I drink again, knowing I might not have the opportunity later, before making my way along the riverside, intent on finding the door.

I'm focusing so hard, I almost walk straight past it.

If not for the light shining upon it, creating a myriad of rainbow streaks, I wouldn't have noticed it at all: a door made entirely of water, protruding from the edge of the river.

It's the same height as me, with strange symbols glittering on its surface in what looks like sparkling gold ink. I blink, but when I try to focus on one of the runes, it flickers and moves, scattering the rest in a dizzying dance, like dropping oil into water.

Reaching out to touch the shimmering surface, I'm mesmerised once again as the runes scatter away from my prying fingers. When I place a hand against it gently, I'm surprised to find it feels firm beneath my palm.

I look down at the doorknob, crafted expertly from some kind of jade. It's shaped to resemble a creature's head, though not one that I've ever come across before, with small green tufty ears, a rounded, tiny jawline – which I hope indicates that it has small teeth – and curly tufts of fur. Its eyes take up most of the creature's face: dark and soulful. I remain fixated on its stare for a moment, before shaking myself out of its magical grasp, covering the doorknob with my hand to suppress its hypnotic effect.

The handle feels pleasantly warm, and with no more than a gentle push, the door silently slowly slides open.

Taking a deep breath, I step inside.

The space is dimly lit, and I stand still for a few moments, my hand placed firmly on the now-closed door at my back so as not to lose my way, as I give my eyes time to adapt to the dark. It's like waking up in the middle of the night and trying to work out where everything is around you, except this time, it isn't my quiet attic bedroom at home, with the steep, sloping ceilings that I'm forever knocking my head into, but somewhere entirely new.

Even when my eyes have adjusted as much as is possible, I can barely make out what is in front of me. I'm not in a room, but rather a long, cavernous tunnel that stretches out further than I can make out. Taking a few wary steps with one hand still on the door, I trail my hand around until the surface changes.

"Stone?" I murmur, trying to work out where I am.

The walls underneath my hands are no longer smooth; instead, jagged rock greets my probing fingers. *Some kind of cave?* I brush my feet experimentally along the ground, pleasantly surprised by the flat, seemingly dry surface they encounter.

I reach down cautiously and roll a piece of debris between my fingers, feeling it disintegrate into small particles. It feels more like dirt than rock.

"I wish I could see," I grumble, annoyed by my limitations, wondering if fae can see in the dark.

As the words leave my lips, light begins to flicker; not from lamps or wall fixtures, but from strange spheres suspended in the air, all scattered around the tunnel at varying heights.

I gingerly let go of the door and put one hesitant foot in front of the other, creeping towards the closest flickering light.

I'm about an arm's width away from it when my immediate surroundings suddenly come into sharp focus, and I promptly fall backwards in a desperate, flurried attempt to retreat.

A creature clings to a branch, protruding from the cave's wall. Its long arms end in sharp, tiny claws that help it cling on, along with its long tail, wrapped around another branch slightly higher up. Its green fur is softly tousled and pulsates with light, along with its blinking, sphere-like eyes.

The lights aren't lights... but many, many blinking eyes.

I stand staring at the creature for what feels like an eternity, but truly is only a couple of heartbeats. I'm reluctant to break eye contact, scared a sudden movement will have it leaping across from the branch straight onto me.

After the petal creatures in the desert, I'm distrustful of anything I don't immediately recognise.

"What are you?" I whisper.

I gulp when a little pink tongue darts out of the creature's mouth as it attempts what can only be considered a smile.

"We are the Mirrors."

Its voice is so breathy it takes me a moment to convince myself that I actually heard it speak.

"The... the Mirrors?" I stutter, when the creature doesn't deign to say more, blinking slowly at me.

"Care for me to demonstrate?" it offers, edging slowly forward along its branch.

Its manner *seems* gentle, but I'd rather not take any chances.

"Um, no, I'm okay, thank you." I hold up my palms placatingly, leaning back on my heels, ready to run if it gives any indication of attack.

Not that there's anywhere I can run *to*. I don't even know if the door will open again if I try it, and besides, if this is the way towards Aalto, the only option is forwards.

I'm desperate for this trial to end. It feels like I've been trekking through this strange landscape forever, and it's impossible to tell how much time has actually passed. I usually rely on my stomach as an indicator, but with the stress of the attack and the dehydration of the desert, I haven't been craving food at all.

"When one sees oneself reflected, one may decipher what one is lacking," the creature whispers in its strange lulling tone. "But of course, there is always free will." It releases its tail from the branch, pointing further into the cave. "You may continue along this path..."

As it speaks, tiny circular lights flicker to life, forming a lined pathway along the tunnel. At the end, a white door glows enticingly.

"... to the door beyond which your final goal lies. But if you continue, you will never know if there was something here that you will be lacking once you get there."

As it wraps its tail back around the branch, I flinch; a second and third creature have joined the first, slowly clawing their way onto adjacent branches. One tilts its head at me questioningly; the other more interested in licking its paws and wiping its tufty ears than studying me. With a sharp pang, I'm reminded viscerally of my cat May, back home.

"Why do you magical creatures always have to speak in riddles?" I huff.

I suppose they've been placed here for a reason, but if I'm as close to Aalto as they say, I'm reluctant to waste any more time, both for his sake and my sanity.

"Why do you humans demand that everyone speaks in a way that suits you?" one of the other creatures retorts, scraping a claw along the branch it is clinging to.

"Do you not think that is rather egotistical of you?" another hisses, flicking its ears irritably.

"Sorry, I didn't mean it like that," I quickly stutter, terrified of insulting them and dealing with whatever repercussions they might shoot my way in retaliation. "I just don't know how to answer you when I don't understand what you're asking of me." I bite my bottom lip, worrying it between my teeth, frustrated but trying my best not to show it.

"How about we demonstrate?" The creature who originally started our conversation holds out a claw to me enticingly. "Come, hold my claw and look into my eyes," it lures me in with a soft whisper.

I can feel my feet dragging me towards the creature, like I've been hypnotised.

"I-I'm not sure," I breathe, but find myself reaching out a hand towards the Mirror's outstretched claw anyway.

I take a deep breath in, noting an unexpected scent as I draw closer. *Why does it smell of rosemary?*

The thought comes too late, for my hand has already reached out for the creature's claw, and with a slow, single blink of its moon-like spheres, the cave fades to black.

CHAPTER TWENTY-TWO

My sense of smell awakens first, the familiar essence of rosemary, so unexpected in the cave of strange creatures, kicking my body into action.

My eyesight returns next.

I lurch back instantly.

"How?" I gasp, a thought that echoes multiple times a day now that I've entered the fae world.

But that's just it – I'm no longer in the fae world.

I'm in my kitchen.

Except... it can't be my kitchen. Not my *real* kitchen. If it was, my mother wouldn't be standing with her back to me, her long red hair tied in a messy plait; her favourite yellow dress drowning her fragile body, the fabric covered in splotches and stains but so beloved that my father would never even consider throwing it away, despite his jovial teasing.

"Mother?" I whisper, my heart in my throat; the pounding beat in my ears drowning out any other sound as I struggle to understand what is so clearly in front of me and yet is equally impossible.

My mother carries on kneading the bread on the table in front of her, studded with sprigs of rosemary. It is a smell and sight so achingly familiar that my eyes well with joyful tears and painful yearning.

"Mother?" I say a bit louder, not sure if she heard me the

first time.

Normally I'd rush to her and envelop her in a firm hug, easily sweeping her off her feet and spinning her around in circles, ignoring her giggling protests of 'put me down, silly!'.

But something is holding me back.

The last time I saw my mother alive, she'd been lying in bed, patchwork quilts piled high around her bony, frail body, listening to me read. A beautiful smile had been stretching her face, tinged with the pain she always tried so desperately to hide from me.

Hours later, she was gone.

I take a deep, shaky breath and edge towards the figure that my eyes tell me is my mother, but my heart tells me is not. When I get within touching distance, I reach out a trembling hand and gently touch her back.

I flinch back in shock, retracting my hand to cup against my chest. The figure's body is warm!

In a transfixed horror, I watch as it slowly turns around to face me.

Two cerulean blue eyes blink at me: round, kind, and full of warmth. My mother wipes her flour covered hands on her pinafore, tied haphazardly around her waist, before extending them in a wide-open gesture.

I can't stifle the sob that spurts from my mouth as I half stumble, half trip over my own feet in my hurry to reach her embrace, falling into the warmest hug I can ever remember receiving. The smell of rosemary and yeast tickles my nose as I bury my face in my mother's shoulder.

"There, there, love. No need to cry." My mother tilts up my face, looking into my eyes lovingly before wiping away the tears that are streaming down my cheeks. "Ah, I've made flour rivers down your face! Come here!" My mother laughs, pulling me across to the kitchen sink.

I can only follow in a sort of dazed wonder as I allow her to wet a soft yellow flannel and gently wipe away at my face. When she's finished, I immediately bury my face into her shoulder again.

"How?" I whisper, my voice muffled by my mother's dress.

"How what? Come, let's sit down, it looks like you've had quite a day," my mother says as, with her hands on my shoulders, she firmly leads me into the adjoining sitting room.

The furniture is simple and rustic – a small three-seater faded blue sofa, with a threadbare quilt draped over it to hide the holes; a large sunken grey armchair that my father tends to occupy; two bookcases crammed with books, piled haphazardly on top of one another, and a low, oblong table with a brown jug of daisies placed just off centre – but it's always been one of my favourite rooms in the house.

My mother leads me over to the sofa, and I instinctively curl up, pulling a pillow tight to my stomach, my muscles remembering the familiar position. Leaving the room briefly, she soon returns with two cups of steaming mint tea, placing them on the table and joining me on the sofa.

I take a sip, closing my eyes in bliss, before I can even process that my mother has handed one of the mugs to me. It's like my eyes can't keep up with my brain, my mind too full of questions shouting over one another to allow me to focus on anything.

"Now, tell me what's wrong?" My mother returns my cup of tea to the table, before taking my hands between her own, rubbing calloused thumbs across the back of my palms soothingly.

"I-I," I stutter, not sure where to begin. "I shouldn't be here."

"Of course you should – this is your home! That will never change, Rosalind," my mother insists, gripping my hands tightly as if she can convince me of the words by squeezing them into my skin.

"No, I mean... I was in the fae world just a few seconds ago. I-I'm in the trials. It's... it's hard. I'm so scared." Another sob sticks in my throat, all the emotions of the past few days catching up with me.

I've been bottling up all my fears and worries in order to keep going, but being here in the comfort of my own home, with my mother in front of me, I no longer have the willpower to be strong. My walls have finally broken down in one crumbling mess.

"Oh, chicken, it's okay. It's okay," she reassures me, looking concerned.

My childhood nickname prompts a deluge of tears, my messy, heaving sobs almost choking me; loud cries punctuated by gasping breaths as my mother wipes at my eyes and nose. She rocks me in her arms, rubbing soothing circles over my back, but rather than helping, this seems to fuel the tears more. Now that my body feels like it has a safe place to break down, it appears to be doing just that, tearing me apart one seam at a time.

"You're stronger than you give yourself credit for, kinder than anyone I know, and full of more resilience than a determined wasp."

She strokes my hair, holding me until my sobs calm. Not once does she tell me to stop crying, and for that, I'm grateful. This release has been a long time coming.

"I-I d-don't want to d-do this a-anymore, I-I j-just want to c-come back h-home." I'm aware I sound like a sulky toddler, but I'm driven by a primal need to feel my mother's love and reassurance in this moment of pain.

As she pulls back to look at me, I try to ignore the sickening lurching feeling that something is incredibly wrong with this situation.

"I know, chicken, but you're here on borrowed time," she whispers, as if she doesn't want to be heard even though no one else is here.

I lean in, desperate not to miss a single word. "I don't want you to go," I choke out, feeling my heart clench in pain. "Not again."

"You know I'm not truly here, chicken," my mother says, and I blink, surprised to hear my thoughts confirmed.

"Please, please don't leave me again," I cry, clinging tightly to her arms and squeezing my eyes shut. If I can't see her, the image will stay; my mother will stay.

But what if I close my eyes and my mother disappears? What if I never see her again? My eyelids shoot open. I can't miss a single moment of this second chance.

"I'm already dead, my love," my mother breathes, her smile suddenly tainted with a slight smirk.

I blink, confused, and it disappears, making me wonder if it was ever there at all.

"You know it was for the best," she continues, her sombre expression transforming into a horrific grin.

What?

I pull back, still holding my mother's arms but shocked by the words leaving her mouth.

"What... what do you mean?" I whisper, terrified of hearing

my worst fears voiced aloud. To hear her speak the words would breathe life into them; make them real. I don't know if I can bear it.

My mother laughs remorsefully. "I was in so much pain, it wasn't fair. I was so tired of living." She shakes her head, ignoring my look of absolute horror.

"No," I exhale, letting go of my mother's arms and grabbing the pillow once more. I hold it tightly to my chest, a shield against my mother's words; a bandage for the pain they are inflicting upon my heart. "No," I repeat, more firmly this time. "You never would've left us willingly. You said you were happy, hearing about our lives; seeing us continue..." My words trail off as doubts begin to paint black streaks across my colourful memories.

"Happy? How could I have ever been happy confined to that bed?" my mother snarls viciously, prodding a finger in my direction. "I laid there in pain *every day*, watching you and your father and sister swan around, living your lives while mine was over."

"You *loved* us," is all that I'm able to force out.

It feels like someone has grasped my throat, effectively cutting off my breathing and my ability to speak. I begin to hyperventilate, sobs threatening to drown me once more in salty waves.

"You're right." My mother gives a bitter laugh. "I did once love you. But that quickly died when you stopped caring."

My eyes are wide. Without realising it, I'm shaking my head back and forth. "I never stopped caring, how can you say that? I read to you every day! I brought you your favourite foods; went searching for your favourite flowers to cheer you up; sacrificed my own hunger to keep you from wasting away!"

"Ha!" my mother barks. "Such pity! How do you think that made me feel? That you were able to go outside, whilst I was stuck indoors, staring at the dead plants you brought back in; watching them wilt and die as my body did the same alongside them? And food! Food that I could no longer taste, that mocked me with memories of a joy that I could no longer experience! I used to scrape it into the bin as soon as you left the room."

My mother's words are worse than any slap, and I'm left reeling. "You... you never said anything."

"You... you never said," my mother mimics cruelly. "You never asked! You just presumed! It's always been about you! It always was! You and your disgusting father and useless sister!" My mother is visually shaking in her anger as she spurts forth vicious, poisonous words one after another.

It is too much. I can't take it. All my worst fears coming into being.

"It would have been better if *you* had been the one to take ill and die. Not me. Your father would have been happier that way."

Her words slice through my heart, eviscerating me. I can hardly breathe, clutching my pillow and rocking back and forth, silent tears cascading down my face as I listen to my mother tear me apart.

My mother.

Who is dead.

Who can't possibly be standing in front of me.

"This isn't you," I whisper, closing my eyes tightly, trying to push away the familiar sights and scents that are trying to trick my brain into thinking otherwise.

This is a fae trick. It has to be.

I focus on what I know to be true: my mother is dead; I'm in the midst of a trial; I'm supposed to be rescuing Aalto.

Hells, Aalto. How had I forgotten about him? I can't let him die too, not after everything he's done to help me so far.

I have to pass this test.

As I come back to myself, my distress transforming into resolved determination, I realise the vision of my mother hasn't spoken in some time.

I open my eyes hesitantly.

She is staring at me, but her gaze is unfocused, almost as if she is looking over my shoulder rather than directly at me. As I inspect her carefully, I realise her figure is shimmering at the edges, a strange flickering skating up and down the outline of her body.

Suddenly, her focus returns, and her eyes bore into mine.

"Of course it is! You just don't want to face up to the truth! I've waited so long to say this to you!" My mother runs a finger down my face, causing me to shiver.

I'm torn between the desire to flinch from her words and seek comfort from her familiar form. Instead, I shake my head.

"This isn't you. The mother I remember was selfless to a fault. She adored us all: Father, Taz and me. She encouraged my love of reading; relished the time we would sit and read together. She would *never* have resented me for living. She was proud of me for keeping going, even when all I wanted to do was curl up in bed alongside her. I kept going because *she* made me strong enough to do so. Not you. You. Are. Not. My. Mother!"

Every muscle in my body tenses as I pronounce the words, yelling them out – words laced with pain, loneliness, and a yearning for what once was.

My breath is coming in quick gasps, my chest straining, but I'm resolute in my beliefs, my resolve further solidified when I notice the effect my words are having on the figure. With each firm statement, the figure flickers a bit more, whole fragments disappearing, taking on an almost haze-like quality, showing glimpses of the room behind her.

I leap to my feet, slinging the cushion to the sofa and running from the room.

"Where do you think you're going? Stop! I haven't finished with you!" the figure screams.

My heart pounds frantically, my ears ringing with white noise as I sprint to the stairs – for one moment, I could have sworn it wasn't my mother's voice coming from the figure, the tone strange; high-pitched; almost demonic.

I don't dare look back as I run for the stairs, taking them two at a time and using the banister to propel myself up the threadbare carpeted steps. I can hear the figure stumble along with clunking steps after me, but the more I remind myself that she isn't real, the more power seems to leak from the creature's grasp.

Finally reaching my destination, I swing open the door, locking it firmly behind me.

It is exactly as I remember.

Just as I left it.

The windows are open; the lopsided, bright yellow curtains that I sewed myself swing softly in the gentle breeze. There is a small table littered with a tower of paperback books, and a cold glass of apple-green drink, dripping a gentle puddle onto the table's surface.

But I don't have eyes for any of these things, my gaze drawn to the figure lying on the bed.

A sudden bang against the bedroom door shocks me back into motion and I afford it a quick glance, checking that the door is still locked, before straightening my back and hurrying to the bed.

The quilt is tucked up tight, just the way my mother liked it.

My mother, who is lying peacefully asleep in the bed.

My mother, whom I know has passed. Who passed with a gentle smile on her lips.

I let out a gentle breath that I hadn't known I'd been holding and stroke a shaking hand over my mother's forehead.

A breeze through the window flickers over the bedcovers, ruffling them gently, and I swear I hear my mother's voice in the air.

"I love you. I always will. Now and forever, chicken."

It's her true voice.

I close my eyes, smiling, a tear trickling down my cheek. "I love you too," I whisper, my hand finding my mother's and gripping it tightly. Although it's cold to the touch, I feel buoyed up and energised, ready to take on whatever is coming next.

I stay like this for a few heartbeats, expecting the door to slam open.

When it doesn't, I reluctantly open my eyes.

"Argh!" I scream, falling onto my bum and shuffling frantically backwards.

I'm face to face with one of the Mirrors, its large eyes looming barely a hand's distance away from me.

"You passed!" it squeaks, before erupting into a cloud of smoke, leaving only two of the creatures on the branches, blinking at me solemnly.

Looks like I'm back in the fae world.

CHAPTER TWENTY-THREE

I leap to my feet, angrily addressing the two remaining Mirrors. "What in the Hells was that trauma you just put me through?"

For their part, they don't look fussed in the least; one is still calmly grooming, and the other is carefully making its way down to the central branch that the other had been sitting on before it disappeared.

"What kind of test *was* that? How *dare* you besmirch my mother's memory!"

I'm fuming, my pulse ringing in my ears, and for once I don't take calming breaths to try and recentre myself. Instead, I allow my rage to take over, the red mist filming over my vision, my heart galloping in my chest as I rant at the creatures.

The Mirrors merely blink at me, not bothered by my change in temperament or volume.

"Are you ready for the second vision?" one of them asks.

"Weren't you listening to what I just said?" I all but scream, covering my eyes with my hands as I struggle to cope with the situation.

I rub my hands against my eyelids, wishing more than anything that I no longer had to take part in these stupid trials; that I'd never been dragged across to the fae world in the first place.

Seeing my mother alive, albeit in a possessed form, and then reliving her death, has left me feeling desolate. Losing a loved one is not something you ever get over, and what people say about the pain lessening over time is a lie. It never lessens – you just get better at suppressing it; at putting more and more bandages over the aching wound.

But this experience has ripped off all my carefully applied plasters in one awful, vicious rip.

My nails press sharp crescent moons into my skin, the physical pain focusing my mind; momentarily taking me away from my mental anguish.

The Mirrors don't answer. They sit patiently on their branches, awaiting my reply to their question.

I'm hit with a sudden wave of exhaustion, leaving me feeling empty. I don't know whether I'm supposed to do as they say, or follow the path to the door. *Is Aalto even behind that door? Or is that just another trick?* I'm so tired of thinking. I want to feel nothing; I don't want to deal with my messy, heated emotions anymore.

Somehow, I doubt I'll get a reprieve.

"Will it be the same as... as what I just went through?"

The Mirrors, again, don't answer.

I sigh. "I need to get to the end of this challenge. Aalto is waiting for me. I don't know what state he's in. Should I keep going or let you show me another vision?"

"When one sees oneself reflected, one may decipher what one is lacking. But of course, there is always free will. You may continue along this path to the door beyond which your final goal lies. But if you continue, you will never know if there was something here that you will be lacking once you get there." The Mirror's eyes blink as it speaks in its soft, trance-like voice.

I roll my eyes. *That's exactly what you said last time,* I think bitterly, tilting my head to look at the rock above me, as if someone will open the ceiling of the cave and answer all my questions.

I sigh, rubbing my tired eyes once more. Ignoring the Mirrors and walking to the end of the tunnel seems like the easier option. But based on what I've experienced so far, nothing is ever that straightforward.

"Fine. I might as well keep playing your twisted game."

"Very well."

The Mirror on the middle branch begins waving its tail back and forth like a metronome. It glows a soft rose pink, and as much as I try to focus my eyes on the creature, I find my vision drawn repeatedly back to the tail that flicks back and forth, back and forth... back and forth...

CHAPTER TWENTY-FOUR

I'm rocking from one foot to the other, feeling my body sway with the movement. I blink, my vision refocusing as I realise all too late that I'm in another vision created by the Mirrors.

"Isabel?" I gulp, my eyes meeting those of the girl whose embrace I'm in.

Two sparking green eyes glint at me, her lips twisted in that sideways smirk that I had once adored.

"The one and only! You've only been dancing with me for the last twenty minutes, how much punch have you had?" Isabel giggles, a surprisingly deep, throaty laugh that sends shivers up my spine. "Should I be offended that you aren't paying attention to me?" Isabel pouts, her hands tightly gripping my waist.

I can smell the familiar rose scent of her perfume, and I can't resist running my fingers through the long blonde hair that falls in waves across her back.

She's exactly the same as I remember. Yet, as far as I know, Isabel *is* back at home, alive. So why have the Mirrors brought me here?

"Are we at the Harvest Festival barn dance?" I ask, blushing, struggling to think of something to say.

I realise I can easily confirm my surroundings if I just look around, but I can't bear to take my eyes off her. I know she isn't real, but it's been a long time since I've seen her look at me with such love in her eyes.

Isabel laughs again, spinning me without warning before swinging me back into her body, bringing us closer together than before.

"I better check what Jack's put in that punch, you're even more doo-lally than usual! Still..." She runs a soft finger across my lips, making me part them open. "... I'd rather hold off for a couple more minutes and keep you all to myself."

She giggles as she leans in close, and I flush.

"Don't go shy on me now," she whispers, as she softly presses her lips against my own.

I close my eyes, welcoming her sweet, gentle kiss. When I don't break the contact, I feel Isabel's mouth stretch up into a smile before she hungrily dips her head closer and deepens the kiss, twirling her tongue against my own.

"You normally pull away when there's other people around, my flower." Isabel's eyes twinkle happily, wide with pleasant surprise. "I might have to keep some of Jack's punch for later," she teases, a soft look in her eyes.

I try to focus and work out exactly what I've been sent here for, aware that my mind is becoming increasingly distracted by the beauty in front of me.

The night of the last Harvest Festival dance is a clear memory: I'd danced with Isabel; lost her briefly amidst the revellers after stopping for a drink; bumped into her again; danced some more, then called it a night when she tired. Then, on the way home, Isabel had broken up with me, completely out of the blue. I'd never been able to work out why, eventually putting it down to her fierce independence and refusal to be 'tied down'. Trying to contain Isabel in a relationship was like trying to cup water in your hands. She was always desperate to be free.

"Isabel... you know I love you, right?" It feels important that I tell her this, though the words feel strange in my mouth, like I'm betraying another by speaking them.

I suddenly feel sick to my stomach, my heartache rearing it's head as I remember the long lonely month I spent reluctant to leave my house, using my ailing mother as an excuse, while I struggled to recover from losing my first love.

This isn't real.

I have to remember why I'm here, and not let my emotions consume me. Maybe the purpose of this vision is to suffer the pain of my breakup with Isabel all over again? Though I can't see how that's testing anything. Perhaps the fae who design these challenges just enjoy tormenting us?

Still... as long as I don't have to go through the whole month, I'll cope. It will hurt, but only as bad as poking at a bruise does. My pain over Isabel's rejection is a remembered pain, but I've healed from it.

Besides, they can't keep me here for a whole month if I'm supposed to save Aalto.

Fear jolts through my body as I consider whether I made the right decision by listening to the Mirrors, until Isabel's voice pulls me back into the vision.

"Of course I do." Isabel tugs my plait playfully.

I notice that she doesn't return my declaration. Not that I'm surprised. I'd always felt our romance was a bit one-sided. Yes, Isabel was intense, and proudly demonstrated how much she cared through physical acts of affection, but I had often wondered if her visible displays were simply intended to garner attention, rather than because she truly cared for me.

I swallow down the rising pain in my chest, frustrated that

all these old worries still have the power to overwhelm me.

"Look, there's Jack!" Isabel squeals, waving her hands manically at the boy on the periphery of the dance floor.

Seeing us, Jack grins and begins making his way through the other dancing couples, holding three orange paper cups that he balances precariously between his fingers.

"Quick, take one before I drop them all!" He grimaces as vibrant blue liquid sloshes over the rim of one of the cups and down his white shirt, instantly staining it.

Isabel laughs, grabbing a cup and handing it to me, before reaching for a second one, which she immediately drinks.

"Woah, slow down! I'm not joining the queue again, Izzy!" Jack admonishes as Isabel finishes downing the drink and scrunches up the cup in her hand.

I roll my eyes, lost in the memory as I visualise nursing a worse for wear Isabel at the end of the night. I sip at my drink mindlessly, grimacing at the sharp, unexpected tang.

"Urgh, just how many *jsal* berries did you sneak into this, Jack?" I take another tentative sip; the taste is still just as tart, but is becoming more palatable the more I drink.

Jack grins. "Sorry I didn't have time to expertly blend them in, Your Highness." He bows theatrically. "Teacher was watching, so I just chucked them all in and mushed them with the serving ladle. Some cups may be... ah... more potent than others." His grin is infectious, and I find myself smiling back at him.

It's good to see my friends again.

The muscles in my face ache, but in a good way; it's been a while since I properly smiled without restraint or force.

The pain reminds me that I'm here for a reason. *Aalto. I have to hurry.* The clock is ticking faster with every second I waste trying to work out what I'm meant to be doing.

"Let's get off the dance floor if we're just drinking," I suggest, leading us back off to the side, ignoring Jack's cries of 'but I just got here!' and Isabel's exclamation of 'I've already finished mine!'.

I scan the venue, trying to see past the orange streamers and the carved pumpkins with their flickering candle-flame eyes. Everyone is dressed in deep reds, cheery oranges, and dusky pinks to fit the season, and it's difficult to separate out individuals in the crowd. Looking down at myself, I realise I'm wearing the clothes I was dressed in that night: plain trousers and an obnoxious orange shirt – one of my father's and the only thing I could find in the correct colour scheme. Isabel, on the other hand, looks devastating in her short, fitted red dress; like a spark of flame.

She stops abruptly, causing me to bump into her.

"I'm just going to the bathroom," she tells me, and I run a reassuring hand up her back, looking at her face, concerned. Colour is flushing her cheeks a rosy pink, and she looks strangely nervous.

"Are you feeling alright? Shall I come with you?" I ask, just like I did that night, assuming the alcohol has hit her system all at once.

"No, no, I'm okay," Isabel hurriedly stutters, already breaking apart from us and making her way towards the trees that line the left-hand side of the dancefloor. "I'll be fine. Don't let me ruin the evening. I can look after myself. Back in a sec!"

A particularly raucous group of boys passes us then, all cheering each other on as they chug their drinks, and I quickly lose sight of Isabel in the mass of bodies.

A large hand on my shoulder makes me jump, and I turn

around to find Jack staring at me, a strange expression on his face.

"The bathrooms are that way," he says simply, the eerie, glazed glint to his eyes making me shudder as he points to the right.

His smile doesn't quite fit right on his face, as if his muscles have forgotten how to stretch. I wrack my brain for my own memory of this night. Had he said the same thing? I can't recall.

Message relayed, he immediately starts walking off in the direction Isabel had gone, a strange stiffness to his limbs, as if he is a puppet and a puppeteer is directing his movements with strings.

I stare after him, confused, before his words finally sink in.

Isabel said she was going to the bathroom. *Why did she go the wrong way?* Had the same thing happened in reality? I struggle to pull the truth from my addled mind, and after a moment, the memory surfaces: Isabel walking in the direction of the treeline while I waited for her by the dancefloor. Why hadn't I realised at the time?

My feet begin moving before my mind can catch up, and it isn't long before I find myself staring up at the trees that stand around the square like tall, silent sentinels.

I'm peering through the tree trunks, worried that she might have passed out somewhere, when I hear a throaty chuckle: unmistakably Isabel's. Without thinking it through, I desperately push through the undergrowth, cursing when a particularly thorny tendril snags in my hair.

As the noise of the party dims to a gentle hum, and Isabel's laughter begins to fade, I'm struck by another, all too familiar noise.

One that, prior to our split, I'd only ever expected myself to elicit from Isabel.

But I'm standing here, very much on my own.

I remain motionless for a while, my hands scrunched up tightly as I try to control my breathing. I can't come up with any other logical reason for the sounds, and when Isabel's voice is joined by a second – another woman's – I feel the alcohol begin to swirl in my stomach and threaten to travel back up my throat.

I close my eyes, but I can't escape the noise, and as much as my brain screams at me to forget it all – Isabel is going to break up with me anyway, I really don't need to add insult to injury – I can't force myself to head back the way I came. I'm too transfixed; too compelled to finally confirm why Isabel broke up with me in the first place.

A dread settles in my stomach. Would turning back even end this nightmare? Are the fae controlling my movements? Forcing me to go through this pain?

Anger swirls around my mind in an agitated cloud, prompting me to grit my teeth and edge forward through the trees.

I feel like I've been punched in the stomach.

I want to stagger back and look away, but it's as if I'm trapped in place.

Isabel is locked in the embrace of another woman, but I can't tear my eyes off my former lover's face for long enough to work out who she is. The familiar way Isabel scrunches up her nose in pleasure; the twinkle in her eyes; the flush on her cheeks; the sound of her desire... all being elicited by someone other than me.

It's more than I can bear.

I feel like a burning dagger is being plunged into my heart, ripped back out and shoved back in.

Again, and again, and again.

I hold a hand over my mouth, not wanting to draw attention to myself as great wrenching sobs tear themselves forcibly from my lungs. I bite down on my hand to try and quieten my grief, allowing the tears to stream down my face.

We hadn't 'grown apart'. She'd just grown apart with someone else.

I squeeze my eyelids shut. *I've seen enough.* It shouldn't hurt this much, yet the pain feels new; just as raw as I remember; tinged with layers of salt that sting my re-opened wounds.

I contemplate confronting her; making her apologise for lying to me. But it won't change what she's done.

It won't change the pain of her rejection.

You've got through this once. You can do it again.

Steeling myself, I open my eyes.

CHAPTER TWENTY-FIVE

Two orb-like eyes blink back at me.

"Only one remains."

Disorientated, I glance around, realising I'm back in the tunnel of Mirrors. I don't know if I'm grateful that I've been spared the confrontation with Isabel or disappointed.

"It's over?" I croak, brushing the tears away from my face. I'm not sure how much more I can take; this constant switching between strong emotions has me feeling completely wrung out.

I suppose it's a good thing I wasn't given time to approach Isabel. I couldn't have faced any more rejection.

Hope flares in my chest. What if Isabel didn't betray me? What if this was all a trick, like the vision with my mother?

Almost as if it can read my mind, the Mirror shakes its head. "You must face the truths that have been hidden from you. Your mother loved you, but seeing the pain her illness put you through left her guilt-ridden; you both needed closure," it explains, clicking its claws against the branch in a rhythmic manner. "Likewise, you never learnt of your lover's infidelity."

"Why did I need to? I could have gone my whole life not knowing that Isabel betrayed me, and I would have been a damn sight happier than I am now!"

"You would rather live your life shrouded in lies? Are you not brave enough to handle the truth?"

The creature's question halts my angry tirade and I pause. I've never thought of myself as someone who hides from the truth. "I... that's not... of course I can handle the truth," I stutter. "It's just... I don't think it's always necessary."

"You would rather lie to yourself and others than deal with the pain of reality? Do you not think yourself a coward for making such a choice? Though I suppose you are a *human*." The Mirror's disdainful reply is at odds with the intensity of its gaze.

"Being *human* has nothing to do with it! Stop acting like you magical creatures are so much better than we are!" I yell, becoming more frustrated with every passing moment. "Not wanting to experience pain doesn't make me a coward; nor does wanting to protect my loved ones from pain. I would lie to my own family if it meant they were saved the pain of the truth. Just because *you* have no empathy for others, doesn't mean *I* don't!"

The creature's tail flicks. "The choice remains in your hands, Rosalind. Do you wish to depart, unknowing? Or face your final truth?" Its tail begins to glow an electric blue. "The one you have been hiding from yourself?"

The fight drains out of me as quickly as it came. I have no desire to experience yet another vision, but I don't feel like I have a choice. Surely the fae wouldn't give us the option, if they wanted us to take the easy path?

"I'm not hiding anything from myself," I tell the Mirror, straightening my back and shifting my feet to stand with my legs slightly apart. The feel of the stone, firm beneath my feet, is grounding. "Let's end this."

Despite feeling that I haven't blinked or taken my eyes away from the creature for a second, I still sway dizzily when my eyes refocus on my new surroundings.

Strange, I don't recognise this place.

I'm in someone's bedroom by the looks of it, a giant four poster bed taking up most of the space, the covers pulled back and several plush, blue blankets slung haphazardly over the top. I spin on my feet, looking for the room's occupant. Clearly someone was sleeping in here only recently.

Or they're messy and didn't make the bed this morning. Unless it's morning now? I scan the room for windows to try and guess the time, but there aren't any. Instead, the room emits its own light, the walls pulsing with a gentle blue glow, just like the room I found myself in before the first trial.

Two cosy-looking armchairs are nestled in the corner, arranged around a small table upon which lie several paperback novels and two empty mugs, alongside a teapot.

"Cold," I murmur as I touch one of the mugs. "Can't have been drunk from recently."

I briefly peruse the books, noting with surprise that they're the type of novels I'd normally pick up myself. *At least the owner has taste.*

Glancing to the left, I notice the room has two doors, one of which has a soft light flickering underneath it. Looking down to inspect it more closely, I realise the floor is decked out in thick, plush carpet.

I wriggle my feet instinctively, startled when I feel the fibres between my toes. I've no shoes on.

With a sharp intake of breath, I realise I'm not wearing many clothes either: just a thin silk nightgown that only reaches my mid-thigh. Feeling vulnerable, I'm just eying up the bedcovers, considering if I can fashion some kind of coverup, when the door closest to me swings open, and a man strolls confidently into the bedroom.

A man I instantly recognise.

CHAPTER TWENTY-SIX

What in all the Hells...

"What are you doing here?" I exclaim, before my eyes catch up with my brain and I hurriedly avert them. "Aalto! Where are your clothes!" I hold one arm over my eyes and wave at him to go and get dressed.

To my growing horror, Aalto merely laughs as he moves across the room towards me. He pulls my arm gently away from my face, but I keep my eyes firmly closed.

"Very funny, my love," Aalto chuckles, pulling my face towards his own.

What?

His hands fit perfectly around my face, almost as if I was made to be held securely between them. My cheeks stain crimson, even as I try to push him away. A feat that is seemingly impossible while I still have my eyes closed.

"Ah!"

Suddenly, I'm airborne, my eyes flying open as Aalto scoops me into his arms. He presses my barely clothed body against his naked form and I'm suddenly grateful for his strength and our height difference. The position is still far too intimate for how little we know each other, but at least I'm only pressed against his chest.

"What is this?" I gasp, looking up at his face – the only safe option in our current position. "This isn't... this isn't one of my memories... is the trial finished? Aalto, will you please just put me down and explain!" I fight against his grasp, but for whatever reason, Aalto takes my growing frustration as playfulness and tightens his grip, laughing as he bumps open the door to the next room with his hip and carries me through.

"Explain what? I'm rather offended you consider our activities a *trial*. It certainly didn't sound like you weren't enjoying yourself. Have I truly ravished you so thoroughly you don't remember?" Aalto smirks as he places me back onto my feet and pulls me towards him.

I sidestep backwards, looking up at him warily.

I try to keep my eyes from looking lower than his chest, but it's extremely hard to do so when he is just – well – *there*.

And there is a fair amount there.

For the first time, I'm grateful for the thin fabric of my nightgown as the telltale heat of a blush spreads over my face and down my neck.

The vapour wafting from the giant stone bathtub in the centre of the room isn't helping. It's filled almost to the brim with steaming blue water that looks strangely like the sea; little wave-like crests move back and forth across the surface like they're being pulled by the tide. It also has a faintly salty scent to it that isn't altogether unpleasant, just unexpected.

Another, more familiar scent momentarily steals my breath.

"I added lavender, your favourite."

Aalto swirls the water enticingly with his hand, a soft smile painting his face. He frowns when I don't reply.

"Are you alright, my moon?" Concern clouds his eyes, making him look unusually vulnerable.

I feel a tug on my heart at the endearment, but I don't understand why. He's never called me that before. Why would he have? And yet... it's too familiar a name to call someone you barely know. I find myself blinking rapidly, a sharp pain streaking across my forehead, like a knife slamming into my skull.

Aalto tilts my face, running cool fingers across my forehead, studying me attentively. "What happened, Ros? Did I hurt you? I'm so used to you speaking up about your wants and needs, I didn't think to check in earlier. Did we go too hard?"

His expression shifts, only slightly, but we're so close I can't help notice the subtle change in his eyes. His fingers begin to trace down my throat, halting at my collarbone.

"You're so beautiful, I just can't stop myself. The things I want to do to you..." He closes his eyes, sighing. "I know I have to restrain myself. It's not your fault your human body is so fragile. Although..." He twirls a strand of my hair between his fingers, a hungry look in his eyes.

I suddenly come back to my senses, realising our bodies are mere inches apart, my breaths coming out in laboured pants.

I push him away.

He looks genuinely hurt, holding his arms open wide as though he expects me to fall into them. He lets them drop when I stay where I am.

"Although what?" I ask, wrapping my arms tightly around myself, feeling suddenly cold, though the room is still warm.

Aalto raises an eyebrow and shakes his head, rolling his eyes. "We're not having this argument again," he huffs, stepping into the bathtub; letting the water spill over the edges.

"You're the one who started it!" I exclaim, not understanding what on earth he's going on about and yet feeling a strange sense of déjà vu.

It makes me feel sick to my stomach, like I've just stepped

off a too-fast carousel ride – I'm still spinning, but the ground isn't moving.

"If you would just let me turn you fae then we wouldn't have to argue about this at all! I wouldn't have to worry about my fae strength hurting your delicate human body; about risking losing you because I wasn't careful enough! How do you think *this*" – he gestures between us – "is going to last if you remain human? What happens when you get old, Ros?" Aalto drops his head into his hands, massaging his eyes.

I can only stare at him in bewilderment, my mind so overwhelmed I can't string a cohesive thought together.

When he looks back up at me, I'm surprised to see genuine pain reflected in his gaze.

"I will love you no matter what you look like, or how frail your body is. I will take care of you until the very end. But my heart? My soul? I won't cope if you step away from this world without me, Ros." He chokes on his words, pools of misery welling in his eyes. "If you were fae, we could grow old together. I just don't understand why you're so against it... do you really hate my species that much? I thought you loved me?" He looks up at me, his long eyelashes sweeping over his pleading eyes.

After all our time together, he knows exactly how to stab me where it hurts. Of course I love him, how could I not? I'm just not ready to fully trust him on this one, not when what he is asking from me is irreversible. What if he only wants me because of my human vulnerability, the thrill of it? Will he still want me when I'm fae?

Wait. What's happening to me? Aalto is practically a stranger. Why am I thinking these thoughts? Why do they feel as familiar to me as breathing? As if I've spent night after night chasing them around in circles through my mind?

I sink to my knees, grabbing hold of my head as I'm hit by another burst of pain.

Water sprays everywhere as Aalto leaps from the bath, scooping me into his arms and rocking me gently.

"I'm sorry, my moon, I'm sorry. I'm just so scared of losing you. I can't lose you... not after it has taken me so many years to find you. I'll do anything to keep you. Whatever you want."

His breath is warm against my ear as he carries me back to the bath, stepping inside and bringing me with him. With my back against his chest, he gently slides the straps of my nightgown down my shoulders, replacing his fingers with his lips as he teases the fabric down my body, until it slips off my feet and into the water. His body is warm against my skin; familiar. I can't get my head around it, but every time I try, stabs of pain ripple across my skull.

So... I stop trying, relaxing into the familiar feeling. The comforting feeling of having someone take care of me.

Aalto rubs lavender-scented lotion through my hair, combing it gently with his fingers.

"You're the first one to ever say no to me." He chuckles, wrapping my hair around his fist and pulling my head gently back so he can meet my eyes. He kisses my forehead tenderly. "Not many people dare say no to a prince. You would make an excellent queen," he breathes, brushing my lips softly with his own.

He bites my lip teasingly, encouraging me to lean in and deepen the kiss, before he pulls away, his eyes smouldering.

"Rule alongside me as my queen, Rosalind. I promise you will never regret it. I will spend my whole life devoted to you. Every second of your existence will be ecstasy."

I twist my body, pressing my lips to his, unable to resist his kiss. I can feel his eagerness at my reciprocation as he moulds his body against my own, the heat of him searing into my skin, making me gasp in pleasure. I reach out a hand to run it through his hair, playing with the tips of his gently pointed ears. I can't stop my grin at his groan, as I recall how sensitive they are.

The ground shakes.

I blink, confused. "Did you feel that?" I ask Aalto.

Pushing myself upright, I immediately scan the room, looking for the source of the tremor. Everything looks the same as it did before: not a speck of dust out of place.

When I turn back to face Aalto, I recoil.

He's shaking, performing jerky, repetitive moments, as if he's stuck inside his own body, trying to get out. If I lean in, I can hear him murmuring a response to my question, repeating the same phrase over and over again.

"Feel what? Feel what? Feel what?"

I turn around fully, a feat made surprisingly easy by the sheer size of the tub. Reaching out a hand, I shake Aalto, only to find that my hand goes completely through him.

I flinch. His ghostly body feels deathly cold, like putting my hand into a bucket of ice – if that ice was made of treacle.

Almost as if Aalto is reluctant to give up my touch, my hand resists being pulled back towards me, and I grit my teeth against the sensation as I focus on retrieving my hand.

The ground shudders again, and Aalto fades a bit more; I can see straight through him to the bathtub beyond.

Feeling decidedly nauseous, I close my eyes.

CHAPTER TWENTY-SEVEN

When my eyelids blink back open, I'm kneeling on the floor, fully clothed. Aalto and the bathtub are nowhere to be seen.

"What the—" *What just happened?*

My body is still trembling, overwhelmed by Aalto's frighteningly familiar kisses and the weird phenomenon of him fading away. I stand abruptly to my feet when I hear loud shouting coming from somewhere behind me. I've only a second to turn around before I feel Aalto, dressed and fully formed, push me behind him protectively.

It seems that we've jumped into a different vision. *Are these Aalto's memories?*

"No! You can't! She's *mine*," he all but growls at the three fae standing in front of him. "I'll kill you if you so much as lay a finger on her!" A sword glows in his hands, the rich blue flame flickering angrily.

The three fae look completely indifferent to his show of bravado.

The male and female dressed in long, green robes – one sporting a white sash; the other black – are the oldest-looking fae I've ever seen. They both have vibrant white hair, so pale it almost seems to glow, but whilst the man wears his long, the woman has shorn hers close to her skull.

The third fae, I recognise. Her long plum hair is slightly shorter than when I saw her at the trials, her golden-brown skin positively shining beside the pale, milky complexion of the others.

Remora.

I look completely out of place standing next to them, dressed in a skin-tight black dress; boots laced up to my thighs.

Remora has an excited glint in her eyes, watching the interactions between us all hungrily.

"What's going on, Aalto?" I lay a reassuring hand on his arm, shocked by the blind panic in his blue eyes when he turns to look back at me.

"You know the rules." Remora shrugs nonchalantly, the glint in her eyes and the smirk on her lips showing she's enjoying every second of Aalto's discomfort. "Nature chooses which human she wishes to take part in the trials, and Rosalind was her choice. You never turned her fae; she's still human, so she's fair game."

"I'll turn her now then!" Aalto growls, pointing his sword towards Remora so that the tip is mere inches from her neck.

She merely blinks, smirking at him as she raises a finger and flicks the blade away with a sharp flare of her own fiery magic.

"It's too late now. Besides, I don't think she wants that, do you, honey?" Remora is aiming for sympathy, but she ends up looking like a shark staring down its next meal.

I shake my head, agreeing with Remora, but feeling like every muscle in my body has tensed up, alert to a wrongness I don't understand.

"Ros..." Aalto grips my face between his hands, eyes flicking over me, desperate. "You can't enter the trials. Hardly any humans survive. I can't lose you. Please! You don't have to stay with me, just let me turn you fae, alright? Then you'll be free. I'll let you go, I promise. Just... please." His eyes are locked onto mine, searching for the answer he so frantically craves.

I feel tears well up in the corners of my eyes, hating that I'm causing him so much pain; overwhelmed by the range of emotions his memory is making me experience. *This isn't about me*, I remind myself. The Mirrors are just making it seem that way. *But then why does this all feel so familiar? Why do I feel like my heart is breaking all over again?*

Remora beckons to me. "Come, Rosalind. It's time. We'll wipe your memories of the fae world so it's fair on the other contenders. Don't worry – you won't remember anything of your dear Aalto either."

She grins a truly evil smile as a heartbroken cry wrenches itself from Aalto's lips, holding out a hand to me, gesturing for me to go with her.

She turns to look at Aalto. "And don't you even think about trying to remind her," she sneers. "If Nature finds out she's been cheating, she'll kill both of you." She looks to the two older fae for backup, who nod solemnly, confirming her words.

As I move to follow her, a slow understanding dawns on me in a horrified wave. "Will I... will I ever regain my memories?" I whisper.

"Not a single one, but don't worry, I'm sure the Elders will make it as painless as possible. Nature is benevolent in this, at least."

"But I don't... I don't want to forget. You can't, please... don't do this. Aalto..."

I reach for him, tracing the necklace he wears around his neck, a simple woven string with a shell attached, trying to use it to focus my mind. *This* is *my memory. Aalto is no stranger. He's* mine.

He reaches for me, but the two other fae suddenly spring into action, grasping his shoulders and clamping his arms to his sides. He tries to struggle against them, but to no avail.

I cry out then, lunging for him, but Remora catches me, binding me with her magic.

"You had your chance, human," she trills. "No dawdling, it's time."

"I'll volunteer for my court; I'll choose you as my partner," Aalto promises desperately. "You won't go through this alone. We will survive this. Nature won't take you from me."

I nod, tears falling silently down my cheeks, my lips sealed shut by Remora's spell.

Struggling once more, he manages to break free from his captors long enough to draw my face to his, kissing my forehead then my lips, as if it is the last taste of me he will ever have.

Maybe it is.

The fae behind Aalto begin to shake at the seams, as if someone is trying to wipe them out, smearing them in front of me. Remora's spell suddenly snaps, and I cling to Aalto desperately, even as I feel him slip through my grasp. I keep trying to focus on his image in my head, refusing to forget what I've just been shown, as I'm bodily pulled back to the Mirror's lair.

At the last moment, I reach up for his necklace, tugging sharply on the woven string around his neck, feeling the sharp edges of the shell scrape into my palm.

I can't forget. I won't.

But clinging to the memory is like trying to grasp a fountain of water with my hands, and as I feel the ground shake, something gouges the images once more from my mind.

CHAPTER TWENTY-EIGHT

It's the third time I've been brought back to the Mirror's lair, but I don't feel any less dizzy for it. I look around for them, but they've all disappeared.

"Oh, of course, just disappear why don't you! Good thing I don't have a million and one *questions*!" I scream hysterically into the empty cave.

I'm even more furious than last time, snapshots of the last vision flickering in my mind but failing to solidify. All I know is that whatever just happened made me cry.

Nothing new there.

Pulling my foot back to angrily take out my frustration on the cave floor, I manage to stop myself just in time.

It must have appeared when I was screaming, because I could have sworn it wasn't there when I'd first returned. Just where I'd been about to kick now lies a long sword. Its hilt is a deep blue colour, with swirling white motifs etched along it; the blade sparking with fizzes of sky blue magic.

Magic that I'm beginning to recognise.

I pick it up, being extra careful not to touch the sparking blade, and as I do so, a door outline slowly appears in the cave wall in front of me.

Gripping the sword firmly, I slowly walk towards the door, steeling myself. The stone moves inwards, creating a small gap for me to slide through. I can only assume this is the correct way to go, rather than using the other door I'd been shown earlier, further down the tunnel.

Before my eyes can adjust, I'm hit with a wall of sound. A cacophony of cheers and yells cascade over me like a tidal wave as I enter what is clearly an arena; longer at the sides and curved at the ends. The walls are formed from solid rock, a bit like the cave I've just come from, and far taller than anything I can climb.

Towering above me, and the cause of all the noise, are rows upon rows of seats, filled to the brim with fae and magical creatures. I'm overwhelmed by the sheer array of colours; no one seems to be sitting in any order, so it looks like a rainbow has just thrown up over the crowd.

There's simply too much for me to take in.

Disorientated, I try to focus on the arena itself, and hesitantly walk further in, away from the overhang of the wall that is shadowing me and blocking off some of my view. I flinch at the sharp increase of noise as my appearance sets off another wave of cheers from the crowd.

I peer cautiously around, wondering what I'm about to be faced with next. The sword remains firmly in my hand; I'm not letting it out of my sight any time soon.

That's when I see him.

Aalto is in the centre of the arena, head bowed; kneeling on the floor with thick metal chains coiled around his body, attaching him to a giant metal ring that is drilled into the ground. His hands are pinned together, as are his legs. Seeing him makes my chest ache and I immediately want to run towards him.

His ears prick up, head tilting in my direction.

"Stop! Who goes there?" Aalto demands, his voice clear

and confident despite the situation he's in.

A bead of sweat drips down his forehead and his beautiful hair is matted, stuck to his skin. I've no idea how long he's been trapped here, but the afternoon sun shining directly overhead cannot have made the experience pleasant, no matter how long it's been.

"It's me..." I trail off, halting my steps as I hesitate.

"Rosalind?" A wave of relief seems to travel through Aalto's body.

He looks up, opening his eyes, and I flinch – his pupils and irises are entirely gone, his eyes nothing more than milky white film.

"Don't move," he insists. "Describe for me all that you can see."

How does he still manage to be so demanding at a time like this?

"Hurry!" he orders, just as I'm opening my mouth to respond.

I swallow an angry retort. Now is not the time to be getting angry. *He's probably scared*.

I scan the arena floor, but there isn't much to report back.

"We're in an arena." I ignore Aalto's impatient huff and eye roll, which is decidedly creepy given his lack of pupils. "There is what looks like a large trapdoor some ways behind you." I strain to see. "It's about the size of, um..." I've never been very good at measurements. "Three of me lying down by, um, three of me?"

"Nothing else?"

"No."

"Alright. Come slowly forward until you reach me," he orders.

Repressing my own eye roll – going to him was my original plan, before he stopped me – I start to walk slowly towards him.

I'm only five paces away when a violent earth tremor and a loud bang shakes me off my feet and hurls me to the ground.

Aalto swings his head back and forth, assumedly trying to gauge what is happening. I'm about to tell him everything's okay when an army of large, pointed wooden pillars pierce their way out of the ground.

They encircle Aalto, with just enough gap between them for me to slip through. The top of them is too high for me to reach.

I don't want to think about what would've happened to me if I'd just run across to Aalto like I'd originally been planning. My heartrate races wildly in my chest, and it takes me a while before I feel reassured enough to stumble to my feet and continue moving.

The sword feels heavy in my hands as I drag it along, but I'm reluctant to leave it behind.

I eye the pillars dubiously. I no longer have clear line of sight to Aalto, and this makes me feel more nervous than I care to admit.

"Aalto? Are you okay?" My voice trembles slightly as I yell out, echoing loudly around the space. The crowd appear to have quietened, watching with bated breath.

Are they expecting something else?

"What's happening?" Aalto sounds annoyed, but his voice is clear and confident

I find myself breathing a sigh of relief. At least he hasn't been impaled.

"What's taking you so long?" he adds, and I instantly

prickle at his impatience.

I peer intently at the pillar closest to me, curious about the angular shaped runes around the base.

"Describe. What. You. Can. See!" Aalto all but screams at me when I'm silent for too long.

I ignore him, crouching down to get a closer look. If he'd only shut up, I might be able to work them out.

I'm just reaching out to trace the shapes when a fizzing sound makes me hesitate. Little holes appear up and down the wooden pillars closest to Aalto, sharp, vine-like tendrils lashing out from within the wood, threading through the holes and forming a lattice between the pillars, creating an impermeable mesh in between them.

My arms shaking, I drag the sword through the other pillars towards the cage now surrounding Aalto, attempting to scrape the blade through the vines; then the pillars. Just as I'd feared, it doesn't even shave off a slither. Strangely, the runes at the bottom of the pillars have gone, leaving me to presume that they were some kind of summoning spell for the vines.

The pillars and the lattice make for a very effective cage around Aalto, although what with him tied up, I don't quite understand the added dramatics of it. It seems a bit over the top.

Classic fae.

"There are several wooden pillars around you, Aalto. They've just shot out some kind of vines, which have lashed together to form a wall. I can't break through," I yell into the darkness.

I catch what I think is the tail end of a response, but the vines have done more than just shut off my vision of him; I can no longer hear him properly either.

"What to do. What to do," I mutter to myself. Now that I've found Aalto, and have seen, if at least temporarily, that he's okay, I can feel myself calming slightly.

You can do this, you just have to think.

The crowd has suddenly woken up again and are stomping their feet in a frenzy. Glancing towards the sound, I catch sight of the trapdoor in the corner of the arena. I'm not entirely sure, but it looks as if it's opened a crack, though it's too dark to see inside the tiny gap.

"Curious," I murmur, before dragging my attention back to my current problem.

I walk carefully around the cage of pillars, searching for a gap, pushing against the vines with my sword every now and again to check for points of weakness.

I find none.

I tap my foot against the ground, thinking. Shielding my eyes against the harsh sunlight, I look up.

Of course!

Slipping my fingers into the vine lattice, I begin to climb. It's hard going, what with trying to drag the sword along with me, and it's not long before I'm sweating and panting heavily.

Aalto must hear me approaching, because he starts yelling again when I get close to the top.

"Took you long enough. Now will you kindly untie me before the yag appears? You collected the three items on your journey through the fae passages, right? One to unlock me, one for my sight, and one to return my magic."

I just stare down at him in panic.

Aalto's expression morphs into one of horrified realisation as I remain silent. "You did collect the three items, didn't you? It was a test of sloth, after all, and if there is one thing I know

208

about you it's that you're too stubborn to sit back and take it easy…" He tails off, swapping his panicked rambling for action as he struggles against his bonds.

"I… what… how was I supposed to know? No one told me! I didn't know!" I jump down and begin to tug at his chains, screaming in frustration as they refuse to budge.

I turn to look at the sword, contemplating whether it might help, but a loud clang from the arena grabs my attention, and I scrabble back up the vines.

The trapdoor in the corner of the arena is slowly lifting, a long taloned claw reaching out from under the gap, scraping along the arena floor.

"Rosalind, what's going on?" Aalto asks, panic lacing his every word.

"Umm… do yags have long talons about the size of my arm, by any chance?"

Aalto begins to fight against his bonds with even more ferocity.

"Cut me loose, now!" he yells, and I reach for the sword once more, this time not hesitating as I lift it above my head with a groan.

"Hold out your chains tight!" I command between gritted teeth, and Aalto quickly obliges, his hands outstretched in front of him.

With a loud cry, I swing the sword down, stumbling a bit as it slides through the chains with surprisingly little resistance.

"You passed the challenge of memories. You dealt with the binds of your past, so you were able to cut mine," Aalto says commendably, clearly pleased.

I ignore him as I focus, my muscles screaming in protest as I lift the sword once more to slice through the chains at his ankles.

"What now?" I snap, aware that we still have a very real threat trying to break through the trapdoor.

"Having some sight would help." Aalto rubs at his eyes, turning to blink at me with an eerie blank stare. "Or, you know, my magic?"

I grimace, thinking of the hill I didn't climb at the start of the challenge.

The hill called Sight.

Perhaps the water up there was magical, and I could have used it to clear whatever it is that's blinding him?

Aalto sighs, reaching blindly for me. I take his hand between my own, helping him to his feet. He stumbles a bit, the blood rushing back into his legs after being prone on the ground of so long, and I struggle to support his bodyweight, the sword clanging to the ground next to me as I drop it to free up both my hands.

Wait. I scrutinise my wrist, convinced that I saw something flicker beneath my skin. I stare at it, unwilling to look away. *There!* It's faint, but I definitely saw it. A band of lavender light under my skin. *Zaidan's magic.*

"Say someone else gave me their magic. Is there a way for me to transfer that to you? Would it restore your magic?"

"Another shared their magic with you?" Aalto frowns. "That could work. But you'll have to kiss me."

"Excuse me?" I squeak, mentally trying to wrap my head around the idea. "How would that help?"

"Because we need a connection for the magic to transfer between us. And you have to mean it, otherwise the magic will know that your intentions are false." His frown turns into a mischievous grin as he tilts his face expectantly.

I reluctantly step closer.

Biting my lip, I can't help but feel curious. I wonder what his lips feel like... what he tastes like? I guess if this is the only way, I have to at least *try*.

I shut my eyes and close the distance, softly pressing my lips to his own. My body's reaction is instant, and I can't stop myself from reaching for him, deepening the kiss. He hungrily reciprocates, but I realise he is still letting me take the lead; letting me stay in control, when he could so easily take over. It feels only natural to wrap my arms around his neck, letting my hands wander through his hair. I accidentally brush the points of his ears and he breaks away with a shiver, a soft blush tinting his face.

"Careful Rosalind, have you forgotten that we have an audience?"

I flush as I look up into the crowd, who are watching us rapturously. I pull away from him, immediately embarrassed, only to realise it worked. Aalto is surrounded by a lavender mist, wafting around him like he's immersed in a cloud.

"How do you feel?" I ask, flustered as he runs a finger across his lips thoughtfully.

"It's cold," he mutters, flexing his hands in front of me. "It doesn't feel like borrowed power, more like my own has been returned. Perhaps you were given healing magic." He extends his hands in front of him, and I jump out of the way as a flurry of snow-flecked mist descends.

"Careful!"

"Hm, it's my magic, alright," Aalto says, grinning. "We might actually have a chance of surviving this thing. We'll just have to hope my magic is enough on its own." With an energetic twirl, he shoots more icy streaks, forming frozen puddles on the ground.

"Oh, well, that is excellent news," I say sarcastically, almost slipping on an icy patch he's made as I try to dodge another of his streams of magic.

"I hope you didn't have to *kiss* anyone else to get this?" he says, with a teasing glint in his eyes, and I stop in my tracks as it dawns on me.

"I just had to *touch* you to transfer the magic, didn't I?" I hiss furiously.

His grin widens. "But a kiss was so much more fun, wasn't it?"

The crowd suddenly cheers, halting Aalto's gloating.

A sinking feeling of dread washes over me.

Reaching for the top of the vine cage, I haul myself up, my eyes darting around the arena.

The trapdoor hangs wide open.

"Where is it?" I whisper, leaning forward slightly to try and see into the darkness beyond the trapdoor.

I flinch, slowly raising my hand to my neck, where my fingers meet a thick, viscous droplet of liquid. It's unpleasantly warm, sticking to my fingers as I pull my hand away.

"Gross," I mumble, flinching as yet another blob hits me.

A draft of icy cold air has me thinking instinctively of Aalto, but strangely, it isn't coming from his direction.

It feels like it's coming from above.

CHAPTER TWENTY-NINE

I'd never experienced the sensation of my heart literally stopping until that moment.

Above me, held up by two scaly, green wings the length of my body, hovers the infamous yag.

It's looking down at me with one huge, blinking yellow eye, it's long, serpent-like body slithering through the air as it beats its wings slowly to stay above me. Its tail ends in a sharp point, oozing a strange gloopy substance that I can only assume is what's now decorating my skin. I watch as another blob wells at the tip and falls to the ground.

"Aalto?" I stutter, leaning slowly back, not wanting to break eye contact with the yag, but starting to panic when I see the blob fizz as it reaches the ground, creating a small crater in the arena floor.

I run a terrified hand down my neck, but when the yag opens its mouth and roars, it plasters me with speckles of thick spit, the same as the globs already running down my face.

The roar of the crowd shocks the yag out of our staring contest and I dive back into the cage as it swoops down, its tail thrashing. Grabbing Aalto's hand, I drag him up the opposite side of the cage, pulling him to the ground just in time as the yag tosses an acid ball at us from its tail.

I weave my way through the pillars, aiming for the trapdoor, hoping we can hide there, but as I catch a glimpse of it my heart sinks. It's shut.

We're flung off our feet as the ground shakes again, hitting the ground with a loud smack. The yag is desperately trying to reach us, but it can't seem to fit through the narrow maze of pillars, screaming in rage as it's talons tear into the wood, trying to claw a path through.

"It's a stupid creature, but it won't be stopped for long," Aalto pants.

I look up at him as I struggle to breathe, the air pushed out of me when I hit the ground.

"It'll realise that it can't get through soon and start aiming at us from the sky."

I feel my anger rising at his pointless commentary. "What do you suggest we do, then?" I snap, looking across at the sword, trying to wrack my brains for a solution.

"Well, if you'd just gotten the item that gives me back my sight, this would be a hell of a lot easier," Aalto grumbles, stopping to sit cross legged, his chin resting in his hand as he thinks.

"Seriously? We are about to die, probably slowly, poisoned by some grotesque creature, and you want to argue about me not completing the task correctly that I was told *absolutely nothing about*? I got two of the objects!" I scream at him, flinching when my raised voice seems to aggravate the yag further, prompting it to slam into the pillars, causing one to wobble alarmingly. "Remind me why we can't just stab it with the sword?" I ask, exasperated when Aalto continues to sit there in contemplative silence.

He barely flinches when the yag slams to the ground, prompting another tremor beneath us.

Sparks of blue energy flicker at his fingertips as Aalto taps his fingers together contemplatively. "Look at it closely." He gestures towards the noise, where the yag is now trying to dig up the pillars with its talons.

The dirt sprays up around it, chunks of gravel harmlessly bouncing off its shiny, green-plated body.

"Natural body armour," I sigh, glaring angrily at the sword as if this is all its fault. "I'm guessing it doesn't have a weak spot, like monsters always do in fairytales?"

Aalto laughs. "Indeed. Only mortal tales have an easy way out. Although..." He gets to his feet and walks over to me, only stumbling slightly despite his blindness.

"What?" I ask bitterly when he grabs me by the sleeve.

"You can be my eyes," he says firmly, and he pulls me so that my back is against his chest. He grabs one of my hands, placing it behind his other hand so that I can direct his movements.

He lets off an experimental shoot of magic and I shiver, feeling the slight brush of icy power through the back of his hand, but I manage to keep our hands aligned.

"Our movement will be limited, but it's better than nothing. You'll just have to aim," he says, as if it's the simplest thing in the world for me to take down the yag this way. "We'll probably only get one chance; my magic won't go through its armour either, so we are going to aim for the only soft spot I can think of. I need to shoot at full power to kill it. I can probably only do that once."

Aalto pulls me snug against him. I can feel his warm breath against the side of my neck, and I shiver again, feeling strangely comforted by his closeness.

I close my eyes and nod. *I can do this.* "Okay. How will I know when the right moment is?" I ask, watching the yag intently as it strikes its tail against one of the pillars, its poison dripping against the wood, making it sizzle but otherwise doing little damage.

"When it's just about to eat us." I hear the grin in Aalto's voice, his lips brushing against my ear.

"What do you mean?"

"You'll know. Now focus!" he instructs, and I feel his hand become noticeably colder as he begins to concentrate his magic. "We can do this," I hear him whisper in my ear, the lightest of kisses fluttering against my earlobe that I'm not entirely sure if I've imagined, but have no time to think about – the yag has finally taken to the air.

Flicking its long, serpent-like body, it swings its head back and forth as it hunts for us. Its wide powerful wings move up and down, causing our clothes and hair to flutter in the sharp gusts of air. I grit my teeth, holding firm, my fingernails digging sharply into Aalto's palm as I hold onto him tightly. If it's hurting him, he doesn't say anything.

I'm not sure how I'm meant to know when to tell him to shoot, but the pressure is making me feel ill. Still, I dig my feet into the ground and try and take comfort in knowing that we are in this together. I know he wouldn't risk his life alongside mine if he didn't have faith that we could survive.

"Hold firm," he growls as the flurry of wind around us picks up.

The yag is going to dive soon. I go to close my eyes as dirt is kicked up around me, but they snap back open when I feel the warm, putrid breath of the yag as it opens its mouth to roar.

I barely have a chance to panic before it is swooping down through the sky, its tail lashing angrily as it dives towards us. The wind threatens to push me from my feet, but Aalto is firm against my back, and my muscles tense, holding fast.

Not yet. Not yet, I think as the yag gets closer, my heart beating rapidly against my chest.

"Now!" I scream, digging my nails into Aalto's palm, moving his hand slightly upwards, directly into the path of the yag as, with a snarl, it opens its mouth. I feel globules of its saliva against my skin, but it's the sudden cold of Aalto's magic that has me shaking and struggling to keep his palm facing in the right direction.

He shoots off a stream of fierce glacial power directly into the yag's open jaw. I can hear the crackle as it solidifies into sharp spikes of ice, piercing the soft delicate skin of its mouth. The yag tries to backtrack, swooping its body around in a desperate attempt to escape Aalto's power, but it's like the creature is frozen in place, and it thrashes in the sky helplessly.

I watch, spellbound as it begins to falter and slow, its wing movements growing sluggish. I can also feel Aalto begin to falter, his hand warming ever so slightly.

"No!" I whimper, gripping him tighter.

I close my eyes, focusing on his magic, praying for him to stay strong, to last just that little bit longer.

A flash of beautiful blue-white light shines behind my eyelids, making me grateful that I closed them mere moments ago. I hear a shriek of rage.

Then silence.

Blinking open my eyes, my ears are overwhelmed with the cheers of the crowd, roaring in their seats as I look around in dazed wonder.

The yag lies on the ground, completely encased in white, pearlescent ice, like a sculpture made of snow.

"How?" I whisper, stunned, finally dropping Aalto's hand as I slump to my knees.

"Power," Aalto whispers, stroking my hair as he kneels behind me, pulling me into his arms.

I turn, burying my face into his chest, too exhausted beyond measure to realise what I'm doing.

"I thought you said you only had enough for one shot," I murmur, my voice muffled by his shirt.

"The sculpture is white," Aalto says simply, like that answers my question.

I'm shaking too much to respond with my usual exasperation.

"My magic is blue," he whispers in my ear, and I turn to look up at him curiously, not understanding his meaning.

The change in position presses my body more firmly against him, and I feel something solid poking at my ribs. Reaching into my pocket, I curl my fingers around a small object.

My mind is hit with a carousel of memories so vivid that I gasp aloud, pulling the object from my own pocket and deftly slipping it into Aalto's. He looks at me curiously, reaching for it, but I stop his hand from pulling it out into the open air. I see his eyes light up in shocked recognition as his fingers trace the familiar shape.

"My shell charm?" he breathes, his eyes wide. "Why do you have this, Rosalind?" He tilts my chin up to look into my eyes.

"You called me your moon," I whisper, studying his facial expression intently.

Understanding and awe sweeps across his face. "You remember?"

I nod. "The Mirrors showed me some of my memories. From when we were together. I couldn't remember them before, but your shell charm... I remember everything now. I remember *us*." I pause, a sob threatening to choke off my words. "I remember being taken from you."

Grief flickers across his face before his expression settles into a look of determination. "I had no control over what the Mirrors showed you. They shouldn't have showed you anything from before..." His voice trails off, low and contemplative.

"But they did," I muse thoughtfully. "So... if not you, then who?"

"Nature is in control of any magic used in the trials. She's never interfered before. I think the more important question here is not who, but *why*? What does Nature want from you, my moon?"

A spark of electricity jolts up my spine at the nickname, the urge to leap into his arms almost overwhelming.

I shake my head, trying to clear my thoughts. "We can't let anyone know. Not until we find out why Nature is interfering. Maybe there is a deeper reason for why she selected me in the first place." I shuffle away from him, knowing if I stay close, my willpower to not touch him will quickly expire. We can't risk anyone finding out that my memory of him has returned. "My heart could never forget you," I whisper. "You're an idiot if you thought otherwise," I add, unable to resist a cheeky grin as I chance a look back up at him.

Aalto winks at me, allowing a beatific smile to paint his face. "Welcome back, my love. Took you long enough," he says gently, and for a heartbeat I forget the crowd. Hells, I even forget the competition.

All I see is the pure adoration that he has for me, despite all that we've been through.

A grating voice snaps my attention away. "Congratulations Prince Aalto of the Winter Court and his human tribute Rosalind for completing the trial of Sloth!"

CHAPTER THIRTY

Remora's voice echoes around the arena, causing the crowd to erupt into noisy cheers, their clamour a gentle backdrop to the thudding of my heart as I stand next to the fae I now remember. I look up at him, my body shaking slightly from the adrenaline still coursing through it and I can't help but admire the way the sun is glinting upon the strands of his white-blonde hair.

Of course he still looks beautiful, despite all that we've just been through. This fae may have my heart, but the return of my memories hasn't erased the fact he annoys the hells out of me. And yet, I also remember the fiery passion between us; the temperamental disagreements and the makeups afterwards. I try to suppress a grin that threatens to bloom across my face as I recall some of our more passionate moments.

He grabs my hand, and I automatically interlink our fingers as he holds them up to the sky in a victory salute. A gesture that causes the crowd to erupt in further screams of raucous joy.

I look at our entwined hands, pondering our future. It's going to be hard to force my body not to respond to him, if we don't want others to know that my memories have returned. Reluctantly, I take a small step away when he brings our arms down, wringing my hands miserably. I'm desperate for this challenge to be over so that we can sit down and talk properly. *Privately.*

And *catch up* of course.

I exhale softly, trying to calm my fluttering heart as I chance a look at Aalto. He's grinning widely at me, as if he can read my thoughts, and I roll my eyes. Would it kill him to make this easier for us and not look at me as if he wants to jump me right here, audience be damned?

"Ouch," I mutter, as one of my fingers sends a tiny icy spark of magic to another. It feels like trying to hold an ice cube when your hands are too warm: piercingly sharp.

I shove my hands into my pockets. That's yet another thing I need to address with Aalto when this is all over. How in all the Hells do I have access to magic? Is it temporary? Permanent? Either way, it shouldn't be possible.

I'm human, not fae; I know this as confidently as I remember my own name. It isn't anything I've ever desired, despite numerous attempts by Aalto to convince me otherwise.

I sense Aalto moving slightly closer to me; his sensitive fae hearing must have picked up on my muttered words of pain. In response, I shuffle my feet slightly, broadening the distance between us. He must take the hint, for he doesn't try to move closer again.

I shudder, overwhelmed by the noise of the crowd cheering, and the aches in my body. The urge to slump to the ground in an exhausted heap is overwhelming, but I'm determined to remain standing. I can't help still feeling on edge, the adrenaline still pumping through me.

A flicker in the periphery of my vision has me startling, but I take a deep breath when I realise it's only Remora, who has entered the arena and is walking towards us. My body stiffens; she isn't someone I feel safe around and it's even worse now that I know she was an instigator in erasing my memories.

She saunters across the arena, taking her own sweet time.

Probably wanting to show off that monstrosity of a dress, I think cruelly, my strong dislike for the woman momentarily making me forget my exhaustion. I try to stand up straighter and brush down my battle-stained clothes.

I hear a chuckle from Aalto. "Easy Ros," he whispers flirtatiously, "you know you're the only fire that lights my heart."

I struggle to come up with a snappy retort, perplexed as to why he'd think I'm jealous of her. He's never been the narcissistic type, and as far as I remember, I've never been one overly prone to jealousy. I just have a certain degree of pride, wanting to ensure I look as presentable as I can.

When I don't respond, he starts walking towards her, and I sigh, reluctantly following him. I notice his ears prick up at my exhalation and I try not to frown as he chuckles once more.

He's just trying to get a rise out of me. I look down, letting the mess of my red hair hide my smile as realisation dawns on me. *Let the games begin fae,* I think to myself, amused.

Unless... A more sinister thought curls its way into my mind. *Perhaps he's trying to distract me so that I don't unintentionally give away that my memories have returned.* She was present when my memories were taken, after all; surely, she's going to be the one that has us under the most scrutiny?

I study her thoughtfully, her dress looking more extravagant now that I can see it up close. What I mistook for a smoky black ballgown, corseted at the top, and tapered out into a wide floating skirt at the bottom, is far more complex. As she moves, streaks of ember, red, oranges and golds stream across the fabric, shooting out sparks of literal fire as it flutters around her. I'm reminded of how much of a mess I am as I look down at my road-weary dirt-encrusted clothing and finger my sweat-matted hair.

The woman smirks as she notices my comparison, before wrinkling her nose distastefully. "Well, you've certainly seen better days." She grins widely, turning up her nose at me as she approaches Aalto.

He runs a hand down his shirt, flicking off specks of dirt distastefully. I clench my hands in my pockets, resisting the urge to shove her away from his body. I'm shocked by my fierce possessiveness towards him. So far in these trials, my tolerance of Aalto has been lukewarm at best: I mustn't show any kind of reaction now.

"Your beautiful dress doesn't hide the ugliness inside you," I mutter, instantly regretting my words as she spins rapidly back to me with an angry scowl.

I curse my stupidity for forgetting how sensitive fae hearing is, wondering if my tiredness is finally affecting my judgement, until I recall that these trials aren't the first time we've met. Insulting her comes as naturally to me as berating me does to her. I smirk to myself, stopping her in her tracks. She looks surprised to find me not flinching from the rage she is directing at me. Too late, I realise I should be acting afraid of her. *Hells, keeping this hidden is going to be harder than I thought.*

"Ah, I think perhaps the trial of sloth has rather exhausted my little human." Aalto holds up a placatory hand towards Remora, stopping her as she stalks towards me.

She turns to him with a growl.

"Don't mess up your dress by touching the filthy human, Remora." Aalto says the words easily, a comment that would have once annoyed me, but I now know is just for show. He lowers his voice. "Nature wouldn't want you to damage one of her tributes."

His warning must be enough because she looks away from us, turning to address the crowd.

I ignore Aalto's stern look, my heart pounding as I realise how close we came to slipping up. I'm not even sure who knows that my memories have been wiped. How public was our relationship before the trials? In my exhausted state, the memories are hazy. Did Aalto show me off, or was I kept hidden? Did I mingle in the fae world, or did we just spend time together in the human world?

I have so many questions for him.

"Witnesses of the trial of sloth... our tribute Rosalind and her fae partner Aalto... have passed!" Remora yells once more, a gust of wind swirling around her, lifting her voice up and carrying it across to the crowds in the stands.

It's obvious where Aalto's court is sitting; whoops and cheers erupt in a tidal wave from the centre section. Perhaps I should have realised it sooner from the swathe of blue and white outfits, but until now, my mind has been focused elsewhere. Namely, on rescuing Aalto and not getting killed.

"There are three trials left for our tributes to complete. Pride. Envy." She pauses, turning to smirk at us, before adding, "And my favourite... Lust." She draws out the word in a seductive hum, much to the amusement of the crowd.

Her Summer Court brethren light up their area of the stands in clouds of fire, showing their appreciation of her words.

I see Aalto grin as his court stand as one, raindrops falling onto the Summer fae, creating a mass sizzling steam and prompting a dismayed out-cry, much to the amusement of the Winter fae.

"Handle your court," Remora growls at him, clearly not amused.

Aalto shrugs, but raises a hand, clicking his finger in a patronising manner. A box of water appears over his court, shielding them from the angry Summer fae that are edging towards them, retribution clear in their eyes. Simultaneously, the raindrops stop falling. My eyes widen; I'd forgotten how powerful Aalto truly is.

I gulp, risking another look at him. How did I attract a fae so powerful? *What does he see in me?* I shake my head. These feelings of low self-worth around him are annoyingly familiar. Surely, I shouldn't still have these insecurities? Am I still missing key memories, or was our relationship not as strong as I would like to believe?

I want to escape to a room where I can just sit and be quiet with my thoughts for a while; try and piece together what I do and don't know and fill in the gaps. But I feel like, until these trials are over completely, I won't get a chance to do so.

I take a deep breath. At least I can take comfort in knowing that I'm no longer going through these trials alone. It's very different tackling what's ahead, knowing that Aalto does truly have my back, and can be trusted. Even if I do wonder what happened in our past, for us to get to where we are now.

When the fight in the stands begins to settle back down, Remora sighs, and my eyes flickers across to her. She's looking at the Summer Court fae almost protectively, and it makes me warm up to her for just a moment.

But when she turns back to us, her words remind me of why I dislike her.

"Even for a human, you completed that trial *painfully* slowly, Rosalind," she drawls. "I suppose your bond with you fae partner is weaker than your fellow tributes'. Though I guess that can't be helped. He is a powerful fae prince, after all, and you're just a pathetic human farm girl."

Her words hit harder, now that I remember my relationship with Aalto. How dare she mock us so openly, especially when she knows? I clench my fists, resisting the urge to bite back. I can't even defend us! I glare at Aalto, who is staring into the crowds, his eyes narrowed and his lips thin. I recognise that he is equally annoyed, and that helps me rein in my anger.

When I remain silent, Remora smirks and waves her hand, almost as if she is dismissing us. I don't have time to react before I feel Aalto's firm hand on my shoulder, and that wrenching feeling in my navel as he teleports us away.

Finally, I think, as we reappear in a room that is surprisingly familiar to me. *We're alone.*

I realise that this time, the teleportation didn't make me feel violently sick, and I wonder how long into our relationship it took for me to get used to it. My mouth opens to ask Aalto just how long we've been together for when my breath is taken away in a gasp, two strong arms suddenly crushing me to his chest.

Finally. I close my eyes, leaning into his embrace, breathing in his familiar sea-salt scent.

"I've missed you, my moon. I've been so lost without you," he whispers, holding me just as closely as I'm holding him.

"Let's get through these trials." I respond simply. "*Together.*"

Acknowledgements

If you are reading this section, that means you are holding this book in your hands – whether that be on the screen of an e-reader, or a physical paperback – and for that, I must thank you, the reader. The fact that you have bought my book absolutely blows my mind – a writer may have a story to tell, but it means nothing if there is not someone to hear it. You mean the world to me.

Of course, you would not be holding it right now if not for the people that have helped me on my journey to get it there. My very own mischievous fae-like husband, you keep me on my toes, and have kept me going. I wouldn't have got this far without you. You are my everything.

My parents: thank you for helping to develop my imagination and nurturing the creative seed that has finally sprouted into this book. My in-laws: thank you for being like a second family and encouraging me to follow my dreams. And of course, thank you to my two beautiful daughters – Imogen and Athena – for being the sparks to my flame. I love you more than I could express in words.

My bookstagram community – I first started my reading journey on Instagram and I'm so grateful for all the friends that I've made along the way. My street team have been a great source of support, and I would honestly have been lost without them. Thank you for being my first set of cheerleaders!

I wanted to particularly mention my besties – Taz, Lou & Liv, who always match my crazy, and Jade, Julisa, Nessa & Iris, who have hearts of gold. My AIB sisters – Kyri, May, Sanity & Jess – if I ever get kidnapped into a crazy fae world, you'd be the girls I'd want to have by my side.

If you found the character art as stunning as I did, please go check out @reirashiver (Luna) on Instagram. Thank you so much for bringing my characters to life! Also @ tammykingofficial, an amazing voice actor who gave voice to Remora (see if you can find the old post!).

Finally, for the team at Cranthorpe Millner, thank you for bringing my baby into the world. You all deserve special recognition, but in particular, I wanted to thank Vicky who logged in during the festive season to push an edit through (!), and Lauren for being my hype woman behind the scenes.

If you've enjoyed my crazy world of the fae, please do leave a review on Goodreads or Instagram; I'd love to read your thoughts! Also, please come join me on social media – I can be found hiding behind my TBR pile on Instagram under @ jadeford_writing – I'd love to see you there!